When We Say Goodbye

Copyright When We Say Goodbye ©2021 by Michelle Vernal

All rights reserved.

No portion of this book may be reproduced in any form without written permission from the publisher or author, except as permitted by U.S. copyright law.

Also by Michelle Vernal

Standalone titles

The Cooking School on the Bay

Second-hand Jane

Staying at Eleni's

The Traveller's Daughter

Sweet Home Summer

When We Say Goodbye

Series Fiction ...

The Irish Guesthouse on the Green

Book 1 - O'Mara's

Book 2 – Moira Lisa Smile

Book 3- What Goes on Tour

Book 4 – Rosi's Regrets

Book 5 – Christmas at O'Mara's

Book 6 - A Wedding at O'Mara's

Book 7 – Maureen's Song

Book 8 – The O'Mara's in LaLa Land

Book 9 – Due in March

Book 10 – A Baby at O'Mara's

Book 11 – Rainbows over O'Mara's
Book 12 – An O'Mara's Reunion
Book 13 – The O'Maras Go Greek
Book 14 – Mat Magic at O'Mara's
Book 15 – Coming soon, Matchmaking at O'Mara's

Isabel's Story

The Promise

The Letter

The bestselling - Liverpool Brides series

The Autumn Posy

The Winter Posy

The Spring Posy

The Summer Posy

The Little Irish Village Stories

Christmas in the Little Irish Village

New Beginnings in the Little Irish Village

A Christmas Miracle in the Little Irish Village

Coming soon – Secrets in the Little Irish Village

Available on Amazon in Kindle, KU or Paperback

Prologue

Do you ever wonder what our lives would be like if we could see around the corner? Imagine if we knew what was going to happen next. Remember that childhood Paper Fortune Teller game? You know the one where you fold up a piece of paper a certain way, and then someone picks a colour and then a number after which you lift a corner to reveal what your future holds.

If all we had to do was take a peek under that paper to know what was going to happen tomorrow then maybe we'd be able to avoid the bits we don't like the sound of. The painful stuff. The hard stuff. I suppose the downside of that would be we wouldn't be able to stand on tippy-toes and grab hold of the highs—not if we meandered along never feeling the lows. I wouldn't change what Sam and I had, not even if I *had* played Paper Fortune Teller, but I'll never understand why it had to end the way it did for us. Life can be cruel and it can be unfair, but you know what? Sometimes it can be wonderful. I'm Ellie Perkins, and this is my story.

Chapter 1

It wasn't any one particular thing that had upset my normally easy-going disposition that leaden-skied afternoon in August. It was a culmination of small, annoying things mingled with a lack of sleep. All of which put together meant I'd not had the best day at Teeny Tykes Early Learning Centre.

There was the irate mother who said greedy George had stolen her little Sadie's lunch. I'd feigned sympathy as she prattled on, tutting and nodding et cetera, all the while reciting *Georgie Porgie Pudding and Pie stole the other kids' lunches and made them cry* in my head. Then there was the staff meeting that had dragged on and on. Boring! Not too, mention the paperwork I'd had to fill in on the lunch theft incident before I could leave for the day. All of this meant my nerves were pinched and on edge by the time I dragged on my coat and ran out the door of Teeny Tykes Early Learning Centre.

I didn't notice the patches of blue sky breaking through all that grey as I stomped across the carpark, perhaps if I had my mood would have lifted.

I'd only had five hours' sleep, and I was very much an eight hours a night girl or the world as I know it goes pear-shaped and I can't cope. I believe the saying goes I'd been burning the candle at both ends. This wasn't because I'd spent the night before making the most of the all-night seven-dollar drinks special at the Empire Bar with my friends. It was down to my other job. I waitressed three nights a week at Nummy-Num-Num in my Tum BYO Restaurant because I was determined to pay off my student loan as fast as I could.

Nummy-Num-Num in my Tum was an Asian Fusion restaurant in the city, and just quietly the food was rubbish. I could never figure out what was fusion about Pork Wontons, Combination Fried Rice and Black Bean Beef, standard Chinese fare if you ask me. Mrs Zheng, my boss, thought it gave the restaurant a broader appeal, and you didn't argue with Mrs Zheng. She was third generation Chinese, but for the sake of authenticity, she liked to dress in traditional silk dresses. She had a different-coloured one for each night of the week, and when she wore the black one on Thursdays, she looked like an oriental version of Morticia Addams.

I worked at her restaurant for minimum wage plus tips, which were virtually non-existent. New Zealanders are not tippers; it isn't in our DNA. I had a secret fantasy that one night I'd take an order for Lemon Chicken from a Texan oil baron over on business who'd just really fancied a Chinese for dinner. Sadly this didn't happen, and the majority of my customers were either couples on their way home from the movies, students looking for a cheap night out, or patrons from the pub next door trying to soak up their ale.

My hours were six p.m. until closing, Thursday through Saturday, and what I earned put petrol in my car, and, on occasion, let me join my friends at the Empire Bar. My wages at Teeny Tykes covered my board at Uncle Colin's and Aunty Paula's and helped pay a chunk off my student debt each week.

I didn't mind the weekend night stints at Nummy-Num-Num because I could lie in the next morning, but given I started work at

Teeny Tykes at eight a.m., I didn't much look forward to Thursday nights—especially when you had two tight-(five-letter word beginning with 'A' ending in 'S') who'd shared an entrée. Okay, I got that but sharing a main too? No, I'm sorry that's plain mean, and I'd never seen anybody chew their food as slowly as those two did that night either. Mindful eating gone mad. I'll grant you the strips of beef could be a tad fatty, but the masticating cows act they had going on was way over the top.

When I suggested dropping some subtle hints that it was closing time like taking their plate and turning the lights off Mrs Zheng, ever hopeful that a dessert might be ordered, hissed that we would not be closing until the fat lady sang. She did actually say that, and when the couple left some time in the small hours having swiped up any evidence of there ever having been black bean sauce on the plate with their respective index fingers, they didn't leave me a tip.

Hence, my temperament was tired and grumpy as I reached my car that Friday afternoon. Back then I was driving an old Nissan, which I'd bought with the money Nan and Pops put in trust for me until my eighteenth birthday; the remainder had gone toward my university fees. I slid behind the driver's seat, relieved that I wouldn't need to speak to anyone between now and my next shift at Nummy's. I planned to go straight home, knowing the house would be empty. Uncle Colin and Aunty Paula were both at work, and my cousin Gemma was in Auckland for a long weekend at a sales conference. It would leave me free to curl up on the couch and have myself a nice little half-hour nana nap before work.

It was as I tootled down Ilam Road that a car pulled out of a side street ahead of me. It was one of those low to the ground Japanese things with a modified exhaust. I could hear the dunk, dunk, dunk beat of the music blaring out of it from inside my car and I shook my head as though I were a middle-aged woman and not a twenty-one-year-old barely out of university. My blood boiled a second later as I pulled up alongside the ridiculous-looking import at the lights and glancing over witnessed the driver toss a half-eaten pie, still in its wrapper, out the window.

The cheek! The arrogance! I reached over and wound down my passenger window; there were no electronic windows in my Nissan, my trust money didn't stretch to that.

'Oi! What do you think you're doing?' Confrontation isn't big on my agenda, I'll avoid it if I can, but this needed confronting. Kiwis do not litter.

"What?' A face that whispered of potential inbreeding peered out from inside a hooded sweatshirt.

'You know what—chucking your pie out like that. Get out of your car, pick it up and take your mess home with you!' My voice rose to a borderline hysterical pitch on that last sentence.

'Fuck off.' His words, not mine.

He flicked me his finger, and his window slid up. I wished I didn't have to lean over to wind mine up because it ruined my street cred. I heard his engine rev as I sat back in my seat and my lips set in a grim line. Not only was this loser making a mess of our environment he was polluting it too. Something came over me then. I think I'd bypassed tiredness, and moved right on into road rage. As the lights turned orange, my foot took on a life of its own tapping down on the accelerator, and I gripped the steering wheel so hard the muscles in my arms cramped. I stole one more glance over at him noticing the Billy Goats Gruff sprouting of hairs on his chin. Oh, how I'd have liked to have pulled them out, one by one with a pair of tweezers. Our eyes locked briefly, and I knew he'd read the challenge in mine.

The lights turned green. GO! Adrenalin slammed through me as I pushed down hard on the accelerator. Eat my dust. I was jubilant and hopeful that no police cars were lurking nearby because a speeding ticket would mean an extra shift at Nummy's. It took a moment for it to dawn on me that I hadn't gone anywhere. Ahead of me, boy racer had burned off down the road in a cloud of exhaust fumes, while I was still sitting at the lights. My Nissan had died. I muttered a bad word or two before going through the motions of trying to get my car to turn over. *This was not happening.*

A burst of honking behind me made me jump. I was in no state to deal with another arrogant 'A' word and not thinking about what I was doing I got out of my car. I slammed my door shut and marched over to the offending van idling behind me. Anderson's Electrical was sign written along the side. I tapped on the window indicating Mr Electrical should wind it down.

'Honking like that is not helping my situation,' was all I said as I registered his eyes were hidden behind dark glasses. He had a cap on too, his longish dark blonde hair curling out from under it. He must have picked up on my being slightly unhinged because he didn't say a word as he gestured toward my car with a questioning expression.

I didn't trust myself to say anything else so I left Mr Electrical to head back to my car and face the music. I had a plan; I'd ring Uncle Colin, he'd come and fix everything. My face was flaming as I walked away because of the slow build of backed-up vehicles also beginning to honk. It was beginning to sound like rush hour in Manhattan. It was at that moment something squished beneath my foot before I began a slow skid. I was aware of looking like I was attempting a body twerking booty dance as I flapped my arms and tried to stay upright. Maybe I should have just gone with it because if I'd hit the tarmac, I might have got some sympathy but my survival instinct had kicked in. It was one of those moments I'd have sold my soul to click my fingers and magic myself away from the mess I was in.

I heard Mr Electrical call out. 'What's the problem?'

I looked back and saw him get out of his van, and I was fairly certain he was trying not to laugh.

'My car won't start; the engine's died,' I answered, this time doing an impersonation of a horse pawing the ground as I tried to get the pie off my sneaker.

'Well, we'd better get it off the road. You hop behind the wheel, and I'll get someone to give me a hand pushing it out the way.'

I did as I was told, grateful to have received a clear set of instructions. A moment later Mr Electrical and a Good Samaritan in a suit told me to release the handbrake before pushing me over to the side of the road. 'Thanks very much,' I said, getting out of my car relieved to be out of the way of the traffic. I got a nod from the man in the suit as he hurried back to his latest model Porsche, keen to be on his way, and I offered up an apologetic smile to the po-faced drivers giving me the hairy eyeball as they snaked around Mr Electrical's vehicle.

My Knight in Shining Armour was behind his wheel once more, and to my surprise, I was disappointed. I'd have liked to have seen what he looked like with his glasses and cap off because, despite the drama that had just unfolded, I'd noticed he was hot. Not in an overstated bulging muscles gym way but a nicely toned hard-working way. I'd have also liked to have said sorry for being snarky with him.

Instead of driving off, though, he veered in behind my Nissan before getting out once more. It crossed my mind that he might want to be paid or something. I think maybe I was still in shock over my pie skid.

'Are you okay? Is there someone you can call to come pick you up?'

'Um, I can ring my uncle; he'll sort this out.' I gestured toward my car resisting the urge to give it a good kick for all the upset it had caused me. Instead, I let the side down, and on behalf of strong women everywhere I apologise, but I started to cry.

That's when Mr Electrical lifted his glasses and pushed them up to sit on the peak of his cap. His eyes, I saw through my blurred retinas, were the most gorgeous shade of blue. I've never been to the Med but I thought to myself they were Mediterranean blue. Every cloud had a silver lining, I decided, blinking those traitorous tears away and hoping my mascara hadn't run.

'Listen, your car will be okay there for a bit, but you look like you could do with a drink. It's a little early in the day for that so how about grabbing a coffee? I can run you to wherever you need to be afterward?'

'Could we get some chocolate too?' I sniffed hopefully.

He smiled. 'We can do that. I'm Sam by the way.'

Chapter 2

♥

'Hey, Sam.' I leaned down and kissed him on his forehead, smoothing the dark sweep of his hair away before straightening up. I wished he'd reply, but he didn't. He stayed silent while I gazed at him, knowing that if someone were to take a photo of me at that moment, I'd look very much like a poster girl for ice-creams. It would be down to the sappy look of yearning I knew I was wearing because I loved this man. I had from the moment I met him. Well, maybe not that first moment, because as you know I had my knickers in a right knot the first time we laid eyes on one another.

Sam and I had been together for four years and three months, and the sight of him still gave me that same exquisite sensation as cracking the chocolate on my all-time favourite ice-cream, a Magnum Double Caramel, each time I saw him.

My life wasn't perfect, though, even if Sam was pretty close to it. In fact, for the last ten months, it has been, and this was putting it mildly because I'm not one for swearing, like someone peed in my bowl of soup. It's a phrase I stole from William-Peter who's one-half of the four-year-old, redheaded Richards twins I look after during the day. Their mother, Nervy Caro as I call her, has a low stress threshold hence her need for a nanny.

William-Peter's the most precocious pre-schooler I've ever met, and I've met a few. He's also the older twin by three very important minutes, and he coined that particular gem the day I served up a homemade vegetable soup for lunch.

The soup was a mix of lentils, pumpkin, peppers, carrots, and turnip and yes, okay, I could have given the stick blender a more hands-on workout, but it had already taken me the best part of the morning to peel, chop, simmer and blend. I was over it. I hold my hand up to the turnip being a wild card too but they were in season, and I could never resist a deal. Anyway, I'd adopted this phrase as my own because I thought it was a nicer way of saying that things had gone to shite.

A 'somebody-peed-in-my-soup' afternoon was also the kind I'd just had thanks to the aforementioned twin.

'Sorry I'm late, hon.' I shrugged out of my coat and chucked it down on the end of the bed. I didn't know why I was bothering to apologise either because Sam didn't give a toss what time it was but I suppose it's down to manners born out of habit. 'William-Peter called Saffy-Rose a little pig and then bit her on the hand, and all hell let loose. Honestly, you'd have thought she'd lost a limb, the racket she was making. I'm shattered.'

To prove my point, I sank down into the faded old armchair. Its rose and yellow flowered fabric lost its bloom a long time ago, but it was comfy enough. My gaze flicked to the window. The last of the day's watery sun was streaming through, and I could see the glass needed a polish. I hate cleaning windows; it is the most unsatisfying of household chores as I can never quite get the glass streak-free. It's right up there with ironing in my opinion, and I did both at the Richards house. My nanny job had a very varied job description.

I tugged my boots off and curled my legs up beside me on the chair, and even though it wasn't cold—it was never cold in here—I pulled the multi-coloured, crocheted Afghan blanket draped across the arm of the chair over my lap. It always made me think of my nan, that blanket; she had one just like it.

Sam's mum, Gina, must have popped by today, I realised noticing the Twix bar wrappers in the bin. She always brought two Twixes when she called in, eating his for him. The chocolate, caramel biscuit bar was Sam's favourite treat. We were both chocolate/caramel fiends and I used to say that's why we were a match made in heaven. I can't help but think as I eye those wrappers that it might be nice if Gina left *me* the extra bar instead of snaffling it herself.

On the side table next to me steam was rising from my mug. It was sitting on the coaster with its stained rings from all the other cups of tea and coffee that had gone before it. Sam bought me the mug for our six-month anniversary. 'You make me a Happy Camper' was emblazoned in black swirly text against a plain white background. It was tongue in cheek given he loved nothing more than loading up his four-wheel drive and getting off road, pitching his tent wherever the mood took him. I think in another life he fancied himself a bit of a Bear Grylls.

Back then I took some convincing that there was pleasure to be found in eating baked beans from a tin, tending to nature's call behind a tree and not showering for an entire weekend. What I refused to go without, though, no matter how off the grid we got was my morning cup of coffee. Hence the mug. Do you know what? I'd have given anything to go camping with Sam again. Why do we learn so many lessons through hindsight?

I drifted back to the present and raised my fingers to my mouth, kissing them. I touched them to his face, feeling the prickles beneath my fingertips as I stroked his cheek. The sensation made me smile at the recollection of him catching hold of me to rub his stubbly chin against my cheek. I used to squeal at him to get off! Only he wouldn't, and we'd wind up kissing, stumbling backward in a well-practised dance toward the bedroom.

The memory was so sharp it hurt. It really did. Surely Sam must have felt it too? I studied his face looking for a flicker, anything. There was nothing though—just the familiar, gurgling, sucking sound of his airways being cleared.

We'd never know for certain how his accident happened. The police said black ice and speed were involved. What I *did* know, though, was the terms for the equipment he was surrounded by and the names of all the procedures that had been done to him since that horrible day he'd gone off grid. It was a trip that saw him somehow drive off a bridge and wind up being helicoptered to the hospital. Terms like endotracheal, ventilator, tracheostomy, catheter a port-a-cath and heart monitor were part of my vocabulary these days. Who would have thought me, a nanny, would need to know what anti-embolic stockings were for? I wished I didn't, I really did, and incidentally, they stop clots forming in Sam's legs due to his immobility.

'Alright, Ellie love?'

The voice startled me. It was Fran. She's my favourite night nurse. I always found the sight of her mumsy figure doing her rounds reassuring. She was kind and gentle, and I was okay leaving Sam for the night knowing she'd be watching over him.

'I'm okay,' I said as I wiped away the rogue tears I hadn't even known were there. I hoped she hadn't noticed them.

'Ah it's not easy, I know, love, but I'll keep an eye on him for you.'

I didn't trust myself to speak, so I stood up and busied myself folding the blanket before draping it back over the arm of the chair.

Fran took the clipboard from the bottom of the bed and scanned the notes, then gave me a sympathetic nod as she carried on with her rounds.

I bent down and kissed Sam goodnight. His lips were paper-dry beneath mine and I pulled the balm I keep in my bag for him out. I smeared my finger with it and rubbed it gently across his lips. 'I'll see you tomorrow,' I said satisfied that at least he wouldn't get cracked lips, not on my watch anyway, and I swung my bag over my shoulder. I didn't look back as I strode out of the silent home. If I stayed a second longer, I was frightened I'd crawl into bed next to him. I can't do that, though, and believe me there have been times I have wanted to lie next to him, close my eyes and not wake up; but I can't do that either. This neverland had been our normal for ten months now. I leave, and Sam stays, and my heart breaks all over again every single time I go.

Chapter 3

It was getting on for half past six when I left Briarwood House; I could smell that fusty smell of hospital food as I walked through the dully lit corridors toward the exit. It signalled dinner time. I always felt withered when I left the care facility, as though something had been sucked from me. I thought, perhaps, it was hope. A little hope seeped away each time it hit me afresh that Sam wasn't going to be coming home with me. My hand slipped inside my bag, and I fossicked for my keys. I needed to think about something else, so I began to do the mental math as I retrieved them.

In eighteen hours I'd officially become a home owner. My eyes burned once more, and my vision became soft around the edges; this time there was no need to hide the tears. There was no one around to see them anyway, so I let them form an orderly queue down my cheeks from which to plop down onto my chest.

The automatic doors slid open, and I stepped outside. The sharpness of the air outside was biting, and as it enveloped me, I thought it must be what a butterfly experienced when it emerged from the dry warmth of its chrysalis. What a shock to realise there was a different reality to the safety of that cocoon.

I got in my car and sat in the darkness. I needed to pull myself together before I turned the key. The thought that this wasn't how it was supposed to work out ran through my head. There was anger in it, and I smacked the steering wheel. Sam and I should have been toasting the purchase of our first home together; Gina should have been getting up my nose with all her helpful advice on the subject. We'd be planning our wedding too, not that Sam had asked me to marry him, but I liked to think he would have by now. I *knew* he would have by now. We'd talked about what the day would be like.

Sam wanted family and close friends only. A backyard barbeque wedding followed by a honeymoon in a tent in the middle of nowhere. I used to joke that wasn't happening. Oh no, I wanted the white, blingy works. I wanted to be a princess for a day. I might even go so far as pumping for a horse-drawn carriage. Sam was adamant he wasn't the suit type and I'd tell him he could pull off the Metro Man look for my sake, for one day. I missed those silly discussions. Yes, I thought frustration welling, by now I should be anticipating where I would fit in the Anderson tribe of six's pecking order.

Sam, at twenty-seven, was the second youngest of the four Anderson boys and, in my opinion the most normal of his brothers. Justin, he's the oldest, owns a sports shop and is into bodybuilding in a big way. He's always on a strict protein diet and brings a can of tuna with him to family get-togethers. I've learned not to stand by any windows if I wanted him to listen to what I was saying, because the distraction of his reflection was just too much for him. He's single because he's in a deep and meaningful relationship with himself. The tuna breath doesn't help much either.

Zac, who's only a year older than Sam, thanks to Mr Anderson not being able to keep it in his pants—Gina thinks it's hilarious to drop this clanger whenever his birthday rolls around—contracts as a courier. He's married to Moany Mandy, a hypochondriac. You know the type. If I said, 'Hi, Mandy, how are you? I've got a cold.' Her reply would be, 'Oh I've got the worst case of the flu the doctor has seen in years.' My headache was her migraine. They were the most money-hungry couple I'd ever met too, and even though it was their choice to pay their mortgage off in the next ten years, they cried poor a lot.

I'll give you an example. Say I were to ask them if they'd seen a film Sam and I had enjoyed or maybe been to a restaurant we liked, you know, normal chit-chat stuff, they'd look at me like I was on drugs and say, 'We can't afford to do that, we've got a mortgage.' I tell you, it was a real conversation killer.

The baby of the family's Lucas; he's the only one of the four boys to go to university. He qualified as a lawyer and has been trying to bonk his way into partnership at the firm he's worked at ever since he started his internship there. It was a source of consternation to Zac and Mandy that he got to live board-free at home while he studied. They asked Gina and Phil if they could move back into Zac's old bedroom so they could rent their house out as a way of paying their loan off faster. Gina managed to wiggle out of that one by telling them she was looking into using Zac and Sam's old rooms for Airbnb. It was a total lie, but Zac and Mandy thought it was a fantastic idea, and they ran with it. They regularly have foreign tourists staying in their spare room now.

I loved Sam's dad, Phil, best; next to Sam of course. I'd have liked to have been his daughter-in-law. He's into camping, surfing, all those outdoorsy things Sam was into, and I could see a lot of his son in him. He wasn't much of a talker, my Sam, and Phil's the strong silent type too, which is just as well because Gina's not. She's the one who wears the underpants in their family, and they're one big pair of bloomers.

I remember a conversation I had with my cousin Gemma, and I can't help but smile.

'Ooh, he took you home to meet the family. Things are getting serious, girl. What were they like?'

'Well, his dad was a lot like Sam, and his brothers are—' I cast about for an apt word '—characters but his mum—' I took my time in finding the right description, and it came to me in the form of Marlon Brando. 'If she were Italian she'd be a Mafia boss. Think the Godmother.'

Gemma sniggered. 'Mothers of sons are always scary. It's a territorial thing. They're like hippopotamuses.'

That made me snigger.

'What does she look like? Is she frump or glam?' The physical appearance of a person is important to Gemma; it's the world she moves in. Me, I couldn't care less although the hippopotamus analogy did strike a chord and I had noticed Gina's trousers.

'She does this thing with her trousers.' I demonstrated, pulling my jeans up as high as I could. 'I mean the waistband's nearly under her arms. And she tucks her tops in.' I did the same, and Gemma snorted. I was in the swing of it now. 'She told me having four boys who all entered the world weighing in at over ten pounds doesn't do a girl's waistline any favour.'

'Or her nether regions.' Gemma's expression was one of distaste as she unwittingly crossed her legs, tightly.

'She's doing that thing too—you know where women go grey.'

'Transitioning.'

'Yeah, but she has a matching whisker, which has already successfully transitioned on her chin. It was so hard not to stare at it when I was talking to her.' Gemma and I looked at each other, and I knew my tummy was going to hurt by the time I'd finished laughing.

The smile that conversation evoked slipped as I recalled another more recent one we'd shared.

'I thought you and Sam were for keeps—you had such an easy way with each other.' Gemma sniffed, needing my shoulder as much as I needed hers. 'You were one of those couples that always seemed to work better as a pair than on your own.' Her use of the past tense had irked me, but I stayed quiet on that occasion because I could tell she needed to talk, too. I had to remind myself here and there that Sam's accident wasn't just about me, he'd touched lots of people's lives. I knew Gina loved him too, differently obviously, but the bond between a mother and a son was a powerful thing. I remembered her saying on one of a myriad of nights I'd needed her shoulder to cry on what had happened to Sam was hideously unfair, and in some ways, it was worse for those around him.

Too bloody right it was (I'm sorry).

Take Gina and me; there used to be this underlying competitiveness for his attention between us, not that we'd ever admit to it. We were all warm hugs and kisses on cheeks when we saw each other, but secretly, we'd be trying to outdo one another. She was forever giving me impromptu cooking lessons when I popped into the Andersons' home to say hello because 'my Sam likes his mashed potato fluffy, Ellie; watch, it's all in the wrist.' And if I'd heard how he had hollow legs as a teenager and the only thing that filled him up was a big bowl of Mum's mac 'n' cheese, one more time...well, I would've hit her over the head with a block of the tasty cheese she reckoned was her secret ingredient.

We have a new understanding of each other these days, and I feel guilty about having laughed about her with Gemma. She's a good woman and a good mother. Our hugs are from the heart because both our hearts are broken. We're by no means besties though, don't get me wrong, because sometimes I find it hard to be around her grief when I'm not grieving. I refuse to because Sam's not dead. The effort we'd put into all that vying to be number one seems so pathetic in hindsight. It was such a waste of energy to get wound up over mac 'n' cheese. It's useless telling yourself not to sweat the small stuff when life's ticking over in an orderly manner, though. Us human beings, we're not made like that.

So yeah, I thought, turning the key and reversing out of the parking space in a *Sliding Doors* moment, Sam and me, we'd still be arguing over whether to splurge on a big white wedding or go budget, barbeque and put our money into the house. Zac and Mandy would be advising us to put it into the house and sniffing behind our backs that they hoped we weren't expecting anything extravagant for a wedding present because they had a mortgage to pay off. Justin would tell us to elope, so he didn't have to get a custom-made suit to accommodate his biceps, and Lucas would be insisting on meeting my bridesmaids so he could have his wicked way with them. Meanwhile, I'd be threatening to call the whole thing off if his mother didn't keep her nose out, and stop insisting on inviting all her long-lost friends she hadn't seen in years but who'd known Sam as a baby. You know normal stuff! Life stuff.

Instead, I was stuck in this alternate reality where Sam had wound up in the land of sleep. It was as if the pause button had been pushed on his life when he left to go camping that day, but for the rest of us, it had to keep playing. I indicated out onto the main road and turned my car right into the gap in the traffic. Tomorrow I'd be turning left because I wouldn't be heading home to the apartment I've shared with Gemma since the accident. I'd be heading to my new home, a place I've lived before, number 16 Radford Street.

Chapter 4

♥

It was a stifling late summer's day when Gemma, a high-end real estate agent who fancied herself a dead ringer for Meghan Markle—only a blonde-haired, blue-eyed, fair-skinned version—informed me the house on Radford Street was listed for sale. She breezed in through the door of her parents', my Aunty Paula and Uncle Colin's who've been like a Mum and Dad to me, where we'd been invited for a barbeque lunch and announced, 'Nan and Pops' old house has just gone on the market and guess who got the listing!'

I listened to her tell us that the family who had called number 16 Radford Street *their* home for the past ten years had decided to sell. They'd bought the house that once belonged to our grandparents, as a deceased estate soon after Nan and Pops passed away in short succession of one another. The decision to sell was down to Mother Nature, Gemma said. That *and* a very nice cash settlement from their insurance company.

It had been eight years since the earthquake that had brought Christchurch to its knees. Gemma's clients, fed up with the insurance wrangling over what damage the quake had done to their home, had opted to take the money and run having finally reached an agreement with both the Earthquake Commission and their private insurers.

They'd decided to start afresh, having no wish to think about repairing dodgy foundations, and cracks in walls, not while juggling two full-time jobs between them, five kids and an elderly mother who Gemma said, from what she'd seen when she'd gone around to do an appraisal, was very fond of her bed. She hadn't gotten out of it the entire time Gemma was there.

Thus, the old house had been listed ludicrously low as an 'as-is where-is' property. She patiently explained to me—as Uncle Colin, still in earshot, turned the sausages on the barbeque outside—it was basically an uninsured, bargain-priced home. A steal for a savvy investor who had the foresight to see the value they could add to the property.

'It's not my usual style of listing, but you know with the family connection, I thought I should be the one to see the old place to auction.'

I looked at my cousin, trying to process what she'd just said, and registered that even though it was Saturday and the rest of us were dressed casually, she was in a figure-hugging suit with a pair of heels on her feet I couldn't fathom staggering about in. She was a bit like Wonder Woman, my cousin. You know a mild-mannered Diana Prince sort, but when she spins around really fast a few times, she transforms into a superhero.

Gemma's a phenomenally successful mover and shaker in the real estate world. Her picture's even emblazoned on the back of the red Metro buses chugging about the city along with the heading, '*Meet Gemma Perkins, The Property Pro's Top Salesperson 2018*'. Underneath that's a profile shot that makes her look golden and ethereal, yet professional at the same time, with the slogan: '*Your Guiding Light Leading The Way To Your Next Home*', printed across her chest. I nearly drove into the back of the bus the first time I saw her grinning down at me. Honestly, the state of those teeth—any whiter and you'd need to wear sunglasses in her presence.

Gemma did her Wonder Woman twirling around thing of an evening, figuratively speaking, of course, because by night she became 'That Girl'. Ta-Dah! Otherwise known to her 150K Instagram followers as Gem. She created the persona of Gem, *a girl about town who frequents the best bars, restaurants, and cafés while showcasing the latest looks from the city's young designers,* while the earthquakes continued to belch up the Canterbury Plains around us.

'Ellie,' she said to me shortly after the big one. The phone was in her hand, and she was angling it for the best light as she posed in a black jumpsuit by emerging fashionista Rain Robards. 'The student army might be your thing but it isn't mine, and this is my way of giving something back to the city I love. I'm doing my bit for the earthquake effort by putting it and its style on the world map.'

At that time, I was waiting for the term to begin at Canterbury University where I was going to study for my Graduate Diploma in Early Childhood Teaching. I'd been keen to join in with the student army—a force who'd banded together to help clean up the silt and sand that had flooded people's homes, gardens and streets after the shakes—both to do some good and as a way to get to know new faces. That way I'd figured campus wouldn't seem so big and scary on my first day. And yes, I did think this hard labour was a more proactive course of action than strutting about in haute couture like Gemma, or rather 'Gem'.

She tossed the property portfolio down on the table and headed into the kitchen to give her mum—who was busy whipping up a salad to go with the meat—a hello kiss on the cheek. I sat down at the table and snatched the portfolio up greedily, hearing the fridge open as Gemma retrieved a cold drink. The bones of the house were the same but it looked tired despite the carefully angled shots. Gemma returned, beer in hand, and finished explaining the finer points of buying and selling earthquake-damaged properties. All I heard though was that the bank wouldn't loan on a property that wasn't insurable. The buyer would need to be cashed up, and that there was good money to be made on these sorts of properties if you were in a position to move on them, fast.

My finger traced the flowery prose beneath the photograph. She was good my cousin—sun-drenched, generous living. What it didn't say was this was a house filled with happy memories. My memories and they were precious. This was where my mother, Nicole, or Nicky as she was always called, grew up alongside my Uncle Colin—where I spent so much time as a kid myself.

It was then—having never had any previous thoughts of buying a home, not without Sam anyway and certainly not on my nanny salary, even if it was generous—that I knew it had to be mine.

'But if I can't get insurance, then I won't get a loan.' My mind was racing.

'What are you on about? You don't want to buy it do you?' Gemma gave me an incredulous look before taking a swig of her beer.

She might drink straight from the bottle, but her tastes veered toward champagne, and the house where our grandparents spent their entire married life was definitely of the pale ale variety. Her facial expression said that, after everything I'd been through this last year, I needed her. I know she's been on hand to mop up my tears, and entertaining the idea of living on my own in a broken-down house seemed mad. But hey, maybe I was a bit mad. I wouldn't be living there on my own long term though.

Gemma and I had lived together in her smart, two-bedroom apartment since I moved out of the townhouse Sam and I rented. I couldn't afford to stay there on my own and moving in with Gemma had always been to my mind a stopgap. The living room overlooks Hagley Park and my rent helps to pay her mortgage. The arrangement suited us both even if she could have pulled her weight a bit more when it came to the housework. On the whole, though, we rubbed along well and the location's fabulous. It's only a stone's throw to the city, and I could see why she'd think I was barmy to consider leaving all that for a circa 1950s house with structural issues in a less than sought after location. The thing was that buying Radford Street was the first coherent thought I'd had since the fog descended after Sam's accident.

The last time the house at number 16 was for sale, I'd been too young to have a say in anything. This time was different. I couldn't, wouldn't let it slip through my fingers a second time. It represented something to me that Gemma would never understand. That was the moment Uncle Colin swooped in from the deck, entering our conversation like a caped crusader wielding a slightly charred sausage on a fork. All the while, Aunty Paula carried on dicing tomatoes.

'Listen, Ellie.' He thrust one hand into the bowl of peanuts on the table and waved the fork he held in the other. The sausage on the end of it wobbled precariously. 'Your Aunty Paula and I talked about this a while ago—we helped Gemma into her apartment when she turned twenty-five, and we'd like to help get you a foothold on the property ladder too. I know a bit about 'as-is, where-is' properties through a couple of my clients who have gone down that track.' He paused to snaffle a handful of the salty nuts and proceeded to talk with his mouth full. 'The bank will loan you a percentage of the land value of the property, and it's a good solid area.'

Gemma snorted, and I shot her a look, not wanting Uncle Colin to get distracted. I had no idea where this conversation was headed, but I wanted to find out.

'It was good enough for your grandparents to bring your Aunty Nicky and me up in,' he said eyeballing Gemma. In that moment I could see my mum in him. They have the same eyes and their mouths curl the same way when they're making a point. 'Don't go getting ideas above your station, young lady. Ellie spent a lot of her early years there too. I can see why she has a connection to the old place, and, with everything that's happened, a project might just be what you need—aye, love?'

I nodded. That was exactly it. The house would give me something to roll up my sleeves and get stuck into until I could bring Sam home.

'It's a good investment, Gemma; you know that. It sits on the fringes of a blue-chip area and it's in a good school catchment area.'

'Fringes? Outer Mongolia you mean, and you could use the living room floor as a ski ramp,' Gemma muttered sulkily, feeling herself lose the battle.

I squirmed and wished she'd shut up.

'I like the idea of what was my family home returning to the family.' Uncle Colin licked the salt from his fingers—food always diverted his train of thought. 'Paula, you've got to stop buying these. I shouldn't be eating them. They're not good for my cholesterol.'

'Or, your belly but there is such a thing as self-discipline, Colin,' Aunty Paula called back, inspecting a pepper. Looking at Aunty Paula I could see what Gemma will look like one day. Her face, though, is softer than her daughter's, and she has the figure of a mum who gives great cuddles. The pepper was a green one, and I hoped she didn't decide to add it to the salad because they repeat on me something terrible.

Uncle Colin ignored her. 'So, Ellie, here's the deal. If I think the structural work involved to get the house to an insurable level isn't ridiculous, and if Gemma here can negotiate you a good price at auction, your aunt and I'll stump up the cash you'll need to buy it. We'll loan you enough to get the necessary repair work done, too. I know a good builder with a solid team behind him who can come around pre-auction to give us an idea of the work involved and if it's viable get the job done properly.'

Uncle Colin runs a successful architectural design firm; he knew what he was talking about, I thought as my mouth fell open. I hadn't expected this. Yes, my uncle and aunty were more than comfortable financially but this, well this offer was so generous, and it showed a lot of faith in me.

'Stop catching flies. Here have a peanut.' He thrust the bowl toward me. 'You can make weekly repayments back to us like you would the bank, only it will be an interest-free loan on the full amount needed to buy the house and get it to an insurable level. Clear?'

I nodded dumbly.

'Right. I'll get the necessary paperwork drawn up. We'll keep it all official,' he said gruffly before taking a swig of his beer.

I threw my arms around his toddler-rotund frame not caring that the sausage had flopped onto the table and mouthed, 'Thank you,' over his shoulder to Aunty Paula. She gave me the thumbs up and sliced into the pepper.

Chapter 5

♥

The sun decided to shine on moving day and I decided the gods must be on my side for once because I'd only had to deal with one dramatic event that morning at the Richards house. It unfolded while my back was turned and William-Peter seized the moment to pick up a black permanent marker pen. He'd decided Saffy-Rose needed a tattoo. Nervy Caro got hysterical when she saw it and was adamant that her daughter was not going to visit her grandmother with the words 'Big Poo' emblazoned across her cheek. I remained silent but to tell the truth, I was quite impressed by William-Peter's neat handwriting. It wasn't bad for a four-year-old, I thought as I soaped up a flannel and got scrubbing.

Amazingly, I managed to leave their house with ten minutes spare in which to get to the lawyers' and collect the keys to my castle before the suburban office closed for lunch. I climbed in my car and set off. Yes the gods were on my side, I thought again as I sailed through yet another green light five minutes into my journey.

I pulled up outside Fraser Norton Wright, grateful for the hassle-free park. I can't parallel park to save myself and raced inside. I was keen to get my keys and be off. Sarah on reception looked startled as the door jingled shut. She was chewing frantically and I caught a whiff of egg. 'Sorry.' She flapped her hand and then pointed at her mouth. 'It's stuck to the roof. Give me a sec.'

I grinned, and waited in front of her desk for her to dislodge her mouthful.

'Sorry about that, I was starving. I'm not supposed to eat at my desk but I was about to start chewing my arm off, so egg sandwich it was.'

'Don't worry about it—a girl's got to eat.'

'Mr Fraser's just on a call but I messaged him to say you're here. He'll be out with your keys soon. Congratulations by the way.'

'Thanks.' I didn't want to stand there watching her snaffle the rest of her sandwich and I was too antsy to sit down so I moved over to the window. I stood there watching the traffic and as a bus rumbled past and I caught sight of Gemma's whiter than white smile I thought about how she'd held my hand at the auction, despite her misgivings.

She'd tried to talk me out of bidding numerous times before the big day rolled around saying, 'I just don't think you should be living on your own, not with everything you've been through.'

'I could get flatmates in,' I told her knowing I wouldn't.

'You won't, though, I guarantee it. Besides, you can't expect anyone else to live amongst the mayhem while the work gets done. And why that old heap anyway? I mean come on, Ellie, I can be as sentimental as the next girl.' That wasn't true. Gemma leaned toward ruthless rather than sentimental. 'And I get you were happy staying with Nan and Pops as a kid. I loved Nan's scones and eating Pops' home-grown peas fresh from the pod too, but I think you're crazy. You've got this rosy picture in your head of how it *was*, not how it is, and I'm telling you: the area has gone downhill. Radford Street ain't the land of vegetable gardens, home baking, and white picket fences anymore.'

I did think about what she was saying, but what I kept coming back to was that I hadn't 'been through' anything where Sam was concerned, because I was still going through it. There was no end to it. The house would be my project, something to occupy those dark, murky corners of my mind during those awful in-between hours when I wasn't working, and I was away from Sam.

Gemma had one last shot at talking me out of going through with the purchase as we sat in the auction room waiting for the house our grandparents had spent a lifetime paying off to come up. The house that would be perfect for me and Sam. My stomach was in knots, and I had horrible sweaty palms.

'It's not too late you know, Ellie, we can leave now,' she said. 'You're going to have to live with all that upheaval while the building work goes on for months. Don't you think you've had enough upheaval in your life?' She squeezed my hand and let it go pretty quickly, screwing her nose up.

'No.' There was a steely determination in my voice that neither of us recognised. I could sense her eyeing me. I know she has us pigeonholed, and I wasn't doing what she expected me to do. I'm the easier-going, malleable one of the two of us. It's the role I play. She's right, too—normally I am. I'm not one for rocking the boat, because I figure my mum's done enough of that for all of us, but this, well this was different.

I sat up a little straighter and smoothed the creases in my purple jeans. I'd teamed the jeans with a white ruffle shirt reminiscent of the flounces way back in Madonna's 'Like a Virgin' heyday and black spike-heeled boots. I'd asked Sam what he thought of my outfit choice as I stood in front of my dressing table mirror before Gemma arrived to pick me up. He approved. He especially liked the purple jeans because I had to lie on the bed and sort of shimmy into them. Oh, I knew he wasn't there but the leprechaun-sized Sam I visualise sitting on my shoulder was. I don't think he'd be too enamoured by my referring to him as a leprechaun but having the pint-sized version of my partner sitting on my shoulder is keeping me sane.

I think I got the whole leprechaun thing from the snow globe Nan's friend had brought back for her after holidaying in Ireland when I was small. I'd been fascinated with the way the green glitter would fall like snow over the funny little man dressed in green trapped inside the dome. I'd shake it and shake it until Nan told me to be a bit gentler or I'd make the poor man sick. I loved the story she told me, too, about how he had a pot of gold hidden at the end of the rainbow. We could all do with one of those.

I like unusual things and my hobby was buying vintage-style outfits from the second-hand stores. I revamp them to give them a Queen of Pop flavour. I adore Madonna; it comes from listening to Mum play her CDs when I was a kid. She'd dance around the room with me, and whenever I hear one of her old songs, it makes me happy.

I put my spin on Madge's different looks with the aid of my sewing machine. I call these creations Mad Ellie Originals. I even have labels with this printed on them that I sew into my designs. The machine was a gift from Nan. It's a Bernina and she had it for as long as I can remember. She taught me how to sew on it but she also passed on her love of creating something from nothing. As for the purple jeans, well they're *my* take on Madge's style.

I sewed the ruffles onto the shirt myself, having unpicked them from a frilly white skirt off the fifty-cent rack. I was quite pleased with the result, but Gemma said I'd look more at home strumming a guitar in an old Prince video she'd seen on MTV recently than sitting in an auctioneers' room.

I once asked her if she'd consider modelling one of my outfits for That Girl, but she said she'd rather go naked than wear a Mad Ellie

Original. I know for a fact she pinched that off the PETA anti-fur campaign even though she denied it.

Prince wasn't the look I'd been aiming for either, I thought, silently humphing after she dropped that little pearler. Sam loved my Mad Ellie Originals, and if he were here in the auction room with me now, I mean *really* here not the leprechaun Sam I can only talk to when no one else is around, he'd squeeze my hand. He wouldn't care that my palms were clammy, and he'd tell me my outfit was perfect. So there, Gemma Louise Perkins, in your boring old Ms Markle twinset, I thought mentally poking my tongue out at her.

The tension of life-changing decisions about to be made as we sat in that light and airy auction room was palpable. Gemma broke it. 'Ellie, you're a pretty girl, and you know I covet your olive skin, but even pretty girls need makeup. A slick of gloss at least.' She rummaged around inside her Marc Jacobs bag—a gift to herself when she closed her first house sale—and produced a tube of lip-gloss. I looked at her pink sticky lips before taking it from her.

'If I put this on will you stop staring at me? You are not going to psych me out; my mind's made up. I want the house.'

'Okaay,' she drawled, 'but if we do this thing promise me you'll get your butt down to the hairdresser's and get something done with your hair. Those split ends are the stuff of my nightmares.'

Jeez, it's pick on Ellie day, I thought gathering a handful of hair and studying it. It *was* getting long, and the ends looked like I'd been chewing on them. This was a habit I'd long since grown out of. I'd always worn my hair shoulder length, and I used to have my dull brown tresses livened up with copper highlights. Sam always said that when the sun shone on my hair, it turned the colour of fire.

Now that he couldn't see my hair, stroke it the way he used to, there didn't seem much point in bothering. It wasn't like I had to maintain a professional image, like Gemma. William-Peter and Saffy-Rose couldn't care less if I wore my bear suit onesie to work although Nervy Caro would probably have something to say about it! Mostly I pull my hair back into a ponytail, and I regretted my decision to let it hang loose today.

'Well?' Gemma asked as she tapped a high heel impatiently against the floor.

'Alright, it's a deal.' I didn't have a choice; I needed Gemma on my side, so I dutifully applied a smear of pink to my lips.

And, forty minutes later the deal was done. We walked out of the auction rooms with matching pink sticky grins. Gemma had done the bidding, and for a steal, she'd successfully purchased on my behalf the three-bedroomed house with a lounge floor you could roly-poly down, that I'd known I was loved in. I pinched myself knowing I'd soon be calling it home. *Sam and I would be calling it home.*

'Where to now?' I'd asked thinking a nice celebratory lunch was in order. I'd even treat. My mortgage-paying austerity measures could be put in place tomorrow, but Gemma was on a mission. She'd driven me straight around to her favourite stylist, Jerome.

'For me, he'll fit you in,' she'd said bustling me in through the glass doors of his modernistic upmarket salon.

Jerome was horrified by my split ends and said he was duty-bound by the hairdresser's code to squeeze me in. I was a little bit taken aback by the head massage I received mid conditioner. When did all that tapping on your scalp become a thing? I didn't realise I'd had my bottom clenched the whole time until it was over.

'Ellie, congratulations!'

My solicitor Ken Fraser's booming voice intruded on my thoughts. I saw Sarah, the receptionist, looking at me strangely and I realised I was clenching. I released in time to shake his hand and agree that it was very exciting before taking my keys and racing out the door.

Chapter 6

Here I was swinging my car into the driveway of our new, my old home! My mobile burst into song as I wrenched the handbrake up and I debated ignoring it. The only thing I wanted to do was get inside the house. It was Gemma's name illuminated on the screen though and I sighed. *Best answer it*. A second later after she'd congratulated me on becoming a homeowner, she launched into her reason for calling.

'Does it mean I'm a cougar if he's two years younger than me, Ellie?'

I wished I hadn't bothered picking up now.

'How would I know?'

'Hmm hang on a sec I'm just googling it.'

I took the opportunity to get out of the driver's seat and put my phone down on the car roof so I could haul my case out of the boot. My white Honda Jazz was an upgrade from the unreliable old Nissan. Sam spotted it online for sale a few years back. The price was right, and he suggested, given my lack of spatial awareness when it came to parking and the Honda's compact size, we take a look. Gemma wouldn't be seen dead in it; she reckoned it was a granny car. Her mode of transport was a shiny, black jeep—she needed it to show her clients around and tried to justify her ludicrous repayments for it by spouting off about success breeding success. I take secret pleasure in watching her try to manoeuver it into those ridiculously skinny parking spaces when we go to the mall together.

As far as I was concerned, though, my Honda was pure gold and bonus! I owned it outright. It was a trusty stead, easily spotted on the roads (white is the safest colour, and if anyone knows how important that is, it's me), and it never let me down, which was more than could be said for my cousin. She was supposed to be here with me now helping me move in. Instead, she was googling the definition of a cougar, and I was guessing she was perched on a barstool eyeing up a younger man. I picked up my phone again in time to hear the answer.

'Oh phew you've got to be over forty to earn that title.' Gemma giggled—at twenty-seven she had a few years to go before she'd be tarred with that particular brush.

'Well, I can breathe easier now knowing that.' I rolled my eyes, picturing her wineglass in hand, toying with one of her carefully curled Hollywood waves as she adopted a glossy pout and batted her lashes. I'd seen her in action before, more than once, and it always had the same stupefying effect on her target. Gemma was like a spider's web to a fly. Her latest target, the newest salesman at the real estate agency where she worked, was Regan Bryant or, as she called him when he wasn't in earshot, Stud Muffin. I knew that he didn't stand a chance if she'd set her sights on him, which she has.

She'd been twittering on about him since he started at her firm, The Property Pro, a fortnight ago. She'd given me a detailed description of the way he filled his suit trousers out just so and the way his shirt strained against his chest and how she could see a smattering of chest hair but not enough to warrant a wax—over our respective cereal, pretty much every morning since.

'Oh, don't be snarky, Ellie, it's Friday afternoon. I'm just going to have one little lunchtime celebratory drinky-winky. I deserve it because my sale in Idris Road finally went unconditional this morning. Thank God!'

'That's great, Gemma, congratulations!' I meant it. I knew the homeowners had been tricky clients who had her pulling her curls out on more than occasion. She deserved the sale; she'd worked hard for it.

'Thanks. I promised the team I'd shout them all a drink and then I'll be straight round to help you get unpacked.' Her voice was nearly drowned out by the music and shouts of laughter in the background.

I wasn't holding my breath, because I suspected she'd be far too busy weaving her sticky web to come and help me unpack. 'Ah, whatever, Gem,' I said. 'Have one for me.' I wasn't surprised she hadn't shown up, although it would have been nice to crack open the bottle of bubbly Aunty Paula had promised to bring over with her later. Aunty Paula and Uncle Colin might have generously stumped up the cash to help me buy and fix up 16 Radford Street, but it was Gemma who'd held my hand these last ten months.

She tried to get me to come out on the town with her sporadically, she'd tell me I was in my prime and life was passing me by, but I didn't want to. I was only twenty-five, and other girls my age were out having fun, but I didn't want to be one of them. It wouldn't have seemed right to twirl on a dancefloor or make small talk over a dinner table. How could I? What could I contribute? I would be the proverbial party pooper. The girl with a face on her like a wet weekend. That's why I didn't want to socialise. It was too hard, and I didn't have the energy for it.

'Life's short you have to keep moving forward, Ellie,' Gemma would say to me before muttering that it was like talking to a brick wall. She even tried the tough love conversation. You know, laying it on the line by telling me the doctors have said Sam's not likely to wake up, and if, by some miracle he does, the brain injury he's suffered will have left him with permanent damage. He wouldn't be the same Sam who left on a freedom camping quest that day. I knew this, but I still got mad and yelled at her in a way that isn't like me. I shouted that no matter what, I would not give up on him because he'd never give up on me.

It's different when someone dies; people know how to react. They bring you flowers and offer sympathy, but Sam hasn't died, and my friends have run out of things to say to me about him. Sometimes I feel so old compared to them. It's like I know something they don't because when something bad happens, and I mean BAD, it doesn't always work out okay. I've learned that sometimes the worst thing you can imagine happening does happen.

Don't get me wrong, they're still my friends, but they're doing what they did before Sam's accident, whereas I'm not, and I don't know where we slot into each other's lives anymore. Sam has a few loyal mates who visit him; he was never the kind of guy who had a big circle around him, just a few good pals he could count on—Connor being one of them. He calls me most weeks to check how I'm getting on and sometimes he comes over with a few beers and we talk about Sam and stuff we all used to do together. He misses him, and I get that, which is why he's easy to be around.

Despite my having shouted at her, Gemma hasn't given up on me, and I love her for that. The property I was standing in front of now represented more to me than a place to live, it's somewhere I'd been cared for and known I was secure, somewhere I hope Sam will feel like that when he finally comes home. All that's worth more than living in a posh suburb, because it's something I haven't felt since last August. Besides, I spend five days a week working in a posh suburb, and it's overrated. Nervy Caro never seems all that chipper despite her luxury surrounds. Maybe that saying's true: money can't buy you happiness.

I think Mum thought it was a bit weird me buying the place she grew up in because she went quiet when I telephoned to tell her, which was unusual. She was lucky I didn't just text her the news. There wasn't a lot she could say on the matter, though, given it was Uncle Colin and Aunty Paula stumping up the cash for me to buy it.

I caught sight of myself standing with the phone pressed to my ear in the reflection of my car window outside my house. My free hand smoothed my hair. To be fair, Jerome did a good job of transforming me. 'Thanks, Gemma.'

'For what?'

'For being you.'

'You're not being sarcastic I hope.'

'Nope.'

I disconnected the call and took a moment to survey the neighbourhood. The gnarled, leafless limbs of the trees that, in the summertime, would form a green arbour line either side of the street. A navy blue two-seater couch sat abandoned under the trees on the grass verge across the road. The garden behind the couch was full of car parts. It was easy to spot the homes that weren't owner-occupied because their lawns were overgrown or full of detritus and the paintwork tired. They gave off an uninviting air of neglect. Next door, for instance, I thought as I peered over the top of the rickety paling fence separating our two properties, was a prime example.

A trike lay abandoned alongside an old tyre on the muddy patch of lawn where the grass had died. The patch was car-sized, so I guessed it was used as a parking space. A woman was sitting on the front doorstep smoking, a phone in her hand. Inside the house, the shrieks and thumps of small children running amok were drifting through the open front door, mingling with the plumes of smoke and drifting off down the street.

She looked about the same age as me, young to have a brood thudding about inside her house. I smiled and waved as I caught her eye. I wasn't expecting her to leap up and magically whip up a welcoming plate of scones, or bottle of wine; a wave back would have done the trick, or a simple 'howdy neighbour'.

Instead, I got a scowl before she ground out her cigarette on the step and flicked it into the garden bed beside the steps. A solitary rose bush was valiantly holding its own amongst the weeds and no doubt, butts. She got to her feet, pausing to hoist her grey hipster trackie bottoms up before stalking inside the house. The door closed behind her with a resounding and unfriendly bang.

Charming, I thought shivering, and for the first time since I heard Number 16 was for sale, I was pricked by doubt that I'd done the right thing buying it.

Chapter 7

I decided to put my encounter with my surly neighbour to one side. Nothing was going to suck the joy out of this moment for me and so, unloading my boot, I began dragging a case along the cracked concrete path to the front door. The front lawn could do with a mow and the weeds either side of the path were having a jolly old time, I noticed, thinking Pops would be horrified. You could have used it as a bowling green when he was in charge of it. It occurred to me then, I didn't have a lawn mower. Maybe there'd be some kid in the neighbourhood keen to earn a couple of dollars. Failing that Uncle Colin might let me borrow his until I could pick up a reasonable second-hand one. Either way sorting that out was going to be a priority. I didn't want number 16 looking like the scrap yard across the road.

The front door, roof, eaves and window trims were all painted in the same shade of forest green. It had been all the go in the nineties, and I wrinkled my nose at the flaking patches on the sill under the bedroom window next to the front door. It had been Nan and Pops' room and I didn't think the paint had been touched up since Pops had last swung a brush. I stood there for a moment visualising a hot summer's day many moons ago. There was Pops with his flannel beanie hat pulled low to keep the sun off his head, paint-and-oil-splattered overalls on as he stood in the front garden bed applying a lick of that forest green paint to the sill. I was sitting on the doorstep watching him and not really paying attention to the bottle I had jammed in the mouth of Baby All Gone.

'Ellie, do you want a turn?' Pops asked.

I did indeed and poor Baby All Gone's bottle was wrenched from her mouth as she was unceremoniously dumped on the porch. 'I won't be able to reach, Pops,' I said looking up at the sill.

I should have known he'd never make a suggestion that he couldn't carry through on, unlike my mum who'd perfected the art of dangling carrots and snatching them away. He dipped the brush into the green paint, wiping the excess on the side of the pot. He handed it to me and then lifted me up. Holding me there as I swiped it over the sill. 'There we are, now, gently does it back and forth. That's it, Ellie, you're doing a great job.'

God I loved Pops.

Nan appeared in the doorway. 'You two are crushing my dahlias!' Her voice was stern but her smile wasn't and she had a plate of hot buttered pikelets in her hand. 'I think it might be time for the workers to take a break.'

God I loved Nan.

I smiled at the memory and put my key in the lock and turned it. As it clicked and the door opened nerves fluttered up through me like startled sparrows flying away from crumbs of bread. What would I find inside? I'd seen the photos in the brochure Gemma had shown me but photos didn't catch the aura of a place. Whatever the vibes would be I needed to get a move on, I thought glancing back to see a hoodie-clad youth shuffling up the street. Otherwise the contents of my boot would have gone walkabout by the time, I'd finished dithering about.

I hefted the case over the threshold and stood for a moment in the hallway. The door to the lounge was open and I could see dust motes floating in the winter sunlight pouring in through the windows. It had always been a suntrap in there. I shivered in the hallway though; the air was cold and spoke of an empty house even if my nose was catching a whiff of fried food and cigarettes.

I left my case leaning against the wall under the shelf were the telephone used to sit and ventured forth, moving through into the lounge to stand in a puddle of sunlight. The busy red Axminster carpet beneath my feet was the same, but the drapes pulled either side of the window were different. A homage to the seventies, I thought shuddering. I remembered stretching out on this carpet in front of the television while Nan told me I'd get square eyes sitting that close to the screen. The patch I was standing on was faded pink from the harsh UV rays but the carpet had lived up to its reputation for durability. Nan would be pleased to see it had lasted so well, even if the rest of the room was in a sorry state.

Would there be ghosts here? I stood still, ear cocked, but there were no sounds other than a faraway shout, children playing. Pops' armchair—the La-Z-Boy I'd get told off for flicking the footrest in and out of—was no longer there, nor the matching two-seater Nan had commandeered for *Coronation Street*. My beanbag too, was long gone. I could still see the three of us in here though. Nan with her cup of tea and biscuit, Pops stretched out on his chair sound asleep, mouth hanging open as he gave the odd little snore, which made me giggle from where I'd be, book in hand, on my beanbag throne. If there were ghosts, I decided, then they were happy ones.

I poked my head in their old room next. This would be Sam's and my room. He'd recoil in horror if he could see it at the moment. Pink, pink and more pink. Somebody had obviously gotten a deal on candyfloss-coloured paint. I couldn't wait to unload my photographs though and put them on the dressing table when Uncle Colin arrived with it. Seeing Sam smiling at me from within a frame was as close as I was going to get to sharing the room with him in the meantime.

I made my way through the rest of the house, ignoring the damp smell in the bathroom, the cracks in the wall and the uneven floors. One step at a time, Ellie, I told myself. It can all be fixed and made better. Sam's face floated before me and I wished I could make *him* better.

Chapter 8

♥

The next day at ten a.m. I was where I always am at that time on a Saturday—at Briarwood House sitting cross-legged in the armchair beside Sam. Sometimes I don't want to talk, so instead, I play music. I've put together a playlist of our songs, downloaded onto Spotify, and on those afternoons when I push *shuffle play* the memories flow. I like to pull the chair closer to him and rest my head on the bed alongside his. Some of the songs make me cry, especially the Ed Sheeran numbers. His lyrics remind me how much I miss hearing Sam's voice, the way he'd laugh so hard sometimes, he couldn't breathe.

There are other songs on that list that make me smile. He loved Coldplay and when I hear their songs, I remember what a terrible dancer he was. There was no holding him back from busting out his moves, though, if it was a song he liked. He took 'dance like no one's watching' to another level, and I loved him for it.

Today was not what I thought of as a wallow day. Those are for when I want to wade through our memories and not be reminded of where we are in the present. I usually round wallow days off with a walk along Sumner Beach. It's where I whiled away many Saturday afternoons sitting on the hot sand watching Sam surf. It's a beautiful stretch of coast, but beautiful places can be deceptive, and the sea there has a nasty rip. I'd scoop up a handful of sand and let it run through my fingers, trying not to worry about him getting caught in it, even though he was a strong swimmer.

Today, I'd woken up in our new home, and I had plenty to tell him. I reached over and rested my hand on top of his, ignoring the rigidity of it. His hands were splinted to stop contracture, that's something else I've learned about since his accident. I stayed like that for a moment before settling back in my seat to begin filling him in.

'I only woke up once last night.' This was very exciting because I haven't had a full night's sleep unaided since August. I have nightmares about Sam lying hurt on his own for hours. 'And that was down to the lemon tree branches tapping on the window. You want to see it; it's laden with them. I don't know what I'll do with them all. Nan used to make the yummiest lemon curd; she'd put it on my sandwiches. Maybe I'll have a go at that, but you know what I'm like in the kitchen. It's more likely to turn out as lemon slop. Or, I might put a bag of them at the gate, you know help yourself sort of thing.' I paused remembering the girl next door. 'Then again they might be used as a weapon. I saw the neighbour when I was unloading my car, and she wasn't exactly friendly.'

I hadn't had time to go shopping yet, so breakfast this morning was a date scone I picked up on my way over. I broke off a piece and popped it in my mouth. They could have been a bit more generous with the dates, I thought chewing. I'd do a proper shop on the way home. It was going to be strange cooking for one after so many years of living first with Sam and then Gemma. The thought of not being asked what the calorie count is in the meals I prepare whenever it was my turn to cook dinner was quite an appealing one though.

'I didn't think I'd get much sleep at all. I thought I'd be listening out for strange noises, but by the time Aunty Paula, Uncle Colin and Gemma left it was nearly eleven and I was pooped. I went out for the count the minute my head hit the pillow. Mind you that might have been down to the bottle of bubbles Aunty Paula cracked open!'

Gemma, in true form, had shown up just as the Lindauer was being popped and somewhat conveniently after all the hard work of unloading and unpacking was done. Still, it was nice that she'd made it and that she'd gotten to christen the house with the three of us. Clearly, a better offer hadn't been forthcoming from the Stud Muffin. I knew, too, there wouldn't be a chance to ask her how she'd gotten on, not with Uncle Colin and Aunty Paula in earshot.

'Uncle Colin got his mate Jeff—remember him? He's an electrician too—to help move my gear. It only took one trip because we got most of it in the back of his van and the rest of it went in Uncle Colin's Hilux. I'll have to buy them both a box of beers because between them they lugged all the heavy stuff inside. They even got the fire going for me. I've put a beanbag in front of it for now because there's no point setting the lounge or the spare bedroom up properly until the work's been done around that side of the house. I'm going to use the kitchen as my living space until it's finished.' Yes, I still have a thing for beanbags.

The piles under the house are damaged, and the house is going to be wedged up room by room, which means I can continue living in it while it's repaired. The interior is going to need re-gibbing, plastering, and painting once the foundations are strengthened. Uncle Colin explained all of this to me before the auction.

'Connor rang yesterday morning and offered to come around and help too, but I didn't think it was fair on him to give up his Friday night. Anyway, between the four of us we got it all done. I'll invite him over in a week or two once I'm properly settled in.' Sam's dad and his brothers would have helped me if I'd asked them, but I haven't told his family about the house. I don't want them to think I'm moving forward or more to the point moving away from Sam because I'm not. I don't want to tell them I've bought it for me and Sam either because we've never talked about what will happen next. I'm not stupid, I do know that Sam will need care, and lots of it when he finally comes home, it's just I prefer not to dwell on that.

'Aunty Paula and I gave the place a good going-over and, ugh! Guess what? I found mouse poo in the back of the kitchen cupboard.' The recollection makes me shudder. I'm not good with rodents.

'I'm going to pick up a couple of traps on my way home although I don't know how I'll cope disposing of the culprit. Do you remember that mouse we had that used to do danger runs from behind the fridge to the table when we were watching TV?' I don't expect him to answer, but I pause for a second anyway. 'Remember how I nicknamed it Jerry? Because it reminded me of those old *Tom and Jerry* cartoons and I thought it was cute. You wanted to set a trap, but I wouldn't hear of it until that night we were in bed and something tickled my hair. I thought it was you until I realised you were asleep and I spied a tiny shadow scampering out the door. Oh my God, that still makes my skin crawl.'

I rubbed my arms and grimaced, remembering with a tremor of guilt how I made a protesting Sam get out of bed and go down to the twenty-four hour supermarket. I'd ordered him to pick up a trap calling after him, 'Get a block of cheese too—there's to be no mercy!'

'Mum sent me a bunch of flowers as a housewarming welcome. They arrived first thing this morning. It must be kind of weird for her, me moving back into her old house. She wants me to send regular photo updates of the work being done. Did I tell you Gemma's given me her couch?' I'm keen to move on from the topics of mice and my mother. 'She said she's been wanting to get a new one for ages.' I flick the crumbs off my lap. 'I'm not sure whether I believe her, but she was adamant I have it.'

I haven't told him that I gave our battered old leather couch to Zac and Mandy—the one Sam had insisted come with him when we moved in together. Their guests use it, and to be honest I was glad to see the back of it. The worn-out three-seater had been the source of more than one argument between us. I wanted to upgrade but Sam said it was perfectly fine and we should be saving for a house, not buying furniture we didn't need.

'I've put it in the kitchen for the time being, and I'm going to make some new cushion covers to match the curtains I've got in mind for the living room. The ones hanging in there at the moment are revolting. Actually, all the curtains in the house are revolting.'

The offending drapes are a swirling mix of mustard yellow and poo brown. The people who I bought from must have hung them and I definitely can't live with them; they're like stepping back into a seventies time warp. Still, I'll have plenty of time to make some new ones while the work is being done.

I think about making a list. A list would be an organised, professional way of going about things and it would be satisfying ticking each thing off. I like the idea. New curtains for the lounge will be the first thing to be crossed off. I've never tackled a mammoth job like full-length drapes, but I'll give them my best shot—failing that, there was always the duvet and curtains for the guest room to make a start on.

I had the basics of setting up house from when Sam and I moved in together, couch aside. The new fridge I managed to talk Sam into buying against his better judgement, a rustic second-hand dining table with matching sideboard we bid for and won in an online auction, and the coffee table he'd made at a woodwork class. I love that coffee table even if it does wobble thanks to a short leg. It was currently propped up by a phone book, and our old TV is sitting on it in my temporary multi-purpose living, dining, kitchen space.

Then there's all my kitchen paraphernalia, boxed up as it was surplus to requirements at Gemma's. The practical pieces of mine and Sam's life together—given I'm not a talented cook there's an abundance of cookbooks, presents from an ever hopeful Sam—tucked away and stored in the corner of Uncle Colin's workshop. Uncle Colin and Jeff followed my directions as to where it all should go, and it's been strange seeing our furniture in an environment that was foreign, yet familiar at the same time.

'There's not going to be a lot left for the fun stuff after I make my repayments to Uncle Colin and Aunty Paula. I'm going to have to do the decorating on a shoestring but I can make a lot of things, and Connor's said he'd help with the painting. He can get the materials at cost for me.' I sent up a silent thank you to Connor for choosing painting as his trade, thank Spotlight for its array of affordable fabrics and Nan for teaching me to sew. I know from trawling the eco recycling warehouses, too, that there's a lot of good stuff to be picked up for a song. Given Sam always thought I was a spendthrift, I think he'd be proud of me. I've long suspected the reason he's always enthused about my Mad Ellie creations is because they're cheap.

'Uncle Colin's lined up the builder to do the repairs. His name's—' I try to retrieve it, but my mind's gone blank. 'James, John? Oh, I can't remember, but he's going to oversee the repairs from start to finish. He's got a lot of experience with earthquake-damaged properties according to Uncle Colin. And he's got a team of subbies, so all I have to do is keep out of their way.' He was supposed to be coming around to make a start on Monday but I'd yet to hear from him to sort out where to leave the key and that sort of thing.

'It was strange waking up this morning; I didn't know where I was at first. I opened my eyes, and all I could see was this candyfloss-pink-coloured wall. I mean, pink. Who paints a whole bedroom pink?' I flashback to the curtains—the same kind of people who can live with swirly seventies soft furnishings. 'And it's the master. When Nan and Pops' had it the walls were papered. I think they just painted right over the top of it.' Getting the walls painted is high on my 'to do' list.

'Anyway once I spotted the Dappledawns on my dressing table I remembered.' I watched Sam's face intently and fancied I saw a flicker of movement beneath his eyelids at the mention of my Sylvanian rabbit family. He knew that where I go, my miniature toy rabbit collection goes too. It's been that way since I tore the wrapping paper off and discovered the little bunny family of six and their cosy plastic thatched cottage on my seventh birthday.

The expensive present came from Nan and Pops, and it meant far more to me than they'd ever known—or maybe they did know. They were pretty wise my grandparents. The world I created around my Sylvanian family with their warm and welcoming home was my happy place. The Dappledawns' had a mother who baked, a father who fixed things when they broke and brothers and sisters to play with and, from time to time, squabble with too. They were the perfect family I didn't have.

When Sam and I moved in together, just like him with that horrible couch, I insisted the Dappledawns take pride of place on top of his old chest of drawers in our bedroom. I gave him short shrift for picking up Mr and Mrs Dappledawn and telling them that they had to stop going at it like rabbits because four kids in an overpopulated world was enough! I told him in no uncertain terms that my Sylvanian rabbit mother and father did not do things like that and the baby Dappledawns had been delivered by a stork!

We'd fallen back on the bed laughing at that and begun to kiss. Sam had broken away, a serious look in his eyes, as he asked, 'We've never talked about it, and I suppose I just assumed with you being a nanny, but do you want kids one day?'

I hadn't hesitated. 'With you, one day yes.'

'Four? Like them over there?' He gestured to the drawers.

'Hmm, we'll start with one and go from there.'

'But not yet. House first, then backpacking around Asia and then— '

'A big, white wedding.'

'A barefoot backyard wedding, and then kids.'

A teeny flash of irritation flared. He had everything so mapped out but I nodded my agreement. I'd argue my point when the time came. That was my way.

'And when we do can we make them the fun way? I'd rather leave the stork out of it.'

'Okay.'

'Can we practise now, you know just to make sure we know what we're doing when the time comes?'

I looked into those deep blue eyes of his and said, 'I think that's a great idea.'

Now I wished we hadn't waited to start a family of our own. Why had Sam been so bloody pig-headed about doing things in the order he'd mapped out for us? Look where it had gotten us. So what if we were young, and not financially set up yet? So what if we hadn't travelled? If you were to go back in time, it had been the norm to be married with children at our age. People didn't flit off exploring the world. We could have done that when we got to the retirement end of things. We'd have bumbled along and made it work. People did. You could always find reasons why you shouldn't do something but did those reasons matter in the big scheme of things?

Look at Nervy Caro, a woman who appears to have everything. She's married to a good provider, has two beautiful children, lives in a flash house, drives a big car, has expensive overseas holidays and boasts a wardrobe to rival Duchess Kate, but she's never happy.

One thing I've learned since Sam's accident is that it's not the things around us that matter, what matters is time. Time spent with the people you love. No amount of money can buy that. And when it runs out, you can't get it back. If me and Sam had thrown caution to the wind, I'd have a little piece of him to help me fill in the hole he's left in my life by taking time out. I looked at him lying there and watched the steady rise and fall of his chest. My breath was tight. It caught in my throat and my heart began to hurt. Heartbreak isn't just emotional, it's a physical pain too.

If we'd had a baby, Gina would have a grandchild—something of her son to hold on to while we waited for him to come back. It seems such a waste now that we didn't because I'd have made it work. You have to when a child is involved unless you're my mum, that is, but I'd had Nan and Pops. Instead here I am with a resident mouse or two, my Sylvanian Rabbit family and Leprechaun Sam to keep me company.

I stared at my half-eaten scone and pushed it back into the telling brown paper bag before tossing it in the bin. I'd lost my appetite. I felt cheated. How'd I gone from telling Sam all about our house to being emotionally bereft over a child we never had? It was as stupid and futile as all those what-if scenarios that plagued me in the early days when the reality of him not opening his eyes and being okay began to set in.

What if I'd told him I didn't want him to go away that weekend? What if I'd stamped my foot and told him he was selfish leaving me on my own? What if I'd made him take me with him? But I didn't, and you know why? Not because I'm an understanding girlfriend who got his need to get off grid and back to basics, because I don't—not really. I mean I think there is a lot to be said for creature comforts, so no, the reason I'd let him go without a word of protest was because I wanted to binge watch *13 Reasons Why* on Netflix.

The bubbles of excitement that had fizzed once I'd gotten my bearings that morning and realised I was back at Radford Street popped and a surge of my old foe anger shot through me. 'It's not fair, Sam; it's just bloody well not fair.' I looked at his still form, and this time I'm not apologising for swearing.

Chapter 9

♥

Looking back I think I knew Sam was going to be someone special in my life from the moment he gave me his chocolate-coated bean over coffee that first time we met. There was that and the way he sat with his head tilted to one side, listening to me talk. I could tell he wanted to hear what I had to say. His hair had the slightest of waves, and it needed a trim but his unkempt look added to his appeal. And those eyes, OMG those eyes. He was a little rough around the edges but give me that over a manscaper any day—in my head, I was giving him a ten out of ten and a big red tick. It's a habit of mine, the mental tick. I can't help it; it's the early learning teacher in me and all the risk assessment forms I have to fill in.

'I've only got half an hour, and then I'll have to head home. I'm working tonight,' I said sliding into the booth opposite him. 'I waitress,' I added hastily lest he jump to conclusions as to my night-time occupation. He'd taken me to a coffee house near the mall, and I'd used the short drive to the café to phone Uncle Colin who'd still been at work to tell him my car had conked out. Sam had already said he'd drop me home and Uncle Colin being Uncle Colin said he'd sort the car out for me. I sometimes wish if I could franchise him—0800unclecolin. I'd make a fortune.

The café was quiet given the lateness of the afternoon, and the food cabinet was limited to thick gooey squares and an obscenely large triangle of cheesecake. I'd told Sam I wasn't hungry because I didn't want to look like a greedy girl with my caramel shortbread and I didn't know him well enough to share but my stomach was growling and I folded my arms across my middle hoping he hadn't heard it. The barista was busy frothing our milk with an intense frown on his forehead and a tall, skinny girl with her hair done in Princess-Leia-style buns, was wiping down tables; apart from them, and a woman leaning into her laptop at a table near the entrance, we were the only ones in there.

Sam was fiddling with our order number, and I wondered if he was nervous. I was. It wasn't something I did, go for coffee with a stranger—even if he was an Adonis. 'So, you're an electrician?' Not the most original opening line but a girl's got to start somewhere.

'Yep, I followed in my dad's footsteps. He's had his own business for years, and he wanted me to go into partnership with him when I finished my apprenticeship, but I wanted to do my own thing. I guess I needed to prove to myself I can make it on my own steam.' He shrugged. 'I've been in business for about six months, and it's going okay. I like being my own boss even if the paperwork's a pain. What about you?'

'I know what you mean about paperwork,' I said going on to tell him about my job at Teeny Tykes and why I waitressed at Nummy-Num-Num. He was laughing at my description of Mrs Zheng when our coffee arrived.

'You're a busy lady,' he said ripping a sugar sachet open and stirring it into his.

'I am, but it's not forever. Once I get my student loan paid back, I'll ease off.' I watched as he picked up the chocolate bean from his saucer. He obviously had a sweet tooth.

'Would you like it?'

But of course, it was chocolate, wasn't it? I took it from him with a smile, popping it into my mouth and licking my fingers afterward where the chocolate had melted.

Twenty minutes passed as I told him a bit about me and listened as I learned a little about him. He still lived at home with his mum and dad and one younger brother who was studying law at university. He was one of four boys; he told me, adding that he wasn't in a rush to move out, not while there were home-cooked meals on offer each night and his business was still in its early days. 'What about you?'

'There's just me, but my cousin Gemma and I've grown up together. She's two years older than me and more like a big sister than a cousin.' I don't normally like to say too much about my mum and what my home life was like growing up, but with Sam, I found myself explaining how she'd left for Australia when I was fourteen and Uncle Colin and Aunty Paula had taken guardianship of me. I told him it was a relief to stay put after years of ping-ponging between wherever my mum was living at the time and my grandparents' house.

Nan and Pops had strong Christian morals, and they'd been strict but fair when I'd stayed with them. They gave me routines and security, and I relished my times living with them. It was those morals my mum Nicky spent her entire life bucking against. There were eight years between her and Uncle Colin, and she was the proverbial wild child, into anything and everything until it caught up with her, and I was born. She's never talked about my dad and believe me I've asked, but she always shut me down. We had a couple of humdinger rows about it when I was younger, but she never caved and told me. I've come to the conclusion she doesn't know who he is and if she does, well maybe I'm better off not knowing him.

My birth didn't slow her down for long though because when the going got tough, she'd drop me off at good old Nan and Pops. The boundaries they set when I stayed with them were what I needed after the disorderly existence I shared living with Mum. She bounced me around the city, moving from job to job, and in and out of the flat she shared with her boyfriend, Steve, with whom she was forever calling it quits. I didn't like Steve much—he was always angry. The stability Nan and Pops' home offered was something I craved.

When I reached my early teens, Nicky finished it with Steve once and for all by moving for good to the Gold Coast. Nan wasn't well by then, and it took all Pops' strength to look after her. He had no energy left in him for me too. Nicky turned to her brother and his wife Paula, crying that with everything that had happened with Steve she couldn't look after herself let alone me as well. She wasn't cut out for life as a single parent. She'd been far too young when she had me, blah, blah, blah. Given Gemma was an only child, she reasoned, having her cousin stay with her would do her good. We'd be as good as sisters.

Looking back now, I know Uncle Colin and Aunty Paula had no choice in the matter. I don't know if they'd wanted a second child or if they'd opted just to have one. I do know they couldn't stand by and see their niece left to her own devices in a strange country while her mother lived the life she seemed to think she was owed. They never once made me feel anything but loved by them though, and as for Gemma, despite being very different personalities we've grown up alongside each other, and just like Mum prophesized, we're more like sisters than cousins. She's definitely the bossy older sister.

'I found a proper home with Uncle Colin and Aunty Paula—they're brilliant,' I said draining my cup. I didn't want to leave that coffee shop. I wanted to know more about him, and I would've whiled away the entire evening talking to him, but I didn't want to risk the wrath of Mrs Zheng by being late. This man who just over an hour ago I'd never met before was easy to be around and well, let's face it he was more than hot he was gorgeous, and I've already mentioned his eyes. I had somewhere I had to be, though, and unlike my mother, I'm an extremely reliable person. I pride myself on it.

Sam took my cue, and we left the café. The traffic was moving into rush hour mode as he drove me home and while we idled behind a line of vehicles all waiting to turn right, he looked over at me. 'You're not going to be late for work are you?' I could see genuine concern on his face, and I melted around the edges just like that coffee bean he gave me.

The clock on the dashboard told me I'd be cutting it fine, but I'd get to the restaurant by the skin of my teeth thanks to Aunty Paula kindly texting to say I could borrow her car. 'I should be alright, thanks. What are you up to tonight?' The question popped forth, sounding like an invitation that I wasn't in a position to offer.

Sam was concentrating on his next manoeuvre so seeing my chance I studied his profile; he needed a shave, I thought, imagining stroking his cheek. His hands were wrapped around the steering wheel as he swung the car right. They were strong worker's hands, and he had long fingers. I don't know what it is, but I have this thing about men with short fingers. They're up there with skinks, you know those baby-sized lizard things? But that's another story. I experienced an unnerving jolt down yonder at the thought of what those strong, long fingers could do to me and blinked as he braked suddenly.

'Sorry, the asshole didn't indicate.'

'They're out there,' I said. Inwardly I told myself to get a grip. I don't usually start envisaging *Fifty Shades* scenarios with men I hardly know, but Sam was different. Like I said, I'd known it from the moment he passed me his chocolate bean. I hoped my face wasn't as flushed as I felt inside as he turned toward me with a grin.

'Didn't answer your question, did I? I'm meeting a mate for a drink. I've got a couple of jobs on tomorrow morning, so it won't be anything wild.' He indicated into my street, and I chewed my bottom lip. Should I be forward and ask for his number? I wanted to see him again, but maybe he was just a nice guy who liked rescuing damsels in distress and would think nothing more about this afternoon once he'd dropped me off.

'That's me over there, the two-storey red brick.' I pointed reluctantly to the house, seeing smoke curling out of its chimney. That was another thing about living with Aunty Paula and Uncle Colin; I never came home to a cold house. There's a lot to be said for that, the warmth and smell of food cooking in the oven when I walk through the door envelops me and I know I'm loved and safe. It's a sensation I've never stop appreciating because I know it isn't one you can take for granted.

'Nice house.' Sam pulled over to the kerb, and I reached for the door handle.

'Yes, it is. My uncle designed it. He's an architect. Thanks for the coffee.' *PLEASE, PLEASE, PLEASE ask me out.* I opened the door reluctantly.

'Hey uh, would you like to go out for dinner sometime?'

YES! 'Yes, I'd like that.'

'Um, should I get your number then?'

I nodded and waited while he retrieved his phone before giving him my number, I enunciated the digits slowly and clearly, and I made him read the number back to me to be sure he'd entered it right. Then, out of nowhere I said, 'I'm free on Sunday night.'

'Sunday it is then. Shall I pick you up at seven?'

'Seven's good.'

We grinned at each other, looking rather pleased with ourselves, before I got out and tried not to skip up the path. I played a silly game, telling myself that if he was still there waiting to see me go inside, then he was the one. I slotted the key in the door and looked back over my shoulder before turning it. His van was still idling, and he grinned, giving me a wave before driving off.

I let myself in and called out hello, hearing Aunty Paula banging about in the kitchen as I skipped straight up the stairs to my room. I wanted nothing more than to throw myself down on the bed and re-hash our conversation, but there was no time. I needed to get changed for work. It was only when I went to give my teeth a quick brush to get rid of my coffee breath that I spied the brown kernel of coffee bean wedged between my teeth. *OH MY GOD! Why didn't he tell me?* My insides scrunched up with embarrassment; it could only happen to me. I was amazed he'd asked me out. Perhaps he was short-sighted or something and hadn't noticed. I could only hope.

Chapter 10

♥

I was lying in bed thinking about candyfloss. It's not because I want a bag of it, although I'd stuff great big pink tufts of it in my mouth if I had one. It's these four walls that put the thought of it in my head. I can't paint them yet though because Connor says the paper's got to be stripped first—he's given me that task. He left a scraper for me in the letterbox the other day so I can make a start. There's an awful lot of wall in here. I just hope there's only the one layer of wallpaper stuck to them.

Uncle Colin went through the Scope of Works with me, and there's a lot of other non-cosmetic stuff that needs to be done to get the house to an insurable level. I wouldn't have a clue where to start or how to go about getting it all rolling. I'm glad Uncle Colin's in the trade, sort of, and has a builder he trusts lined up to do the job. I might not know much about the industry, but I do know that good tradesmen are gold. Sam told me more than once that he'd been on some jobs where the post-quake repair work would make you cringe.

My builder's name is Joel. I repeated it to myself ten times once I'd gotten off the phone to him to imprint it on my brain; it's a good solid name, which I hope reflects his workmanship. I mean you wouldn't put your faith in a Duane, would you? That, to me, screams Cowboy

Builder. Joel rang me yesterday and said he and his crew would be onsite at eight a.m. Monday morning. He sounded professional, for which he got a tick.

I hope none of his team are the kind of creepy tradesmen that go through your knicker drawer. It's not that my mind's in the gutter, it's because I saw this programme years ago and it scarred me. There were hidden cameras put up in a house, and this plumber was called in to do a bogus job. The knicker thing did happen. It's one of those TV clips that once seen you can't unsee, and I decide I'll put my period knickers—they came in a five pack and were bought solely for comfort and have no aesthetic qualities whatsoever—at the top of the pile. A deterrent for anyone that way inclined.

The rain was hitting the window and the light in the room was dull, not giving me any clues as to what time it was. Yay for Sunday, I think, snuggling back down under my duvet and ignoring the wallpaper stripping, which is something I could be getting on with. I was reluctant to get up because I'd already tested the air by sticking my foot out from under my bedding. It shot back under the covers pretty darn quick, too, because it was cold. I don't mean a little bit nippy either, I mean sleep with a hat on bone-chillingly freezing.

I've gotten used to living with modern creature comforts such as double glazing and heat pumps. I didn't appreciate how magical it is to get out of bed and flick a switch or even better have the heating set to a timer. Voila! You've got a toasty house. Like I said, magic.

Radford Street, I know from the building inspection, has a few pink bats in the ceiling, single glazing throughout and one log burner in the living room. I love the idea of having a fire. It's a cosy thought, curling up on the couch and watching the flickering flames in the depth of winter, but I'd love it even more if I had a servant who would lay it and light it for me. I go one step further and get them to bring me in tea and toast on a silver platter because it is breakfast time after all.

At least I've got Uncle Colin. All young people venturing out on their own should have an Uncle Colin. Like I said before 0800unclecolin. If it weren't for him, this Joel and his crew would find me frozen to the couch come Monday morning, but I won't be because Uncle Colin dropped me off a cord of wood yesterday, along with a gas heater and full bottle. The heater's a temporary fixture in the kitchen while the lounge is out of action. I hadn't thought about practical stuff like keeping warm; I'd only thought about fun things like wall colours and curtain fabrics. Wallpaper stripping does not fall into the fun category. I wished Sam was here; he'd be a dab hand with a scraper.

I keep imagining what it would be like living here with him. To sit in front of that cosy fire with him. Then I get frustrated that he's still at Briarwood House; it's why I've been fixating on my bedroom's pink walls and the sanctity of my knicker drawer.

Once I'd put the groceries away yesterday afternoon, finished unpacking and set my mouse traps, I spent the rest of the daylight hours stacking the wood down the back of the garden. There's a small shed there, and the wood's stored under the eaves where it will stay dry. It was surprisingly hard work and I think that when I get up I'll find my arms are sore thanks to my efforts.

I'd just gotten the fire going as the afternoon began creeping toward evening, deciding to make the most of it before the work starts on Monday, when my phone rang.

'Hi, how's it all going?'

'Hey, Connor. All good here.' He's breathing heavily and I figured he must be jogging. It's the second time I'd heard from in the last couple of days. 'You running?'

'Yeah.'

'You're mad.'

'Ellie, I want to ask you something.'

'Oh yeah?'

'I'm thinking about organising a sponsored run for Sam. Well for Brain Research New Zealand but I want to donate the money raised from it in his name. I just need to do something.' I could hear the frustration in his voice and I knew what he meant. There is a feeling of inertia, of powerlessness where Sam and his never-ending sleep are concerned.

'I think it's a great idea.'

'You do?' He sounds relieved.

'I do. So long as you don't expect me to run.'

'I reckon November will be a good time to hold it. That gives you plenty of time. You could come for a run with me tomorrow if you want?'

'You've got selective hearing, Connor. I don't want, but thanks.' No way am I pounding the pavement with him. For one thing he's super fit and for another, I hate running. I'm more a 'recline on the couch, eat chocolate' kind of girl.

'Three months, Ellie.'

'Yeah, yeah.'

'Hey, before I go do you need a hand unpacking? I know you said you had it under control yesterday, but I know what it's like to stand in front of a pile of boxes with no idea where to start or where the can opener is.'

I laughed at that. 'I'm pretty sorted I got a lot of it done yesterday and I found the can opener, so I won't starve.' I thought about asking him if he wanted to come around and toast the house with me, watch a movie, do a spot of wallpaper scraping or something later on, but held back. I needed time to settle in myself. I'm going to be living here in this house on my own until Sam wakes up so I might as well get used to it. 'Enjoy your run.'

'Twelve weeks,' he managed to get in before I hung up.

The movie I chose was a thriller, and I regretted my choice when I went to bed because I'd lain there wide-eyed in the darkness listening out for strange bumps in the night. I'd also begun hating the lemon tree and its window-tapping branches. I didn't have half a bottle of bubbles soothing me off to sleep this time either. I wished that I'd stoked the fire before I went to bed too because the lounge will be like a fridge in the morning.

Now as my phone rang, I crept my hand out from under the covers to pat around on the bedside table until I found it. It was Gemma. I meant to call her yesterday to drill her about how she'd gotten on with Regan at her Friday drinks session. By the time I'd come back inside though, my top covered in wood splints, I was knackered and I knew if I spoke to her she'd try and talk me into coming out with her for the night. I'd no energy left to be bothered arguing with her, and no intention of going out, hence no phone call.

'Morning, rise and shine, oh cousin of mine!'

She was ridiculously cheerful, and I was immediately suspicious because Gemma's not a morning person. My eyes narrowed, as I deduced she must've had sex last night with the Stud Muffin. What else would have her chirruping like a randy cockatoo this early on a Sunday morning?

'Hi. What's got you so perky then? Or should I not ask?'

'I'm psyched for the gym that's what.'

'Did you pull an all-nighter? You'll pay for it on Monday.' She must be drunk because like me with running, Gemma does not do the gym.

'No and before you ask, I haven't had sex and I haven't been drinking either, only a green smoothie and it was delish. What are you doing?'

'Having a Sunday morning lie-in and wishing someone would light the fire for me and whip me up some breakfast.'

'Well you've had your lie-in. It's nine o'clock and coming to the gym with me is a great way you can warm up and get into shape at the same time. Exercise is good for your state of mind too you know, Ellie. So come on up, up, up and get your workout gear on!'

What is with people trying to make me exercise? I don't know when Gemma, the girl who drives to the shop for milk even though it is less than five minutes on foot, became an authority on the benefits of exercise. And, I'd rather walk naked through the Antarctic than go to the gym on a Sunday morning. I don't like this amped-up, cheerleading version of my cousin either, so I said, 'Piss off, Gemma.'

'Ah come on, Ellie. You can't expect me to go on my own.'

'Yes I can, and anyway it's a well-known fact that the gym is where hot-fit people go to meet other hot-fit people. It's the hot-fit person's alternative to a bar hook-up. You don't need me to hold your hand.'

'But I'm not fit, and I don't know how to use any of the equipment. I need you to show me.'

Sam and I had gone through a keep-fit phase for all of two months. We'd both put on a few pounds in our loved-up state, thanks to snuggling up together on the couch, watching TV and eating chocolate caramel ice-cream treats. This was despite our regular vigorous after-dark workouts. So, we hit the gym, but we packed it in when the lure of lounging on our settee watching *Game of Thrones* and eating chocolate caramel ice-cream treats outweighed pounding it out on the treadmill. To Gemma's mind, those eight weeks qualify me as a personal trainer, but I'm not giving in without a fight. 'Why the gym? You hate the gym.'

'No, I don't.'

'Um, short-term memory. What about when we did that circuit class a few years back? You said you would never set foot inside a gym ever again.'

'Oh right. Well, you can't blame me. The way that awful woman with the huge thighs shouted at me for not doing those burp things properly was not called for, but I've moved on from that.'

'Burpees,' I murmur, and to be fair, the trainer had been a bit scary. She'd have been more suited to a Russian Weightlifting Olympic Training Centre than the fitness class she was in charge of.

'Whatever, it's a stupid name for an exercise anyway. This time around I'm going to try out the equipment. Have you heard of Fitbods? It's on the city end of Fendalton Road—you might've noticed it on your way to work.'

I do know it because each morning when I stop at the lights I stare in at the row of sweaty people on the treadmills. Their faces are set with grim determination as they gaze out the big glass window, making the rest us of us who're sitting in traffic feel slovenly and unmotivated. I still haven't solved the mystery of why Gemma wants to go to the gym though.

'Yeah I know it but why now, on a Sunday morning, have you decided you need to go and work out?'

'Regan works out there. I overheard him on the phone saying that's where he'd be on Sunday morning.'

And there we had it. The truth of the matter. 'I see. I thought you might've got together with him at your Friday drinks session. A bonk after a few drinks would have been much easier than trying to impress him at Fitbods.'

'Tell me about it, but it was a waste of time. He had to dash off to meet a client before I could make my moves, and Fitbods is Plan B. I think where Regan is concerned I'm going to have to play the long game. Besides, I've got the most gorgeous Jo-Jo Runs purple mesh, racer-back vest top and matching pink leggings with a mesh insert up the sides to wear. I'm modelling them on That Girl, and I promised Jo-Jo I'd upload my shots tonight. I need to take a couple of action pics while we're there. It's called multi-tasking, my darling cousin, and Regan won't be able to resist.'

Modest, Gemma is not, and I pictured her get-up. It sounded like the type of outfit you needed to have been working out seven days a week for at least six months before even considering squeezing into it—that, or be genetically blessed like my cousin. The thought of her striking a pose on the cross-trainer made me smile. Poor Regan was probably at this moment happily lifting weights, oblivious to the fact that a purple vision in full makeup was on a mission and heading his way.

'I'll swing by in twenty, okay?'

'Gemma, I haven't had breakfast and I've got stuff to do. I'm not go—'

'Grab a banana,' she said before hanging up.

I know when I'm beat so with a sigh as weighty as my duvet I pushed it to one side and got up. I looked at my dishevelled self in the mirror and muttered to Sam on my shoulder, 'How come I always let her get her way?'

Leprechaun Sam shook his head slowly and said, 'I don't why. You always have. How many times did I tell you to stand up to her?'

'I know, I know.' I think we wasted a lot of time on that discussion and I replied the way as I always did, 'But she's my cousin.'

~

I heard Gemma toot, and I tossed my banana skin in the bin before hurriedly pulling my hair back into a ponytail and racing out the door.

'How's your first couple of nights been in the old place?' She asked as I clambered in alongside her.

'Good. It's funny, but I thought I'd get a real sense of Nan and Pops once I moved in, but I haven't.' The house with its tired and almost garish interior isn't the way it was when they had it. There are no echoes of them left behind, but it is familiar.

'Is that a good thing or a bad thing?'

'A good thing I think.' I can decorate it the way I want without guilt at the thought I'm tearing down parts of Nan and Pops. I remind myself I'm going to go easy on the feminine touches because it's Sam's place too.

'You're right about it not being the way it was when Nan and Pops were still around. I saw a teenager with a hoodie on and his jeans were hanging so low he took builder's crack to a new level. He was casing the street when I pulled into it.' Gemma shook her head causing her topknot to bob precariously 'Not a good look. I told you the area wasn't what it used to be.'

'He's a product of his upbringing, and everybody's got to live somewhere.' I buckled myself in. 'And besides, the kids round here they don't you-know-what in their own patch.'

'Shit? And you're obviously voting Labour this time round.'

'Yes, that's the word,' I answered ignoring the latter remark.

As Gemma concentrated on her reversing camera, I spied one of my unfriendly neighbour's children tootling up and down their driveway on a scooter, and I waved over, offering a beaming neighbourly smile. I got a two-fingered salute in return.

'I saw that.' Gemma said primly. 'And I rest my case.'

Chapter 11

The gym was busy. Who'd have thought? What happened to people going to church on a Sunday morning and having morning tea afterward? I used to love going with Nan and Pops for the spread laid on once Sunday school was finished. Or, when I got older, having a decent lie-in. Gemma and I paid our casual entry fee and loitered in the foyer, soaking up the scene. Hip-hop music was playing, competing with the sound of grunts and pounding feet. The video screens up on the walls were tuned to MTV with near-naked women doing booty dances and the air smelled of sweat and perfumed deodorant.

My gaze swept the facility, and at the far end, I spotted a row of cross-trainers stationed in front of a wall of mirrors. They were alongside the rowing machines and exercise bikes and were all currently in use. The treadmills were positioned in front of the big expanse of glass that looked out to the road, with puffing, panting people striding it out on all of them. I spied a gruesome-looking stair machine in the corner. No one was on it, not that I was surprised. I'd already made my mind up I wouldn't be climbing that today. A revolving staircase is the stuff of nightmares. Men and women were on the various weights and muscle-strengthening machines, stretching ahead on either side of where we were standing. It's a serious business, working out, because no one in the whole gym was smiling and an awful lot of them were looking in the mirrors.

I haven't seen Regan before, and I scrutinised faces waiting to see if I could pick him out from Gemma's numerous descriptions. *No definitely not him. It would take super glue to rip that mat off his chest.* I needn't have bothered because she was already making a beeline for a vicious-looking contraption with a man wrapped around it. A cable machine, but to the uninitiated, it could be mistaken for bondage equipment. Checking him out before I followed her over, I could see why she was smitten. He was handsome in a Hollywood blonde, Hemsworth brothers way and I gave him a big red tick for wearing appropriate gym attire. That would be a vest and loose-fitting shorts with skins underneath them. Not just skins thank you very much!

Nervy Caro's husband Mr Richards or 'call me Doug'—his catch-phrase when our paths sporadically cross—is a keen road cyclist. I've seen him in cycling shorts—say no more. I'm not entirely sure what he does but so far as his job title goes, I've heard the phrase ED being bandied about. You know what I'm thinking, don't you? Erectile Dysfunction. Yes, it's immature, but it always made me laugh to think I have a boss with ED and a love of Lycra.

Regan's forehead glistened with sweat and the strain on his face was evident as he pulled the handles he was gripping down into his abdomen. I could tell that beneath that sweaty shirt he had a six-pack. He spotted Gemma—she was hard to miss—and looked surprised. His face broke into a grin. I shuffled from sneaker to sneaker trying to look innocent as I listened to her lie about what a coincidence it was seeing him there. Just as I was about to leave them to it, because I was worried Regan might think I was a bit weird lurking alongside the bondage equipment, she introduced me.

'Regan, meet my cousin, Ellie.'

Under normal circumstances, we might have reached out and shook one another's hands, but that's not protocol when you've been breaking a sweat like Regan has. So, I gave him a little wave and said, 'Hi.'

'Ellie, right?'

He blatantly gave me an approving once-over even though I was wearing grey leg warmers with green stripes over my leggings. Gemma had tried to make me take them off on the drive over but I found them ages ago in my favourite little second-hand boutique, and this is their first outing. Besides, it's payback for her dragging me down here. I thought about wearing my net skirt over the top of my leggings too; that would've really wound her up, but I decided there's a time and place for going all-out eighties and Fitbods probably isn't it. I have got on my grey crop top though.

'You remind me of someone?'

'Probably Madonna when she was young,' Gemma said. 'Ellie's a big fan of all her retro looks.'

He nodded slowly, and I had the weirdest sensation that he had X-ray vision and he could see what lay beneath my crop top. If that was the case he'd be disappointed by my matching grey sports bra. It used to be white. Either way, I could tell this was a man who liked women, and I've already decided that if Gemma has anything other than a casual romp on the photocopier at work planned for him, she might get burned. He oozed arrogant confidence, and I think it was this—coupled with his good looks—that had Gemma drooling. She doesn't like a pushover when it comes to her men.

'Gemma talks about you a lot.'

'In a good way, I hope?' I side-eyed her but she ignored me.

He grinned but didn't answer my question. 'You bought at auction recently didn't you?'

'Yes, the house is where Gemma's and my grandparents used to live. It settled on Friday.'

'Ah yeah that's right. I know the story.'

I knew then that Gemma had told him about Sam. I can always tell. It's in the flicker of sympathy, however brief, that flashes in someone's eyes when they're talking to me. It's an odd feeling, like I'm avoiding the elephant in the room by not bringing Sam into the conversation even in the teensiest-tiny way but what would I say? And I'm protective of whom I choose to mention him to. I don't want sympathy or pity from strangers.

'Well congratulations,' he said, sidestepping the elephant and smoothly moving on. 'Are you all settled in?'

'Yes, thanks, I got most of my unpacking done yesterday.'

'Great. Did you two ladies come for a class?' He gestured toward a room leading off the main gym where several people were laying mats out before his attention flitted back and settled on the purple and pink gym bunny. I wanted to say that I'd come under duress and would he not just whisk Gemma off to the showers for a quickie and be done with it. That way I could head home and burrow under my duvet once more. My leg warmers and crop top had had enough of an outing. I was ready for the off.

Gemma's topknot was bobbing once more as she shook her head in response to Regan's question, but I could see a way to extricate myself from the conversation. 'Nope not doing a class but I am going to hit the cross-trainer, and there's one just come free. It was nice meeting you, Regan.' I put my earphones on to avoid any more conversation and headed over to the empty machine before scrolling through my Spotify listings. I didn't want one of my Sam playlists because having a blub session at Fitbods was not on the cards, and searching *workout*, I chose a random compilation of dance music.

My legs were like lead weights as I began pumping them back and forth to Rihanna and reflected in the mirror in front of me I could see Regan demonstrating his prowess on the cable machine while Gemma did a couple of leg stretches nearby. It made me smile because they were such a pair of preening peacocks; all that was missing was an elaborate display of plumage. I turned my attention to the screen in front of me and watched the calorie counter tick over. Five minutes in, my legs had loosened up, and I was beginning to find my pace.

Gemma, I saw looking up, had left Regan to investigate the stair machine. The woman on the machine next to me looked over as I laughed out loud before quickly refocusing on the mirror in front of her. I lost my rhythm watching Gemma in the reflection; it was much more entertaining than the MTV video overhead. She had her foot resting on the first stair, and her leg was bent, hip thrust down, one hand was resting on that same hip, and in her other hand, she was holding her phone aloft. She was wearing her Victoria Beckham pout as she snapped away.

Gemma has three stock-standard expressions for That Girl, which she rotates. Today was the Victoria Beckham. This is the one where she sucks her cheeks in and glares straight at the lens. The look on her face always makes me think that if I waved a cheeseburger under her nose she'd have my hand off. Then, there's the wide-eyed and kissy lip, baby face Kylie Jenner close-up; but my personal favourite is the young Angelina Jolie. Think index finger in the mouth—whoops I've been a naughty girl, come tell me off pout. She does that one really well.

I kept gliding back and forth, watching as she put her phone down on the ground. The will I or won't I debate was obvious in the way she was tapping her fingers on the rail of the stair machine. She decided she would, and as she clambered aboard, I noticed something white on the ground to the side of the machine. It looked like a piece of paper, or maybe it was one of the antiseptic wipes used for wiping the equipment down. I'll pick it up when I'm finished. Turning away and checking out my calorie counter once more I saw that it had nearly reached one hundred! Surely that was enough to have earned a toasted ham 'n' cheese sandwich for lunch? I could really go a toastie today. Or, better yet, a pie.

I was enjoying myself. It was good to lose myself in a repetitive beat where I wasn't thinking about anything other than just being in the moment—and toasted sandwiches or mince pies. I could squeeze in a half-hour session before work, I thought, wondering what membership would cost. It would be an added expense on a tight budget, but I don't do anything else, and this would be good for me.

The sweat was trickling down my forehead, stinging my eyes. Wiping my brow, I looked over to see how Gemma was getting on. Wow, I thought watching her go, respect, she's moving! She should've worn a bra under her vest, though, even if it is racer-back because her boobs have got more bob in them than her topknot. My earlier irritation at being dragged down here was disappearing. It was replaced with admiration because given the way she was running up and down those stairs it was obvious she didn't come down here just to prance around and take a few pics. That girl meant business.

Why's she got that weird look on her face though? I noticed her mouth was open in a silent howl. It was like she was being tasered. I could see her knuckles stark and white against the rest of the skin on her hand; that was how hard she was holding on to the rail. Her other hand was jabbing at the control panel too, the movements were frantic, and my breath caught. *Oh my God. Maybe she's having a seizure.* Her body could have gone into shock at the sudden burst of intense exercise.

I slowed my steps and jumped down, disentangling myself from my phone and earplugs before jogging over to her.

'Gemma, what's going on?'

'The fucking machine's jammed,' she gasped before pointing at the wall. 'Switch it off.'

I couldn't help but flinch at her language. I hate swearing, heard too much of it when I was young. 'What's the problem?'

'I said the machine is jammed. Switch the bloody thing off at the wall!' A few bodybuilders turned our way, and I swung into action, flicking the main switch off. I saw the white thing I spotted on the floor before was a piece of paper and picked it up. It was a handwritten notice saying Out of Order. Too late for poor Gemma—she was almost on her knees as the stairs slowed and with a final shudder, stopped. She thrust her hand out to me, and I helped her down.

'Are you okay?'

'No—' she gave a rasping breath '—I'm bloody well not.' She leaned against the wall and slid down it to slump on the ground. A hand fluttered up. 'Water.'

I handed her her drink bottle, wondering if I should try and find her a paper bag to breathe into or something. Her face was the same purple shade as her top and tendrils of damp hair were plastered to her forehead and cheeks.

She drank deeply before looking up at me. 'I could have died.'

'I don't think that's likely.'

'Yes, it is, you can die from exhaustion. It's a real thing.'

I could see there was no point arguing with her, not when she was in drama queen mode. 'The machine's broken.' I showed her the sign before putting it down on the steps for all to see. 'It must have fallen off.'

'I might sue.'

'You are not going to sue Fitbods because you couldn't get off the stair machine.'

She looked at me mutinously.

'Why didn't you ask someone for help?'

'I couldn't could I? Not with Regan right there. He kept looking over at me and I could tell he was impressed by how fast I was going.'

I looked around, but he was nowhere in sight.

'He's in the showers. I saw him head over just before you rescued me, and I haven't got the energy left to even think about joining him.'

A giggle escaped my mouth and Gemma nudged me with her foot.

'It's not funny.'

'The look on your face,' I managed to choke out before I began to laugh. I demonstrated the taser howl, and her mouth twitched. I did it again, and she began to giggle. 'One more time,' she demanded, and I pulled the face again. We both erupted into a fit of the giggles and laughed so hard we were clutching our bellies. People were looking at us now. We'd broken gym protocol, but I didn't care. It was the best laugh I've had in...well, you know.

Chapter 12

Briarwood House's carpark was nearly full, and I'd just about resigned myself to parking on the street when I saw a space at the end. I squeezed in nicely next to the maroon People Mover. Sunday afternoons were always busy here. It was an unspoken arrangement with the Andersons, but we all have our times in the week when we visit Sam. The weekends, however, were free for all.

I managed to get out of my car without knocking the People Mover, although it was like taking part in a new version of the limbo. I was itching to tell Sam about how Gemma staggered out of the gym today. My tummy still hurt from laughing. She dragged me along behind her looking like she was about to draw her pistols at dawn, desperate to make her exit before Regan emerged from the shower. We made it, but I didn't stop laughing until she threatened to hit me with her Fitbit.

Poor old Gemma—she reckoned she'd need a hoist to be able to get on and off the loo for the next week. On the bright side, she got some great action shots for That Girl, and she gets to keep the Jo-Jo Runs gear, which she's offloaded to me. She's sworn off the gym. On the ride home told me she planned on spending her afternoon soaking her aching muscles in the bath and coming up with a Plan C where the Stud Muffin's concerned.

'Why don't you come and see Sam with me this afternoon?' I asked as we pulled out of the gym carpark.

'You know how I feel.' She had that expression on her face that makes her look like she's forgotten to put her false teeth in.

'I'll do the talking; you just say hi.'

'Don't push it, Ellie.'

I flared up. 'So, you think I'm a nut job for sitting there having a one-sided conversation?'

She hesitated. 'No, but it's how it makes me feel when I visit.'

I thought she was being selfish, but I let it slide and changed the subject. 'I think I might join the gym.'

'Okay, *now* I think you're a nut job. Arse!' She pulled the middle finger at a middle-aged man who nearly cut us off with his lack of indication.

'I enjoyed it. I got into this rhythm where it was just me and the music, and it was good. I wasn't thinking about stuff. Oh and I forgot to tell you, Connor phoned me yesterday. He's thinking of organising a fun run in November to raise money for The Brain Research Foundation. He'll expect me *and you* to take part, so that's an incentive to get fit between now and then.'

'I'll walk it,' Gemma said. 'Shall we hit the bakery? I could really go a sausage roll after all that exercise.'

As I made my way across the carpark to the care-home entrance, it hit me that deciding to go to the gym would be what that counsellor I'd gone to see at Uncle Colin and Aunty Paula's bequest would consider a step in the right direction. I thought she was a waste of their money at the time. I was so raw and all I'd done was rant while she sat with her legs crossed making little 'mmm, I see' noises while scribbling on her notepad. I couldn't see how she was supposed to help me. Now I think perhaps the offloading of emotion on to someone neutral had done me some good because I vaguely remember her saying—on those rare occasions she'd actually contributed to our conversation—I needed to hold on to my positive emotions.

What I was feeling now I'd made my mind up to go to the gym was positive. I wasn't going to analyse it though. I'd simply go do half an hour on the cross-trainer before work tomorrow morning. I had a definite bounce in my step as I barrelled in through the main doors. I waved to a man I knew from a few brief chats in the communal kitchen. His face had gotten greyer over the months since his wife was brought here. I'm not sure what's wrong with her. I think she may have had a stroke, but he's never said, and I don't like to ask. Just like there's a gym protocol there was protocol here at Briarwood House, too.

I wound my way down the corridor with its tasteful but dated prints on the wall. My feet were making the floor hidden beneath a worn grey carpet that had once been green creak as I headed toward Sam's room.

I heard Gina's voice before I saw her. She's got one of those voices that carries even when she's trying to be circumspect, and I caught the tail end of: 'It's not her decision. It's not as if they were married.'

Now, I know Gina's a big fan of *Married at First Sight*, so the odds were she was talking about a couple from her favourite TV show. She tended to chat about the stars of her number-one programmes as though they were good friends of hers.

I'm getting off track, and she might not be talking about Sam and me and how we were merely cohabitating and not married. It seemed a pretty archaic difference to point out, and it might have been paranoia on my part, but there was something in the way the conversation stopped as I stepped through the door that made me uneasy. It was in everyone's flushed faces and the way Gina began chatting randomly about this week's episode of *Britain's Got Talent* while hoisting her trousers up to the point of no return. Like I said we've never talked about what will happen when Sam wakes up.

They were all there, the whole Anderson gang, and it struck me as it always when did they gathered en masse how strange it was that Sam wasn't included in the tableau. Instead, they were all squished around his bed like he was Snow White or Sleeping Beauty. *Why were they here?* It wasn't his birthday, or anybody else's so far as I knew and I'm pretty good with that sort of thing. There'd been no change with Sam's condition, or I'd have been notified. The snippet of conversation I'd overheard and the unexpectedness of the whole clan being here had me on my back foot—what were my rights where Sam was concerned?

I didn't want to share him this afternoon; because now I wouldn't be able to tell him about the gym and how I was going to join. There was no way I was mentioning the 'g' word in Justin's earshot. He'd have a field day giving me helpful pointers about what equipment to use for strengthening that or toning this, and then he'd remind me he'd give me a ten per cent discount on sports shoes. It would be incomprehensible to him were I to say that I only wanted to go to get some blank headspace.

'How're you doing, Ellie?' Gina ended her BGT monologue and homed in for a hello hug. She smelt of Opium and chocolate chip cookies. It was a strange mix and a little overpowering given our tight quarters.

'I'm okay thanks, how are you?'

'Oh, you know. It's not easy.'

God, I wish she would pluck that chin hair; it was so distracting. I wasn't feeling the love, not after what I'd overheard. 'No, it's not.'

She released me, and the three brothers said hi in varying forms of nods, eyebrow raises, and a wave. They didn't do the whole kissy-hug thing, unlike Phil who stepped forward and wrapped me in a bear hug; I squeezed him back. There was something about his hugs that made me feel safe. His scent is a mix of Brut aftershave and cigarettes. He started smoking again on the sly after having given up for over ten years, once it became clear Sam wouldn't be coming home for a while. It was a smell I usually hate, but I didn't mind it on Phil, and I was disappointed when he let me go. He didn't ask how I was he just rubbed my back for a second, and that gesture meant more than any pleasantries. I have this thing for older men. Not in *that* way but in a looking for a father figure way. I know I do, I can't help it, and you don't have to be Freud to figure out why.

Then, it was Moany Mandy's turn, and I breathed freely as we embraced our hello because she doesn't wear perfume; it's too expensive.

'How are you, Mandy?' I was only asking to be polite, and I didn't want a long-winded answer. A simple 'good' would be fine, but I knew I was going to get one. She didn't let me down.

'I've not been well since you ask.'

I thought a bad word and snuck a look at Sam, half expecting to see him bite his lip the way he did when he was trying not to laugh and roll his eyes at the oncoming inevitable information deluge. Something inside me twisted at the sight of his face in repose.

'My stomach's been playing up for weeks, and I've had lots of bowel issues as a result.'

I dragged my attention from Sam and made sympathetic noises, but in my head, I was beginning to chant, la, la, la, la. It wasn't helping though. I could still hear her.

'It's taken weeks to narrow down the culprit.'

'Oh really, what is it?' I didn't care, but I had to ask.

'Gluten. I've cut it out of my diet, but it's come at a cost—the price of GF foods is horrendous. I think it's appalling that you take an ingredient out of a product and then double the price. It makes no sense.' She paused, waiting for me to nod my agreement, which I did because it was way easier than arguing her point.

'It's stretching us, but Zac says my health comes before our house.'

I gave Zac a good-for-you smile. He was standing on the other side of his brother's bed near the window, and he didn't meet my eye. That made me more suspicious as to what they were talking about when I walked in because under-the-thumb Zac usually laps up any praise tossed his way. A dog being thrown a bone.

'It wouldn't be so bad but the bread tastes like cardboard, and I bought a packet of GF biscuits because you've got to have some treats in life, don't you?'

I automatically nodded, hoping she was finished. She wasn't.

'But Zac helped himself.' Her eyes narrowed as she darted a look across the bed. 'It annoyed me because there was a packet of digestives he could have had, chocolate ones too, but I can't touch them. The last time I did, well let me tell you I thought I'd lost my insides.'

LA, LA, LA! Too much information! Poor Zac, I bet he's never heard the end of the great GF biscuit heist. I hoped they were worth it, but from my limited tastings of gluten-free products, I'm guessing they weren't. I found myself asking, even though I didn't want to encourage her, 'So is it helping?'

'It is actually.' I could see her drawing breath. We'd only just scraped the tip of the gluten-free lifestyle iceberg, and I sincerely hoped she was never struck down with piles or vaginal thrush; the ins and outs of that would be too much. I looked to Phil for help because once Mandy's off on a tangent, she can go for hours. He came to my rescue.

'So, what have you been up to, Ellie love? We haven't seen you in weeks.'

It's closer to a couple of months since our paths last crossed, and I knew it had been deliberate on my part. I could cope with my grief at Sam's situation, but not everyone else's too. 'I bought a house.'

I saw an expression so fleeting I wonder if I imagined it flicker across Gina's face. It was of surprise, but at the same time, there was a spark of resentment. I'm a reminder to her of how Sam was before. When I moved out of our townhouse, I think she saw it as a sort of betrayal that I wasn't keeping the home fires burning for him, so to speak. I told her it wasn't that I'd given up on him coming home, it was that it was too hard being on my own there without him and, of course, it made no financial sense. Gemma said I didn't have to explain myself to her, but I wanted her to know that I would never, ever give up on Sam. Having overheard what I heard today, I wondered if they'd given up him.

I could sense that Gina wanted me close to her with a neediness that was almost scary at times. It was as if by being around me she could hold on to a part of her son's adult life she wasn't privy to. At other times I know she can't bear for me to be near her. I understand all of this because it's exactly how I feel about her. There have been moments when all I want to do is sit and listen to her stories of the little boy I never knew and other occasions where I want to push her away because it hurts too much.

My relationship's different with the Andersons now. When Sam was with me, we'd bowl around for dinner with the casualness of a weekly catch-up, and although they invited me regularly in the early days after the accident Sam's absence left a gaping hole at the table. As the weeks dragged by with no change in his condition, I began to make my excuses.

'A house. Wow. Congratulations,' Phil said. 'How did that come about?'

Once I'd filled them in on the familial connection and seen the expression of horror on all their faces at the street address, I asked what it was that had brought them all here today.

'I suggested we pop down and see our Sam.' Gina's tone was defensive.

It *was* me she was talking about when I arrived, and my body temperature plummeted. What was not my decision to make? No one can give us an answer as to how long Sam will stay like this, but at least there's hope. I wanted to cry, but I wasn't going to in front of them all. So, I swallowed the golf ball lodged in my throat, and continued to make polite conversation until they said their goodbyes and shuffled out of the room.

~

That night I dreamed that Sam and I were climbing Cave Rock at Sumner Beach. The tide was in, and the breakers were crashing angrily against the rock, turning it into an island. We were marooned, and Sam had his hand held out to take mine so that I wouldn't fall into the surf below, only I couldn't reach him. The rock was slick beneath my feet, and as I stepped, I lost my footing and tumbled off the edge. I woke before I fell into the water, but my pillow was wet and, disorientated from the dream, I thought it was from the sea.

Chapter 13

♥

Shit! Whoops, I know, double standards, but I'd forgotten to set my alarm, and I'd slept in. It was already eight o'clock, and I was due at the Richards' in half an hour. So much for hitting the gym. This was not a good start to the week. I tossed back my covers and hotfooted it straight to the shower hoping the hot water would throw off the befuddlement from my rude awakening. Five minutes later I'd stepped into my dungarees, worn with a woolly jumper underneath, when I heard knocking. With one sneaker on and the other in my hand, I went to answer the door wondering who on earth it would be at this time of the morning and on a Monday.

A man was standing there, and he was smiling at me, which made me instantly suspicious. He had a nice smile; it stretched all the way up into his eyes. It was a 'spread the good word' kind of a smile. That was neither here nor there, though, because nobody should be smiley at this time of the day even if they did have a message. I dimly registered two younger men milling around on the path behind him. It was drizzling softly, and they were rugged up with woolly hats on. Don't tell me the flipping Mormons have cottoned on to the best times to catch people like those power company salespeople. I groaned inwardly. They always managed to show up right when you sat down to eat dinner. Maybe they'd agreed to split shifts; you get the morning run, we get the evening, that sort of thing.

'I'm not interested. Thank you,' I said politely but firmly and tried to shut the door. The man stuck his boot in the doorway.

'Excuse me?' I ignored his outstretched hand. Today was not the day to annoy me. I'd already had a crappy start. Besides which I DIDN'T HAVE TIME for religious instruction this morning.

'I'm Joel King, your builder.' He looked bemused and dropped his hand to point to the truck parked behind my car. It was emblazoned with the words King Builders; there were planks of wood with an orange cloth tied to the end of them sticking out of the back. A truck was parked on the street with the same name on its side. Mormons ride bicycles, and they don't wear woolly hats, old jeans and fleece tops. They do have nice smiles though; I knew that much. The Americans know how to look after their teeth.

He interrupted my train of thought. 'I spoke to you on Saturday. We arranged for the boys and me to meet you onsite at eight.'

What a ditz. 'God! Sorry! I am so not with it. I slept in, and now I'm running late.' I held the door open wide. 'Please come in.'

He didn't move. 'We're going to be working outside today, getting the house into position so don't let us hold you up.'

I managed a smile. 'Sounds good, I'm Ellie by the way, and I really am sorry.'

That smile again. He must be used to dealing with demented homeowners, I thought. 'This is Jonno and Mikey.' He nodded to the two lads behind him.

Joel looked young to be running his own team, around thirtyish, but then what did I know about the building trade and Uncle Colin said he knew his stuff. He stepped aside, and the taller of the two younger men stepped forward thrusting out a hand. This time I took it.

'How're you doing?'

'Good thanks apart from being late and feeling a bit foolish for not knowing who you guys were.'

'Don't sweat it. I'm Mikey,' said the other fella following Jonno's lead and shaking my hand. He had a cigarette roll-up tucked behind his ear I noticed.

'Um, should I give you guys a quick tour around? I've got a spare key in the kitchen for you.'

'We don't want to hold you up.'

'It's no problem.' It was a problem. I was going to be soo late, but I felt bad about being disorganised.

'Well if it's no bother, is it alright with you if we use the kettle for smoko?'

'Yes of course, please come on in.' I urged once more, keen to get this show on the road. 'I'll show you where the kitchen is and then I'd better be going.'

'Cheers.' Joel moved to take his boots off, but I told him not to worry. I've big plans of getting the floorboards I have a suspicion will be hiding under Nan's prized Axminster sanded back and varnished. I liked to think she'd understand.

'Nice sock,' he said following my lead down the hall. 'High Viz. They'd see you coming in the dark with those on.'

I wasn't offended. I had the fluorescent yellow merino ones Aunty Paula bought for me online on today, and he's right: they are bright. Fluoro ankle socks were all the rage in the eighties in case you didn't know.

The key was on top of the fridge with a tag saying 'spare Radford St' on it, and I handed it to him before gesturing toward the kettle. 'Help yourself to milk—it's in the fridge—and you'll find the tea, coffee, and sugar in the pantry. I don't have any biscuits sorry.' I should have done some baking for them or something; Aunty Paula would have.

'Cheers and no worries we'll be fine. Mikey's got his eye on the fish and chip shop he spotted at the end of the road for lunch.'

'Right, well I'll grab my other shoe and leave you to it. Thanks. Oh—' I remembered something. 'Do you see that cupboard behind you?'

'Yeah?'

'Would you mind checking inside to see if there's a dead mouse in the trap? I don't think I could face it.'

'It's not in the contract, that.'

I wasn't sure if he was teasing me or not.

'I'm joking. I'll add mouse removal service to my résumé.'

'Thanks.' I smiled relieved I wouldn't have to deal with a dead rodent when I got home. 'Right, I've got to go. Have a good day.'

As I headed back down the hall, Mikey was standing there with an old tape deck radio. 'Is it okay if I plug this in?'

'Go for it; the lounge is straight ahead through that door.' I assumed he was going to put it by the window, so they could hear it outside.

As I tied my laces Led Zeppelin blared forth, and I grabbed my bag, glad to make my escape because it was way too early for 'Stairway to Heaven'.

~

The traffic was bumper to bumper, and ten minutes later the heater finally kicked in, and I sat at the lights tapping the steering wheel, trying not to look over at Fitbods. I couldn't help myself though, and I stared at the row of motivated people who, despite the wintry morning, all managed to set their alarms and get up on time to pound it out on the treadmill. I knew Nervy Caro was going to be in a right stew by the time I arrived. She doesn't do well when things don't run to plan, and Mondays are not her best day, having been without me for the weekend. She'll be chomping at the bit to make her escape.

The light finally turned green, and the traffic sneaked forth. I veered into the Richards' driveway, parking alongside Caro's Range Rover a full twenty minutes late for work. The Richards lived in a modern house that reminded me of a white Rubik's cube but with windows. It was in a quiet cul-de-sac nestled amongst a variety of old and new homes all with one thing in common—they're huge, and they're expensive.

I picked my bag up off the passenger seat and hurried toward the front door. It swung open before I got the chance to fish my key out. Caro was stood in the entrance looking manic and yet resplendent at the same time in her yoga attire. 'Where've you been?'

'Sorry, Caro, I forgot to set my alarm, and then the builder and his team showed up ready to start work, and I thought they were Mormons.' Seeing her expression, I cut it short. 'I slept in, sorry.' I made a contrite face. I couldn't lie and say I got a flat tyre on the way over or something like that. I'm no good at that sort of thing; Gemma says I'd make a terrible real estate agent, far too honest for my own good.

'Well, you're here now. Come in.' Her toned arm reached out and dragged me inside. I could hear screaming coming from the end of the entrance hall and was guessing from the pitch it was Saffy-Rose. Caro, reassured by my presence, shrugged into her coat and scooped up her keys off the side table where a huge bunch of fresh flowers were displayed. 'William-Peter's not having a good morning, which means Saffy-Rose is having a terrible one. You would not believe the weekend I've had with the pair of them. I have to go, Ellie, or I'll be late for class, and Swami Laghari makes anyone who's late for class do a headstand.' I must have looked stricken because she patted me on the shoulder. 'You've got them wrapped around your little finger; they'll be good as gold for you. You're the Twin Whisperer; you know that.'

The headstand is the yoga version of the naughty step, I think, but saying that I or anyone else had the twins wrapped around their finger was a gross exaggeration. I knew if neither of them was having a good morning, then my day was only going to get worse.

'Give me the low-down on what's been going on,' I sighed. Forewarned is forearmed.

'William-Peter pinched his sister this morning. He was watching *Little Einsteins*, and she switched it off at the exciting bit. The world according to William-Peter. Anyway, I dealt with that but now he's busy flicking Cheerios at her, and you know how she gets over messes.' Caro tossed this last bit over her shoulder as she made a dash for freedom toward her Range Rover. 'Shut the door, Ellie, you're letting the cold in,' she said before clambering inside it.

I did as I was told and felt momentarily trapped. I knew exactly how Saffy-Rose gets—hysterical. This is why William-Peter does things like flick Cheerios or whatever else he has to hand at her. I've told her time and time again that if she didn't react or, even better, if she simply flicked whatever delicacy he'd tossed at her right back at him, he'd soon get sick of it. She can't seem to help herself though, and reluctantly I moved down the hallway toward the kitchen light where all the ruckus was coming from.

I walked in on a scene with William-Peter looking jubilant on one side of the kitchen island he and his sister were perched at. He was sifting through his bowl of cereal looking for the next suitable candidate to biff. Opposite him, Saffy-Rose's face was streaked with tears, and her nose was bright red. I could tell she was undecided whether to scream again or to pick the soggy Cheerios off her dressing gown.

'OKAY,' I bellowed, and they both looked up, startled to hear my voice. 'I'm here now, and that means this stops. RIGHT NOW! Do you hear me?' I can be quite scary especially if you're only four years old.

Two tousled red heads bobbed up and down emphatically, but I wasn't convinced. 'William-Peter, apologise to your sister, or you'll find yourself on the naughty step.' This was the last step on the sweep of stairs from the entranceway to the first floor where there's a second adult-only living area, guest room and master suite along with a gazillion bathrooms. William-Peter finds it extremely difficult to sit on the naughty step for any length of time, and his punishment ultimately becomes my punishment. But hey, I've done the training and one day it will have the desired effect of getting him to do what he's been told. Although maybe I could try making him stand on his head—it works for his mother. Now there was a thought.

The children's bedrooms were downstairs toward the back of the house with a playroom sandwiched between them. They each have their own bathroom. I'd hate to be the lady who comes in and does the cleaning on Tuesdays. I had many household chores here at the Richards' but cleaning the toilets isn't one of them. Once I'd managed to get them to finish their breakfast I sent them off to get washed and dressed while I tidied up calling after them, 'It's going to be a home day today.' This means they have free rein in the wardrobe department.

On Mondays there's always a pile of dirty laundry to get washed and dried, a hangover from the weekend. I hate ironing, and I especially hate ironing 'call me Doug's' shirts. Caro gave me a demonstration when I first started as to where the creases need to be because he's very particular as to how they're done. I live in fear of burning a hole in one of his Ralph Lauren's. I'm glad that my Sam, as an electrician, owned one good shirt that only came out for weddings, or funerals and, on occasion a christening.

I decided to make a batch of play dough before I tackled the washing and once it had all been mixed in the pot and tipped onto the breadboard, I began to knead it. I liked the feel of the dough—the oil I use in it always makes my hands lovely and soft. Caro won't have anything but extra Virgin olive oil in the house. I'd chosen blue food colouring today to tint it; this would save arguments over it being orange, Saffy-Rose's favourite colour, or green, William-Peter's go-to colour. Believe me, stuff like that matters. Once it was ready, I headed down to the playroom to retrieve the plastic table and chair set. I had a big plastic sheet, which I laid out on the floor before putting the table and chairs on it; this makes for easy clean-up later. By the time it was all set up the twins had reappeared.

William-Peter had opted for the deranged Highlander meets Guns N' Roses look today with his sister's red tartan skirt worn over his jeans. He'd had the sense to put on a fleece top and the sight of him looking pleased with himself as he twirled around in the skirt made me smile. Saffy-Rose, meanwhile, had gone for her Elsa dress; she would need to put a warmer top on, I thought, noticing she'd forgotten to brush her hair. As she pirouetted in an attempt to outdo her brother, I spotted an angry red mark on her forearm.

I pursed my lips. Caro said she'd dealt with the earlier pinching incident, but that looked nasty. William-Peter's been getting a little heavy-handed of late, and it needs to stop. For the moment, though, they were both happy and I left them to their play dough, cutting, rolling and shaping while I put the first load of washing on before setting up the ironing board in the kitchen. The basket with last week's five shirts now freshly laundered and dried over the weekend by Caro was waiting for me on top of the machine. I stuck my tongue out at it before picking it up.

By eleven a.m. the washing was tumbling in the dryer, and the shirts were hung on the back of the laundry door. The novelty of the play dough was also wearing thin, and there were bits of blue dough spread far and wide. So much for easy clean-up. I bit my lip, to stop from grumbling out loud. I was out of sorts today. It wasn't all down to having slept in, I was edgy and rubbing my temples. Those edges frayed even more as William-Peter picked Sardine up and began carting the poor cat about the kitchen. She mewed pitifully.

'She'll scratch you if you don't put her down,' I warned.

He ignored me, his pudgy hands holding on to the poor Persian for grim death as he attempted to swoop her through the air. 'I'm pretending she's an aeroplane. The big one you took us to see.'

The cat was overweight, which was why he wasn't doing a good job of swinging her about, and he was referring to the Emirates A380 Airbus, which we parked up outside the airport to watch land a week back. Saffy-Rose stood alongside me in bossy princess mode as she pointed at her brother and lisped, 'You'd better put Sardine down, or you'll be off to the naughty step, and you won't like that.'

As predicted a beat later Sardine lost the plot and swiped William-Peter who dropped the poor animal and began to howl. 'There's blood; there's blood!'

Give me strength, I thought, cleaning his scratch before letting him pick a plaster from the box of *Frozen* novelty Elastoplasts.

'Yucky, mean Sardine,' he hiccupped admiring Elsa for a tick before letting me unpeel it and stick it on.

'The Elsa ones are mine.'

'But you're a good sharer, Saffy-Rose.' She thought about that, and it was touch and go, but to my relief she conceded.

'And you should have put Sardine down when I told you to. You know she doesn't like being carried around.'

William-Peter looked sulky. We still had another six hours in each other's company. The cabin fever was setting in. Sod home days, I thought, telling them to fetch their coats and gumboots. There was nothing else for it; if we were to stay sane then we were going to have to go to the park. Rugged up we headed out the door, and I caught a whiff of flowers from the bunch I hadn't had time to admire earlier that morning. 'Call me Doug' had gone to town with the enormous bunch of pink, yellow and red blooms on the antique telephone table in the hall. I wondered as I closed the door behind us whether he and Caro had a fight and how flowers were supposed to make everything alright.

Chapter 14

William-Peter was splashing in every puddle he could find as we walked to the park. The weather was clearing, thank goodness, and the twins' moods and mine were lifting with the fresh air. Saffy-Rose was finding treasures. In her coat pocket, she had an acorn cup, a red leaf and a sprig of rosemary. I snapped it off on our way past the grand old two-storey weatherboard I covet. The spiky herb was peeking between the gaps in the mansion's fence, and I couldn't resist. The look on her face as she sniffed it was magic, and I had a warm fuzzy moment where the reason I chose to work with children became clear. Now, she spotted a red and white polka-dot toadstool nestling on the grass verge separating us from the street and exclaimed delightedly.

'That's rather special,' I said crouching down beside it and looking up at her. 'But you mustn't touch it because it can make you sick.'

'Why's it special?' Her freckled face was a picture of wonderment, and it egged me on.

'Because it's a fairy meeting house, that's why. Of course, they'll only come out at night when the rest of us are in bed because they're very shy.' I smiled over at William-Peter who'd left the puddle he was playing in to come and listen to the tale I was telling his sister. His head was cocked to one side; there was something about his expression though. 'William—'

Too late! He took a running jump and stomped on it. The toadstool lay broken on the grass.

'The fairy house—NO!' Saffy-Rose fell to her knees. Her wails were ear-splitting. She was singlehandedly bringing down the property prices in the neighbourhood, and I could sense the curtains in the houses up and down the street twitching.

My reasons for having chosen a career in childcare became murky once more as William-Peter gave the toadstool a kick for good measure. It was time to bring out the big guns, the ace I held up my sleeve for desperate times like this. 'Cut that out,' I said to him in my most menacing tone before grabbing hold of Saffy-Rose. 'Breathe,' I dictated as she hiccuped and gulped in a lungful of air. 'The fairies will find another toadstool and William-Peter's very sorry for jumping on that one, aren't you?'

His wily blue eyes met mine. He's wise beyond his years, I thought as I watched him weigh up his odds. He could sense I'd reached the end of my tether and knew that if he played the game right, there might be something in it for him.

'Sorry,' he finally mumbled scuffing at the ground with his gumboot, refusing to look at his sister.

'Alright, Saffy-Rose, your brother's said sorry. Let's move on. We're nearly there now.'

Saffy-Rose's tearstained face was heartbreaking. She, too, sized up the situation, and I could see her tossing up between going all-out Oscar for the best dramatic actress and carrying on the short distance to the park to where the slide is. She loves the slide.

I gestured toward the gate at the end of the street. 'If you two play nicely when we get there I'll stop at the shops on the way home and buy you both a lolly mixture. Deal?'

Just like that the sun came out as the twins nodded their heads and beamed at me. It's pathetic really, but a bag of sweets is a rare treat indeed. Caro is of the belief that William-Peter's challenging tendencies and Saffy-Rose's dramatic turns are exacerbated by sugar. The twins skipped happily ahead, and before I could wage a mental debate on my feelings about the so-called white poison, my phone rang. It was Gemma.

'Hey, I'm in between clients. How's your day going?'

I filled her in on Joel and his team showing up.

'Was he good-looking?'

'Who?'

'The builder of course. God, Ellie, you're on another planet sometimes.'

'I don't know. I guess so. I wasn't checking him out, Gemma.'

'Not for you. *For me.* I'm not getting anywhere with Regan. I'll give it another week or two, and if nothing's happening, I'll cast my net wider. A girl can't wait around forever.' She hesitated realising what she'd said. 'Shit, sorry. I didn't mean it like that.'

'It's okay. I didn't take it like that.'

She must have picked up a tone in my voice. 'Are the twins giving you a hard time?'

'They've been a little challenging, but we're under control now. I bribed them with the promise of sweets.' And, yes, I know I shouldn't bribe them, especially not with food, but they're kids, and it works. So, today we're rolling with the sugary stuff and what Caro doesn't know won't hurt her.

'Nothing wrong with that. Worked for me as a kid especially if they were spearmint leaves. They were my favourite. You used to like those awful little pink ones remember.'

'Smokers.'

'Yeah, weird name for a sweet.'

A pang of nostalgia shot through me. 'I haven't seen them around for ages.' Sam was a fan of them too.

'So, what's the dynamic duo been up to then?'

I filled her in on toadstool Armageddon. 'It makes me sad you know, Gemma. I'm sure William-Peter only acts out because he wants attention. Honestly, I want to shake Caro sometimes. Their little faces light up when she comes home. All they want is for her to read them a story or sit down and help make a play dough snail, but she's always got something else more pressing she needs to do.'

The Richards' lives are a little bit Victorian in so much as they seem to subscribe to that adage of children being seen but not heard. I think that's why William-Peter is so set on making sure he *is* heard. I thought my childhood was disjointed with Mum and my periodic stints at Nan and Pops' when I was getting under the feet of her boyfriend, Steve. I don't remember all that much about him, but I do remember being aware he found me a nuisance. He used to shout a lot too and drop the F-bomb. The twins are also ignored by their parents. The only difference is that it is in an affluent and, therefore, acceptable manner.

'You don't have to be Supernanny to work out that if their mum and dad spent more time with them William-Peter's behaviour would pick up, which would mean Saffy-Rose would stop being so emotional,' I added.

'Yeah. I know their type, been there sold their house. From what you've said Mr Whatsit is a workaholic and she's one of the "ladies who lunch" brigade.'

It was true, Caro does do lunch a lot, in between her hot yoga sessions, hair appointments, and manicures. Still waters run deep, though, and I'd like to think there's more to her than meets the eye. As for 'call me Doug', Gemma's nailed it. I had him labelled under Workaholic, and when he wasn't working, he was gadding about in his cycling shorts, instead of spending time with his family.

I watched Saffy-Rose follow her brother through the gate and disappear through the trees either side of it into the park. 'Got to go, Gemma.' After she said goodbye I shoved my phone back in my pocket and picked up my pace. When I caught up, I saw there were only two others out braving the cold weather. A woman pushing a bundled-up toddler on the swing. I gave her a friendly wave and watched my charges run past the seesaw and the spinning bucket—I hated that thing; I got stuck in it once and nearly threw up and I was so dizzy by the time I wriggled free—over to the slide, each desperate to beat the other to it. It had the added attraction of being a waterslide today thanks to the big puddle of water sitting at the bottom of it.

The park bench was damp, but I'd brave a wet bum, I decided sitting down. It had stopped raining, but it was still freezing, and I shoved my hands in my pockets, shivering. A hazy sun was trying to push its way through the cloud cover, but it was fighting a losing battle. I wondered how things were going at Radford Street. I'd no idea what was involved with raising a house, but I was picturing something along the lines of an extra-large tyre jack hoisting it up.

I heard the gate squeak open behind me, and a moment later, a lady tucked up inside her coat being pulled along by a panting Golden Retriever passed by me. I watched the dog squat on the grass and shuddered as she scooped up the deposit into the blue plastic bag she was carrying. Rather her than me, I thought as my phone rang once more. What did Gemma want now? I dug it out, but when I glanced at the screen I saw it was Lucas. That was weird. He never rang me. My antennae quivered, and I hesitated, frightened to pick up. Should I let it go to voicemail? A need to know overrode my wariness though and, taking a deep breath, I answered his call.

Chapter 15

'Ellie?'

'Hi, Lucas, what's up?' Energy was coursing through my veins making me jangly like I'd had way too much coffee.

'It's Sam. It's uh, well it's not good. You need to come to Briarwood now.'

Oh God, oh God, oh God.

'Ellie?'

'Yeah, I'm here. How bad?'

'Bad. Just get here. If you don't think you can drive get an Uber, but you need to come now. Do you understand?'

'Okay.' I hung up, and the blood roared in my ears. I didn't move from the park bench as I tried to arrange my racing thoughts into a sequence of actions. *What should I do first?*

A piercing siren roused me, and a police car screamed down the street galvanising me into movement. *Breathe, Ellie, breathe. Right, now think. Okay first things first, get the twins home.* Oh, FUCK why did we walk? There was no point calling anyone to pick us up; it would be quicker on foot. William-Peter was about to climb the slide once more, and Saffy-Rose was running toward the swings as I beckoned frantically at them to come over to me. Their noses were running, and their little faces were flushed pink with the cold air and excitement as they rushed toward me. They must have seen something in my expression though because their pace faltered as they drew closer.

'Come on! We've got to go right now.' For once they did as they were told. 'We're going to walk home as fast as we can,' I told them, taking each child firmly by the hand and pulling them along behind me. The poor wee things' legs were like windmills on a gusty day trying to keep up. My heart was pounding, and my head hurt. I wanted to step outside of myself and for this not to be happening. We made it back to the house in under ten minutes, and to my relief, Caro's Range Rover was parked in the driveway.

William-Peter exclaimed, 'Mummy's home.' I think he was as relieved at the sight of her car as I was, the children sensed something was wrong. They must have because neither of them mentioned their promised bag of sweets.

I unlocked the front door and pushed them both inside, calling out for Caro. She appeared, knotting her dressing gown at the top of the landing with her hair dripping from her shower.

'Ellie's, what's with the shouting? Are the twins okay?'

'They're fine, but I have to go. I've got to get to Briarwood House; something's happening with Sam.'

'Oh. Is he—'

I think she was about to ask if he was coming around, but I cut her off, 'No—I don't know.'

And I turned to leave, but she called out after me. 'Wait! You're not driving yourself there. Not in that state. I'll take you.' She raced barefoot down the stairs and grabbed her keys from the hallway table casting around for her shoes, kicked off and left outside the door when she got home from her hot yoga session. She ordered the twins out to the car as she slid her feet into the sneakers. They both looked terrified but grateful for a directive, and they did as they were told. 'Come on; I'll get you there in no time, I promise,' Caro said pulling me by my arm and herding me down the drive behind them.

'Okay, Briarwood House is on the Memorial Ave end of Greers Road, not far from Burnside High School right?' she asked reversing down the drive and out onto the street.

I nodded buckling in. I didn't know how she knew where it was, and I didn't care. I just wanted to get there. My nerve endings were stretched tight like a rubber band ready to be fired from a slingshot, but even in my state, habit still made me turn my head to make sure the twins had their safety belts on too. They were sitting in their car seats strapped in, Saffy-Rose was clutching her bunny, and both their eyes were saucer-like as, with a squeal of rubber against the slick road, their mother accelerated down the street.

This time when we raced through the green lights, I looked upward and mouthed a thank you.

'It's there up that driveway with the plum tree beside it,' I managed to say in time for Caro to indicate and turn into it. The care home was set back from the road, and she followed the sweep of drive to the entrance.

'Do you want me to come in with you?'

She couldn't leave the twins in the car, and I didn't know what was going on with Sam. It was no place for them to be; besides she was in her dressing gown.

'I'll be okay, thanks, Caro.'

She reached over and gave me a quick squeeze. 'Go, and let me know won't you?' Her sentence hung unfinished as I opened the door and all but fell out in my haste to get to Sam.

I jogged all the way to his room.

Chapter 16

♥

I heard sobbing. It was bouncing off the walls, eating into my brain. When I burst in through the door, Sam's room was full. A sea of familiar and unfamiliar faces. I swung from one to the other trying to guess what was going on. Phil had his arms around Gina, her face buried in his shoulder, and I understood then it was her cries I'd heard. Lucas and Justin were talking to a doctor, and there was a nurse I didn't recognise next to him with a clipboard in her hand. Zac was slumped in the armchair, his head in his hands. As for Sam, well he looked peaceful. I couldn't figure out what was going on. I cocked my head. The background noise that had become as familiar as a fridge humming or the sighs of a house settling was still clicking and whirring. He was still attached to all those wires and cords.

I looked to Phil questioningly, and he shook his head. My hands flew to my head, and I held it because I was sure it was going to explode. *What was happening?*

Justin said something to the doctor who closed the distance between us in a few short steps. He needed to shave and looked like he'd been running his fingers through his thatch of grey hair. 'Ellie, I understand you were Sam's partner.'

'Am Sam's partner,' I automatically corrected him.

He nodded. 'I'm very sorry, and it was quick, but Sam's suffered an embolism, which caused a clot to travel from his heart to his lungs. It stopped his breathing and he suffered an irreversible loss of brain function as a result.'

I looked at Sam. His chest was rising with rhythmic breaths, and I pointed, not trusting myself to speak and not understanding why this man was saying what he was saying to me.

'We haven't turned the equipment off. The ventilator's keeping his heart beating in order for blood and oxygen to keep flowing to his organs. Sam's listed as a donor. I believe you were walked through what would happen when his accident first occurred.'

Yes, I remembered. It was a conversation I closed my ears to because I wanted no part of it. I still didn't. All I wanted to do was scream; instead, I threw myself down beside the bed and stretched my arms across Sam protectively. He was still warm. I wasn't going to leave him. I'd stay right where I was until someone told me everything would be okay. A hand rested on my back. It was solid and real, and I wanted to shake it and its meaning off. I just wanted Sam. I held him tighter.

'He's at peace now,' Justin said. 'It's a good thing he's doing.'

His words bounced off me because this couldn't be happening. We'd been through too much already for it to end like this. I squeezed my eyes shut as I wheeled back in time ten months to that weekend when my life with Sam imploded.

Chapter 17

'Sam, get off I'm nearly finished.' I was trying to sew a panel of leopard print fabric onto the lapels and cuffs of a black fitted jacket. It's a nod to Madonna's *Desperately Seeking Susan* look, Mum's favourite film. I'd been delighted when I'd pulled the jacket from the rack of my local SaveMart and seen that it was my size. Sam wrapped his arms around my middle and I wriggled to make my point. His lips grazed my neck, causing an instant jolt to my womanly bits that resulted in me putting my foot down hard on the treadle and the needle running off the fabric. 'Look what you made me do!' I swivelled in my seat to face him.

'Sorry.'

He wasn't. I could tell by his wolfish grin. I spotted his bulging rucksack behind him in the hallway.

'You off then?'

'In a minute.'

'Is that all it's going to take?' I gave him a cheeky grin.

He laughed and pulled me to my feet. 'I might last for two.'

Ten minutes later I was pulling my jeans back on before kissing him goodbye at the front door. I watched him walk over to his wagon and as he opened the driver's door, he turned to look at me. The sun was illuminating him and he looked golden. 'What are you going to do without me?'

'I'm catching up with Lisa this afternoon.'

'Lisa?'

'You know. Tall girl, short black hair. We worked together at Teeny Tykes. I haven't seen her since I left, so we're going to meet for an overdue coffee, and then, this evening I have a Netflix binge planned, after which I am going to starfish in bed all night long.' I stretched my arms wide to demonstrate.

'Ah, you'll miss me.'

'I won't miss your snoring and you'll be back tomorrow,' I said waving him off. I wanted to get my jacket finished so I could wear it on my coffee date.

~

I'm glad Lisa and I opted to meet at the Starbucks by the entrance to Westfield. I shuddered as I glanced into the mall. The centre was heaving with Saturday afternoon shoppers. She'd beat me there, I noted, spying her dark head bent over a magazine. She looked up and waved out, gesturing to her cup to let me know she'd already ordered. I got in line and waited my turn to ask the young dreadlocked girl with the scarf pulling her mountain of hair back from her face for a flat white before greeting Lisa with a hug and sitting down.

'You look great.' I beamed. 'I love the hair.' Her pixie cut had grown into a short bob. It was less severe and softened her jawline, which always reminded me of that actress, Olivia something-or-other.

'So do you. Only you could rock a jacket like that. Is it a Mad Ellie Original? How's yummy Sam?'

I nodded. 'Thanks. I finished it this morning. And Sam's great. He's in his happy place out in the wilderness as we speak. How's it all going with you?'

'Work wise or non-existent love life wise?'

'Um let's start with work.'

'Well...' She stirred her cappuccino and then licked the foam off the spoon. 'We miss you, me especially. I've got no one to bitch about bossy bum Cherry with.'

We smiled conspiratorially over our mutual dislike of Teeny Tykes' head teacher and manager, Cherry, as my coffee was deposited in front of me. 'Thanks,' I said but the dreadlocked girl was already moving on. 'I miss you guys, too.

'I still think it was on the nose for Caro Richards to poach you the way she did.' Lisa held up a hand. 'I know, I know she made you an offer you couldn't refuse, and you don't have all the form filling out at the end of the day, but how you deal with William-Peter day in day out, I don't know. I thought Cherry was going to spontaneously combust the day he peed all over the Fisher-Price Happy Sounds Home his sister was playing with.'

'Oh my God that's right, and he said he only did it because he thought it should be raining like it was outside.'

We can laugh about it now, but at the time it wasn't funny.

It was the final act that had seen William-Peter asked to leave Teeny Tykes and Caro resort to asking me if I would come and work for her. She'd pleaded she wouldn't be able to cope if I didn't. She called me the twin whisperer.

'I love the twins even if they are a handful,' I said simply.

We hardly came up for air as we chatted and an hour passed by quickly. I was thanking my lucky stars I wasn't single having just heard all about Lisa's latest disastrous blind date, when we decided it was time to make a move. With another hug and promises to catch up again soon, Lisa headed into the mall, and I clasped my keys in my pocket. I wasn't quite ready to go home. I decided to call in on Aunty Paula and Uncle Colin to say 'hi'.

'Stay for dinner?' Aunty Paula asked.

Inhaling the aroma of something spicy I decided it was a better offer than the pizza I was contemplating picking up on my way home.

I was comfortably full of Moroccan lemon chicken and couscous by the time I left, and I made one pit stop on my way home to pick up a bottle of red and some dark chocolate. Tonight was going to be binge television viewing at its best, and besides, I'd read in a magazine last time I was at the hairdresser's that dark chocolate was full of antioxidants. I'd decided to take that to mean the benefits offset the calories and planned on demolishing the whole bar.

By one a.m. I'd kept to my plan by watching three back-to-back episodes of *13 Reason's Why*, polishing off half a bottle of red, and the chocolate was a distant memory. It was time for bed. There was no word from Sam, I saw checking my phone, but Gemma had messaged. *You should be here*, I read, before scrolling down to a picture of her hair tossed back necking a shot. Hmm, I bet Meghan Markle doesn't carry on like that, I thought; mind you that Prince Harry was a wild one in his day. I didn't bother to reply. I switched my phone to silent before putting the lights out because Gemma could be persistent when she's had a few.

I wondered if Sam was asleep. I didn't expect to hear from him; cell phone coverage in the places he likes to disappear to can be patchy.

I stretched out scissoring my legs back and forth like I said I would, but it was weird being in bed without Sam, and I didn't sleep well at all.

I woke to banging on the door and, bleary-eyed, picked up my phone. I'd slept late, it was nearly ten o'clock, and I could see missed calls on my phone. Shrugging into my dressing gown, I padded out to the hallway to answer the door fully expecting it to be Gemma still tipsy from the night before come to tell me about her Saturday night escapades.

Uncle Colin was standing there, and his usually red face was alabaster white.

'What's happened, is Aunty Paula okay?' *Oh God, maybe it's Gemma.* 'Gemma, is she alright?'

'They're both fine. Listen, Ellie, it's Sam; he's had an accident. The police called around to Phil and Gina's. Phil tried calling, but he couldn't get hold of you.'

I curse my silenced phone and my drunken cousin.

'He rang me to come and get you. Sam's being airlifted to the hospital now. Go get dressed, and I'll take you there.'

'Is he hurt?' A stupid question but my brain was still trying to process what I'd just been told.

'It's serious, sweetheart, but Phil doesn't know any more than that.'

~

Uncle Colin dropped me at the hospital entrance, and I told him to go home. 'I'll phone you as soon as I know what's happening.'

'I can park and come in with you,' he offered but I didn't want him to. It was going to be okay, and I told him this. A taxi was pulling up behind him in the drop-off zone, and he had to move on. If he'd wanted to say something else, it was too late because I was already making my way to the enquiries booth.

I found the Andersons clustered together in a nondescript room overlooking the treetops of the Christchurch Botanic Gardens nearby. A coffee table had a few dog-eared magazines spread out on it and a Dick Francis book; there was a water cooler in the corner making a random gurgling noise. We were near the entrance to the intensive care ward. Lucas was sitting on one of the seats against the wall with his hands clasped in his lap, legs jiggling up and down. Zac and Mandy were next to him, her head resting on his shoulder. Justin was pacing, phone in hand, and Gina was looking out the window. Her eyes were closed, and I thought she might be praying even though she doesn't go to church.

Phil, who was leaning against the wall with a cup of water in his hand, dropped it in the bin as he pushed himself forward to pull me into the room. His embrace enfolded me so tightly it squeezed the breath out of me. The fierceness of it frightened me.

'What happened?' I asked when he let me go.

He shook his head. 'All we've been told is that he drove off a bridge inland from Arthur's Pass. A hiker found him this morning. He's got swelling on his brain, and he's going to be brought up to the intensive care ward once he's been assessed. We'll be able to see him then.'

I nodded because I didn't know what to say.

Gina opened her eyes and beckoned me over. I moved next to her and she took my hand. I held hers with the same fierceness her husband had just held me. He's going to be fine, I told myself. There was power in positive thinking, so I kept repeating it.

The hand on the clock on the wall above the water cooler moved with an audible tick, and I'd lost count of how many ticks I'd heard when at last a nurse appeared. She told us we could go and see Sam, no more than two at a time.

'Doctor Hammond will come and explain the situation to you,' she said, and I could see compassion on her face as we filed past.

We took it in turns to see him, Phil, Gina and I go first ignoring the 'in twos' rule. Sam's got equipment on either side of his bed; it was connected to the tubes snaking their way from his body. A bandage was wrapped around his poor head. I wanted to push it all out of the way and hold him, but I hung back suddenly frightened at the reality of what was in front of me. Phil had dragged a chair in from the corridor, which he put beside the bed for Gina to sit down on. She sank onto it and rested the hand I'd been holding a short while ago on top of her son's. A sob caught in my throat, and I looked to both his parents. 'I just want him to be okay.'

'I know you do, so do we,' Gina said softly, and I wondered how it was possible for someone to age so much in a few short hours.

Doctor Hammond, when she arrived, was young with straight brown hair pulled back in a no-nonsense Alice band. She wore no makeup, and her accent had an American twang to it as she explained the gravitas of Sam's situation. He wasn't awake, or aware of his surroundings, which meant he was in a coma. His RAS, which she told us meant Reticular Activating System, wasn't responding to any stimuli and this wasn't a good sign.

'But when will he wake up?' Gina demanded before I could. I looked to the doctor silently beseeching her to tell us that it would be any minute now. I wanted her to say that all we had to do was keep doing what we were doing, talking to him, and stroking his hands. She didn't say that though. She told us she didn't know and all we could do was wait. And so we waited.

It was two weeks later when she told us if Sam regained consciousness, in the best case, he would have severe cognitive and physical limitations. I heard the words but I couldn't accept them. Doctor Hammond's face was grave as she said, 'These limitations will be permanent. In the worst case, he'll never regain consciousness.'

'But there's hope,' I interrupted.

'There's always hope, Ellie,' she says. And I could see she wanted to believe that, too.

Chapter 18

♥

There we were all were gathered again with Gina sitting in a chair dragged in from the corridor. Her hand was veiny as it rested on top of Sam's. She was on the opposite side of the bed to me, her head bent, and the line of grey hair was stark against the reddish brown ends. We were watching over him together like we did when this horrible journey first began. I had no idea how much time had passed since I'd arrived because I'd been kneeling there beside Sam's bed lost in my thoughts. I heard a cough and recognised it as Uncle Colin's. I blinked to try and clear my vision, which was furred from unshed tears, and I raised my head to look over in his direction. His large, comforting frame was filling the space in the doorway. I didn't know who'd rung him, but I was glad he'd come because he always fixes things. He'd make things alright. Remember 0800unclecolin?

'Gina, Phil, boys,' he said nodding to them all. 'Paula and I, we're so very sorry for your loss.' He coughed again. I understood it was to cover his uncertainty as to what the protocol was for this situation. None of us knew, because we had no precedent. Phil stepped forward and put him at ease, always mindful of others, even now.

'Thanks, Colin. I'm glad you've come. Ellie needs you.' His voice wavered slightly before he held his hand out to shake my uncle's. Uncle

Colin stepped forward into the crowded room and grasped his hand with both of his, trying to convey his sympathy through touch. Each of the boys followed suit, their faces pale and drawn. He embraced Gina last. She'd gotten to her feet and had come around the bed to stand by her husband. It was a clumsy hug, but I could see it was heartfelt, and my eyes prickled and burned once more. They were slits, heavy and puffed with the weight of the tears they'd shed.

I turned my attention back to my lovely Sam. I could hear low murmurings and catch snippets of words, bits of sentences, but none of it made sense. Organ donation—take her home—ambulance coming. I held on to my Sam tighter.

Uncle Colin's weighty hand settled on my shoulder. 'Come on, sweetheart. It's time for Sam to go now. You need to say goodbye, and then I'll take you home.'

'No, I want to stay here.' I saw several people in the green uniform of ambulance officers talking to the nurse whose face I didn't know. There was no room in here for them, and they were standing outside the entrance. Respectfully waiting.

'Love, he's gone. He's going to help someone else now. It's what he wanted.' It was Gina's voice.

How was this what he wanted? I didn't understand. He was still warm. He was still here.

'We all need to say goodbye now,' she said.

I got pulled to my feet by Uncle Colin who ushered me away from the bed. I stood in the protective cocoon of his arm while Gina leaned down and kissed her second youngest boy. Her remaining sons stood back and let their mother say goodbye. Phil was next and he, too, kissed his son, his mate. 'We'll see you again soon, Son. We'll bring you home one last time. I promise.'

Justin, Lucas, and Zac with Mandy—I hadn't been aware of her arriving—filed past his still form, touching his hand, patting his arm, laying a hand on his chest.

Then, the room was empty except for me and Uncle Colin. He nudged me forward. I'd sat by this bed day after day talking about something and nothing for the last ten months, and now I was supposed to say goodbye. The word stuck in my throat. I couldn't, and I wouldn't say it. 'Goodnight, Sam, sleep tight, my love.' My lips rested on his forehead, and then Uncle Colin led me from the room.

The journey back to Uncle Colin and Aunty Paula's was a blur as I wrapped my arms around myself trying to keep warm. Aunty Paula was at the door when we arrived, and her arms were outstretched to envelop me. I collapsed into her, grateful for her familiar scent.

'I'm so, so sorry, sweetheart.'

Her breath was soft on my hair. 'Make it better, Aunty Paula.'

Her voice caught. 'Oh, my girl. I wish I could.'

She led me through to the living room. 'There we are, darling. Lie down for a bit.'

I sat down on the sofa and then laid my head down on the cushions while she took my shoes off. A blanket was draped over me but I was still freezing and I curled up as tightly as I could. Aunty Paula knelt down on the carpet beside me just like I had with Sam and stroked my hair. I squeezed my eyes shut wanting nothing more than to climb out of my body and join him because I didn't want to be here without him.

'She's trembling; I'll get another blanket.'

'It's the shock, Colin. Doctor Bayfield will be here any minute. I explained what's happened, and she said she might need a sedative. Sleep's the best way for her body to handle the trauma.'

'Mum.' There was desperation in her voice as Gemma burst into the living room. 'I came as soon as Dad called. Is she okay? What happened to Sam?'

'A clot travelled from his heart to his lungs and stopped his breathing. It was quick,' Uncle Colin added this last bit as though that made it all okay.

Their voices ebbed and flowed over me, and I felt weight by my feet as Gemma sat down. She rested her hands on my huddled form, and I must have drifted off because suddenly there was a woman I didn't know talking to me. I had to sit up and shake or nod my head accordingly in response to her questions. After a minute she got up, and I heard her talking to Aunty Paula, but I didn't know what she was saying. Gemma crouched in front of me.

'We'll get you through this, Ellie, I promise.' Her eyes were red. She'd been crying, and I reached out to pull her to me. We were all hurting. We only let each other go when Aunty Paula reappeared with a glass of water. She handed me a tablet.

'Here we are, Ellie, the doctor's prescribed this to let you sleep. It's the best thing for you right now. Gemma and I will stay right here with you until you do.'

Gemma nodded, and I took the drink and swallowed the pill before lying back down. Closing my eyes, I drifted off into blissful oblivion.

Chapter 19

The weekend dragged the way it does when you're waiting for something special but finally, the hour rolled around when I could begin to get ready for my dinner date with Sam. I liked saying that and had been driving Gemma mad by constantly dropping it into our conversations. She'd say something like, 'I'm doing an open home at eleven a.m. today.' To which I'd reply, 'Did I tell you I've got a dinner date on Sunday night?' Or she'd say, 'Mum, I'm not going to be home tonight.' And I'd butt in with, 'I'm not going to be home tomorrow night either, Aunty Paula, because I've got a dinner date.' I think Gemma was just as keen for Sunday evening to arrive as I was so that I'd shut up about it.

I'd decided, after careful consideration, to wear a black knit dress. It was proper vintage high street, not quite Dolce & Gabbana but the odds of coming across a genuine Italian couture design in my local seconds store was slim. I was teaming it with a denim jacket and black ankle boots. Think Madonna, during her 'Ray of Light' phase. You know, the long dark hair, almost gothic clothes.

Mum had all her CDs, and I can remember her turning the volume up so loud the neighbour would bang on the wall of our flat, but she'd just giggle and pull me up to dance with her. We did have some fun times, me and Mum. When she was like that, full of energy and laughter, there was nobody else I wanted to be around. She wasn't always like that though.

So, having channelled my inner material girl with my outfit, I was standing in front of my dressing table mirror applying my lipstick and wondering if Gemma would let me have a squirt of her Tom Ford, Jasmin Rouge when she barged in.

'You are not wearing that!'

'What's wrong with it?'

'You look like you're off to a funeral, one that was held twenty years ago, make that thirty years. I mean it has shoulder pads. What are you thinking, Ellie?'

'I like shoulder pads.' I was on the fence when it came to shoulder pads, but I wasn't telling her that.

'Could you not have splurged on a new dress for your big date?'

'No need, there's nothing wrong with this one. Besides buying recycled clothing is sustainable shopping. *I* am doing my bit for the planet.' Sanctimonious I know.

'If you wear my red Next dress with the spaghetti straps, I'll let you have a spray of my Tom Ford.'

Sanctimonious shamancymonious the red Next was gorgeous. 'Deal! But can I keep the denim jacket?'

Gemma nodded and disappeared off to her room to retrieve the goods.

Sam arrived on the dot of seven as we'd arranged. He got big red ticks for being punctual and for coming to the door. Good manners go a long way—this was drummed into me by Nan, and I put a lot of store by them. He also told me I looked great (giant red tick) and I could tell he meant it. That was what struck me straightaway with

Sam; apart from the fact he was gorgeous he was also genuine, and I could sense that he was kind right through to his very core.

Uncle Colin and Aunty Paula were trying to look casual and relaxed in the kitchen when I brought him through to say hi. They put down their glasses of wine and came out from around the breakfast bar where they'd been nibbling on a platter of cheese, crackers, and olives to shake his hand. They liked him, it was obvious in the way Uncle Colin got all blokey, and Aunty Paula got giggly. Gemma sauntered in eager to check out the man who'd gotten me in such a spin. I held my breath while she said hello because sometimes she can be a tad overprotective by pulling the bossy big sister act but she behaved herself.

'I booked Hot Salsa; you know the new Mexican place in town,' Sam said as we walked outside to where a shiny Hilux was parked. 'I hope that's okay?'

'I love Mexican food.' The evening was cool, and I was glad I'd gotten away with keeping my jacket. The red dress was floaty and romantic, and I did feel rather princess like as he held the wagon's door open for me. I don't know how ethereal I looked clambering up into my seat though.

'I borrowed the Hilux from my dad,' Sam said climbing in behind the wheel. 'The van's always dusty from work and I have a four-wheel drive I go off road in but that's not the cleanest inside either.' He flicked me a shy smile and I was touched by his thoughtfulness. I wouldn't have cared what he was driving; I would have walked around with dust all over my backside if it meant I was with him.

He reached over to lift the handbrake and our hands grazed each other's. It sent a current of nervous tension rocketing through me, and as we drove into the city, I began babbling on about Mexico being on my travel wish list.

'Yeah? It's pretty dodgy isn't it?' He glanced over at me, eyebrow raised, before turning his attention to what was in front of him. He tapped the steering wheel as he waited for the lights to turn green.

'Not where I want to go. I'd like to see the Mayan Pyramids on the Yucatan Peninsula. That's right down the bottom; it's very touristy. All the drugs and murder stuff is further up.' For a girl who hailed from a small city in the South Island of New Zealand, who'd only been to the North Island once, and Australia a handful of times, I sounded pretty worldly. It was true, though, ever since I'd seen a picture of those big rock monoliths built by the Mayan Indians in an encyclopaedia Nan and Pops had on their bookshelf, I'd wanted to go and see them for myself.

'I'm into camping,' he said the truck moving forward as the light changed. 'I've got an old four-wheel drive I load up and take off grid.'

'Oh, I love camping!' I lied and reaching up I smoothed my hands over my hair hoping it hadn't frizzed on the short walk from house to vehicle.

He flashed me a grin. He had a lovely smile, and it made me happy to see that he was pleased to have found a kindred spirit. I resolved that if I hadn't loved camping before, I did now.

'Yeah, you can't beat getting out in the middle of nowhere away from it all. So you're into the outdoors?' he asked, and I could hear the hope in that question. It felt like a test, and the short answer is no. Like I said I hate camping, and I'm NOT an outdoorsy girl. I'm very definitely a sit at my sewing machine making things or curling up with a book, indoorsy girl—and there's always chocolate involved when I do either. I don't get camping, all that packing and unpacking not to mention walking to and from the kitchen block and the toilets continuously. And, Sam here was talking about the kind of camping where this is no kitchen and worse, no toilet. Where was the fun in that?

The last time I'd helped pitch a tent was with my friend Chloe from my uni days. The crowd she got round with were going up to Nelson for New Year, and she talked me into going, too. I got bitten on the eyelid by a mosquito overnight and woke up looking like Quasimodo. I'd refused to leave my tent until the swelling went down, which meant I missed New Year altogether. The toilets in the campground got blocked too. It was horrible and not my idea of fun. As for freedom camping—horrors! Did I say this to Sam though? Um not exactly.

'Yeah, it's great! All that clean air, love it.' I didn't know who this person speaking was and all I needed was some pom-poms. Give me a 'C', give me an 'A', give me an 'M', you get the idea. The thing was, I desperately wanted to impress this guy and if it meant lying through my teeth, then so be it. It's not much different to posting your best five years out-of-date, ten-pounds-lighter profile pic on a dating site right? He was worth it.

Sam scrubbed up well, and I'd lodged his outfit of crisp blue shirt that matched his eyes, brown bomber jacket and jeans that fitted him just right in the compartment of my brain where I would bring it out later for further inspection when I was in bed rehashing the evening. His hair was damp and curling around the neckline of his shirt. He smelt of the sea (not salty or like seaweed, I mean he smelled fresh) and a pine forest after the rain, with a bit of musk thrown in there too. I'd had crushes before, I even fancied I'd been in love, but no one's physical presence had ever affected me like his was sitting in his truck that night.

I don't remember much about our meal. I know nachos were involved and more than a couple of craft beers but all I could think about the entire time was what it would be like to kiss him. I had to force myself to lift my gaze from those soft lips and concentrate on what he was saying because my mind kept conjuring up all these scenes. It was like watching a movie. There was me and Sam rolling around in the surf snogging; there we were kissing over a tennis net at the end of a match (no idea where that one came from; I think you've probably guessed I'm not sporty), oh and there we were getting hot and heavy in a cinema. I can tell you though not once were we at it in a tent!

The waiter asked if we'd like dessert, but neither of us fancied it; Sam asked if I fancied moving on to a bar, there was one a few doors down that was a popular spot. I said yes, and he picked up the tab, which I know might not be PC and I am a feminist, aren't we all? But it made me happy just like his holding open the door thing had. We didn't have to queue for long and once inside the bar I could tell that conversation was going to be impossible with the pulsating music, but there was a great atmosphere and we kind of went with the crowd moving toward the dancefloor.

I wondered whether he might be a bit of a Justin Timberlake. I hoped not because even though I love to dance I don't have natural rhythm and I'd never keep up with Justin's fancy footwork. Nan put me in ballet lessons for a term when I was eight and wanted to be a professional ballerina like the pretty lady in the painting on my bedroom wall. I imagined myself twirling on my pointes effortlessly, but I was a Heffalump with heavy feet, so I moved on to Brownies.

This was our first song and inching onto the edge of the dance area we began to sway in front of one another to 'Blurred Lines'. He was more Redfoo than Timberlake, and like I said while I might covet Madonna's style there's no way I could emulate her moves, but we had fun. I kept smiling up at him. I'd been to the loo after our meal and checked, and there were no stray bits of mince stuck in my teeth, and he kept smiling down at me. A part of me didn't want the night to end, but another part did because then we'd get around to the goodnight bit. And I REALLY wanted that kiss.

It was in the wee hours by the time we left the bar. The temperature had plummeted, and Sam said, 'You look cold.'

I was frozen thanks to the sheer red number I was wearing, but even if I hadn't been, I would have faked a bit of teeth chattering and shivering because I wanted him to put his arm around me. He did and nestling in under his shoulder it was like we slotted together perfectly—the last two pieces in a jigsaw puzzle. Sam had had too much to drink to drive us home, so tucked in under his arm, we walked in a natural rhythm with each other's steps toward the taxi rank. 'I've had such a good night,' he said before we reached the line of cabs. 'I'm really glad your car broke down.'

'Me too.'

'It was like we were meant to meet.'

That was exactly how I felt too. We stopped walking then, and I looked up at him vaguely aware that we were standing in the shadows of an abandoned building. It loomed spectre like over us. The moon was trying to peep out from behind the clouds, and in the distance, I could hear drunken shouts and hoots of laughter. All of that noise disappeared, and there was only him and me as he pulled me into him, then, cupping my face with his hands he tilted it toward his. The instant our lips connected was the sweetest moment of my life.

Chapter 20

♥

I wished I was a Buddhist. Buddhists don't mourn or fear death. I know this because Sam once read me an excerpt from the *Lonely Planet Guide to Asia* he liked to thumb through. He had this thing about scuba diving in Thailand where that old film *The Beach*—the one with Leonardo DiCaprio in it—was filmed. It was under the Religion section and I remember him telling me they believe in the impermanence of life—that our spirit remains and seeks out a new body and a new life. He thought that was cool; I wished he'd stop banging on about Asia.

Like the camping I went along with the grand backpacking plan but I'm a homebody. I didn't have itchy feet like Sam. I suppose I didn't own up to the fact I didn't want to pack my bags or backpack and explore Thailand, Vietnam or wherever because I don't like confrontation. There was too much of that in my life when I was little. What I'd wanted was security, stability and love. All of which had been ripped away three days ago.

I woke up that first morning and lay in my old bed, in my old room and for a moment I didn't understand why I was there. Had I called around to have dinner with Uncle Colin and Aunty Paula and had too many wines to drive? A hangover was a distinct possibility with my fuzzy head and thick tongue but then as if somebody was pressing down as hard as they could on my chest, I remembered. I didn't get out of bed all day. I pulled the covers over my head because the world outside my duvet was overwhelming. The same thing happened when I woke up the next morning too but Aunty Paula came in the room and pulled open the curtains. She was insistent I get up and move to the couch at least. Even locked in that weird land between what was real and my memories I knew that if I didn't do what she said, she wouldn't budge from the foot of the bed. I got up but I didn't get dressed and I told Aunty Paula I didn't want to see anyone.

I couldn't stop Gemma buzzing in and out between meetings with her clients though and I appreciated her trying, I really did but to be honest, she was annoying. It was because she was tiptoeing around me, and Gemma never tiptoes, she thuds. She'd exclaim over the flowers that kept arriving and read all the inscriptions in the cards out loud. She didn't get it; I wanted her to be normal. I needed her to be normal. Okay so refusing to move from the couch and refusing to eat or get dressed wasn't exactly normal but when hit with an unimaginable pain double standards are allowed.

Uncle Colin and Aunty Paula understood that. They weren't making allowances, but they were there with the soup and cups of tea. Uncle Colin still called out that some selfish so-and-so scraped out the last of the peanut butter and put the pot back in the pantry. Aunty Paula still called back that it wouldn't do him or his belly any harm to have cereal for a change. There was comfort in that sameness.

Aunty Paula made all the necessary phone calls for me over those first couple of days. 'No, she's not up to seeing anyone, Lisa. Not yet but she will be, sweetheart. Don't forget her, she's going to need you.' She'd even managed to fend off my mother who seemed to be having a maternal fit at the news of Sam's death. She picked her moments to play Mum, and I couldn't handle talking to her yet because I knew she'd turn his death into her drama. It's what she does. There's never been any middle ground with Mum. She's all or nothing and right now I'd rather have nothing.

I stayed away from Facebook and the likes too, but Gemma said there'd been loads of messages of support on my page. Uncle Colin got the paper on Saturday and cut out the obituary for me to keep. I'll put it in a memory box along with all the cards. Aunty Paula suggested drying some of the flowers when they've lost their bloom. The roses will hold together well, she said telling me about a trick for drying them using hairspray. I liked the idea.

I was grateful to Gina and Phil for mentioning me in the short paragraph in the paper along with Sam's closest friends. They've been generous with their grief. I was bemused, too at the request for donations instead of flowers to be sent to the Fiordland Conservation Trust, but I shouldn't have been because it's fitting. Sam loved Fiordland, he loved the wilderness, and what are they supposed to do with flowers anyway? I've got more than enough for all of us; the house smelled like a florist's shop.

Connor called around the fourth day after Sam passed. I'd managed to shower and get dressed and was flicking through our photo albums when he knocked on the door. He was always the well-groomed, fashion-conscious one of the two of them. Sam's hair always grew a tad too long before he'd get around to having it cut and he only shaved when he had to. Camping wasn't Connor's thing either, but he and Sam having decided the cricket of their youth was too time-consuming, it left no time for surfing, had become good squash buddies and, on occasion, drinking buddies in the latter years.

I looked at him as he stood talking to Aunty Paula. His six o'clock shadow was dark, and for once he wasn't wearing his baggy crutch jeans, the ones Sam always took the mickey out of. Instead, he'd thrown on trackies and a hooded top.

Aunty Paula made him a coffee, and he came and sat down next to me. He'd bought an envelope with him, and he opened it, pulling out a stack of photographs. He sifted through them before handing me an old class photo.

'That's us there.' He pointed to two knobbly-kneed teenagers sitting in the front row. They were clad in the boys' high uniform of blue jumper and grey shorts, socks pulled up to the knees and folded over at the top.

'You both look so young.'

'We were. That was taken in Year Nine. We met on the first day of high school.' He ran his fingers through his hair, which didn't have its usual slick of product in it. 'Shit I was scared walking in through those brick gates for the first time. I didn't know anyone, and he was the first kid to talk to me. Then we wound up in the same class, and cricket team.' He tapped a tubby, teddy-bear-like boy in the back row. 'We went to our first party when we were fifteen, at his house. We used to call him Paddington.'

The reason for the nickname was obvious, I thought. I'd heard the story about the party before, but Connor needed to tell it again, so I listened quietly.

'I got seriously pissed, made a right dick of myself running around with a light shade on my head and pretending the sizzler sausage I'd swiped from the barbeque was a gun. Sam managed to get me back to his place, so my folks wouldn't find out. He snuck me in the back door and up the stairs to his room once Gina and Phil had gone to bed. I had to pay Lucas ten bucks not to say anything.' He laughed at the memory, and then his face crumpled. I reached out to him then, and we comforted each other.

'It's shit, Ellie; it's just shit. I miss him.'

'I know. Me too.'

We broke apart, and Connor cleared his throat and busied himself shuffling through the pictures, passing them to me. It was a slide show of two best mates through the years, bad haircuts, pimples and first cars.

'Do you want to stay for dinner, Connor?'

I hadn't noticed the smell of frying garlic and onions until then.

'Thanks, Paula, but I'll take a rain check. I might borrow your niece for a while, if that's okay though?' He got up and held his hand out to me. 'Come on, I've got something I want to show you.'

'It will do her good to get some fresh air.' Aunty Paula smiled over at us, but I could see the concern etched around her eyes, and I was nearly toppled by a wave of guilt. Connor promised he wouldn't keep me out late.

'Hey, you two, I'm not twelve.'

Aunty Paula flapped her tea towel at me. 'Go on, off you go.'

'You'll need your coat, Ellie, it's cold out,' Connor said.

I thought about telling Aunty Paula not to worry about dinner for me as I took myself off to my room to get my jacket. Gemma had brought some of my things around for me. I bit the words 'I'm not hungry, Aunty Paula' back though because I knew they'd fall on deaf ears. She's a feeder, and Uncle Colin is a fixer. Maybe I should make that number 0800unclecolinandauntypaula.

I was small and shrunken inside that jacket, a shadow of who I used to be as I followed Connor outside. I hadn't stepped outside since I got back here on Monday night and it was as though my senses had been swaddled in cotton wool. My legs were wobbly like they didn't belong to my body, but curiosity as to why he had a tree sticking out of the boot of his Holden penetrated the fug. It had blousy magenta blossoms clinging to it, and I shot him a questioning glance.

'I thought we could plant it in your garden. It'll blossom each year on Sam's anniversary. What do you think?' He sounded nervous, like he was worried I'd think he was overstepping the mark, but he needn't have been. I thought it was a beautiful idea and I told him so.

We drove around to Radford Street, and as we neared my house, I saw that someone had dragged an old fridge out on the street. They'd dumped it on the grass verge, leaning it up against one of the trees in the interim since I'd left for work on Monday. 'So that's it there,' I said pointing to number sixteen, ignoring Connor's raised eyebrow at the whiteware appliance free for the taking.

He pulled up the drive. 'When do you think you'll come home?'

'I don't know.' Being a weekday, I couldn't tell you which, I'd lost track of the days, I was perturbed there was no sign of Joel and his team. I hadn't given any thought as to how they were getting on until now. 'It's weird no one being here. I thought there'd be all sorts of activity going on.' I was relieved though that I wouldn't have to explain why Connor and I both looked like wrung-out ghosts, or why we'd decided to plant a tree when most people were at work.

'They've probably gone to another job for the day. They won't be onsite every day, Ellie, that's not how it works.' Connor shrugged and taking in his surroundings once more he locked his car before following behind me. The smell of wood fire's burning was thick and someone somewhere was having curry for tea. A car backfired in the distance and I jumped. It was all normal life stuff but it seemed so strange that life should be carrying on as normal for the people on my street when my world had just imploded. How could they not know what had happened? That was how momentous it felt.

'You haven't seen inside, yet, have you?' I made myself focus on Connor.

'No, only the outside when I dropped the scraper off.'

I unlocked the front door and stepped into the hallway. It was cold with that unlived-in atmosphere that said it had been abandoned; it was how I felt. I led Connor through trying to see the place through his eyes.

'This was where I used to stay when I was a kid,' I said opening the door to the smallest room. 'It was Mum's room before me. I'm going to use it as a sewing room and the room next door, which was Uncle Colin's, is going to be the guest room.' I didn't tell Connor I'd planned on turning it into an office for Sam, for when he eventually went back to work. I'd thought we could put one of those bed settees in there for when guests came to stay. I knew Sam would be pumping to get Mum over; he was forever trying to get us to mend bridges.

Connor made appropriate enthusiastic noises, and I loved him for it because I knew he was dead inside and didn't give a toss what I planned to do with the rooms. Right then I didn't care either.

As we wandered through to the lounge, the worst room in the house, I was aware that the floor no longer sloped, but there was a gaping hole in the middle of the floor. No wonder the house was an igloo. There were cracks in the walls and the ceiling—with bits of plaster dangling like icicles—was worse than ever. I concluded that if I were Connor I'd think I was mad for buying the house in its current state.

'The piles under here were the most damaged but not enough to rebuild them, the builder and his team began relevelling them on Monday.' The significance of Monday hung between us for a beat, but I didn't want to talk about what happened, so I kept talking. 'It's only this side of the house that was affected: the lounge and the two spare bedrooms. They'll repair them in stages by packing them with treated timber or something.' I didn't understand the process, but I'd give spouting the terminology I'd been told a go.

Connor nodded. With him being a tradesman, I figured it made sense to him and if he did think I had a moment of madness when I bought the place, then he was far too polite to say so until we reached my bedroom.

'Whoa! It's the pink palace.'

'I know, right? It always makes me think of candyfloss. I get hungry all the time in here.'

'Yeah, good thing you know a decent painter.' He raised a wan smile.

I stood in the doorway gazing around the bedroom while Connor went to use the bathroom. It would just be me sleeping here now. Sam and I would never get to argue over the throw cushions I was going to insist we had, or who got which side of the bed and how I took up far more than my share of the wardrobe. I bit down on my bottom lip hard; I wanted to feel another sort of pain.

'Are you ready, Ellie?'

I hadn't heard Connor come up behind me. I wasn't ready. I wasn't ready at all but I followed his lead outside and helped him unload the tree from the boot. He carried it while I brought the spade around the back of the house. I could see the lounge was propped up by a hydraulic jack, or at least that's what Connor told me it was called. That gaping hole in the lounge floor beneath it felt symbolic.

As we cast our eyes around the backyard looking for a suitable spot to plant the tree I noticed the lawn had been freshly mowed. I'd have to remember to thank Uncle Colin, I thought, smelling wet, cut grass. There were the raised voices of children over the fence, squabbling over a scooter. I hoped they were properly wrapped up playing outside at this time of the day. 'What about over there?' I said pointing to a large bare patch of soil on the fence-line between a hydrangea bush just beginning to bud and the dark green leaves of a camellia tree. Whatever had filled the gap between the two before must have died, so it seemed kind of apt to plant new life there.

Connor set about digging the hole, which didn't take long as the dirt was loose, but he still managed to get a bit of a glow on despite the chill air. He placed the tree, a crab apple, in it. He picked it, he said, because he liked the colour of the blossoms—magenta was more masculine than the pale pinks of some of the other saplings on offer. We piled the soil up around it before staking it securely. Job done and with dirt under our fingernails we stepped back to admire our handiwork before taking hold of each other's hands. There was a tremor in Connor's voice when he spoke. 'I think we should say something profound but I don't know what. "Rest in Peace, mate" doesn't sum it up.'

I leaned forward and rested my free hand on the spindly trunk. The bark was scratchy but solid. It was real. 'I don't think we need to say anything, Connor. I think Sam would know what's in here.' I gestured to my heart.

Chapter 21

To my surprise the day after we planted the tree Caro appeared, twins in tow on the doorstep, almost hidden behind an enormous bunch of white flowers.

I was glad I'd gone through the morning ritual of brushing my teeth, showering and getting dressed. Aunty Paula wouldn't settle for less. I was sleeping twelve hours at a time of a night thanks to the pills that reminded me of green M&M's, which Doctor Bayfield had left with Aunty Paula. Not enough to get addicted but enough to get me through, she'd said. Despite this I was assailed with exhaustion as I looked at Caro's anxious face.

'They're Kiwiana lilies, Ellie,' she said thrusting them at me. I thanked her before burying my nose in them.

'They're gorgeous. I'll pop them in some water.' The strong scent made my sinuses burn but I was grateful for all sensations that weren't the unrelenting pain of heartbreak. I tried to put a little spring in my step but think my movements still came across as sluggish and slow as though I were wading through mud. We were all out of vases, and I used one of Aunty Paula's old Agee preserving jars instead. I remembered wondering at the Richards' house what seemed a lifetime ago now, how flowers were supposed to fix things. They don't. I understood that now. I placed the jar down next to an elaborate bouquet of orchids, what flowers do is let you know you're not alone. They provide a splash of beauty and colour when everything around you has gone grey.

I was touched that Caro had come to see me. I'd imagine it wasn't easy to go and see someone when the grief is naked and plain to see. I thanked her for her help in getting me to Briarwood House on Monday afternoon. She waved my thanks aside, and I noticed she didn't seem as nervy. I think underneath that polished veneer that always looks like it's about to crack, there's a strong lady lurking. She's a bit lost, that's all. I pulled the twins toward me greedily and inhaled their no more tears shampoo smell. They were subdued and obviously under threat of death should they misbehave. William-Peter had done me a drawing. It was a stick figure standing on top of a slide wearing a skirt, and he pointed proudly at it saying, 'That's me.'

'I can see that it's a very good drawing.'

Not to be outdone Saffy-Rose presented me with a piece of cardboard upon which she'd glued the treasures she'd collected on the morning we walked to the park. She'd added a glitter flourish. 'It's lovely thank you. I especially like the rosemary.' To make my point I held the paper up to my nose and sniffed it. She puffed up proudly.

'When are you coming back, Ellie?'

'William-Peter, I told you Ellie would be back when she's feeling better.' Caro flashed me an apologetic look, but I can see she's yearning for an answer, too.

'I'll be back soon, guys, I promise. I miss you. Once the funeral's over.' I turned to Caro. 'It's on Monday. He's being cremated, and we'll spread his ashes at Sumner Beach in a few weeks. Sam loved the sea; he was a surfer.' I closed my eyes for the briefest of seconds and fancy I can smell the salt tang of the beach.

I heard Caro say, 'I'll be there.'

'What's cremation?'

'It's how we say goodbye to someone's body, William-Peter,' I said opening my eyes and hoping that would satisfy him. I definitely didn't want to get into the nitty-gritty.

It was Phil's idea to scatter Sam's ashes on the beach. He taught his son to surf at Sumner, and Sam and Connor whiled away long hot summers riding the waves tossed up there. I used to sit on the beach watching them, two black seals in the distance. I'm glad he's going to surf those waves once more. I think he'd have liked the idea.

I could smell coffee and Aunty Paula brought out a plate of chocolate biscuits. I had to smile watching the twins' eyes widen as they realised they were for them, before diving on them. They were like seagulls at the beach swooping on a discarded sandy sandwich. She was old-school, Aunty Paula; it wouldn't enter her head that a child might not be allowed such a simple pleasure as a chocolate biscuit—or four. Caro's lips tightened, but she didn't say anything. It was what her offspring had been banking on.

There were other visitors, friends who'd fallen by the wayside of late who'd been waiting for Aunty Paula to give the word and say I was up to seeing them; Lisa, whose hair has grown down past her shoulders now. They're friends I don't often see but I know they're there when needed. They were all welcome distractions to fill the time because we were in limbo waiting for the funeral. I understand why we have a ceremony when someone dies now. It's not just to see them off, to say goodbye. It's so we have something to focus on.

The planning of a funeral gives a sense of purpose when there's no sense to anything at all. For my part I've focussed on choosing a photo of the two of us to have blown up. It would sit there beside his coffin, alongside the other snapshots of his life, as a reminder that he was loved. I've stretched that simple task into something herculean because it seemed so very important I picked the right photograph.

The service was going to be held in the Chapel at the Woodland Memorial Gardens. Sam's going to have a memorial plaque, and it will be placed near the rockery because he wasn't a rose bush sort of guy. There'll be a page open in the memorial book, too, where we can write an inscription. I liked that idea because it will be opened for viewing on that page each anniversary of his passing.

I've left the planning of the service to the Andersons. He was my partner, but he was their son and brother and, well, they're paying for the funeral. That's not the main reason though. Gina brought him into the world, and she should be the one who organises how he leaves. She's called several times to see how I am and to talk about the service. I can sense she's on automatic pilot and that arranging Sam's goodbye is her way of marching forward. Her trousers will be pulled up high, and she will be taking charge, but I'm glad, because she's lost her son. It's incomprehensible, and she needs to find her way to cope. Besides which, I have no idea what Sam would have wanted other than laughter and not too many tears. I can't promise the latter.

Gina wanted to know what music I'd like included in the service. I asked for 'Crazy for you' by Madonna and Coldplay's 'Yellow' to be played. Sam loved Coldplay and I wanted to check in with Leprechaun Sam, be reassured by him that I'd chosen well but he wasn't there. I stood in front of the bathroom mirror for ages, frozen to the bathmat and still dripping from my shower as I kept rubbing at the misted spot on the mirror to see if he'd come. He didn't and the thought that he'd left me too pulled me further down into the quicksand I was slowly being dragged under by.

The family's all in agreement that the service should be a celebration of Sam's life, and the boys have been putting together a video montage.

Lucas was going to speak on behalf of the family, and Connor—as his mate—had asked to say a few words, too. We all knew different sides of Sam, and I was pleased he would talk about the kind of friend he was. There'll be others whose life Sam touched who'll get up, too, when the time to share comes. Phil's brother, Nate, who taught Sam how to scuba dive is going to deliver the eulogy and I've decided to talk about the night Sam and I stood under the stars in the middle of nowhere and told each other we loved one another..

Gina told me most people don't wear black to funerals these days and that I should wear what I'm comfortable in. I've decided to wear my check shirt, sparkly belt and dress trousers. My take on Madonna's cowgirl look in the 'Don't Tell Me' video was Sam's favourite, but I draw the line at wearing jeans.

Chapter 22

Today was the sixth day since Sam died, he'd be cremated on the seventh. I'd woken strangely excited because today I'd get to see him again. I was going to stay the night at the Andersons'. My Sam's been brought home.

~

'You're too pale, and you're too skinny, Ellie,' Gina said pulling me inside. 'I've made a plate of club sandwiches, ham and egg, and there are scones, too, so make sure you eat up. Oh, but don't touch the cheese and onion sandwiches because they're on gluten-free bread for Mandy.' She rolled her eyes and muttered something about fussy eaters and she'll be going dairy-free next, before closing the door behind me. I watched as she paused to adjust her trousers, yanking them up until they were sitting in their customary position, up around her ears, and today, it was endearing. I wasn't sure what I expected, but the house didn't smell sad; it smelt of fresh coffee and baking. It smelt inviting.

'Give me your coat, love. Everybody's in the living room except Zac and Mandy; they'll be along later once Mandy's migraine's eased off. Oh, and Connor's here too. It's lovely that he wanted to be here.'

I shrugged out of my coat, and she hung it up while I hovered in the entrance, unsure whether I should offer my services in the kitchen or go through to the living room. I was desperate to see Sam.

Gina patted me on the arm. 'He looks well, love, it's good to have him here with us again.' Her eyes filled up then, and I reached out to her. We squeezed one another tight. 'You never expect your child to go before you.' She sniffed and then said, 'I wish it could have worked out differently, Ellie.'

'So do I.' All of a sudden I began to shake and I was worried my legs might buckle because it hit me then that the tie that bound me to this family was gone, and all we had left in common was grief.

We broke apart as Phil stuck his head around the lounge door. 'Any chance of a cuppa, Gina love? Ellie, hi, come on through and join us.'

I looked to Gina who gave me a gentle nudge. 'Go, I'll put the kettle on.'

Phil put his arm around my shoulder and led me through.

The lounge was crowded, and every seat seemed to be taken. Justin and Lucas sprawled on the settee while their grandparents were seated king and queen like in the armchairs. I said hello to them all and headed over to Nana Mo and Grandad Don first, telling them not to get up as I bent down and clumsily embraced Grandad Don, apologising for nearly knocking his glasses off. He was Gina's dad, and she'd inherited her propensity for pulling her trousers up past her middle from him. He's a gruff man, but a heart of gold hides beneath his bluster.

Nana Mo, when I put my arms around her, is frailer than I remembered and her shoulders bony. I released her, and she patted me on the cheek, blinking back her tears. 'You're too thin.' She echoed her daughter's sentiment. 'I hope you're eating, Ellie; starving yourself won't do any good.'

'I am.'

She didn't look convinced, and her eyes flitted to the coffee table laden with food. I'd have to prove myself by stuffing down a few sandwiches.

Justin, when he got up, seemed smaller somehow, too, his brawny presence a little shrunken. I'd learned grief did that. He gave me a welcome hug.

'You doing okay?'

I nodded, and then shook my head. 'You?'

'It's not easy. You know how it is.'

I did.

It was Lucas's turn next. 'He looks good, Ellie, he looks like Sam again,' he said releasing me. 'Go and see him.'

I gave Connor a hug hello but didn't embrace him for long. I was desperate to stand beside the brass-handled, walnut box I'd seen the moment I stepped inside the room. You'd think it would feel bizarre to walk toward a coffin positioned by the entertainment unit, but it didn't. The lining was white silk, I saw when I reached it, and there was Sam. *Oh, my love.* He was lying there against his snowy backdrop looking ever so peaceful. I wasn't sure what my feelings were about his body being used for organ donation. He'd suffered enough and I didn't want him ravaged more. Seeing him now, though, he looks as though he's still sleeping. He's at peace and I'm glad he's helping someone else. It was what he'd wanted.

I leaned over and kissed him on his forehead. His skin was waxy beneath my lips. Then as I stood back up and looked at him properly, I couldn't help but smile. He was dressed in his beloved check flannel bush shirt and jeans, his hiking boots on his feet.

I'd slept in one of Sam's shirts for weeks after his accident until I eventually had to wash it. I kept another under my pillow, which I refused to wash, but it's lost the musky scent of him. There was a pale blue baby blanket folded up next to him and a couple of trophies from his younger years. I dug into my pocket and pulled out a tissue-wrapped charm. It was the first charm Sam ever bought me for my Pandora bracelet. I slipped it beneath his shirt to rest on his chest and kept my hand there. His body was cold beneath my touch and I knew for certain he was gone but I could sense him there with me. I stood there for the longest time and the tears fell freely.

Zac and Mandy arrived later. I couldn't help noticing that Mandy had pretty rosy cheeks for someone recovering from a migraine. They were all just in time for a helping from the enormous casserole dish of macaroni cheese Gina had made in Sam's honour. We toasted my love, their son, brother, brother-in-law, grandson and friend by each cracking open a bottle of his favourite beer, DB Export Gold, and even Nana Mo drank from the bottle.

Then we each found a space to hunker down to watch the family movies Phil had dug out. I fell asleep next to Sam, on the cushions Phil pulled off the couch for me when everybody began making their way home or to bed. The image of him as a young boy, bronzed and skinny with shaggy blonde hair, teaching Lucas to ride a bike burned on my retinas.

Chapter 23

♥

I was in the back seat of Gina and Phil's car, squeezed in alongside Nana Mo and Grandad Don. We were following the hearse the short drive to the crematorium. The boys, along with their Uncle Nate, a cousin whom I'd never met whose name was Liam and Connor were the pallbearers. They were riding in the hearse with Sam. Connor took me aside before they left and said he'd take care of him and in that moment I'd really loved him for it. Mandy was making her own way although she'd offered to drive us all there in her car. We wouldn't have all fitted in it and there was no room for one more in Phil's Nissan. Besides which Phil said he wanted to drive. He needed to do something practical. I could have gone with Mandy but I didn't want to. I wanted to be with Gina and Phil.

My mind played over how hard it had been to place my hand on Sam's chest for the last time earlier that morning. To lean down and rest my lips on his forehead and to tell him I loved him before whispering goodbye. I didn't want to let him go but I had to and Gina pulled me gently away from him and into her embrace. We clung together as Sam's coffin was carried out of the house and it hit me afresh that he'd never be coming home again.

The windows inside the car were fogging up, and I wiped at mine with my sleeve. The day outside was cold and clear; a perfect late winter's day in Christchurch. I couldn't see a single cloud in the cobalt sky. I was filled with the strangest sensation sitting there in the car; it was as though I was disjointed, as if the parts that made me whole no longer fitted together. I tried to pay attention to Nana Mo's story about Sam picking all the heads off her marigolds when he was just a little lad in short pants. Gina's head in front of me was focussed straight ahead as was Phil's; they were both quiet, but then Nana Mo was talking enough for everybody. Grandad Don told her to quieten down.

Poor Nana Mo didn't know how she should be though, and I knew her chatter was anxiousness to fill the void because driving to her grandson's funeral was not the natural order of things. It wasn't how it should be, so I reached my hand across to rest on top of hers, and she patted it gratefully.

I gazed out the window, seeing but not seeing, and when we got closer to the chapel I began to focus on the cars lining either side of the street. There were a lot of people here but then Sam had touched a lot of lives, not just mine. Today, I told myself, wasn't just about me; it was about everybody who'd known and loved him. Phil parked in the allocated family space and I helped Nana Mo from the car before we gathered ourselves. Gina straightening Phil's tie, Grandad Don patting his pockets to make sure he had his hanky. Then, our sombre group of five made our way toward the entrance. Five is an odd number and that's exactly how it felt: odd, one was missing.

People were milling about, some faces I recognised some I didn't. I wasn't sure how I would muster the energy to talk to anyone because my insides were leaden and I was sure if I spoke my voice would sound robotically monotone. I thought I saw Caro. She stood out with her natural elegance but her back was turned to me and I couldn't be sure. Phil shook someone's hand and accepted their condolences while Gina was hugged by his wife. Gemma rushed up and wrapped me in a Tom-Ford-perfumed hugged. I hugged her back tightly, grateful she was here, and when I saw Uncle Colin and Aunty Paula behind her, I told myself I could do this.

I pulled away from Gemma to watch as Sam was unloaded from the back of the hearse, each of the men taking up their position and waiting a moment before the director gave them the signal to proceed. They did so solemnly and the crowd of people began to file inside slowly behind them, filling up the long wooden pews in the chapel.

'Ready?' Phil asked as the director gestured it was time for us to go inside. He took Gina's hand. She nodded and took hold of mine. We walked through the entrance and up the aisle. I could feel the heat of stares, smell roses mingling with heady perfumes and as we made our way to the front row where Mandy, Zac, Lucas and Justin were already seated alongside Nana Mo and Grandad Don, Pink Floyd's 'Wish you were here' played. Justin's choice.

We sat down and I could feel the cool smoothness of the pew through the thin fabric of my trousers. My eyes flitted straight to the coffin where sprays of lilies decorated either side of it. That's not what I was looking for though; I was looking for my photograph oh so carefully chosen. I'd decided the only way I was going to get through this goodbye without dissolving was by gazing upon the pair of us forever frozen in time as we laughed at a terrible cracker joke a few Christmases ago. We've both got silly paper party hats on and our heads are thrown back carefree and happy. The picture always made me smile.

So, as the chaplain welcomed everybody and we bowed our heads in prayer I snuck a peek at our photo. I kept my eyes trained on it as Justin walked heavily to the lectern with Lucas and Zac following behind him. He cleared his throat and thanked everybody for coming before opening the Bible to the page he had bookmarked and beginning to read from Psalm 34:18.

Gina gave a loud sniff as Lucas carried on to talk about Sam, their brother, and what he'd meant to them. I could hear the rustling of tissues and someone coughed.

Phil, with Gina by his side, read John 14:1–3, and, through my tears, which had started despite my staring at that photo so hard my eyes began to burn, I couldn't help but look to Phil. I watched his lip tremble as he tried to get through his reading. He did his son proud, and Gina dipped her head to hide her grief and linked her arm through his, keeping one another steady as they made their way back to their seat.

The chaplain said that we were now going to listen to some pieces of music chosen by Sam's partner Ellie while the video montage played. 'Crazy for You' began and I sat watching the home video clips on the screen behind the lectern. The emotion that swelled inside me was like a powerful king tide. My Sam as Gina's baby. My Sam as a boy, off to school, playing with his brothers, fishing and camping with Phil, family barbeques. My Sam as a young man, so handsome with his surfboard tucked under his arm, a group photo with Connor by his side, beers raised at a stag do, standing proudly beside his van with its new sign writing. And then there we are. I was sitting on his knee, my arms wrapped around his neck as I kissed him on his cheek. A sob escaped and Gina gripped my hand tightly.

When the final chords had played and the video faded Connor was asked to come up and talk about his best friend. I listened as he said how much he missed Sam before sharing the same story he told me—the one about their first party when they were teenagers, and there's laughter. I'm glad because Sam would have wanted laughter.

Then, it was my turn. I looked at that photo and told myself I could do this for Sam and for me. I stood up, swallowing the lump in my throat because I wouldn't let either of us down. I walked up to that lectern on legs that felt like they were no longer part of my body and in a voice I hoped would stay strong and true I began to talk. I told all those tear stained faces turned toward me how I could pinpoint the moment I'd fallen in love with Sam. We were looking up at the night sky which was a carpet of stars and he showed me the Southern Cross. I said that I liked to think Sam was up there in the sky now roaming free and happy. The brightest of all the stars in the sky.

I kissed my fingers and placed them on his casket and then my legs carried me back to the family. Gina reached her hand to me as I passed her by, and stroked my arm, giving me a ghost smile that said I did well.

Phil's brother, Nate, read the eulogy, and another of Sam's friends got up to share what their friendship meant to him, as did his old boss, under whom Sam did his apprenticeship. 'Yellow' by Coldplay heralded the moment we had to say our final goodbyes but in my heart I'd already said mine. We stood and I filed in behind Grandad Don as we each picked up a yellow rose from the basket at the foot of the steps. We climbed the steps, placing our roses one by one on top of Sam's casket, closed now, forever closed to me, before we walked outside to the sunshine.

Chapter 24

'Ellie, I know it's early days, but you can't hide away.'

'You're in your prime,' I mouthed, and on cue, Gemma says, 'You're in your prime. You need to test the water sometime, so why not tonight? Come on, I'm only talking a couple of drinks, and maybe a dance. It's not every day you get VIP passes to the hottest venue in town. Please, pretty please. We can leave anytime you want, and I promise you'll be my date and that I won't talk to anyone else no matter how hot to trot they may be.'

'I don't hide away thank you very much. I'm actually very busy with the house. There's all sorts to do you know, colours to be picked, material to be bought, fixtures and fittings to choose and I can't take my eye off the ball when it comes to the repairs being done.' I spent a lot of time on Pinterest and Uncle Colin came around once a week to check on how things were tracking. He'd explain the finer points of what was actually being done to the house for me. I've been learning a lot.

'That's not exactly venturing out, Ellie. You're becoming a hermit.'

'I'm not! I went for a big walk around Taylors Mistake with Lisa, last weekend.' I'd been glad to escape from the dust the plasterer had left behind the day before. We'd met up at the surf beach and walked the track that cut into the wheat-coloured hills to follow the rocky coastline. The water had been turquoise and frothy and the sky a perfect shade of faded denim with only a smattering of puffball clouds. It was good being out breathing in all that salty air and it had been nice to catch up with an old friend and talk about our Teeny Tykes days.

'Just because I don't want to hit the town doesn't mean I sit around doing nothing.' I chewed my thumbnail—a new habit. That statement might have been a tad hypocritical given it was eleven o'clock on Saturday morning, and I was still in my pyjamas, um, sitting around doing nothing.

I'd had good intentions of going to the gym this morning, I'd joined by the way, and the regular exercise was helping keep me sane, but then, a grief grenade exploded, and that was the end of that. I'd switched the radio in the kitchen on and Ed Sheeran's 'Photograph' was playing. BOOM! So, I took myself off back to bed, assumed the foetal position and had a good cry. Grief grenades can't be ignored once that pin's been pulled; they have to be wallowed in. I've learned this in the eleven weeks and five days since Sam's funeral and now I just go with them when they randomly detonate.

I have also learned that people, my cousin included, seem to think I can draw a line under my life with Sam. They think because he was asleep for so long that my grieving was done then, the funeral the closing chapter. It doesn't work like that. Yes, I had to pick up and carry on, I had bills to pay, responsibilities to people other than myself, but I was simply going through the motions. Oh, and that's another thing. If one more person was to give me that look and say, 'It's good to keep busy, Ellie, get back into your normal routines, life goes on.' I'd...I'd...well, I'd use a very bad word.

There have been many somebody-peed-in-my-bowl-of-soup days this last while. There's a hole in the bedroom wall where I gouged it with the scraper when the wallpaper strip I was trying to peel off wouldn't budge. The frustration that Sam would not ever share this space with me bubbled over and I slid down the wall and sat on the floor for an age. I only got up to retrieve Sam's shirt from under my pillow, so I could hold on to that while I cried. I'd felt like I was going under as I sobbed. I couldn't see anyway forward but eventually I stopped crying. That's another thing I've learned. You can't cry forever because eventually you either pick yourself up, or fall asleep from the effort of it all.

Poor Connor would have to patch that hole up before he could paint the room now. On the bright side, there had been a flicker of satisfaction when I ticked 'peel wallpaper off bedroom wall,' on my 'to-do' list, with red pen of course.

Sometimes I made a beeline for the Memorial Gardens to sit near the rockery, my hand resting on Sam's plaque because it made me feel close to him, and other times, like this morning, I climbed into bed and let the duvet swallow me up. Once I was all cried out, I dragged myself back out of bed. I made a coffee and picked up my book with the intention of reading it on the laundry's back steps. It's a sun trap out there and an escape from the chaos of the work in progress going on inside. I'd no sooner plonked my bum down when Gemma phoned.

'Ellie,' she wheedled. 'I promise you can wear whatever you like, and I won't say a word.'

'Even if I wear my corset and tulle skirt?'

There's a choking sound. 'Even if.'

Gosh, this did mean a lot to her, and suddenly I couldn't bear the thought of curling up on the couch, eating my way through a packet of Tim Tams, chocolate caramel of course, while watching *The Crown*.

This is what I'd done every Saturday since Sam's funeral. Okay, I was fibbing a little; Connor quite often popped around of a weekend to do a spot of painting, after which I'd call us a takeaway, and we'd watch a movie. Hang out. Last weekend we watched an appalling action flick, but it was so cheesy we both managed to laugh, and I'm always glad of his company. We're comfortable together.

I've had dinner at the Andersons' a few times too, although I've got mixed feelings about that because I think I'm a reminder to them of the future their son's never going to have. Whereas, when I go there I feel close to Sam because I like to hear their stories. Gemma's right, though, it had been so long since I did anything remotely normal socially. I think I'd probably forgotten how.

'Okay,' popped out of my mouth. I wasn't going to think about it. I was going to relax and go with it.

'Really?'

'Yep.'

'Right. Be at mine for seven. This calls for something bubbly.'

I hung up, and—despite being worn out from all those tears earlier—I was buoyed. Who knows? Maybe I'd enjoy myself. I love dancing, and it would be nice to get dressed up. I didn't feel like reading anymore, and I wouldn't inflict the corset and tulle number on Gemma. I wanted to get something new, and so I headed off to the bathroom muttering a naughty word on the way as I tripped over a claw hammer that's been left lying outside the door. That will be down to Mikey. I've grown used to his habit of leaving his tools lying about. Yesterday I trod on a level; it could have been worse. The joys of living on a building site, I thought, pushing open the bathroom door.

The smell of damp has blessedly disappeared in here now, and I have a modern vanity, and new bath with a shower rose overhead. The old shower curtain that had a knack of sticking to me when I was showering or hanging over the outside of the box, which meant water puddled everywhere, went out with the rubbish. It's been replaced by a glass screen. Aunty Paula presented me with a set of matching teal flannels, big fluffy towels and bathmat to celebrate the first space being completed in the house, and I went out and bought a matching soap dish and toothbrush set.

Once I was presentable, I hopped in my car and whizzed down the road to a seconds warehouse I knew of.

The racks of recycled clothes were endless and coordinated by colour then size. I whiled away a happy hour flicking through them until the perfect dress jumped out at me. Well almost perfect.

It was a pink shiny strapless full-length dress that some young woman back in the nineties must have worn to a school ball. The size was right, and I held it up and imagined it taken up to just above the knees and worn with a sash. I could make the sash from the material I'd take off the length. 'Material Girl' began to play in my head, and for eight dollars I had to have it!

Something peculiar happens to me when I find what I consider to be the perfect bargain. I become like a lion guarding her cub, and if anyone looks sideways at the treasure I have unearthed, I have to stop myself from snarling a back-off warning. I relax once the garment is in a bag, bought and paid for, but I wasn't there yet with the dress, and I muttered a bad word under my breath as my phone rang before I could get to the counter.

There was a redhead who would look amazing in the vibrant pink number currently draped over my arm, and she obviously thought so, too, as she stared at it. I swallowed a growl and checked my phone, the dress tightly held. It was Mum. *Major big I've been holding on for hours pee-in-my-soup.* No way was I answering it. She's taken to ringing me every Monday night since Sam's funeral. It's nice to know she cares but

I find those calls hard work. They're stilted and polite and last week's call went like this:

'How's life at American Nails, Mum?'

'Great, I've got my regular girls who refuse to let anyone else do their ombre finish. I'm only there Tuesdays, Wednesdays and Fridays now, though. I've cut back because I like to spend time with my George.'

Mum has done everything over the years from waitressing, to working in a jewellery shop, to selling makeup at Carrara Markets on the Gold Coast. She's found her niche with nail art at the Pacific Fair Mall, though. As for George, he's a man with an unpronounceable Greek surname whom I refer to as George the Papadum, because it's simpler. She's been with him for a few years now, and she probably didn't need to work because he was rolling in it, but she reckons she likes to keep a hand in.

The house has given us a bit more to chat about and after she'd told me the key to achieving the perfect ombre finish (it's all in the sponging) I told her where the renovations were at.

'Joel and his lads are busy in the lounge now. They've chipped the old lathe and plaster off the walls, and re-gibbed them, the skirting boards are going to be replaced next, and then next week the plasterer is coming. After that, Connor can do his thing.'

'He's doing a good job then, this Joel?'

'Yeah he is.' Uncle Colin picked well. Joel buzzes in and out keeping an eye on the work being done. I like him; he doesn't condescend to me when he explains what stage everything is at and what's planned for that day. It was him who changed my mind about getting the floorboards sanded. He said they'd look good, but they'd be cold. I decided he was right. The carpet and vinyl will be the last job to get ticked off the list. I only really see him and the lads on my way out the door of a morning and occasionally of an evening if they're trying to finish a particular job and stay later. I'm happy to leave them to it. They know what they're doing.

I'm not sure whether they know about Sam or not. I've not mentioned him to them. It's not the sort of thing you drop into a flying conversation as you race out the door. 'Oh, and by the way, my boyfriend's just died so if I have a face on me like a prune soaked in gin, that's why, lads, no need for alarm.'

'I won't recognise the house next time I see it. It's so strange to think of you living back there with all those memories.'

'Happy memories, Mum,' I said pointedly, and she got off the phone pretty quick after that.

This phone call now of hers was breaking the routine. I'd check my messages in a few minutes, I decided, shoving my phone back in my bag, just in case it was important. She means well but it's Aunty Paula who's been making the soup and dropping the casseroles around to make sure I'm eating. Words are easy, it's actions that count and I don't remember seeing her while Sam was sleeping, or at the funeral. To be fair I did put her off that. I didn't want her there making a big show of looking after her daughter. The daughter she only mothers when the mood takes her.

I paid for the dress, and once I was back in my car, I dialled voicemail.

'Hi, Ellie, it's me, sweetie. No need to call me back. I wanted to tell you that George and I have been talking and we agree that now's a good time for me to come and stay with you. I stayed away from the funeral because you said you had lots of people gathered around you and I only agreed to that because I know it's when those people drop away, the going gets tough. I'll ring with my flight details once I've booked. Bye for now.'

VERY BAD WORD. 'No, Mum, you don't know! You've got no idea because when the going gets tough for you, you take off.' I shouted this out loud staring at the phone as though it had committed a criminal offence by relaying her message. A woman with a toddler hanging off her hip walked past my car and shot me a wary glance, but I didn't care. I wasn't finished yet. 'And I don't want you coming here!' I hit number five to erase the message. Mum's never toughed anything out, and if she was feeling guilty about it now, it's not my problem. I don't need her trying to make up for all those lost years. It's too late and who would she be doing it for anyway? Me or her? My mother's motivation is always murky.

I sat there in the carpark racking my brain. *The spare room wasn't ready?* It wasn't true. Hope flared. The foundations are strong now with the lounge, and what was my childhood bedroom and Mum's, along with Uncle Colin's old room having been raised and levelled. I stayed on at Aunty Paula's and Uncle Colin's during that time. There was no point in me trying to live amongst all that mess as more cracks appeared with the movement and clumps of plaster crumbled down. I think I would have lost the plot completely, and I wasn't ready to be home alone. I could barely get out of bed of a morning the first week after the funeral. I was worse than I'd been in the week leading up to it after Sam passed. I think it was the reality of never seeing him again finally sinking in and I needed Aunty Paula issuing me directives to steer me through the days when I eventually did get out of bed.

I'm grateful to have my house. Owning it means I couldn't collapse in a heap, well not for long at any rate. I won't break the trust Uncle Colin and Aunty Paula showed in me by lending me the money to buy it and fix it up. I've got repayments to make, responsibilities, and there's no such thing as a Work and Income Grief Benefit. Besides I missed William-Peter and Saffy-Rose, even Caro to a point. It *was* good to get a routine going because I've learned I need routine. My mother turning up will completely throw my routine and make me insane.

She can't come, I thought turning the key and reversing out of the carpark. The thing is, if I say the guest room isn't habitable, Mum's liable to say she'll top and tail with me—that's not happening. Or, she'll go and stay at Uncle Colin and Aunty Paula's. I'll run it by Gemma later and see what she can come up with, I decided, indicating out onto the road and heading for home. She's good at making stuff up; it's a big part of her job.

Chapter 25

I put the thought of dealing with my mother to one side and whiled away a pleasurable couple of hours hemming my dress and making a sash. I loved the result, and I stood in front of my dressing table mirror admiring it and striking a pose before turning to the side and finally looking back over my shoulder. I have black heels on, and I've put makeup on for the first time in ages. I felt pretty and feminine, and something else—something I hadn't felt for a very long time, I realised as I picked up my black clutch, and headed out the door—I felt young.

Gemma had a random selection of dance hits playing when I arrived. They were the songs we used to play as kids, when all we wanted to be when we grew up was one of the Pussycat Dolls.

'That dress looks fabulous on you. What label?' She raised an eyebrow ever hopeful I would have finally discovered, if not the city's designer stockists, then at least the women's high street fashion chains.

'Thanks, it's a Mad Ellie Original, and you look gorgeous too.' She did. She had her hair pulled back in an elaborately tousled do and was wearing a classic little black dress and killer heels. Her customary glossy pink pout was in place.

'The dress is Fifi Rhodes, I think it's very Meghan Markle, Royal Tour of Dublin. Elegant, yet with a hint of naughtiness. I thought about jewellery—what do you think?'

'Did Meghan wear it with jewellery?'

'No.'

'Keep it simple then.'

Yeah, you're right. Fifi—her real name's Shona; you can see why she calls herself Fifi—launched her label at Fashion Week in September and the dress is a thank you for me posting her designs on That Girl the day she was showing.'

'Well it's lovely, and it fits you perfectly.'

'So long as I don't bend over.'

We giggled, and I sat down while Gemma disappeared into the kitchen. On the coffee table, there was a bowl of chips and dip, and I took a handful of chips, ignoring the dip. I didn't have any dinner. It was a hit and miss affair anyway these days, but I was too busy with my dress to bother. Chips would have to do. I was doing well, I thought shovelling them in; I hadn't thought about Sam once. When Gemma returned she was clutching two bottles of ready-to-drinks, and taking mine, I inspected the label: passionfruit-flavoured vodka. Hmm, looked interesting.

It was yummy lolly water and it slipped down easily. While I was necking it, it occurred to me that once again it'd all been about me this last while. Yes, I know that had been for a good reason, but it was high time I had an update as to how Gemma was tracking with work, the Stud Muffin, life in general. I was out of touch with what was going on with her and although she'd probably told me what had been happening, I hadn't been listening. White noise and all that. The world needed to stop revolving around me starting now.

'How's work?'

'I'm still number one, and I closed the sale on Rossall Street yesterday.'

'Cool, go you! The advertising you've been doing was worth it?'

'Yeah it's pricey, but it's paying for itself now.'

I don't think I'll ever get used to seeing my cousin on the back of a bus.

'What about you? How are the gruesome twosome and Nervy Caro?'

'They're not that bad.' I scooped my chip into the dip this time; it was sun-dried tomato and cashew nuts and it was scrummy. 'Although, William-Peter got into trouble at the music group I take them to sometimes on Fridays. He told the woman playing the piano that she had a big bottom and needed to do something about it.'

'Oh dear.'

'He's very forthright. It will stand him in good stead later in life, just not now, but that's not the worst of it.'

Gemma raised a perfectly shaped eyebrow.

'He said all that sitting at the piano was no good for her and suggested she go to hot yoga like his mother.'

Gemma snorted. 'God where does he get it from?'

'No idea. He is an adult trapped in a little boy's body, and to be fair, the piano lady does have a ginormous bottom. It was hard to keep a straight face when I had to tell him it wasn't appropriate to say that sort of thing.'

'I bet and how's the "lady who lunches"?'

'Caro's okay, she's been good to me since—' I wasn't going to say his name. Not tonight. 'I feel like I've gotten to know her a lot better lately. She is precious, but she can be quite funny too when she wants to be.'

'Really? She always looks miserable whenever I've seen her.'

'I think she's just got one of those faces.'

'RBF.'

'Huh?'

'Resting Bitch Face.'

'Gemma!' I couldn't help but laugh. 'So, how's it going with the Stud Muffin? Have you had your wicked way with him yet?'

'No and I don't know what I'm doing wrong, Ellie.' She looked genuinely puzzled. 'I've dangled lots of carrots, but he's not nibbling.'

'Maybe he doesn't like carrots.'

'Not funny.'

'No, sorry. Perhaps he's got a girlfriend?'

'He's definitely single. I couldn't find any info on Facebook or any other site, so I checked out his file at work.'

'Gemma!'

'What?'

'Isn't that breaching the Privacy Act or something?'

'Oh, probably, but who cares? Nothing's private these days anyway.'

I wasn't convinced—she could get in trouble for doing that. Have I mentioned I could be quite the goody-two-shoes? She was always the instigator growing up and I was the follower and failing that the telltale. A thought occurred to me. 'Maybe he's gay?'

'Nope, no way.'

'How do you know?'

'It would be a sin against womankind, that's how I know. God could never be that cruel to provide a man who looks like Chris Hemsworth, has abs to die for and an ass I could crack an egg on who wasn't up for a bit of Gemma time.'

We cackled like a pair of witches over a cauldron at that, and she got up to fetch us both another bottle of the fruity water. 'Guess what?' I said opening mine.

'What?'

'Mum's got it in her head I need looking after, and she's the one to do it. She wants to come over.'

'Crap.'

'My sentiments exactly. I need you to come up with something to put her off.'

'Um, okay how about —New Zealand Customs is on strike, and as such there are no overseas persons allowed in or out of the country for the foreseeable future. She'll have to stay put. There. Done.'

We grinned at each other, but I was serious I didn't want her coming. 'I hate all these complicated feelings she conjures up in me, Gem. You know I love her, but at a distance; otherwise, we don't work.'

Gemma nodded. 'You'll just have to tell her straight. You know, say something like you need time on your own to heal. That's not a lie, either.' She knows I hate telling fibs; they don't roll off my tongue easily.

'She'll think I'm suicidal if I say that.'

'Hmm yeah maybe. Oh, I don't know, but I always think better after my third vodka.' She got up and came back with fresh drinks and turned the stereo up. I forgot all about Mum as we danced to an old Black Eyed Peas song, both trying to outdo each other as we broke out our Fergie moves. By the time the nice Uber driver arrived, we were both hoarse from singing and ever so slightly sozzled.

Chapter 26

♥

The Terrace Club was the latest hot spot in town, and it was the place to be seen, or so Gemma informed me. There was a queue of scantily clad girls and boozed-up boys already, but of course, she flashed our VIP passes, and we bypassed the line and headed straight inside. I have to admit it was nice feeling important. I can see how celebrities would get used to the special treatment. The interior had been done, I saw doing a quick sweep of the place, in a Cuban cigar bar style and it was packed. I could smell bodies and booze and the temperature was hot, the music pumping. We pushed our way up to the bar and waited our turn to order. I glanced around and saw a girl elbow her friend. They both gawped over at Gemma before making their way over.

'Aren't you Gem? From That Girl?' the taller of the two shouted over the music.

Gemma smiled and nodded, used to being accosted.

'Oh wow! I love your site,' the short one gushed before picking up a beer mat from the bar top and asking Gemma if she'd sign it. She did so graciously as if this was an everyday occurrence, and maybe it was. I was so out the loop, I wouldn't know.

'I love your dress.' She was really fangirling.

'Thanks, it's Fifi Rhodes.'

'Oh wow, I like love her stuff. It's Fifi Rhodes,' the short one bellowed up to the tall one who looked down at my cousin with adoration and admiration. It was getting a bit much, to be honest. She was a real estate agent who moonlights on Instagram, not one of the Kardashians, and, actually having said the 'K' word I don't know what they've ever done to warrant their slavish following either. I pushed my way in front of Gemma. 'My dress is a Mad Ellie Original.'

'Oh, right.' I got a cursory once-over before they stared past me. 'So cool meeting you. Selfie?' They clicked away leaning their pouting faces in next to my cousin's, and I got great pleasure photobombing a couple of the shots before they disappeared back into the crowd.

'When did you get so popular?' I asked once Gemma had given our order to the bartender who, spotting all the fuss being made of her, figured she must be someone important and had ignored those ahead of us.

She shrugged. 'It happens now and then.'

Once we'd both got a bottle each of some ridiculously expensive mix, Gemma led me out to the dancefloor.

I didn't know the song, but after a few minutes I loosened up because the beat was good, and I lost myself in that. I was all floaty and free, and well, like I mentioned before I was a weeny bit (quite a lot actually) tipsy. Gemma and I were garnering a few looks from a group of cute guys all scrubbed up for their night out, and I found myself showing off. I was enjoying being admired, and Gemma was happy, because she could see I was having fun. We danced for ages until we were both dying of thirst and, as we weaved our way back toward the bar, my way was blocked by one of the men I was showing off to a few seconds ago. I may well have had my beer goggles on, but he looked pretty fine to me.

He leaned down and shouted, 'Hi, I'm Troy. I was just admiring your dress. You look gorgeous.'

He's smooth, I thought, and his breath was minty. A big red tick for that. 'Thanks. I'm Ellie.' I batted my eyelashes.

'Can I buy you a drink?'

Why not? Actually, there were quite a few reasons why not, drink spiking at the top of the list, but instead of politely refusing I said, 'Yes please.' I didn't want to be cautious tonight, I wanted to let my hair down and have fun.

Gemma had disappeared somewhere in the throng, and as I trailed behind Troy, I looked around for her. I spotted her talking to some guy and on closer inspection, squinting through one eye always works well for me when I'm a bit squiffy, it clicked that it was the Stud Muffin. I wondered if she knew he'd be here. I wouldn't put it past her but I didn't care either because as Troy turned to ask me what I'd like to drink, I decided I was going to do something. It was something I hadn't done in a very long time, and I might be rusty at it, but I was going to try my darnedest to pour some oil on that rust. I was going to flirt.

'Are you having a good night?' Troy breathed in my ear once he'd ordered.

'Yeah great, you?'

'It just got better.'

I smiled up at him, and my lip got stuck to my top gum. He handed me my bottle of vodka mix and asked if I'd like to dance. I let him take me by the hand, and he carved a path through the crowd to the dancefloor. Gemma who was still sidling up to the Stud Muffin saw us and raised her eyebrows questioningly. I made a circle with my thumb and index finger and held it up for her to see. She looked a little taken aback; it's the signal we used way back when I was footloose and fancy-free, and it meant everything was good. A thumbs down was the sign for 'come rescue me'.

Troy was a good dancer, and I kept looking up at him, checking him out, and he kept looking down at me, and we both keep smiling at each other stupidly. I had that lovely feeling; you know the one where you can't help but feel like an incredibly gorgeous supermodel who also happens to be a fabulous dancer.

'You've got a beautiful smile, do you know that?' Troy leaned down, and I could feel that minty breath hot on my neck. Something inside me tingled.

'So do you.' He really did, and I smiled even more.

We were three songs in and one drink down when he asked me if I'd like to grab a seat upstairs in the lounge bar. I looked around. His mates seem to have moved on, and I couldn't see Gemma anywhere. My feet were sore, unaccustomed to heels, and it would be nice to sit down for a bit. Maybe Gemma was upstairs. 'Sure,' I slurred, so it sounded more like 'Shuuure.'

He took my hand once more, and steered us over to the stairs on the far side of the dancefloor. There was a door at the top, and he pushed it open. It was like stepping through the wardrobe into Narnia. There were armchairs angled opposite each other and couches with couples lounging on them while soft jazz music played. It was packed, but it was all very civilised compared to the party zone we'd just left.

At the far side of the room were French doors leading to a balcony and I could see the glowing tips of cigarettes. Each time the door opened a whiff of cigarette smoke trailed through the room. A tall skinny guy in black stovepipe jeans with a pork pie hat on got up from one of the couches and pulled a packet of cigarettes out of his pocket. Come to think of it, there were two of him, and I blinked as he morphed back into one, watching him hold his hand out for his girlfriend and helping her to her feet. Troy swooped in on the vacated seat, and I was so glad to sit down because with the change in tempo I was suddenly not feeling too steady on my feet.

It wasn't as dark in here as it was downstairs, and I could see that Troy was a little older than I'd thought. He had a nice smile though, he really did but I think I already told you that, and oh boy I wished the merry-go-round I was spinning around on would slow a little.

'So, Ellie, tell me about you?' He slid an arm along the back of the couch, and it slipped down to rest on my shoulders. Well, it was all the invitation I needed. I launched into a no-holds-barred account of Sam and me, and when I'd finished telling him I slept beside him while he lay still in his coffin the night before his funeral, my tummy began to heave. The drift of cigarette smoke from the terrace wafted over once more and I felt as though I couldn't breathe. Oh God, my poor stomach was really beginning to roll and I knew what was coming but there was no time to stop it. I shot Troy an apologetic look and lurched forward, throwing up all over his shiny leather shoes.

Chapter 27

♥

'I disgraced myself, Gemma,' I sobbed burying my poor sore head back under the blanket. Ugh, I could smell myself and it wasn't pleasant. I didn't need reminding of the night before but the odour of vomit and alcohol seeping from my pores meant I couldn't escape it. I'd surfaced long enough to surmise that I was still in my pink dress and I was in my old room at her house. 'That poor, poor man.' I moaned.

'No, you didn't. You just had a little bit too much to drink that's all.'

I told you she could tell a barefaced lie without batting an eyelid.

I peeked out from under the covers, and the light hurt my eyes. Gemma was standing there looking unfairly healthy and freshly scrubbed in her slouch top and leggings; she had a glass of water in her hand. 'Come on, sit up. I've got you a couple of paracetamol; they'll make you feel loads better.'

I'd try anything, and I pulled myself up tentatively taking the pills from her and forced myself to swallow them down with the glass of water. Gemma was opening the window to let some air into the room when my tummy pitched just as it had last night. I threw the covers aside and stampeded to the bathroom, only just making it in time. Why, oh why did I drink so much? I sat with my knees hunched up to my chest on the floor by the toilet, having hot and cold flushes, while beads of sweat peppered my forehead and I vowed never to touch anything alcoholic ever again—not so much as a rum 'n' raisin ice-cream or bourbon cream biscuit.

Once I was sure I wasn't going to be sick again, I held on to the vanity and pulled myself up, peering into the mirror above it. 'A fallen Madonna,' I whispered dramatically because the reflection was not pretty. Last night's makeup was streaked down my face, and there were bits of sick in my hair. My dress in the harsh light of day was crumpled and tarty-looking and very, very bright. I needed a shower, but I needed to sleep more. 'I'm sorry, Sam,' I whispered to the mirror, hoping my Leprechaun Sam would appear on my shoulder and tell me he understood, but he didn't. I'd let him down, as though I'd cheated by flirting with another man. It made me sick to my stomach once more.

There was a knock on the door and Gemma called out, 'Are you okay?'

'No,' I croaked before opening the door and pushing past her to fall back into bed.

When I opened my eyes next, the pounding in my head had mercifully stopped, and I lay there for a bit listening to the drift of voices coming through the open window from the balcony next door. The sun was streaming into the bedroom, and I wished it were a wet, miserable day more suited to my suffering. I couldn't lie there forever, though, and eventually, fed up with myself, I sat up and perched on the edge of the bed for a minute or two, relieved the world had stopped spinning. I desperately needed a shower, and I padded down the hall to the bathroom.

I was a new woman when I emerged from under the hot water to wrap myself in a towel. Gemma had lovely big, soft fluffy ones like you'd get in a hotel. My teeth were brushed, my makeup removed, and I'd washed my hair with some expensive salon-only shampoo that smelt divine. I was very close to rejoining the human race. Or at least I would be when I found some clothes to put on. Gemma was sprawled on her settee watching the TV despite the glorious day outside. She hit pause when she spied me peering around the living room door.

'You're alive!'

'Only just. Can I borrow something to wear?'

'Help yourself—you know where everything is.'

'Thanks.'

I did just that and flopped down the other end of the settee a few minutes later in a T-shirt and leggings that matched hers. 'Please don't say anything about last night.'

'I wasn't going to. I feel bad for not keeping a better eye on you. I'm sorry, Ellie, I let you down.'

'I'm a grown-up, Gemma, not your responsibility.'

'Still—'

'Not your responsibility,' I repeated.

'If you say so.' She carried on watching *Location, Location, Location*. It's her favourite show; she reckons she watches it for real estate research purposes, which makes no sense given the hosts Phil and Kirstie are in the UK. She admitted to me once that she has a secret crush on Phil. Personally, I can't see the attraction but hey each to their own. I once had a crush on Garth Brooks. I was fifteen, and it was the cowboy hat. Please don't tell anyone. I replayed my last memories of the night before and remembered—whatshisname? Troy, that was it, looking shell-shocked as I told him all about Sam. It was not what he'd had in mind when we ventured upstairs to the lounge bar.

'Was I really sick on his shoes?'

'Yes.'

'I can't believe I did that. I hope they weren't Italian leather or something.' I massaged my temples. 'Where did you go? I couldn't find you.' Now I'd decided to try and pass the blame.

Gemma wasn't having it. 'You just said you weren't my responsibility. And you can't have looked very hard because I only went to the loo and when I came back I couldn't see you anywhere.'

'Sorry.' Well, it was worth a go.

'I went upstairs and found you asleep on that fella who didn't know what to do with you. I got some napkins to clean up his shoes, and we managed to get you out of there without a big scene. He walked us to a cab; he was a nice guy, by the way, really understanding about everything.'

I shook my head reiterating my earlier sentiment. 'Poor, poor man.' I remembered then that Gemma had spotted the Stud Muffin in the crowd. 'Did I ruin your chances with Regan?'

'No, he'd ditched me by then anyway.'

'Really?'

'Yeah, he told me he was going to another bar with his mates, and when I came out of the toilets, he was gone and so were you. He could have at least asked me if I wanted to come too.' She reminded me of Saffy-Rose with her arms crossed in a sulk. 'I'm thinking of getting my lips enhanced and I want to try this new henna technique for brows.'

'Where did that come from? Why?'

'Look.' She points to her mouth and then her eyebrows.

I still didn't get why. Both looked perfectly acceptable to me.

'My lips are mean and skinny, and if I don't draw them in I don't have eyebrows. Ellie, sometimes we need to work a little harder with what nature gave us.'

'Gemma you didn't not cop off with Regan because your lips aren't big enough and you don't have high-definition eyebrows. You do know that, right? He was probably having a boy's night, that's all.'

'I'm not stupid, Ellie. It's got nothing to do with Regan,' she lied.

I looked at her sceptically.

'It doesn't. I've been thinking about it for a while now. Just a little plump, not a full-blown Kylie Jenner or anything more of a Kirstie. And if I get my eyebrows done it will save me at least three minutes each morning.' We both looked at the TV screen where Kirstie was giving Phil grief over something. She did have full lips and very expressive eyebrows, both of which are natural, and I looked back at Gemma.

'Getting your lips and eyebrows done won't enrich your life. You've got too much money—that's your problem, Gem. You'll turn into my mum if you're not careful,' I warned. George the Papadum treated Mum to a boob job on a holiday to Thailand earlier in the year. He's given the term 'sugar daddy' new meaning in my opinion.

Gemma poked her tongue out at me. I owed her an apology, I thought, as I had a PTSD flashback of her taking my shoes off and helping me into bed.

'I'm sorry I lost the plot last night. I was having a great time and then, all of a sudden, I just wasn't.'

'Not your fault—you said you didn't think you were ready.'

'I wanted to be, Gemma, I really did. I don't want to feel like this forever.' My eyes filled up partially because of what I've just said—it was disloyal to Sam—and partially because I was still feeling fragile.

'Hey, it's okay. It's just going to take time.' She reached over and gave me a quick squeeze. Then, her face brightened, and she got off the couch to scoop her keys up from the kitchen bench. 'Come on we're doing a McDonald's run. I want a Big Mac and large fries.'

Suddenly the things I wanted most in the world were fries, a thick shake and a Filet-o- Fish. No, make that two Filet-o-Fishes because one is never enough. It's the tartare sauce.

Chapter 28

♥

I left Gemma's around four that afternoon feeling miles better now that I was stuffed full of burgers, fries, and shake. Yes, I know they're not healthy choices in this day and age of keto and sugar-free, but hey, sometimes carbs are the order of the day and lots of them. Besides I figured I'd earned them seeing as I'd been to the gym more these last six weeks than I had in the previous three years. I'm still not up for running a marathon or anything like that, and I closed my ears whenever Connor brought up his fun run, but I thought I could manage to tackle the unit I'd planned on painting when I got home. That way, the day won't have been a complete write-off. First things first, though, I needed to swing by the Memorial Gardens and put things right with Sam.

The gardens were quiet and I was glad because I looked a sight in the clothes I'd borrowed from Gemma and my black heels; she's two sizes bigger than me. There was a posy of flowers by his plaque, freshly cut from a garden. I was guessing Gina and Phil had been there, or maybe Mandy and Zac. Whoever left the flowers, I'm glad I missed them. I couldn't face seeing any of Sam's family, not after my carry-on last night. I'm supposed to be having dinner with the Andersons this Wednesday, everybody's coming, and I hoped the horrible, twisted feeling in my stomach would be gone by then or I wouldn't be able to look any of them in the eye. I sat down on the grass.

'Sam, I got trashed last night,' I said. 'I tried to pretend I was just a normal girl out for a fun night, but it didn't work, and I wound up flirting with this guy.' The rest came out in a big gush. 'I only did it because I was angry with you for leaving me. Nothing happened, because I wound up being sick all over his shoes.' I could see why people go to confession—it was cathartic—and I sat there until my legs began to prickle with pins and needles from being in the same position for so long.

A young family, Mum, Dad and three kids all under ten were making their way toward the rockery and I wondered who they'd come to see. It was time to go, I decided, stroking the plaque and saying goodbye, which is no easier now than it was when he was at Briarwood House, or when he'd come home to the Andersons' that last time.

~

There was someone sitting on my front steps I realised as I slowed and indicated to turn into my driveway. I ignored the little boy from next door on his skateboard, who was poking his tongue out at me. At least he wasn't flipping the birdy like he did the other day. I screwed my eyes up, trying to see who it was, but the sun was sitting low in the sky and was blinding me. It was only when the shadowy figure stood up that I clicked as to who it was.

OH NO, NO, NO! It couldn't be, but it was. There was nobody else I knew in her mid-forties who would wear a boob tube and Daisy Duke denim shorts despite it only hovering around eighteen degrees today. Did I mention the cowboy boots? Mum stood up in all her spray-tanned glory, her suitcase at her side, and waved with gusto. GOD, I wished that woman would wear a bra.

I wished, too that I was hallucinating as part of a freakish delayed hangover response and that the vision jiggling out the front of my house was just that, a vision. It was too late to floor it and take off down the street, so there was nothing else for it, other than to pull up the handbrake and find out what was going on.

'Surprise!' she yelled doing a cheerleader-style jump as I clambered out of my car. She's like an exuberant child sometimes, and she was also going to give herself a black eye if she wasn't careful. I heard the little boy next door whistle; he's all of nine. I shot him a look but didn't say anything because although he's little he has a big mouth and I wasn't able to handle that right now. He dropped his skateboard down on the front lawn and ran inside the house. Good riddance.

'Sure is.' I attempted a smile, and that thing happened again where my lip stuck to my top gum. 'How did you get here?'

'I swam.' She laughed but I didn't join in, and her smile faltered slightly, which made me feel mean. I hate the way she releases all these tangled-up emotions inside me. 'I got a last-minute flight and taxied from the airport because I wanted to surprise you all. Colin and Paula don't know I'm coming, either. I couldn't believe all the changes around the airport since I was last here. There's that new shopping complex and bridge, and Johns Road's a motorway now. It used to be a country road.'

'Yeah, things are moving along.'

'Come here, Ellie,' she said and before I could brace myself I was pulled into her chest. I nearly choked on the duty-free perfume medley she'd been spraying. 'I'm so sorry for everything you've been through. I wanted to come earlier, I wanted to be here for you—he was one of the good ones, your Sam.'

I wanted to pull away from her because the floral bouquet mingled with musk was too much but Mum's grip was tight. Sam would be pleased she'd come. I knew if he were here now he'd be looking at this scene in the front garden with satisfaction. He was always trying to get us to reconnect and it used to wind me up because although I'd told him what my childhood was like he can't have understood, not properly, because he was all for forgiving and forgetting when it came to Mum. I used to wonder with his ability to hold a grudge, whether he'd be so quick to want to mend bridges if his parents had dumped him on his grandparents and then his Uncle Nate so they could flit off to the Gold Coast. I doubted it.

She released me before giving me the once-over. 'You look like shit.'

'Thanks, Mum. I had a bit too much to drink last; that's not helped.'

She narrowed her eyes, and I think she's had permanent eyeliner done because her heavy black liner looks too precise to have been done by pencil. 'You've been through a lot, kid.'

I nodded, unsure what I was supposed to say to that because it's true, but she's not expecting a reply.

'I knew I was right to come and I knew if I phoned you again to talk it over you'd try and talk me out of it. George was a bit surprised I was leaving so soon, but he'll be fine for a couple of weeks. He can get those food bag thingies in. He's been getting a bit paunchy around the middle lately, so it will do him good to be on rations.'

She was right about the trying to talk her out of coming part but a *bit* paunchy around the middle? The last time I saw George, which was when I spent a disastrous week on the Gold Coast—it was Sam's, mending bridges big idea—he was Boss Hogg to Mum's Daisy Duke and boy does he love his bling. It's incredible he can even stand let alone waddle given how weighted down he is by gold accessories. I would not like to be waiting in line behind him to go through the metal detector at the airport.

I must have misheard her too because it sounded like she said she was over for a couple of weeks. My headache had come back with a vengeance.

'So what do you think?' She put her hand under her breasts and wiggled them. 'More than a handful now!'

'Oh um, they look great, Mum, really um—'

'Perky?'

'Yes, that's it.'

'You know people look at you funny when you tell them you're off to Thailand to give Mother Nature a helping hand, but I've got no qualms in recommending Dr Demir or the hospital. It was like staying in a five-star resort but with bandages on and I made some friends for life.'

'Really?'

'Yes, Noelene was over getting her tummy tucked, it was her fiftieth birthday present to herself, and Dulcie had a full facelift. It was a bit unnerving talking to her because she only had holes in her bandages for her eyes, nose, and lips, but I got used to it.'

I couldn't believe I was having this conversation; I steered it back on track. 'Um, it's great you're here and everything, Mum, but you know like I said, the house is still a work in progress. I don't have anywhere for you to stay.'

She looked over at the house, and a funny look crossed her face. 'It's strange the way it's worked out. You buying the old place. I wanted to come back and see it for myself. Maybe put some ghosts to rest.'

I didn't know what she meant by that, but I was distracted from asking her by the little you know what from next door re-emerging. This time he'd brought his brothers and sisters with him. They all peered over the fence, and he said to his siblings, 'See I told you she has big tits.'

Right, that was it. The show was over. It was time to head inside, and I took Mum by the elbow, turning her toward the front door. 'Well, we can't stand around out here all afternoon entertaining the locals. Come on I'll make you a cup of coffee.'

'A herbal tea would be nice. If you've got any.'

That's not like Mum; I thought her catchphrase was always: 'It must be wine o'clock somewhere.' My stomach reeled at the thought of alcohol.

I opened the front door hearing Mum's suitcase bump up the porch steps behind me.

'Like I said, it's a work in progress.' I waved in the direction of the midden that was my lounge. I could smell woodchips and the plaster dust in the air tickled my nose as my heels dug into the carpet on our way to the kitchen.

'The bones are still the same,' she said a minute later, following me through to the kitchen and taking in the original fittings that had yet to be ripped out. 'If I were to close my eyes and open them again, I'd half expect to see your nan standing at the stove cooking up a storm and your pops sitting reading the paper.' She reiterated how I'd felt walking in here that first time.

She flopped down on the couch while I rifled through the pantry knowing full well there was only good old PG Tips in there. 'Will one of these be okay? I held up the box of teabags; I don't have any herbal stuff sorry.'

'Lovely—you joining me?'

Too right. I had a raging thirst. 'Yes, I'm really dry.' I busied myself making tea. 'Would you like me to give Uncle Colin a call?'

'What for?'

'Well, you might want to stay there. It'd be more comfortable for you than this bomb site, and they won't mind, they've plenty of room.'

'No thanks, Ellie, I can make do. The couch will be fine.' She patted it as though to prove her point. 'You're the reason I'm here, and I'll have plenty of time to catch up with Colin, Paula, and Gemma. How is Gemma, by the way?'

'Good, I stayed there last night. She's selling lots of houses. You'll probably see her on the back of a bus while you're here.'

Mum looked bemused but didn't query me. It would be me sleeping on the couch; I was far too well mannered not to give up my bed.

'She got any fellas on the scene?'

'No, but there is one she's keen on.'

'Ah well, only a matter of time then, if I know our Gemma.'

She hasn't seen Gemma in two years so how would she know? I managed to hold my tongue.

'And what about you? How're you doing?'

I don't meet her gaze. 'I'm doing okay.'

'Ellie, I'm—'

Whatever she was going to say, I didn't want to hear it, and I put my tea down. 'You look cold; you're not on the Gold Coast now.' I sounded like some sort of chastising schoolteacher as I got to my feet and fiddled around with the gas heater. The evening stretched long. I was planning on having a cup of soup and some toast, and watching a bit of TV before heading off for an early night. Mum had spoiled that idea. 'Are you hungry?'

'Not overly, I had something on the plane.' A noise that sounded very much like people in the throes of orgasm went off, and Mum giggled. 'George downloaded it; it's his little joke. That'll be him wanting to know I arrived safely.'

'Well, you better take it.' I smiled brightly even though my toes were squeezed so tightly in my shoes they were likely to cramp. I didn't know why I was still in the stupid things and I stepped out of them, grateful to revert to my normal height.

'Hello, Big Daddy.'

Oh dear God, someone, please help me!

Chapter 29

♥

I couldn't sit and listen to their sweet nothings, and I shuddered recalling how I'd lain awake at night when I'd stayed with them in Australia listening to the banging of the headboard on the adjoining wall. That trip had been Sam's big idea. I left Mum to her phone sex and headed for my bedroom, shutting the door behind me. The temptation to fling my shoes hard at the wall was strong but instead I hit speed dial on my phone, tapping my foot until I heard Aunty Paula's voice.

'Hi, Ellie, everything alright?'

'No, Mum's here.'

'Pardon?'

'Mum's here—she was waiting on the doorstep with her suitcase when I got home half an hour ago. She said she wanted to surprise us. Oh, Aunty Paula, she's talking about staying for two weeks!' I remembered she was only down the hall and lowered my voice to a whispered rasp. 'Two whole weeks! Help.' I held the phone away from my ear as she shouted out to Uncle Colin that Nicky had shown up unexpectedly at my place.

'Why's she there, is everything okay?' She'd been prompted by Uncle Colin.

'Yeah, yeah she's fine, still madly in love with the Papadum, and she's got the boobs to prove it. She's here to look after me apparently.'

'Oh, I see.'

'She's adamant she's staying here.'

'Well, you can tell her she's welcome here if it helps. We've got plenty of room. Although you know, Ellie, it might be nice for the two of you to spend some time together.'

'No it won't and I already did.'

'She already did, Colin, and Nicky wants to stay with Ellie.'

I wished she'd put me on speaker. It would be easier.

'Sweetie, you'll have to go with it. She is your mother, and she loves you. Listen, how about we go for a meal tonight? The Lone Star at the Bush Inn at six-thirty? We can all have a good catch-up.'

'If it means not sitting alone with my mother all evening, then, yes, I'm in,' I said. 'We'll be there.' I hung up.

When I walked back into the kitchen, Mum was still on the phone. She was blowing kisses down it and stopped when she saw me. 'I've got to go, lover boy, bye. Bye. No, you hang up first.' She giggled. 'No you. You! Oh alright, then I will. On the count of three, one, two, three.' She disconnected the call and beamed up at me. 'Sorry about that, my Georgie needs a lot of reassurance.'

I shrugged that it wasn't a problem. 'Aunty Paula rang while you were on the phone. I told her you'd arrived out the blue and she suggested we all meet up for a meal at the Lone Star in an hour. That will give you time to have a shower if you want to freshen up and get changed.' Having said that with the restaurant's Wild West theme and Mum's current outfit she'd fit right in.

'Oh I'm fine as I am aren't I?' She didn't wait for me to answer. 'Now, before we go why don't you give me the grand tour?'

It felt strange showing Mum around her old home.

'I've gone all goosey,' she said rubbing her arms as we stood in the doorway of her old bedroom, and what was my sometimes room. I watched her close her eyes, and guessed she was remembering the girl who used to occupy this space. She opened them a few moments later. 'Are you going to use this room as a guest room?'

'No, this is going to be my sewing room. Uncle Colin's old room will be the guest room. That's still a work in progress.' The walls need to be re-gibbed and plastered but I had the fabric for the curtains and the duvet cover I wanted to make. 'I'll show you. I bought an old dresser too, which I'm going to chalk-paint. I've been saving ideas on Pinterest.'

Mum nodded. 'You still sew then?'

'Yes.' I felt a melancholic stab as we stood in the doorway of the room we'd both once slept in. We were so out of date with one another's lives.

Chapter 30

♥

I was shoving down a piece of toast when Mum emerged from the bedroom the next morning. I'd just given her the rundown on where she'd find everything in the kitchen when Joel, Mikey, and Jonno arrived. Mum's not a morning person, and she looked like she'd been dragged through a hedge backward. I glanced at her outfit of silk dressing gown and navy slip nighty and seriously debated not introducing her, but I couldn't do that. So, as the lads trooped in and out of the house unloading their gear, I said, 'Guys this is my mum, Nicky. She's over from the Gold Coast for a couple of weeks.'

'I was very young when I had her,' Mum said fluffing her hair out.

'I can see the resemblance between you.'

I wanted to foot-trip Mikey for that as he passed by me with a stepladder. We look nothing alike, well okay our eyes are the same shape and our noses are identical but my face is rounder than Mum's, and her dark hair's been blonde for years. She's fair-skinned too, underneath the spray tan so I must get my colouring from my paternal side. As for Jonno, there was no need to stick my foot out because he just about tripped over himself as he came inside the front door and caught sight of her twin assets. I would have dearly loved to have told him to pull his head in, and her to go and put some clothes on.

Joel seemed to be the only one unaffected by her arrival. I had no idea how she was going to fill her day, but I hoped it didn't involve hovering around the workmen, distracting them from moving on with my house. I'd been back in the house for nine weeks. I stayed on at Aunty Paula and Uncle Colin's for just over two weeks after Sam's funeral. I didn't want to leave because it was scary knowing that when I went home, I'd be alone. Sam would not be sharing the house with me, not ever. I was over the constant mess of dust, equipment lying about and general upheaval. It was a relief to leave them all to it and head out the door to the gym.

I was doing a slow jog on the treadmill when I glanced to my left and spotted Regan lifting weights. I made a note to myself to tell Gemma I'd seen him here. It was the first time our paths had crossed since Gemma had her near-death experience on the stair climber—a machine I steered well clear of. Our eyes met and I could tell by the blank look on his face he didn't remember me. Perhaps it was because I no longer bothered with the leg warmers. Either way, I felt a bit of a prat smiling at him and not getting a smile in return. He probably thought I fancied him. He's that sort of guy.

I concentrated on my pace once more. I was trying to work off the enormous chicken dinner I'd put away last night at the Lone Star. It was official. I'd taken carb loading to another level. The traffic on the road outside was beginning to bottleneck, and I was filled with virtuousness that I wasn't sitting on my bum staring in at other people exercising. I'd picked a random workout beats playlist this morning in the hope that if I worked up to a fast run, I'd also work off the ginormous slice of Banoffee pie I rounded my meal off with.

I must've been comfort eating over the shock of Mum showing up on my doorstep. I flexed my neck from side to side. I had a serious crick in it from sleeping on the couch. I'd tossed and turned most of the night, too, with my poor digestive system having to work overtime. I woke up feeling crumpled and cricked, but at least there was no sign of yesterday's hangover.

Our Lone Star dinner was pleasant enough. Mum thankfully put a blouse overtop of the boob tube and swapped her shorts for jeans. She kept the boots though, and I got that song stuck in my head. You know the one: 'These Boots Are Made for Walking'. Still, it was an improvement on Peppa Pig's theme song. The kids' cartoon is Saffy-Rose's favourite, and whenever I hear the opening jingle it winds up playing over and over in my head for hours afterward. The oink-oink at the end drives me mad! Oh, and Mum refrained from asking Uncle Colin and Aunty Paula what they thought of her new breasts, small mercies and all that. Although our waiter seemed to think that if he asked her boobs what they'd like to order they might reply.

'Gemma didn't come; she had prior arrangements,' Aunty Paula had said smiling after everybody had hugged and kissed hello. I slid into the booth next to Aunty Paula and we caught up on each other's week. The conversation played out in my head as I picked up my pace.

'What about going to a grief group, Ellie? Have you thought about it?' Aunty Paula blurted out. 'I know you saw a counsellor after the accident but maybe getting together with a group of people who are all experiencing the same emotions, well maybe it could be a good thing?'

It sounded like AA to me. 'I don't think so.' It had come out of the blue and I reckoned Gemma had relayed what had happened on Saturday night to her. I wasn't happy. There was plenty of stuff I could have dobbed her in for over the years, but it's not my style. I stabbed at a potato; I suppose she'd done it out of concern but still...

'I've looked into it for you, sweetheart, and there's a group that meets on Monday nights in the old Knox church hall on Madras Street. It might be good for you.'

I swallowed the bite of spud. I do NOT want to sit in a draughty old church hall in a circle where I'm expected to stand up and say, 'I'm Ellie Perkins and I'm grieving.' I don't know if that's what they do or not but one thing I did know was I didn't want to sit around listening to everybody else's tragedy. I'm sorry if that sounded selfish, but I couldn't see how that was supposed to help me with mine.

Aunty Paula must have seen by the way I was viciously chewing that I wasn't smitten with the idea, but she still made me take the card with the address and details on it in case I changed my mind. 'Gina's going. She said she'll pick you up if you decide you'd like to come along.' Aunty Paula took a sip of her wine and when I didn't reply she carried on. 'She said she finds it therapeutic.'

I didn't know what she expected me to say so I looked across the table at Mum and Uncle Colin; they'd been talking one another's ears off all through our mains. Uncle Colin has got a lot of time for Mum—he's super loyal and won't hear a bad word said about her. He's able to excuse her behaviour over the years too, unlike me. Maybe it's the whole big brother thing, or maybe it's just that he has a big heart and I've have a mean, little one. I asked Aunty Paula about it once, and she said pretty much the same thing Uncle Colin had said to me the one time I broached it with him. They believe that some of us don't cope as well as others in life and need a helping hand; both of them said I shouldn't be too quick to judge her. Whatever.

When she could get a word in edgewise across the table, Aunty Paula tried to convince Mum to come and stay with them. I forgave her for the grief group thing then because she tried hard. Uncle Colin backed her up telling Mum she'd be so much more comfortable with them, especially with the workmen being at the house during the day and me being out at work. Mum dug her heels in though and said she'd be fine.

Uncle Colin picked up the tab, and I felt guilty for ordering such a piggy dessert, but he told me he was pleased to see me eating properly again.

It wasn't late by the time Mum and I got home, but I was pooped, my appalling antics of the night before were still fresh, and that together with Mum arriving, and having excelled myself with what I'd put away at dinner, had all caught up. Mum protested a bit about having my room, but it was my turn to dig my heels in. I changed the sheets for her and apologised for the state of the walls, then told her I needed an early night. I know, I know not exactly the hostess with the mostess, but it's not as if I'd invited her.

I heard her on the phone when I got up later for the loo; I sincerely hoped she wasn't having phone sex with the Papadum again. One day down thirteen to go was my last thought before drifting off.

I came back to the present as I nearly lost my footing on the treadmill, thanks to not keeping pace properly. I had ten minutes to go, I noted wiping the sweat about to trickle down into my eye away and then I'd have a quick shower before heading to work.

Chapter 31

♥

William-Peter was bouncing on the trampoline at the far end of the back garden looking like he was trapped in a cage with all that netting around it. I was attaching a few pieces of paper to his easel, which I'd set up on the lawn so he could do a spot of painting in the morning sunshine. The pots of primary colours were in the holes on the stand as was a cup of water and a clean brush. He was good to go.

He seemed to be going through an artistic phase, and his works of art are on display in the playroom. Caro's talking about private art lessons, and I had to remind her that he is four. I didn't tell her that from what I recall from my Teeny Tykes days, most four-year-olds' artworks tend to look modernistic and that didn't necessarily mean he was a future Picasso. She's convinced he's gifted, though, and I'm waiting for her to suggest singing lessons for Saffy-Rose who's taken to lisping her way through the *Beauty and the Beast* soundtrack.

The garden's a gorgeous, unexpected find at the back of the house. It's encased by a fence almost hidden by the shrubbery that surrounds it. Under the windows and on either side of the expansive glass doors, which slide open from the kitchen, is Caro's pride and joy: her rose garden. It adds a riot of prickly blooming colour to the whiteness of the Rubik's cube. A man I think of as the lawnmower guy, because I can never remember his name, comes to mow the stretch of lawn and maintain the garden once a week but Caro tends the roses herself.

I was intrigued the first time I saw her out there deadheading the faded blooms in readiness for spring, and she saw the look on my face.

'My grandmother had a gorgeous rose garden, and she taught me how to look after them.' There was something wistful about her expression as she tended those bushes. I told her I got my love of sewing from my nan. It was like we'd found our first piece of common ground that day, and I felt a tenuous thread of friendship spike between us. Today, Caro's gone to a Pink Ribbon Breakfast Fundraiser for breast cancer.

Sardine had one wary eye on William-Peter as she rolled around on the bark beneath a particularly lovely rose bush with apricot buds just beginning to unfurl. The sky was big and blue overhead and the day was beginning to heat up. The changing season signals the passing of time since Sam left for good and instead of feeling lifted by today's promise of summer, it makes me sad. I tried not to think about Sam when I was at work, though, because it's not fair on the twins. They're sorely lacking in attention from their parents, and they deserved my full attention.

It might be worth setting the paddling pool up, I thought shaking the sadness off and looking over my shoulder to see if Saffy-Rose was still sitting up at the kitchen island. I'd left her happily threading buttons onto a length of wool to make a necklace for her teddy, but she wasn't there now. She was probably in the playroom bestowing her gift on teddy; I decided I'd better check anyway. William-Peter had begun to attempt forward rolls on the trampoline now, and after I gave him a clap for his efforts, I left him to it. My first stop was the playroom. She wasn't there though nor was she in her bedroom or the toilet.

'Saffy-Rose!' I called out thinking she might be in the living room but no, there was no sign of her. I stood at the bottom of the stairs, and even though she's not supposed to go up there, I looked up at the landing and hollered her name. I was met by silence. 'Saffy-Rose!' I tried again. 'If you don't come out right now you will not be watching *Peppa Pig* this afternoon.' I heard movement. *Ha, that did it!*

She appeared at the top of the stairs just in time for me to see her slide something into the pocket of her shorts. 'Come down, please. You know you're not supposed to be up there.'

She did as she was told and was about to run off, but I blocked her way. 'Not so quick, madam. What's in your pocket?'

'Nothing.' The look on her face said the opposite.

'Saffy-Rose, please don't tell stories.' I held out my hand.

Her little face was pink beneath her freckles. She didn't like being in trouble and looked like she might cry as she put her hand in her pocket and retrieved a bottle of nail polish, which she placed in my palm. 'Thank you.' It was a garish red, which isn't a colour Caro—who is a French manicure sort of a girl—would wear. I shuddered to think what Saffy-Rose had planned for the polish and was sure I'd escaped near disaster. 'Did you take this from Mum and Dad's room?'

She nodded.

'That's not like you sneaking things, Saffy-Rose.'

'Mummy does it.'

'Pardon?'

'Mummy sneaks things. I saw her put the nail polish in her pocket when we were at the chemist shop.'

'I don't think so.' Taking things and making stuff up is really out of character for Saffy-Rose.

'I *did*.' Her blue eyes were wide, and I sensed an impending tantrum, which I could avoid by moving on. I wanted to get back outside and check on Picasso, so I decided to let the remarks go. 'Come on then; we'd better put it back, hadn't we, before Mummy gets home.'

Kids' moods change as rapidly as flicking a switch and the thunderclouds that had rolled across her face a second ago dispersed as she skipped back up the stairs with me following behind.

I've only glanced inside the Richards master suite once when Caro gave me the grand tour on my first day of work. I don't come upstairs because there's never any need to. It's never been said, but I'm guessing that just like for the children their private quarters are out of bounds to me, and it feels wrong to be up here now.

As we entered their room, I was reminded of those pervy tradesmen I was unnecessarily worried might be on my job. I was a little curious too; I won't deny it. There was a navy plaid armchair by the bedroom window, which overlooked the garden. 'I'm just going to check on your brother,' I said marching over to take a quick peek outside. To my relief, William-Peter was still intent on his forward rolls.

The room was decorated in tones of contrasting grey, and there was an enormous arty black and wedding photograph on the wall. Caro looked whimsical and stunning of course in her figure-skimming white dress and 'call me Doug' looks much better in his suit than he does in his Lycra. I couldn't help but cast my eyes over their sumptuous white bed linen. It looked like an advert you'd see in a flyer for beds with the plump comforter, throw blankets and cushions arranged just so. Despite the cushions, it wasn't a feminine room by any means, and it was hard to get a sense of Caro, but I couldn't stand there speculating on the Richards' decorating tastes forever.

'Right then, Saffy-Rose, where did you find it?'

She got down on her hands and knees and fished a large hatbox out from under the bed.

'In here,' she said taking the lid off.

My eyes bulged because inside it were eyeshadows, lipsticks, blushers, highlighters and more. There was an array of nail polishes too. It was like a beautician's in a box with every colour and brand under the rainbow. I didn't know how Saffy-Rose came to find the box under the bed, but I could see how she was attracted to all those bright colours. I popped the polish back into the mix and slid the box back where it came from. 'You won't do that again will you?'

'No.'

'Promise?'

'Pwomise.' She gave me a 'butter wouldn't melt' smile and ran off down the stairs.

I stood there for a sec; something was off. Saffy-Rose's words about her mother sneaking the polish at the chemist and then seeing all those products hidden under the bed—it was odd. None of it was opened, I realised, and the colours were so bright. Not shades Caro would wear. It was bizarre but it wasn't my problem, and I didn't want to be caught looking like I was having a stickybeak at my bosses' boudoir, so I headed back outside to the sunshine and tried to shake off the unsettled feeling seeing that box had left me with.

Chapter 32

♥

I'd stopped at the supermarket on my way home today, and I was staring blankly at the meat trays in front of me. What should I buy for dinner? I usually buy a big tray of whatever's on special and portion it up to freeze when I get home. That or make a supersized meal, which I bag up into little dinners for those nights I don't feel like cooking. I've gotten the hang of cooking for one, although I do get a bit sick of things like cottage pie three days in a row. My repertoire in the kitchen was limited.

While we're on the subject of mince, it was a good price today, and I picked up a tray. Was it mean to buy cheap meat when I had a houseguest, even if it was my mother? Yes, I decided, putting it back and moving further down the aisle. Rump steak, chicken breasts? In the end, I settled for some fish fillets on special. I'd crumb them, I decided, pleased to have made a decision, and I picked up a bag of salad and new potatoes to go with it.

That's something new I'd noticed since Sam died—I dither. I find it hard to make decisions even over stupid stuff like what to have for dinner. I'm even worse when I do the shopping for the Richards, which doesn't involve following a tight budget.

There are five stages to the grieving process. I know because I looked it up. Denial, anger, bargaining, depression, and acceptance. The thing is, though, my grieving began when Sam had his accident, so I don't think I'm a textbook case, and I'm not sure where dithering comes into it, but I definitely didn't dither before. I feel like I've already picked my way through the big five, and now since he died, I'm left with a smidgen of all of them bundled up into one tidy package for me to deal with. A bit like when you read the mild side effects on a box of pills.

I mean, let's start with denial. It took me a long time to understand Sam was not simply going to open his eyes and ask me when he could come home. Once I figured it out, I got mad, I mean seriously pissed off. You can ask Gemma; I was a bit of a nightmare to live with for a while, there. Stupid stuff would make me melt down, like her having used the last of the shampoo and not bothering to replace it. It was like being an older version of Saffy-Rose, but thankfully I seemed to have grown out of it, and I hold high hopes of Saffy-Rose doing the same.

I tried the bargaining thing. I told God I would be the best person I could be for the rest of my life and that I would make a conscious effort to be kind to others. I explained nicely that I probably wouldn't make it along to church—it's not my thing—but to please remember I used to go to Sunday school and that I would send up my thanks to Him every single day if He would bring Sam back to me. Well, we all know how that worked out. Now I ask Him to look after Sam for me up there in heaven.

So far, the depression has been the worst. The bleakness or as I think of it, the grey fog. It's like one of those rogue mists that rolls in from the sea and I feel like I'm standing on a vast plain all alone in Siberia. It's like having all the joy suctioned out of you by a giant happiness-sucking vacuum cleaner. I think joining the gym has helped me with that side of things. Sometimes it's hard to make myself go, but I do feel better once I've been. Of course there are days when I get up and turn the radio on and one of Sam's and my songs will be playing, and a grief grenade will detonate. I don't go back to bed now though, I let myself cry and then I go and get ready to face the day.

I don't think I've ever accepted Sam's accident and I don't know if I ever will. How do you accept a split-second mistake like putting his foot down too hard on the accelerator or braking too suddenly, or whatever it is he did? How do you accept someone who hasn't made it to thirty is gone and yet others soldier on through to their nineties? How do you accept the unfairness and randomness of life? It really is like spinning a roulette wheel. It might stop on 'you get to live happily ever after' or it might stop on 'you've got some serious crap coming your way.'

I put my fish down on the conveyer belt. These thoughts were way too profound to be having at Countdown, I decided as the checkout guy asked me how my day was and whether I'd like my fish in a separate bag.

All the other tradesmen had left for the day, but Joel was still packing his truck up when I pulled into Radford Street. I parked kerbside, not wanting to block him in. As I clambered out of my car and looked up, I saw my little friend from over the fence skating toward me with a parcel of fish and chips under his arm. I decided to be the adult, and I smiled at him. 'Wow, dinner smells good.'

He gave me a gappy grin and said, 'Well you're not having any, lady.'

I thought a bad word and tossed in a rude imaginary finger sign for good measure as he careened into his driveway. He was far too streetwise for his own good that kid. Joel waved over, and I wiped the scowl off my face.

'I'll be out of your hair in a minute,' he said as I walked up the drive with my shopping bags.

'You're okay. Don't rush.'

'Good day?' he asked, just like the Countdown man did, before pulling the tarp down over the back to cover his tools and fixing it into place.

'Yeah, pretty good thanks. I'm loving this weather. Blue skies and sunshine make working with kids a lot easier.'

'Are you a teacher?'

I realised we'd never gotten much further than 'good morning' and 'see you later' in nearly two months. 'Yes, early learning but I'm a full-time nanny to a set of four-year-old twins at the moment.'

'That'd keep you busy.'

'It's never boring, that's for sure.' I give him a naughty William-Peter story, the one where he gave poor Sardine a trim and left him looking more like an Ewok than a Persian. I felt rather pleased with myself when he threw back his head and laughed.

'My sister's got a boy; he's just started school. I can relate.'

So, now he knows I'm a nanny, and I know he has a sister. 'What do you do when you're not building?'

'I like to ride.'

Really??? TMI.

'Mountain biking,' he explained. 'It's my thing, helps me unwind.'

'I've always fancied mounting biking,' I blurted, and it was true. It wasn't Sam's thing though. Mind you, I'd always fancied hot air ballooning and Garth Brooks too.

'Well, I've got a spare bike if you ever want to come and have a blat.'

'Oh.' I didn't expect that. It was, after all, just one of those throwaway things you say. 'Thanks, Joel, I might take you up on it.' I wouldn't, but the offer was kind.

'There are some great tracks around but if you've never been before, McLeans Island is a good starter loop.'

Okay, he was getting a bit carried away now. I only said I liked the sound of it. 'Uh-huh, yeah it sounds good.'

'How's about Saturday morning then?'

'What?' I must have appeared horrified because he looked embarrassed as he quickly added, 'You don't have to. I just thought with you saying you wanted to try it—'

I had foot-in-mouth syndrome. 'No, I'd um, no, that'd be great.' I didn't want to offend my builder. What if he signed off on a dodgy loadbearing wall or something in retaliation? There would be no lie-in with the possibility of a grief grenade wallow on Saturday morning. I'd be going flipping mountain bike riding instead. Oh please, please don't let him be a 'call me Doug' type because if he was into Lycra he would go down in my estimation. I tried to look enthusiastic at the prospect because it *was* nice of him to make the offer and he seemed appeased. Besides it's only Monday—anything could happen between now and Saturday. 'Right well, I better get this lot inside.' I held up the shopping bags. 'I hope Mum hasn't got under your feet today.'

'Nicky? Nah she was fine, she's kept herself busy.'

I bet she has, I thought feeling a spark of irritation.

'The plasterer's done the finishing skim on the lounge walls, and the skirting boards are ready to be painted. It's all coming together.'

'I can't wait for the painting part. That's going to be exciting.' It was true, I was excited about that.

'You've got a mate doing it, right?'

'Yeah, he volunteered, which he might live to regret.'

'Have you got your colours picked out?'

'I did have but I'm having second thoughts. I'm rethinking my colour scheme. It will have to tie in with the material I've already bought, though. I'm making a lot of stuff like the curtains, and cushion covers myself.'

'You sew, right?'

He would have seen the machine set up in my room. I nodded, wondering if he was going to ask me to repair the hole in the knee of his jeans. He followed my gaze and laughed. 'Yeah they're looking a bit rugged. It's a bugger; they're my favourites. I caught them on a nail today. I only asked about the sewing because Nicky was on your machine most of the day. She still made us a couple of brews though.'

'Really?' Mum was sewing? I knew Nan taught her like she taught me but so far as I knew she was never really into it. I remembered his original question. 'And yeah I do sew—it's my hobby.' Some people play sport, some people are movie buffs or travellers, me, I sew, but I didn't say that instead, I found myself saying, 'I can patch those for you if you like.' A favourite pair of jeans is worth saving after all.

'Yeah?'

'Yep.'

'That'd be great, thanks. I would've chucked them. I flunked home ec at school.'

'But not tech.'

He grinned again. 'Not tech.'

'Lucky for me. I'll grab them off you tomorrow.' I realised how that sounded and hastily added, 'I mean you can give them to me tomorrow. See you, enjoy your ride.' And I beat a hasty retreat up the stairs into the house.

'Will do. Cheers,' he called after me, and I heard the truck's engine grumble into life a minute later. It dawned on me as I made my way through to the kitchen that I'd just held the longest conversation I've had with Joel in the ensuing weeks since he began work on my house. I knew nothing about him, other than he's a builder who likes mountain biking in his spare time. Oh, and I'm fairly sure he isn't one of those pervy tradesmen either. He also seems kind. What I mean is, it was kind of him to invite me for a ride because I did open my big mouth and say I wanted to try it. Ah well. I put a positive spin on Saturday's excursion—it'd be good to try something different.

Chapter 33

♥

I could smell something cooking the minute I walked inside the house, and a few flies had buzzed in through the open front door with me. I swatted them away after offloading my bags on to the table. Mum was at the stove stirring a big pot of something that smelled garlicky and yummy.

'Hi, Ellie, good day?' She smiled over, and I noticed she was wearing Sam's 'Licence to Grill' apron over a maxi dress, and her feet were bare. I felt like telling her to take the apron off because it was mine, and only I'm allowed to wear it, but I held the pettiness inside.

'Yes not bad thanks,' I said feeling my shoulders tense like bedsprings as I began to unpack the bags. She could've texted me to say she was cooking and I wouldn't have wasted half an hour debating over what to buy in the supermarket. Just the sight of her in my kitchen like it was a normal occurrence has wound me up, but I managed to ask, 'What's that you're cooking? It smells good.'

'Spaghetti bolognaise—your favourite.'

When I was ten, Mum, you wouldn't have a clue what my favourite is now, I thought trying to arrange my face into a smile, but I couldn't bring myself to say 'yum'. I saw a flash of hurt cross her face and instantly felt bad; I couldn't help myself though. She doesn't bring out my best side.

'The plastering's all done, in the lounge, it looks good. He's a nice fella—Reece.'

I assume she means the plasterer and I haven't met him.

'So's that Joel. I saw you chatting outside just now.'

I wind up a little tighter. 'He's my builder, Mum, that's all.' No way was I going to tell her that I was going mountain biking with him on the weekend. I feigned busyness in the fridge as I put the fish and salad away and then took a deep breath. Start again, Ellie, I told myself. Be nice; she was making an effort cooking dinner, so I needed to, too. 'What about you? I hear you've been busy sewing all day?'

The machine was set up in my bedroom on an old desk for now. I like to leave it out ready to go because I never know when the mood to sew is going to strike and when it does I don't want to faff around hauling it out of its case. It was going to be such a treat to have my very own sewing room.

'I have, it's been years since I sat at the old Bernina. I can't believe it's still going, but then again things back then were built to last.'

'It runs well, I oil it once a month and take it in to be serviced every year like Nan did.' I look after that machine more diligently than my car whose oil would never get changed if Uncle Colin didn't do it for me.

'I used to like the sound of it.'

'Yeah me, too.' The gentle humming was the sound of home for me.

'It took me a bit to get the hang of it again, but once I did I was away.' She chucked a handful of spaghetti noodles into the bubbling pot. 'It brought back memories, that's for sure. Your nan used to sew all Colin's and my clothes when we were kids; she was a bloody whizz on that machine.'

'I know, she could make anything she set her mind to. I remember her cutting her own patterns out when she couldn't find what she wanted. I used to love the dresses she'd make for me when I was little.'

'Your Sunday school dresses. You were pretty as a picture in them.' Mum smiled and looked pensive, which surprised me, and I didn't remember her being around to see me in them much, but maybe she was. I was only little; memories could get skew-whiffed.

'She used to make me little outfits, too. Colin and I were always well turned out. My favourite thing ever, though, was the dress she made for a dance when I was fourteen. I had my heart set on one I'd seen in the shops. I pointed it out to her and dropped big hints about doing extra chores if she'd buy it for me, but you know money was tight when me and Col were kids. I didn't hold out much hope, but on the day of the dance I got home from school and found it hanging up in my room.' She pointed in the direction of the sewing room, my old room too and I saw a softness in her I hadn't seen before.

'She'd bought the fabric, made the pattern and sewed it for me. I couldn't have told the difference between that one and the one I'd fallen in love with in the shops. It was like magic.' She smiled at me, her face glowing from the steam rising from the pot she was standing over. 'I wish I'd appreciated her more.'

I wasn't sure what to say. Mum did give her parents the runaround, the little tattoo on her shoulder of a cartoon devil with a pitchfork was testament to that, but then again their religious views made them tough sometimes. I could see how my free-spirited and, let's be honest here, irresponsible mother clashed with them, but I'd always been grateful for their staid ways, because just like the humming of Nan's old Bernina, they gave me stability. One thing I was learning, though, as time went by, was that life's never black and white and there are always two sides to every story. I'd never really given Mum a fair hearing because I'd never moved past her leaving me. Just like the 'acceptance' part of the grief process. I didn't know if I ever would.

Whenever I felt like Mum, and I were taking steps to move forward, we always seemed to hit a wall too high to scale. Maybe this visit would be different.

'Anyway,' Mum snapped out of her reverie and turned the element down. 'That'll be alright for a few minutes. Come with me, I've got a surprise for you.'

I hoped she hadn't got it into her head to make me a new top or dress or...anything because our tastes were very different. I shuddered at the thought of us in matching mother-daughter outfits, but tried to keep an open mind as I followed her to my guest room.

'Shut your eyes.'

I did as I was told and she took my hand and led me through the door. 'Right you can open them now.'

I blinked and stared because she had been busy. She'd sewn the duvet cover I was planning on making for my guest bed. The bed was still in Uncle Colin's garage, and would be until work on the room is finished. The cover she'd toiled at was spread out on the floor looking just as gorgeous and faded French chic as I'd envisaged. This space when it was finished was going to be very feminine with a shabby chic theme. I couldn't go all out in the master bedroom because I'd wanted to keep the colours more gender-neutral for Sam and I. I loved the charm of the shabby chic style of décor though—and the fact that it means I can add a lick of paint and repurpose an old dressing table I picked up for peanuts at the Eco Store.

'I thought I'd make a start on the curtains for you tomorrow.' She looked thoroughly pleased with the expression of amazement on my face. 'Joel said work on this room is starting tomorrow. It would be good to have all the furnishings ready in time for it being finished.'

'Wow, Mum! I don't know what to say.' I remembered my manners and added. 'Thanks, it looks fantastic. Exactly how I pictured it would.' Then I reached out and put my arm around her shoulder, squeezing it, and it felt good. I was suddenly very glad she was here. Hope was something that was my friend for most of this year, and it was snatched away from me when Sam died, but it's a bit like that hair on Gina's chin. It doesn't matter how many times she plucks it; it always grows back. So, who knows? Maybe there's hope for Mum and me finding how we fit together after all.

Chapter 34

♥

The smell of fish frying hit me as soon as I walked in through the front door after a long day at the Richards'. I poked my head around the guest room door and was pleased to see that the walls were now lined. Day by day the restoration was progressing, and each tick off my list felt good. Once Reece, the plasterer, came back to do his thing, I'd speak to Connor nicely about painting in here. I tried to envisage the finished room in all its shabby chic glory; then I wondered who would come and stay before finding my current houseguest in the kitchen. Mum was pan frying the filets I'd bought the other day and I stood in the doorway watching her as she hummed at the stove. Why couldn't she have been like this all the time? How different everything would have been if she'd been this version of Mum when I was growing up. She must have sensed me there because she turned and saw me.

'Hello, you. Did the twins behave themselves today?'

I sat down at the table. 'They had their swimming lessons today; they're always worn out after swimming so, yeah, we had a good day. What about you? What've you been doing?'

She flipped the fish and checked on the potatoes boiling away in the pot before looking over at me. 'Oh, I've been busy, busy, busy—sewing and things. I've got a surprise planned for you after dinner.'

'Another surprise?' I tried to muster up enthusiasm, but Mum had that look in her eyes. It's a certain gleam I remember of old that makes alarm bells ring. I was suspicious because I'm not big on surprises, especially not where she's concerned.

She giggled. 'Yes.'

'What is it?'

'If I tell you then it won't be a surprise. Could you drain the spuds for me?'

I did as she asked and Mum served up. She chattered all through dinner, talking fast and animatedly. I could see she was excited to get the meal out the way so she could reveal whatever it was she had up her sleeve. As soon as I'd put my knife and fork down on my plate, she pushed her seat back and was out of her chair. 'Come on. The dishes can wait.' She thrust my car keys at me.

'Where are we going?' I asked taking them from her.

'It's not far. Come on, Ellie.'

I locked up after us, and we climbed in my car. 'Do I turn right or left at the bottom of the drive, Mum?'

'Let me think, it's the Fitzgerald Ave end of Bealey Ave, so that would be a—'

'That's left,' I answered for her reversing out on to the street. 'Can I have a clue?' I asked as we sat at the lights a few minutes later.

'No.'

I pursed my lips and tapped the steering wheel. *What was she up to?*

It didn't take us long to reach Bealey Ave, and as we sailed down the wide tree-lined avenue, I tried for another clue. 'Is it a something sort of surprise or a doing surprise?'

'Not saying.' He leg was jiggling up and down excitedly.

Oh for goodness' sake!

A few sets of lights later Mum, nose pressed to the window, shouted, 'Left, left on to Packe Street.'

'Thanks for the forewarning Mum!' I veered off to the left as instructed, indicating at the last moment and receiving a toot from the car behind me.

'Okay we want number thirty-three; that's on your side.'

We drove a little ways down the street until spotting the house we were after, a tired weatherboard with long grass out the front. I did a U-turn and parked out front.

Maybe we were going visiting. Maybe catching up with an old friend of Mum's I hadn't seen since I was a kid was the surprise. I didn't remember any of her friends living around here, though. She was already out of the car opening the gate leading to the front path.

'Shut the gate behind you, Ellie,' she called over her shoulder while ringing the doorbell. By the time I reached her the door had already swung open, and a woman with a halo of grey frizz stood there, a big ginger tabby in her arms.

'Yes?' Her eyes narrowed as she sized Mum and me up.

'Hello, you must be Iris.'

'Who wants to know?'

Mum wasn't perturbed. 'I'm Nicky, remember we spoke on the phone this afternoon?'

She looked from one of us to the other. 'That your daughter? The one you told me about?'

I tried to smile but Iris looked a little, you know, not quite the full packet to me, and I didn't want to encourage her.

'Yes, this is Ellie. Ellie, Iris.'

'Hello, Iris.'

'Come in then.' She looked furtively over the top of our heads surveying the street before urging us to come in once more and closing the door behind us. My nostrils twitched. What was that smell? The hall we were standing in had cardboard boxes lining either side of it, and if we were expected to walk down there, we'd have to inch our way down, side on.

'In here.' Iris's mound of hair wobbled as she indicated we were to follow her. She led us through to the front room, and I sidestepped a bulging black, bin liner bag. The source of the smell revealed itself as I gazed around the room. Cats. Lots of cats. I couldn't count how many.

A Persian sat on the sill of the bay window keeping a watchful eye on the street outside. Two smaller cats, one tortoiseshell and one a sandy colour, had their noses in their food bowls. A row of which were lined up on sheets of newspaper against the far wall. I couldn't help but notice the shredded regency striped wallpaper behind them.

My eyes flicked to a sleek panther stretched long across the top of a saggy old couch; on the cushions below curled in a tight ball was a grey striped feline. I sensed movement and looking up saw a white mound of fur with one eye staring down at me from its perch on top of a bookshelf.

I still had no idea why we were here, and I don't mind telling you, the place was kind of creepy.

'Iris runs a cat shelter.'

Figured.

'Unofficially.' Iris tapped the side of her nose. 'A few of the neighbours have complained about my boys and girls so it's hush, hush.' The ginger tabby fidgeted in her arms, and she placed him down on the ground.

So that explained her furtiveness but not why Mum had brought me around to visit this mad cat lady with hoarding tendencies.

I felt something brush against my leg, and I looked down. A pair of yellow eyes belonging to a big, black cat looked up to me. 'Hello. Where did you come from?' I said reaching down and stroking his head. He rubbed back against my hand.

'That's Pete. He hides under the couch until he decides whether he likes our visitors or not. He was hit by a car last year.'

'Oh! He only has three legs.'

'He's lucky to be alive. I christened him Pete after the old Disney character, Peg Leg Pete. The vet, Trevor, and I have an understanding when it comes to injured cats and nobody came forward to claim the poor fella.' She winked.

Was I to take it she gave the vet sexual favours in exchange for free cat healthcare?

'In those situations he calls me next and tells me what needs doing. In Pete's case, it was an amputation. I foot the bill and pay it off on account. I have a running tab at Poor Paws, and the money I make rehoming these fur babies goes toward paying it off.'

I looked at Mum questioningly. Call me dense, but I still wasn't up with the play as to why we were here.

'You always wanted a kitten, Ellie. You used to ask me all the time if we could get one.'

What she was saying was true. I had. I'd never gotten an animal of any sort because we moved about far too much.

'Well, you've got your own house now. You've put down roots, so I'm going to get you that pet you always wanted. I thought an older cat, one that needs to be loved, and that was already housetrained would be a much safer bet than a kitten. A kitten would run up and down those new curtains of yours and shred your lovely couch. They're too much work.'

Pete meowed, loudly reminding me he was still there. I picked him up and held him close. He purred, a warm furry ball in my arms. 'What do you say, Pete? Do you want to come home with me?'

He meowed again, and Mum laughed. 'I think that's settled then.'

Chapter 35

♥

It was Friday evening, and I was disappointed when I pulled up the drive to see that Joel and the rest of the crew had left for the day. I'd made a deal with myself on the way home that if Joel was still there, then I'd tell him I couldn't make our bike ride tomorrow. I had a story all worked out in my head. I'd say I was sorry, but Caro had begged me to work in the morning, due to a last-minute charity breakfast the Richards were expected to attend. A white lie.

Joel not being there meant I had to go mountain biking in the morning because the deal I'd made didn't include a cell phone cancellation clause. He'd checked in with me this morning before I left for work as to whether I was still up for it and I'd put my happy face on and said yes, I was looking forward to it. So, I suppose I've got nobody to blame but myself. We'd arranged to meet at McLeans Island at nine a.m.

The only person I told about this excursion was Caro. She swanned in from hot yoga at lunchtime and found me in the garden enjoying a picnic with the twins.

'It's gorgeous out here today. I'm going to make green tea and come and join you all. Would you like one?'

I didn't know how she could drink that stuff. Yes, I know it has health benefits, but it looked like pee. I didn't say this, though. What I said was, 'Thanks, Caro, that would be lovely.' I seemed to be saying yes to all sorts of things I didn't want to do. I watched her disappear back inside the house, and it occurred to me that she might be lonely despite all her ladies' lunches.

I reached over to retrieve a grape from Saffy-Rose's ear and gave William-Peter a stern talking-to about the dangers of poking foreign objects in his sister's ear canal. 'Listen, you two, eat your lunch nicely, and I'll tell you all about my new cat.'

That got their attention.

'He's called Pete and he's only got three legs.'

They were all ears now, and I was telling them about the big cushiony cat bed Mum and I had picked up from the pet store on the way home, along with a food bowl, and a scratchy pole, when Caro reappeared. The twins were peeling a banana each as she walked toward us balancing two china teacups on their saucers. 'He settled in like he's always lived there with me,' I finished saying as she passed me my tea and rearranged her long limbs next to me on the chequered rug.

'So, what's new?' she asked frowning at William-Peter as he slapped Saffy-Rose with his banana skin. I quickly removed the weapon and handed him a packet of rice wheels. He couldn't do too much damage with those, or at least I hoped he couldn't. Caro got the rundown on Pete, too. I told her he'd already commandeered the end of the couch as his. I didn't say how nice it was to feel that warm mound beside my feet, and how I slept well knowing he was there.

I held off on saying anything further by sipping my tea. It tasted like wee too by the way. I debated whether or not to confide in her about tomorrow morning. I needed to tell someone, and she was Switzerland, unlike Mum, Gemma or Aunty Paula.

'You know how I'm having building work done at home?'

'Uh-huh.'

'Well Joel, he's the boss builder, he asked me to go mountain biking with him tomorrow morning.' I explained how the invitation came about.

'And you patched his jeans?'

I don't know why she's zoomed in on this aspect of my story.

'What was he wearing at the time?'

'Another pair of jeans,' I replied tartly. He'd been impressed when I handed his mended old favourites back and had fished out his wallet. I'd waved his hand away and told him not to be stupid. It felt good to be admired though, even if it was just for my seamstress skills.

She took the hint. 'So, are you looking for advice?'

'I suppose I am.'

'Because you're worried there might be more to his invitation than just experiencing the delights of rough-riding around a muddy track, and you're not ready for that?'

I thought about it, and nodded. She'd pretty much summed it up. I took another sip of my tea, trying not to grimace because it hadn't gotten any better and, when she glanced away distracted by Sardine trying to catch a butterfly, I tipped it out.

'Well,' she said turning back to face me. 'What I think is that you should take his invite at face value and not overanalyse it.'

Simple really, but easier said than done, I reflected clambering out of my car and heading for the house now.

I'd thought about inviting Caro tonight. We're having a girls' night in at Aunty Paula's, and she wouldn't have minded one more joining us. In the end, I didn't because I'd be on edge making sure she was having fun. It would be nice to chill just the four of us and for Mum and Gemma to catch up. There will be wine, something sweet, and

Mum and I are putting together a cheese board. Gemma's bringing her *Bridget Jones's Baby* DVD around. I hadn't seen it, neither had Mum, and we were looking forward to having a giggle.

I hunted down Pete. It wasn't hard to find him, because just like he'd chosen the end of the couch at night, he was already very attached to his cat bed, or, as I thought of it, his day bed. Mum and I had positioned it in the kitchen where it got all-day sun, and gave him easy access to his food bowl. I picked him up, thinking I'd have to remember to bend my knees next time, because he's a big boy. My cuddles were rewarded by loud purring, and I told him he was lovely. Then popping him back down, I topped up his biscuits before going to say hi to Mum. I'd heard the Bernina humming in my bedroom.

She was sitting at the machine hemming the guest room curtains. The pink and white fabric pooled out to the side. The room smelt of heady Opium perfume, her favourite, and she was dressed in a tropical print sundress with a white cardigan overtop. She'd tied her hair back in a ponytail. A pair of readers were perched on the end of her nose.

'Hi. You look busy.'

'Hi yourself.' She lifted her foot on the treadle. 'I'm nearly done. I didn't want to carry on with those. I decided to wait for you to help.' She pointed to the neatly folded pile of material that is slowly morphing into my living room drapes. 'Too big a job on my own so I thought I'd tackle these instead. Sam's friend Connor was in between jobs today, so he popped in mid-morning and introduced himself. He seems nice.'

'Yeah, he is. It's been tough on him, too.'

'They went way back, he said.'

'High school.'

She nodded. 'Not an easy time for any of you.'

'No.'

Her face brightened. 'He got stuck in and finished the painting in the guest room for you and he's made a start on the lounge.'

This was an unexpected bonus, and I felt the fog that was about to roll in disperse. This was exciting, no more dirty-tea-coloured walls!

'Go and have a look. It looks great.' She put her foot down again, and the old Bernina whirred into life. 'I thought we could hang these before we head around to Paula's. It'll be nice to see the room all put together.'

'Brilliant.' I beamed scooting down the hall. I could smell that distinctive solvent odour of fresh paint before I reached the bedroom. I pushed the door open and the early evening sun spilled into the room, dappling the old brown carpet. It was so light and airy, I thought soaking up the transformation. It was amazing what a difference the off-white wall colour had made. I was glad I'd decided to go neutral throughout the house to lighten and brighten it; it was a good choice and it would give me free rein to be adventurous with the colours in my soft furnishings.

This room had felt dull, like a sepia-toned afterthought. I felt a surge of gratitude toward Connor and his paintbrush. Not just for the wonderful job he'd done but because once we got the curtains up, Uncle Colin could bring the guest bed around and Mum could move her stuff in here. Bring it on! No more couch for me.

I wandered down to the lounge and saw two of the walls were done. They too looked fantastic and I retrieved my phone from my pocket. I left a message when Connor didn't pick up to say how happy I was with how the room looked.

It hit me then, as I stuffed my phone back in my pocket, that I was okay with Mum staying. This week had been good because for the first time in forever we'd been relaxed in each other's company, not tiptoeing around one another politely. It sounded weird, but we'd been bonding over a three-legged cat and the Bernina. I smiled at that because I knew it would make Nan happy.

We'd settled into an easy routine when I got home from work of an evening. Pete got fed and given plenty of cuddles, we had a quick dinner, washed up and then got stuck into a job. Together we'd made a start on the lounge curtains. They were a task and a half with them being full-length drapes, and I'd have struggled on my own. Like Mum had just said they were a two-man job. She was in charge of cutting the expanse of deep red fabric. I loved the rich warmth of the colour and had been drawn to it as soon as I'd spotted it. I was nervous about cutting into it, frightened I'd make an expensive mess of them, so she'd taken on the task. She was pinning the hems too, and my job was the actual sewing.

I'd been waiting for her to finish with the hem so I could run the machine over it when she'd looked up, pin in her mouth. She took it out and sat back on her heels. 'What was he like, Ellie? I mean really like.'

I didn't have to ask who and I didn't have to think about my answer either. 'He was lovely, Mum. He was my rock.' I remembered how I used to second-guess myself all the time, never fully confident in my decisions and how Sam used to tell me to back myself more. I'd still always deferred to him for his opinion as to what I should do.

It dawned on me as I looked down at all that deep red material that I hadn't been second-guessing myself since I moved into the house. I'd grown in confidence with each decision Joel had asked me to make and when it came to the paint and finishing touches, I'd been clear in my mind as to the look I wanted to achieve. Uncle Colin and Aunty Paula had invested in me, and I was stepping up. I was turning something old and broken into something beautiful again. Right then, I felt proud of myself and I knew Sam would be proud of me too.

Mum was looking at me expectantly.

'He was gentle and kind, funny too. He used to make me laugh so hard it hurt.'

'Sounds close to perfect.'

We weren't perfect. I knew that. I suppose I'd always know that. No one's relationship is perfect—how can it be when nobody is perfect? I'd even wondered if one day he might have got fed up with me not sharing the same enthusiasm as him for the great outdoors. Or, whether I might have come clean about not wanting to travel around Asia. Might he have gone without me? The thing is I'll never know what might have happened next. I didn't answer Mum and she popped the pin in the hem. 'Here we are, this is good to go. I'll help you feed it through the machine.'

We'd chalk-painted the older dresser too, googling how to achieve a distressed look. We'd rolled up our sleeves and gotten stuck in. It was against the wall near the window. I walked over to it and ran my fingers along the top. It was dry beneath my fingertips and ready for its second coat. It looked suitably faded and French, and I was so pleased with how it was turning out. My eyes flitted over to the duvet folded on the floor and ready to be put on the bed, when it arrived. The curtains will tie together the whole romantic French look I'm going for.

There's a lot of fun to be had in making something new out of something old, and Mum and I had plans to mooch our way down Ferry Road tomorrow afternoon. Once I got home from the bike ride (I'd told Mum I was going to do a couple of gym classes). There was a glut of antique and second-hand shops over that side of town, and we were going in search of the guest room's finishing touch: a chandelier. I'd quite like to pick up an old chair of some sort, too. It would go in the corner of the room, something we can re-cover the seat with. There's just enough of the lovely rose fabric from the duvet and curtains left to stretch to that.

'Finished.' Mum's voice startled me. 'Come on, let's get these babies hung.'

The radio was on in the kitchen, and I recognised the song. 'Mum, come here!' I called running for the kitchen and turning the sounds up. When Mum walked in I had my arms up over my head and I was doing my best tummy wiggling Madonna dance to 'Like a Virgin'. She clapped her hands and gave me a huge grin, picking up her long skirt and twirling about the room just like we used to.

Chapter 36

♥

We pulled up at Aunty Paula's on the dot of seven and parked behind Gemma's shiny big beast. Mum had the cheese platter we'd put together on her lap; she also had a bag of nasty-looking duty-free spirits and was making noises about mixing cocktails on the drive over.

'I thought you weren't drinking,' I said trying to keep my tone light as she passed the plate to me before picking up the bag.

'I'm not, but that doesn't mean you girls can't have some fun.'

'You never said why you're not drinking.' I looked over at her curiously. Mum liked a drop but she's not an alcoholic and I wondered what her reasoning for going teetotaller was.

'Oh I just decided it wasn't doing me any favours and I don't need it,' she answered getting out of the car. 'I'm better when I abstain, more on an even keel. Did I tell you I like your outfit? It's very—'

She studied me for a moment and I held my breath.

'Madonna when she went through her Vogue phase.'

I breathed out. I knew she'd get it.

The front door was already open as we made our way toward it. Aunty Paula was standing on the porch and as we drew closer I registered the strange look on her face. 'What's up?' I asked nervously.

'It's nothing serious, nothing to worry about.'

Which instantly made me worry.

'It's um, it's just that Gemma's had a reaction after visiting the beauty salon this afternoon. She's a tad sensitive about it, and just bit her dad's head off. He was glad to make his escape. He's going to drop the spare bed in for you, Ellie, and then watch the rugby around at his mate Ron's house. I'm giving you the heads-up so you know not laugh at her or stare.'

From inside the house, a voice shouted, 'Mum, I can hear you!' The speech sounded funny, a little thick and muffled, and me and the cheese platter pushed past Aunty Paula, to see what was going on. I found Gemma reclining on the couch, head dipped as she sipped a glass of wine through a straw.

'I thought we'd outgrown that little party trick in our teens. What are you doing?' On the table in front of her was a bowl filled with Cadbury Favourites all shiny in their foil wrap. I felt like a magpie as I fought the sudden urge to rifle through them, clenching my fists to stop myself from taking out all the Caramello ones to stash for the movie later. That would be greedy.

Gemma put her glass down, and I forgot all about the mini chocolate bars as my mouth fell open. Good grief she'd had her lips done alright! Oh, dear and not just her lips her eyebrows were like Groucho Marx's. My cousin had morphed into one of those Bratz dolls. Her mouth was giving new meaning to bee-stung pout and I expected her to waggle her brows at me and stick a cigar in her mouth. Think Angelina on steroids. 'Gemma, my God what have you done?'

'I just wanted a puller pout and defined bows. I told you I was going to get fiwers and my bows hennaed.'

'I didn't think you'd *actually* go and do it, though.' I knew Aunty Paula said not to, but I couldn't stop staring at her mouth and when

I wasn't staring at that I'd stare at her eyebrows but at least I didn't laugh. I was transfixed by her exaggerated new features as I reached down and grabbed a napkin off the table. 'Here, you're dribbling.'

She dabbed at the side of her mouth. 'It's numb, dats why I'm dwibbling and stop starwing. The swelling will go down in twenty-fouw howrs, the cosmetician said so and I twied scwubbing my eyebows but it won't come off.'

I raised a normal eyebrow because if it were me, I'd be down at the butchers who'd done this to me demanding my money back.

She read my mind. 'They were fweebies; I have to show my new bows and lips off for That Giwl.'

'Well, I'd wait the full twenty-four hours if I were you and keep scrubbing those eyebrows. Then again, you could do a series of photos on why fiddling with what nature gave you isn't always a good idea.'

She shot me a look but opted to slurp the rest of her wine up through her straw, and I shook my head at her sorry state. 'What? I can't move my mowth pwoply I need the stwaw.'

'Gemma darling, long time no see. What's with the straw? Are you playing drinking games?' Mum trilled.

Gemma said no and pointed to her lips. Mum leaned in for a closer look nearly knocking the bowl of chocolates off the table. 'Whoops, but wow! And I mean, wow. Looking hot, babe! I'm loving those luscious lips—not sure about the brows though, maybe a tad too dark.'

Maybe Mum needed her eyes tested I thought, but Gemma instantly looked brighter. There was a cosmetic enhancement kindred spirit in the room, and for that, she got herself off the couch to give Mum a hello hug.

'Thanks, Auny Nicky. I love your boobs by the way.' Mum grabbed Gemma's hand and put it in on her breast.

'Have a squeeze, go on. You'll be amazed at how real they feel.'

I looked at Aunty Paula, and she rolled her eyes at me. I was suddenly grateful for her normal middle-agedness and small breasts. We sat our little unenhanced selves down and listened in as Mum and Gemma talked, well Gemma tried to anyway, about what their various procedures entailed. I was right; Mum has had permanent eyeliner tattooed under her lashes and along the top lid of her eyes. It sounded as though she had been toying with having her eyebrows done next but having seen Gemma's she wasn't so sure now. All I could see was needles and more needles, and it was making me squirm.

I butted in and asked Gemma, 'Did it hurt?' I pointed to my lips.

'Anything worth doing in life is painfuw.'

I couldn't help my mouth twitching at her holier-than-thou tone.

'It's not funny.'

Aunty Paula and I begged to differ and had a bit of a giggle at her expense. She'd obviously forgotten that we weren't supposed to laugh at Gemma. Once we'd sorted ourselves out, she said, 'If she'd told me what she was up to I would've told her it was a silly idea to mess with what she was born with. She was gorgeous the way she was.'

'But I'm more gorgeous now.' Gemma's lips curved into what I thought was a smile, I really couldn't stop staring at them. 'Or I will be tomowwwow.'

My hand twitched with the urge to slap Mum's hand as she helped herself to a Caramello and added, 'But, Paula, God gave some of us a bit less than others in some departments, and that's not fair. We're only evening up the odds aren't we, Gemma?'

I wondered what Nan would make of Mum's religious views as Gemma nodded enthusiastically.

'Have you ever thought about having anything done, Ellie?' Mum turned her attention to me, and I dragged my eyes away from Gemma's mouth.

'Nope, well maybe a tattoo. Sam didn't like them on women though.' It was true I'd always fancied getting something small, and discreet of course. My secret.

'What about you, Paula? Ever thought about a bit of Botox or a spot of filler for those pesky little wrinkles?' She tapped her lips and between her brows, both of which I saw were suspiciously smooth. Mum should have had a mouth puckered like a cat's you know what, with all the cigarettes she'd smoked over the years. She'd finally given up when she met the Papadum.

'They're not wrinkles they're lifelines,' I stated in Aunty Paula's defence. 'They're a map of a life well lived.' I was surprised when she joined in with the peals of laughter coming from Mum and Gemma because I was sticking up for her.

'Oh, Ellie love, you're not there yet. You wouldn't have a clue,' Aunty Paula said. 'I don't like the *pesky* little wrinkles and saggy bits any more than the next girl, but I can't stand needles, and I have a fear of looking like one of those stretched, overdone Hollywood types.' Her eyes flicked to her daughter and I bit back, 'or a Bratz doll.'

'I asked Colin once what he thought about the idea of me giving nature a helping hand, and he said he'd no wish to get about with a wife who looked ten years younger than him and to leave my face alone.'

Well, that told me, I thought helping myself to a cracker and wedge of Brie.

Mum got up from the couch and clapped her hands, 'Paula, how about you and I mix us some mojitos? I've got the rum.' She produced a bottle of Coruba from the duty-free bag she'd toted in and waved it about. 'Your favourite. And for me...voila—apple juice! Did you pick the mint?'

'As soon I got off the phone—there's a big bunch on the bench. I haven't had a mojito in years.' Aunty Paula got up and followed Mum through to the kitchen. 'And good for you, Nicky, sticking with apple juice. I think we'll all wish we'd followed your lead tomorrow morning.'

Once they were out of earshot, Gemma squished up next to me on the couch. 'How's it gowing?'

I refused to look at her mouth because I wouldn't be able to take her seriously 'Surprisingly well,' I said, my voice lowered. 'Mum seems different; maybe the Papadum has had a calming influence on her.' I shrugged. 'Whatever it is she's easier to be around than she used to be. Or maybe it's me; maybe I've mellowed.'

We looked at each other. 'Nah!' It made us giggle, or it would have if Gemma could have moved her mouth properly. She gave up. 'Aunty Nicky was always one hundred miles an hour; she needed to calm down.'

'Not always.' I thought back to the times when she'd go quiet and retreat, and I'd find myself back at Nan and Pops'.

'So you're getting on okay?'

'Yeah, we are. We've been making curtains and things for the house, and well, it's been really good. Like I said before I think the Papadum's a steadying influence even if he is needy. From what Mum says he treats her like a princess. She loves him, and I mean properly loves him.'

Gemma grimaced; she'd seen his photo. 'Each to their own.'

He might not be an oil painting, but he must have something about him other than a fat wallet because those hazel irises of Mum's are worldly with hard flints of a tough life lived, but when she talks about him they soften. This was a new thing. It was a nice thing. She told me he as she snipped the fabric for the lounge drapes the other night that he was the first man who'd ever made her properly happy.

It doesn't take much to treat someone the way they deserve to be treated, and it made me a little sad when Mum said that. I remembered something I'd forgotten or chosen not to think about—I'm not sure which.

I was about ten I think, and I'd been sound asleep but the next thing I knew Mum had me out of bed and into a coat before bundling me out the door to the car. Steve stood in the doorway yelling at her not to come back. I remembered he called her a fucking bitch, and I apologise for the language, but they were his words, not mine. I didn't like that memory, and I tucked it back in with the others that I know are there but which I leave well alone.

'Are you gowing to ask her about your dad while she's here?'

Gemma knew how much this blank spot in my life bugged me. Sam used to push me to do something about finding out about him too but I'd held back. 'I don't know. I don't want to spoil things.' That wasn't the whole story, though. The stuff she'd said about the Papadum made me wonder if I might be better not knowing. What if he was in prison or just a total waste of space? I think it could be true; you know, that ignorance is bliss because that way I can imagine he was a decent bloke who was too young to be a dad. Gemma must have read my mind.

'Do you remember that story you used to tell people? How he was a British backpacker your mum met at the pub?'

'I liked the idea of being able to get a British passport.' It was true. The tale went on that their one-night stand was in the days before mobile phones and social media took off, so Mum had no way of finding him let alone contacting him once she discovered she was pregnant. It was fictional, but it was a palatable version of my conception. So, instead of venturing into that minefield when the opportunities had arisen during the week I'd told Mum stories I'd never shared with her before about Sam and I. I could almost believe he was still with me when I relived those times, and I wished he could have met this version of my mum, not the one who would fly in and out of my life like a hurricane. Hurricane Nicky. He'd be so pleased if he could have seen us now.

On cue Mum appeared with two glasses, a slice of lime on the side. Aunty Paula minced in behind her, a drink in each hand. The ice tinkled as they made their way over. 'Here we are, girls. Ernest Hemingway's favourite drink, the mojito. Just use the straw again, Gemma,' Mum said seeing Gemma size up the glass doubtfully.

'Wait,' giggled Aunty Paula whose cheeks looked suspiciously pink. She's had a head start. Mum was a bad influence, I thought primly as she bounced up and down like a kid with their hand up in class asking if they can go to the bathroom. 'We've got to do the toast, Nicky. We can't drink rum, or apple juice,' she added eyeballing Mum's glass with its crushed mint and ice, 'without making the toast first.'

They raised their glasses and chimed,

'Drink Rum, Drink Rum

Drink Rum by Gum with me,

I don't give a damn

For any damned man,

That won't take a drink with me.

Cheers!'

Gemma and I looked at one another as we all clinked glasses. They'd obviously done that before. Either that or they'd both gone potty.

Chapter 37

♥

'If you *were* to get a tattoo what would you get done?' Mum asked me while vaping as if her life depended on it and then holding the canister aloft and eyeing it with disgust. 'I only feel like smoking when I'm having a few drinks even if they are mocktails and these are just not the same.'

A faint smell of spearmint wafted past me.

'The strawberry flavour's best,' Mum added wrinkling her nose and having another puff.

Rubber lips piped up with, 'Do not say you would ink yourself with, "I love Sam forwever".'

'I wasn't going to.' Actually, I was. I pointed to my hip. 'There, where only I could see it. Something dainty.'

'What about you, Paula?'

Mum had this mad gleam in her eyes; perhaps she'd overdone it with the vaping.

'Oh, I'm with Ellie, something dainty like say a pretty little butterfly.' Aunty Paula patted her shoulder. 'I'd get it done just there.'

What was it I said earlier about middle-agedness? I wasn't sure I knew this rum-loving aunty of mine at all!

Gemma rolled her jeans leg up to reveal an angel on her ankle. She'd gotten it done a few years ago, and Mum sat there going on about how cute it was, but I could see that mad gleam was getting brighter.

'Well, shall we put the movie on?' I asked wanting to move on because I've seen that look in Mum's eyes before and I had a feeling I knew where this conversation was headed. I sneaked the remaining two Caramello bars before picking up the movie and heading over to the TV.

'I saw that,' Gemma said.

'What?'

'The chocolates. I like the Caramello ones too.'

'No idea what you're on about.' I wasn't putting them back.

'Hold your horses, Ellie. We can watch a movie any old time. Why don't we hit the town?' Mum elbowed Aunty Paula. 'Come on, Paula, you're up for it aren't you?'

Flashbacks of last weekend assailed me, and I shuddered, but Mum wasn't done yet.

'And get inked.'

'What?' me, Gemma and Aunty Paula chimed.

'You heard me. Come on, girls, you only live once. What do you say?'

~

I think it's what Mum said that made me throw back my mojito and agree to throw caution to the wind. The 'you only live once' bit resonated because I know how true that is. That's why I found myself standing in a brightly lit room in a central city tattoo studio with my top tucked up in my bra and my jeans low around my nether regions. My tattooist who preferred to be called an artist, Mel, had piercings through every visible orifice and bright red hair. Given how mean she looked I wasn't going to argue with her. Artist it was.

She was slowly peeling away the stencil transfer from my hip to reveal two little lovebirds perched on a twig. She'd already made me fill in all sorts of paperwork and show her ID, which I was a bit indignant about, but Mum said I should it take as a compliment because, before you knew it, you were past forty and invisible. She said that's why she was so gung-ho about keeping young and beautiful, but I didn't think she had to worry about being invisible—not with her fuchsia pink tank top and white jeggings.

Aunty Paula was next door getting a blue butterfly inked on the back of her shoulder. Seeing will be believing because this was so out of character. Gemma, and her eyebrows and lips, had gone with her for moral support, and I wondered how she was getting on as I saw the needles and tubes being removed from their sterile packs. I hadn't heard any screaming, so that had to be a good sign.

'How're you doing?' Mel asked undoing the lid on a pot.

'Okay.'

'This will help the needle run over your skin more smoothly.' She applied a greasy salve over the transfer.

I wavered a little. It wasn't too late, I could do a runner, but I looked at Mum standing there pleased as punch. This was her treat, and she gave me the thumbs up. It struck me as not the norm for one's mother to shout one's daughter a tattoo, but then our relationship had never been what you'd call normal. I chewed my bottom lip. The lovebirds symbolised me and Sam of course, who by the way would so not approve of what I was doing, but then he wasn't here. I was doing this, I realised, for myself. It would also be symbolic of Mum and I moving forward in our relationship. Besides if Aunty Paula with her fear of needles could go through with it, then so could I. 'Don't be a wimp, Ellie.'

'Sorry, what was that?' Mel asked.

I didn't realise I'd spoken aloud.

'It's the first couple of minutes that are the roughest, and then the pain regulates itself.' Mum held her hand out for me to take. I grabbed it and squeezed as hard as I could.

'Breathe slowly and deeply,' she advised wincing at my grip as the tattoo gun began to buzz and the needle came closer. Famous last words. I howled as it connected with my flesh. It HURT! And for the duration of the process, I made a keening, guttural sound while Mum let me grasp her hand so tight I must have cut off her circulation. 'Ellie, I don't rate your chances in childbirth when the time comes. Go with the gas.' She shook her head.

When it was finally, mercifully over Mel gently cleaned the freshly tattooed area, holding a hot towel over her artwork for a minute or two before taking a photo of it for her portfolio.

'There you go. That wasn't so bad, was it?' She wasn't expecting me to answer as she applied a protective ointment over my brand new tattoo and carefully placed a bandage over the tender skin, which she taped into place. 'This will prevent any nasties from getting into it.'

I was almost euphoric that I'd made it through my ordeal and wanted to hug her, but all those piercings put me off, I'd probably wind up hooking her up in my top or something, and that wouldn't be pretty. Instead, I thanked her profusely. I apologised for all the noise I made throughout, but she shrugged it off.

'Everyone has different pain thresholds.'

I took the aftercare instructions sheet and thanked her again. I felt fantastic, and it dawned on me that it was the best I'd felt since losing Sam. Who knew submitting to a legal form of torture would leave one feeling like they were walking on air, like they'd faced the lion and won. I was getting carried away, but I did feel great, and I walked taller as we went in search of Aunty Paula and Gemma.

We found them waiting for us in the reception area seated on the leather couches. Aunty Paula looked like me, pleased as punch and she pulled her blouse down over her shoulder to show me her bandaged war wound.

'She was vewy bwave. I took a video for my site. I'm calling it That Giwl's Mum Gets a Tattoo. The manager agreed to give you two a fifty per cent discount on your inkings.'

'Thanks. It might take the spotlight off your lips.'

She poked her tongue out at me, and it made me laugh because she looked so ridiculous.

'It wasn't too bad,' Aunty Paula said. 'I can't wait to get home to show Colin. How did you get on, Ellie?'

'I was brave, too, wasn't I, Mum?'

'Oh yes,' Mum lied. 'Super brave, not a peep out of her.'

Chapter 38

♥

I woke up at seven the next morning pleased to find myself back in my own bed with the familiar stripped, bare walls. Uncle Colin, always true to his word, had set the bed up in the guest room. He'd even made it up and Mum had slept in there. Pete had taken to his new bedtime location, stalking over the covers, turning around a few times before curling up into a ball, with ease. He stirred at the foot of the bed as I reached over and patted him. I wondered how Mum had slept in the guest room. That's when I remembered what it was we got up to last night. OMG, I got a tattoo!

That woke me up and, sitting up, I rolled my jammies down to inspect the bandage. Mel said I should leave it on overnight and that it would be fine to take off by morning, so I peeled the tape off gingerly before tracing my finger over the two little lovebirds. The area was a little tender but nothing major. I'd put on the ointment I was given to stop it getting yucky after my shower, I decided, and throwing my duvet aside I got up. The sky I saw upon opening the curtains was clear and blue, a good day for going for a bike ride. All was well in my world. I was a warrior woman with a tattoo, or at least I would be once I'd had a coffee and fed Pete.

Mum was still in bed by the time I'd sorted Pete, showered and stuffed down a banana. I didn't bother waking her as I headed outside to my car. My little friend from over the fence was skateboarding up and down his drive. He looked up just in time to give me his one-fingered salute. I was past being shocked by this now, just as his asking me where the MILF was this morning didn't wind me up. I'd come to the conclusion he was bored, and I think he liked to try and shock. I was going to employ different tactics because he wouldn't wear me down. Watch this space because he and I will be on amicable neighbourly terms before the year is out. I would not allow myself to be beaten by a child; I'm a qualified pre-school teacher for goodness' sake! That's why I gave him my brightest smile.

'My mum, if that's who you're talking about, is still in bed. I'll tell her you were asking after her though.' I'm satisfied to see him look surprised.

The traffic was light this early on a Saturday morning, and it didn't take me long to wind my way into McLeans Island, which isn't an island at all. I've no idea why it's called that. It's an area of recreational land near the airport. The carpark was busy, which surprised me. There were an awful lot of energetic early risers in Christchurch—who knew? I pulled into a space between two all-terrain vehicles. I felt dwarfed as I got out and locked up before scanning the carpark to see if I could spot Joel. He was over the other side near the kiosk, lifting a bike off the back of his work wagon. He looked up and spotted me, so I waved out and made my way over.

For the record, he was dressed in perfectly respectable shorts with skins *under* them and a T-shirt. I couldn't help but notice he had a nice physique, gently muscled not chiselled and oversized like some of the weightlifters at the gym. But I was NOT checking him out, nor was I giving him a tick.

'Hi, great morning for it.' He gave me a grin as I reached him.

'Yeah. I'm amazed at how busy it is.' A family of six was setting off along the track. Two littlies were perched on baby seats on the back of their mum and dad's bikes, the bigger kids independently pedalling off. There were also some serious-looking action men and women whom I didn't want to get in the way of on the track.

'It's a popular circuit and this time of day you beat the heat. Did you get up to much last night?'

'I did actually.'

He raised an eyebrow. 'Well, you look pretty fresh for someone who had a big night.'

'Oh no not like that. Well, a little like that—I got a tattoo.'

His eyes widened. I hadn't noticed before, but Joel's eyes are an unusual shade of grey. They're almost silver. 'Yeah?'

I nodded. 'It's a long story, but it was Mum's big idea. Sounds mad right?'

'Uh yeah, it does.'

'Mum *is* a bit mad. You've met my Aunty Paula right?'

'Yeah through Colin a couple of times. She's a nice lady.'

'She is but she's got this whole other wild side to her I never knew existed because she wound up getting a butterfly tattoo on her shoulder. I got two lovebirds perched on a branch done here.' I patted my hip, but that was as far as I was going and he didn't ask to see it. I fished out my phone then because I remembered Gemma was going to load the video she took onto That Girl to show him, but my mouth dropped open when I saw how many likes she'd gotten. I blinked to make sure I wasn't seeing things. This couldn't be right surely? It was though. Overnight my cousin has gotten over eight thousand views, and there were hundreds of comments too. Oh wow, she'd gone viral!

Gemma couldn't be up yet. Otherwise, she'd have been screaming this news down the phone at me. 'I've just got to make a quick call. Sorry.'

'No worries, this tyre needs a pump.'

Gemma answered after a few rings, sounding groggy.

'Wake up!' I yelled.

'Ellie? What's the time? What's going on?' She'd lost the lisp of the night before, and I assumed that meant the puffiness of her lips was receding.

'You've gone viral,' I shrieked, and Joel looked up at me curiously. 'Check it out.'

The next minute she was screaming, and I held the phone away from my ear knowing I had a big stupid grin on my face. I was guessing this meant that even with a set of lips that would be more at home on Lindsay Lohan, my cousin was going to be seriously in demand from here on in.

'I've got to go, Gemma, but it's fantastic! I'm proud of you and Aunty Paula.' And me and Mum too I thought disconnecting the call. She'd be burning her phone line up for the rest of the morning, besides I was itching to see the video myself.

'My cousin Gemma has an Instagram account called That Girl, which has a big following here and overseas. She calls herself Gem and models local designers' gear on it. She showcases new restaurants and bars, that sort of thing. The perks she gets are amazing. Anyway she uploaded the video of her mum, my Aunty Paula, getting her tattoo done last night and—'

'It's gone viral,' Joel finished.

'Uh-huh. I haven't seen it yet.'

'Come on then, what are you waiting for?'

I held my phone up away from the sunlight and hit play, aware of Joel's proximity as he leaned in to watch it. Gemma and her lips appeared on screen as she blew a kiss and said hi.

'They're not her real lips,' I said in case he was wondering.

She introduced the tattooist, who just like Mel liked to be called an ink artist; his name was Aslan.

'Wasn't that the lion from the Chronicles of Narnia?' I asked Joel.

'Rings a bell.'

'I bet it's not his real name.'

'He's probably called Randolph or Rupert, something like that.'

I giggled and hoped for Aunty Paula's sake he was more pussycat than lion. And there she was. She was in a reclining chair similar to those found at the dentist, her naked shoulder exposed, and her rosy mojito-fuelled cheeks pale. Joel and I craned forward to hear what Gemma was saying.

'And this gorgeous lady is my mum, Paula; she's nearly fifty-three.'

'Not for another year thank you very much.' Aunty Paula looked indignant, and it made Joel and I laugh.

'I was a young mother,' she adds. It echoed my own mum's sentiments when she met Joel and his team, and I did the math: Aunty Paula was the same age I am now when she had Gemma.

'Alright, Mum, we get it. Anyway, Mum or Paula here has decided to take a walk on the wild side. Cue the music.' Gemma clicks her fingers, and Lou Reed's famous song plays for a few beats. 'She's getting her very first tattoo.' Gem holds her finger up to her puffy pink mouth and says, 'Shush don't tell my dad—he's got no idea we're here.'

'Colin will think it's sexy,' Aunty Paula pipes up giving the camera a big wink.

I muttered to Joel, 'Is that saucy lady related to me?'

'*Mum*, TMI.'

The video pans out to show some of the framed designs on the walls; they're big, elaborate and very swirly. The ink artist, Aslan, must feel he's not getting enough camera time because he appears in the frame wielding his gun like a gangsta as he homes in on poor old Aunty Paula's shoulder.

I closed my eyes now remembering the pain; I didn't want to see it on my aunty's face. Aslan is giving a running commentary on what he's doing. I took a peek. To my amazement, Aunty Paula looked incredibly relaxed.

'You're doing well, Mum.'

'Gemma—'

'It's Gem remember.'

'Oh right, *Gem*, given you were born with a head like a watermelon on you, this is a walk in the park.'

I clenched my nethers. A watermelon? I sincerely hope that's not a genetic trait.

Aunty Paula tells Aslan all about her birthing experience, and he goes pale, well paler given he's a goth. By the time she's reached the cutting of the cord bit he's done, and we get a close-up of the end result, an exquisite blue butterfly, which Gem exclaims over before asking if Aunty Paula would like to share anything about her tattoo experience.

'I would.' Aunty Paula stares straight into the camera, and you can almost see her thinking this is her moment to shine. To my utter disbelief, she bursts into song. Her anthem, 'Man! I feel like a Woman.' By Shania Twain.

Chapter 39

'That was classic,' Joel said once he'd stopped laughing. 'I can see why it got so many hits.'

I was shaking my head in disbelief at what I'd just witnessed, no wonder my aunt and cousin are internet sensations. They were brilliant. I hope fame doesn't change them.

'Do you have any?'

'Tats?'

'Yeah."

'Just one. I got it after the 2011 quake. I think I wanted to prove that I was still here.'

I looked at him quizzically, but I understood his sentiment. I'd felt the same last night as Mel set to work. I was still here even if Sam wasn't. Joel didn't meet my gaze as he put the bike pump in the boot.

'I was due to meet my girlfriend, Ali, for lunch in City Mall when the shaking started. She was early, and I was late, which meant she was sitting having a coffee waiting for me when the building she was in collapsed.'

'Oh! Did she—'

'She died.'

I was unsure what to say, but then I trotted out what I'd heard so many times. 'I'm sorry.'

He smiled at me, but I could see the pain in those silver eyes. 'Yeah, it was rough.'

'What did you get?' I quickly added, 'If you don't mind me asking.'

'No it's okay. It's a Latin phrase, *Ad Astra Per Aspera*, which means "through difficulties to the stars".'

'*Ad Astra Per Aspera*,' I repeated. I looked at him as he hauled what I assumed would be my bike off the back of the truck. 'That's beautiful,' I said taking the bike from him.

'It was a long time ago.' His voice was gruff, and any thoughts I'd had about telling him about my lovebirds and Sam disappeared.

'The seat might need adjusting. Hop on, and I'll have a look.'

I took the hint to move and got on the bike. I could touch the ground on my tiptoes, but if I had to stop suddenly, there was the potential for serious injury to my womanly parts. I clambered off, and Joel fiddled around lowering the seat before handing me a helmet. I put it on, and it sat loosely on top of my head. I fiddled about trying to adjust the straps but I wasn't getting anywhere, and I felt a bit stupid. I was worried I'd pinch the flesh under my chin.

'Here I'll help you with it.' His fingers brushed against my chin and neck as he tightened the strap and something ignited inside me. I'd forgotten the electrifying effect a bolt of attraction has, and it left me flustered. I didn't know if the feeling was mutual, and I didn't dare raise my eyes to look at him. A second later the helmet was secure, but I could still feel the heat where his fingers had touched me. Surely there must be little scorch marks there? I thought risking a glance at myself in his truck's window. There weren't, but I looked a bit like a spaceman with that helmet on. Joel didn't, he looked cool. How did that work?

Oh well, I didn't care. I was itching to get going and take my mind off my quivering insides. It had been so flipping long since a man touched me that it was no wonder I'd overreacted. Gemma keeps telling me I'm in my prime and that was all it was, I decided, a primal reaction—a 'me Tarzan, you Jane' thing. Or maybe it was because I knew he'd experienced the same grief as I had. I'm sure there was a Freudian link in there somewhere, but whatever it was, it's not what you're thinking. I do NOT think my builder is a bit of alright.

'Right, are you good to go?'

I shook my musings aside and concentrated on balancing. 'Yep, ready when you are.'

Joel swung his leg over his bike and pedalled over toward the start of the track with me off to a wobbly start behind him. It had been years since I'd been on a bike, but it didn't take long for me to gain confidence and up my pace. I'd stopped feeling trepidation as to what was around the bend and had thrown caution to the wind five minutes into our ride. We overtook that family of six, the older girls' bike purple with streamers floating out behind its handlebars. We crunched over the open gravel path before winding our way onto the dirt track, which plunged us into a forest.

The air was cool and fresh, Norse-like. I inhaled the pine scent and made a note to come back here closer to winter with a bag to collect pine cones for kindling. I got the hang of the gears as we headed up sudden dirt mounds and I swallowed my fear as I raced down the other side. I felt alive as I flew along the track.

We burst out of the forest, and the sun was on our backs once more. On either side of us, as far as I could see, was an expanse of blue sky clashing with gold gorse. I was glad I'd been going to the gym because this was hard work and I could tell already I was going to have a sore backside tomorrow, but I wasn't out of breath. Joel shouted over his shoulder, 'You okay?'

'Yeah, all good thanks.' Famous last words.

A split second later I was startled by a whoosh behind me followed by someone calling, 'Coming through.' I veered left and braked instinctively as the blur of spandex whizzed past, and I was aware in that instant as my front tyre hit a rock, I was going to come off. There was that horrible blink of an eye sensation of knowing there was nothing I could do about it and then a burst of pain as I hit the ground. Did Sam feel like that the moment he lost control of his four-wheel drive? Did he know that was going to be it for him? The breath was knocked out of me, and I lay there stunned but still managing a big dose of embarrassment, which meant it couldn't be serious.

I pulled myself upright to check to see if anything was broken. There was a hole in the knee of my leggings and blood was oozing out of a cut. It wasn't life-threatening, but it was a nasty graze, and my leg was going to be stiff as anything tomorrow.

'Shit! What happened? Are you okay?' Joel skidded to a halt in front of me.

Nobody was there to ask Sam that question. He stayed in his vehicle for hours, trapped and hurt. I wondered if Joel's girlfriend died instantly or whether she too lay under the rubble wondering why no one was coming. I looked up at his concerned face blinking at the brightness of the sunlight and opened my mouth to say, 'I'm okay.' But something inside of me snapped before I could get the words out. The pin on a grief grenade I never saw being lobbed at me was pulled, and I began to sob. Great big snot-rendering sobs. I was crying for Sam, for Ali and for all those that have gone before their time.

Chapter 40

Joel walked beside me, but we didn't talk. I was too embarrassed by my meltdown, and I think he was just relieved I'd stopped crying long enough for him to get me moving. One or two people passed us and asked if everything was okay and Joel answered for me, which I was grateful for. 'Yeah, all good, a bit of a banged-up knee but nothing too serious.'

It seemed to take forever but at last, the kiosk came into view. We were nearly back at the carpark.

'We made it.' He flashed me a reassuring grin, and I gave him a watery one back. 'Why don't you sit in the shade over there and I'll load the bikes. I've got a first aid kit in the truck to clean that up, and then I'll get us a couple of drinks.'

I didn't feel capable of driving yet as much as I'd have liked to be as far away from here as possible, so I sat gingerly down under the tree he'd suggested and plucked at the grass. I watched him steer both bikes back to his truck before lifting them in the back. He opened the driver's door and then opened the glove box to retrieve what I assumed was his medical pack before making his way back over. I bet I looked a fright, and I checked out the rip in my leggings. That was the end of my Jo-Jo Runs, the most expensive item of activewear I'd ever owned. There'd be no point trying to patch them; they were beyond repair. The antiseptic wipe Joel used over the grazing a few minutes later stung, and I winced.

'Sorry. You okay?'

'Yes but I've come to the conclusion I have a very low pain threshold.'

He looked at me bemused.

'I wasn't crying because of that.' I didn't want him to think I was a total baby as I pointed at the graze. 'But it does hurt.'

'I figured as much. That's the worst bit done anyway.' He put a sterile dressing over the top of my knee and stuck it down with tape. 'I don't think I'd get any St John's awards for that, but it should see you right anyway.'

'Thanks, Joel.' My voice wavered, and he looked at me in alarm. 'It's okay I'm not going to cry again.'

He got up. 'I'll go and get us a hot drink.' He didn't ask me what I'd like as he jogged over to the kiosk.

I watched him go but I was too tired to feel much of anything other than a fool and all that quivering stuff that was going on earlier when his fingers brushed my chin, and neck, as he helped me with my helmet, was a distant memory now.

He returned a few minutes later holding two paper cups. 'I got you a white tea with sugar in it. It's good for shock. Hope that's okay.'

'Perfect thanks.'

'And a chocolate muffin.'

Well sweetness *is* good for shock, and I'd only had a banana for breakfast so, I hoed in. By the time I was fed and watered I was feeling much better, and I owed this man at the very least an explanation not to mention an apology. 'Joel, I'm sorry and I feel pretty stupid.'

'About what? Falling off your bike or the floods of tears?' He smiled.

'Both.'

'Do you want to talk about it? The tears I mean.'

I nodded and crumpled up the muffin case, sticking it in my empty cup. 'What you said earlier about losing Ali, well I lost someone too. Not all that long ago, although technically he left me over a year ago now.' As the sun worked its way through the spiky pine branches overhead, I told him about Sam and the accident. I told him about those long months of hoping in between, and finally, I told him about his passing. 'I thought I was doing okay but these…' I hesitated. 'I call them grief grenades. They hit me out of nowhere, and it's been a while since the last one. I thought I'd gone past them.'

'Colin mentioned you were having a hard time, and I'm sorry for what you've been through but it's early days, Ellie. Don't be too hard on yourself because it's true you know, about it taking time. Those grenades you mentioned, eventually they stop coming at you.'

'They do?'

'Yep, they do.'

'How did you get through what happened to Ali?'

'I reckon you get through the worst of the pain because you have to, but you don't get past it. I think losing someone shapes you and makes you who you become. It changes you. It can't not.'

'So, you become a new version of the old you?'

He nodded. 'When someone you love dies it's like a part of you does too, and you know when it first happened and people told me it would get easier I didn't believe them. I couldn't imagine my life ever being normal again.'

'Me neither.'

He gave me a wry smile. 'It's true, though, it does. I was a mess after Ali died. I drank a lot, and I got angry with everybody, and eventually I realised I couldn't do it on my own, so I started going to this grief group.'

'Did it help?'

'It did. I didn't think it would but knowing I wasn't the only one going through total crap and being able to speak freely about how I felt to people who got where I was coming from, well that was a good thing. The counsellor who oversaw the sessions gave us strategies on how to cope when things like what just happened to you hit. Have you thought about going to something like that?'

'I did go to a counsellor after Sam's accident and I'm not sure if that was a waste of time or not. It's not like they wave a wand and you magically feel better. Aunty Paula suggested I go to a grief group in town. Sam's Mum, Gina, goes but I didn't want to. It felt like I'd be admitting I couldn't manage and I was scared of hearing Gina speak about her pain because my own seems so big. But I don't know.' I shrugged. 'Maybe I should.'

'You don't have to commit to anything; you can go and see what you think. It might help, or it might not, but it won't make things worse.'

'You're right.' I resolved to ring Gina and ask if I could tag on with her when she next went.

I glanced at my phone, and seeing the time announced, 'I'd better get going. Mum and I have a shopping date.'

'You okay to drive now?'

'I'm fine, Joel. Thanks, you know for—'

'It's all good.' He cut me off and helped me to my feet. 'Do you need a hand?'

I tested my weight on my leg. I'd have liked to lean on him for just a little longer, but that would be overdoing it. My knee ached now, but I could walk on my own just fine. 'No, but thanks.'

He walked me over to my car, and I thanked him again. 'I'll see you Monday.'

Work would start on the kitchen on Monday; it was the final room that Joel and his team would be working on as all the major structural work was now done. There would still be painting and lots of it to be done, but Connor had that under control. I offered to help, but he reckoned he wouldn't work with cowboy painters. I don't think he was impressed when he saw the gouges I'd made in the bedroom stripping the wallpaper. The carpet would be the last thing to go down. It was hard to imagine the house being finished.

I'd grown used to seeing Joel and his team pull up the drive ready for work, too. I'd been enjoying the hustle and bustle of activity around the place and the thought of it all being done and dusted, and an empty house made me feel a little bereft. *Stop being silly, Ellie, it's what you signed up for,* I told myself tooting and giving him a wave as I drove out of the carpark and headed home.

Chapter 41

♥

'Well, you didn't do that at the gym.' Mum had her hair in a towel turban, and she was sitting on the front doorstep removing the bits of polish where she'd painted over her toes with a cotton bud as I hobbled toward her. There was a bottle of remover and polish in a pale shade of green on the step.

Pete was sitting in the doorway next to her. I bent down and gave him a pat before sitting down next to her. 'No,' I said stretching my sore leg out in front of me. Seeing the nail polish made me think of Caro. I'd confided my suspicions in Gemma, and she has taken to calling her Klepto Caro now. She thinks I should confront her about all that makeup I found before she goes and gets herself arrested for shoplifting. She's got a point, but it wouldn't be easy finding the right moment. I eyed Mum's toes. 'Nice colour.' It's a pale green and I can smell the pungent, chemical smell of acetone. 'Did you sleep in?'

'Mm thought I'd try something different and I've got a hair pack on if you're wondering why I have a towel on my head. I got up about nine. The bed was super comfy. I didn't want to get out of it.' She paused, the cotton bud hovering above her toe. 'Are you alright because if you don't mind me saying, Ellie, you look like shit?' She looked at my face and then my taped-up knee.

'Thanks, Mum. You know how to make a girl feel good about herself. That's the second time you've said that to me now.'

She didn't apologise.

I chewed my lip. I knew she was right. I looked at myself in the mirror on the sun visor when I'd pulled up the drive, and I did look like, excuse me, but there was no point tiptoeing around it, shit. 'I'm fine, my knee's a bit stiff but I'll live.'

'And how's the other?' Her eyes flitted to my hip.

'Really good.' I pulled the waistband of my leggings down for her to have a look. 'See.'

'It looks great, nice and clean. Good pick, it's very sweet. Have you spoken to your cousin this morning and heard the news?'

'I watched the video earlier and couldn't believe how many hits she'd had. Who would have thought Aunty Paula would be an Instagram natural? Have you seen it?'

Mum laughed. 'Uh-huh, I sent the link to George. He thought it was hilarious. There's more to Paula than meets the eye. You get a few mojitos into the old girl, and she's away. Gemma's talking Hollywood you know.'

That made me laugh, typical Gemma thinking big but then I sobered as the thought struck me that maybe it wasn't such a big stretch. Look at what she'd achieved with her career and building her social media following already. If she sets her mind to something, she's unstoppable.

Mum opened up her polish once more and applied three deft strokes to her big toenails before screwing the lid back on. 'They needed a second coat. That's me done. Shall we go in? I'll make us a coffee while you tell me what you've been up to.'

'Sounds good.' I got carefully to my feet and hobbled after her as she walked on her heels through to the kitchen. She flicked the switch on the kettle while I pulled out a chair and sat down at the table. We'll be moving the couch and the table and chairs through to the lounge tomorrow in readiness for work starting in here on Monday, and I was going to have to box up everything in the drawers and pantry.

I glanced around at the lemon-coloured joinery that would have been smart back in the fifties and the stainless steel bench. Nan was Queen in her kitchen and it's a little sad to think of it all being ripped out. Then I thought about the gorgeous ready-made kitchen kitset I picked out from Bunnings with its sleek wooden top and white cupboards, and I put those feelings aside. The old memories won't fade. They'll always be here because they're in the very fibre of the house, but it's time to make new ones.

'It must be weird for you, Mum, seeing all these changes being made?'

'I see your nan and pops around every corner. Good times, not so good times. It's time this old place was dragged into the present though.'

She threw a smile over at me before retrieving a couple of mugs from the cupboards. 'So come on then, what happened?'

'I went mountain biking with Joel, hit a rock and came off.'

Her head did an exorcist-style whirl as she faced me. 'Joel as in hunky Joel the builder?'

My shoulders did that coiled spring thing. 'Yes, one and the same and that's why I didn't tell you where I was going because I knew you'd react like that.'

'What do you mean? I didn't say a word.'

'You didn't have to, Mum. It's the tone of your voice and the look on your face.'

'Ellie, you don't have to get defensive. There's nothing wrong with you going out with a guy. I think it's great. Nobody's judging you.

You're only twenty-five, love, you've got your whole life ahead of you.' She turned back to what she was doing, and her voice was quiet as she added, 'And I'm sure Sam wouldn't have wanted you living like a nun for the rest of your days.'

'How do you know? You never met him. You only ever talked to him a couple of times on Skype.' My voice was sharper than I intended it to be but her reference to what Sam would have wanted had struck a guilty chord. I felt guilty about the quivering insides being around Joel gave me today even though I know Sam wouldn't have wanted me mourning him forever. That was just it though, wasn't it? It hadn't even been a year yet.

It was like Mum was reading my mind. 'Oh, Ellie, I'd have loved to have met Sam but you never gave me the opportunity.'

It's true. She did invite us over to stay with her and George. I never told Sam, though, because I didn't want him to meet her. He would have gone in a heartbeat, if I had.

'You can't put a timeline on grief, sweetie. There's no correct waiting period before you dip your toe back in the water. You were grieving Sam long before he died, and it doesn't mean you loved him less if you start dating other people. So, if you want to get back in the saddle, so to speak, I, for one, think it is a good thing.'

She said the 'D' word. I am so not ready for that and today was NOT a date. My hackles rose. 'Yeah well nobody could ever excuse you of living like a nun.' I knew it was nasty, but I'd said it now, and it was too late to take it back.

Mum looked like she'd been slapped because her skin, free of its usual slick of foundation, was red and mottled. She stuck her head in the fridge to retrieve the milk and there in the silence hung the opportunity for me to apologise. 'I'm sorry,' stuck in my throat though and in the end, it was her that spoke.

'I think I'll ignore that comment,' she said breaking the silence and closing the fridge door.

There was an atmosphere in the room now, and it was ugly. I realised subconsciously this was what I'd been waiting for from the moment she'd arrived. The ugly inevitable scene that always played out when Mum was around. Deep down I hadn't trusted the Mary Poppins Mum. She never stuck around for long and I knew the one who always let me down would make a reappearance at some point.

My insides began to churn, and my breath quickened. A rage was bubbling, and I didn't know where it had come from, perhaps I was going mad—sobbing one minute, angry the next. Why did people always leave me? I knew that was what she was going to do—she always did. I could tell by her fidgety stance. She was going to leave just like Sam did and I'd had enough. The finger had been pulled out of the dam.

'Why did you take off to the Gold Coast, Mum?' Bam! I'd said it.

She put the kettle down but didn't look at me. 'I don't think now's the right time to talk about that. You're in a funny mood.'

'I'm not. I'm just saying it how it is. I was only fourteen. Fourteen, Mum. You've never, not once talked about why you dumped me on Uncle Colin and Aunty Paula. You've never talked to me about anything that matters. What about my father? I know nothing about him. Why do I have to pay for your mistake?'

'Ellie, where's all this coming from? There are reasons behind everything I've done and I did them with your best interests at heart.'

'Don't give me that,' I snarled.

I must have looked vicious because she stepped backward. 'You've every right to feel angry about what happened to Sam, but don't confuse your anger at his death with your feelings about me and my actions. Now's not the right time for us to talk about all that.'

I wasn't letting her get off that easy. 'But I don't understand how you could just up and go. Or pretend my father never existed. What kind of person does stuff like that?' I was like a dog with a bone. 'Didn't you love me?' My eyes sent a challenge.

'I've always loved you.'

'Just not enough.'

I'd pushed too far because Mum reared up then and the height of the towel on her head made her seem taller. 'I loved you enough to leave. It was the hardest damned thing I've ever done, but I had my reasons.'

'You don't keep secrets and you don't abandon your child Mum!' I screamed this almost foaming at the mouth. 'You're not right in here.' I tapped the side of my head. 'Why couldn't you be like the other kids' mums instead of a head-case?'

And she walked from the room.

I didn't blame her. The things I'd shrieked were terrible but it was more than that. You see I knew something about Mum, something I'd never talked to anyone about.

Chapter 42

♥

Sam and I had been an item for five blissful months having moved through winter and into summer by the time we had our first proper fight. Since I'd met him, I felt like I was walking around encased in a warm, golden bubble of champagne that couldn't be pierced because nobody annoyed me, not even those mums and dads who parked in *my* space behind Teeny Tykes were capable of ruffling my feathers. I'd turned into one of those people who smiled at everybody. Gemma said I had joined the pain-in-the-arse girlfriends club. She reckoned my first sentence always began with Sam. She was right; it was all Sam said this and Sam did that. I couldn't help it.

We didn't rush things, well having said that we did have sex on our second date because we were in a rush for that, but we took our time getting to know one another. I learned he had a thing about peas, and I didn't even find his habit of picking them out and lining them up on the side of his plate annoying. I knew I might do one day, just like he might find my habit of not shutting drawers irritating one day. Not then, though, we were at that stage of our relationship where each other's little foibles were cute. I loved the way he was so pedantic about things going back where they came from, and how in life you needed a plan. He loved the way I was insistent we play John Denver whenever we went for a long drive, even though he hated country music. He refused point-blank to play Madonna, though.

The Christmas holidays loomed, hot and inviting, and so it was that for our first summer together Sam suggested we go camping. 'Come on, Ellie, you said you loved it. So, let's get right off grid. It'll be great.'

I would rather shave my eyebrows off, but that's not what I said. I'd made my own bed with that one.

'We could always hire a cabin in a campground.' That was a pretty good compromise I felt, but Sam didn't look enthused. 'Or, tag along with Gemma and her mates. They've hired a big pad down by the lake in Wanaka, and there's bound to be a spare room.' I didn't fancy crowding in on someone else's holiday, but I was desperate.

'Nah, let's go away just you and me. I know a great watering hole we could set up alongside. We can catch fish for dinner, swim, and just chill, really get lost. You'll love it.'

I loved that he wanted it to be the two of us and no one else. It was romantic the thought of us alone in the wilderness, and I loved the whole hunter-gatherer scenario too. I had mixed feelings about the swimming. If you've ever dipped a toe in a South Island river, you'll know why. And, I was always up for a spot of chilling but what I didn't love was the idea of taking a spade with me to do my morning ablutions. There was absolutely nothing romantic about that scenario.

Relationships are all about compromise, or, in my case capitulation, and we left with the four-wheel drive loaded with all the paraphernalia needed to get away from it all. There's a lot, believe you me. It was ridiculously early given it was the weekend. The roads were quiet. I was quiet too; I always am when I haven't had my full eight hours' sleep. I'd been snuffling my way into my seventh hour when the enthusiastic knocking on the front door had signalled it was time for me to get my A into G. Aunty Paula and Uncle Colin had waved us off, while Gemma, whose idea of a holiday from hell was camping, sniggered in the background.

I think Sam must have sensed my mood wasn't quite as buoyant as his because he put my John Denver on without me having to suggest it. Now and then he'd interrupt John and slap the steering wheel. It was followed by, 'This is going to be so great.' And, for the first time in five months, my lovely Sam was beginning to get right up my nose. I kept silent counsel, though, trying to admire the burnt summer hues of the wilderness we'd begun bouncing toward. The Southern Alps, stripped of their winter blanket, reared up ahead of us, a rocky arm reaching around to keep us safe on our adventures.

Profound scenic thoughts aside, I wondered what state my hair would be in at the end of our week-long Camp Granada without my trusty hairdryer, and straighteners. It didn't bear thinking about. The road turned to shingle and the further we wound our way from civilisation the more steering wheel slapping there was. By that stage, I'd moved on from worrying about my hair to what state our relationship would be in by the time we returned home.

We were following a river. I don't know what it was called, but it was beautiful. The stuff of calendar shots. The water was turquoise and flowing fast given the time of year. It looked pristine with the faded pinks, purples and blue watercolour splashes of the wild lupins having one last hurrah on its banks. I had a moment sitting there in the passenger seat where I pictured myself in Amish-style get-up perched in the buggy of a horse and trap exploring the frontier. Sam who was holding the reins masterfully and did not have a beard, nor was he wearing a straw hat, and a dark suit. I'm sorry, but that just wouldn't have done it for me.

He finally slowed, and the old Land Cruiser came to a stop in a clearing. This, he informed me proudly, was to be our campsite. I glanced around; there were trees. Well, thank God for that because a girl needs some privacy and, at five months into our relationship, there were some things I was not yet ready to share with him—things I'd never be ready to share for that matter.

I got into the swing of things after that. Sam's excitement was contagious, and he was out of the car now, so all that irritating steering wheel slapping business had stopped. The tent didn't take us long to pitch, and he was busy blowing the airbed up that we'd bought in the Boxing Day sales. He'd conceded that we needed it but only after I told him he could get some serious knee burn from doing it on a roll mat. This purchase had restored my faith that relationships *are* about compromise. So, while he got busy pumping, I unpacked the portable kitchen and began setting it up. I was playing at being married, setting up house *Little House on the Prairie* style and I was having fun.

It didn't take long before we were unloaded and had our outdoor home away from home organised. We stood back, Sam's arm slung across my shoulder, admiring it. He'd even hung a solar shower from the trees. I was glad because he was a bit whiffy after all that pumping and I hoped he wasn't going to take the whole caveman vibe too far. The shower was another compromise in our camping trip.

He suggested we gather sticks for our campfire because we planned on toasting marshmallows later, so we set about the task. First things first though, I retrieved the mosquito spray from the first aid kit and sprayed liberally. The sandflies were not going to have a party at my expense this time around, thank you very much.

We tested out the airbed, and it withstood some trampoline-style bouncing. My mood had swung by the time we sat down for Sam's perfectly cooked medium pork chops with applesauce and the cold potato salad Aunty Paula had pressed into my hands on our way out the door this morning. I was beginning to see what the appeal was in getting back to nature.

I ate heartily because it's true, you know, fresh air does make you hungry. So does sex before dinner. It was wonderful knowing we'd wake up next to each other in the morning and, if we fancied a spot of you know what before our beans on toast, there was no stopping us. We managed to squeeze in the aforementioned shagolympics whenever we were left home alone, which did not happen often enough. Given the paltry board we both paid, we couldn't very well moan about it and both his parents and Aunty Paula and Uncle Colin had a thing about respecting the home. No sex under their roof fell into this category. A bit hypocritical given I'm certain Aunty Paula and Uncle Colin are Sunday morning people but there you go, it is their house.

Sam and I've had to resort to desperate measures on occasion, i.e. the back of the Land Cruiser, or his work truck. This was fine in summer but had proven challenging over winter as the heater was on the blink in the van and the Land Cruiser was squished. So, a week of being able to do it on a bed whenever the mood took us was going to be wonderful!

'See,' he said to me later when the air was dusky, and the campfire was spluttering, 'this is the life.'

I speared a white marshmallow with my stick and stuck it in the embers, nodding my agreement. The sky was streaked with the last of the day's yellows and oranges and once they faded it would grow dark. I inspected the marshmallow, making sure it was properly burnt and crunchy on the outside before popping it in my mouth. It was sweet and gooey on the inside, and I sighed with contentment.

It was around eleven p.m. when things went pear-shaped.

I woke suddenly and was aware of three things. The first that my hip was numb and sore from digging into the ground, secondly I desperately needed a wee, and thirdly there was an almighty ruckus going on outside our tent. Now, I'd seen that Australian film *Wolf Creek*, and at that point, my insides turned icy. It was pitch-black, and we were in the middle of nowhere. Nobody knew where we were. I didn't even know where we were. I did know there was no cell phone coverage here because I'd checked. It would be seven days before anyone got worried about us, maybe longer because they'd all assume we were having so much fun, we'd decided to stay on longer. Plenty of time for a psychotic loner to do his worst.

'Sam,' I hissed.

'What?' His voice was groggy with sleep although how he could have slept with all the noise going on outside, not to mention the flat airbed, I don't know.

'There's somebody outside.' I'm not sure what I expected him to do but I didn't expect him to tell me to go back to sleep because it was probably just a possum. I wanted action, and I elbowed him, hard.

'What?' This time irritation penetrated the grogginess.

'Go and check.'

'Oh for fuck's sake, Ellie, go back to sleep. It will be a possum looking for food. We put everything away; there's nothing it can get into. It'll clear off in a minute.'

I flinched at his language but I wasn't backing down. 'But what if it's a person?'

'Don't be stupid.'

You can call me sensitive, but I didn't like that.

'Why would someone want to hang around outside our tent banging pot lids?'

Okay, good point but still he didn't need to use that tone with me. 'Well, I need to pee, and I'm not going out there while that's going on. The airbed's got a hole in it too.' I hoped we could get a refund and I can tell you, I was fast falling out of love with the great outdoors once more.

I heard him sigh and mutter something I didn't like the sound of either from the depths of his sleeping bag. I think he said, 'For fuck's sake, toughen up,' in fact I was ninety-nine per cent sure that's what he'd said. I itched to give him an extremely hard nudge with my foot for putting me in this situation and for not understanding I was scared. If we were in a room in a swish Wanaka holiday home, there would not be a possum having a party outside our bedroom door, and I'd be able to tiptoe down the hall to the loo without fear of marsupial attack.

'*Sam.*' My tone was insistent.

'Fuck, Ellie!'

I shrank back into my bag while he climbed out of his. I heard him feeling around in the dark for his torch before the tent zipper went up, and he clambered outside, closing it behind him. I sat in the dark with my breath held. The way he'd raised his voice at me had made me feel sick inside. I tried to remember if I'd ever read that possums were dangerous. I didn't think so, but you never knew: it could be rabid or something. I'm sure I'd read about rabid squirrels, and they were all part of the same tree-climbing family, weren't they? The banging and clattering had stopped, and after a second or two I could see the torchlight swishing about a little distance away. The next thing I heard running water and it took me a beat to register it was Sam. Lucky him! The sound made me more desperate to go, and I jiggled on my knees willing him to hurry up.

The torchlight got brighter, but I still jumped as the tent zipper went up once more. All the sounds were jarring and so much more exaggerated in the depth of night. He scrambled back inside and closed the tent down. 'It's cooled down out there; I'm freezing.' He shone the torch under his chin. It made him look like the psycho I'd been envisaging stalking around our campsite.

'Don't do that, it's creepy.' His angry irritation from earlier was gone but I wasn't happy. 'What was it?'

He kept the torch on while he slid back inside his sleeping bag and then shone it in my face. 'It was too big to be a possum; I'm guessing it was a wild pig.'

'Oh God really?'

'Yep, she wasn't happy either. I think she could smell the pork chops we had for dinner. My guess is she's in the bushes waiting.'

'Waiting for what?' My mind went into overdrive, as I envisaged the news headline. 'Young Freedom Campers Gored by Wild Pig, Police are Calling it the Revenge of the Pigs.' AND I NEEDED TO WEE.

Tears pricked at my eyes; I so did not want to be here. I heard a funny noise coming from the sleeping bag and realised Sam was laughing. 'What?' He didn't answer, but I could tell he was still laughing. 'Sam, it's not funny. I can't hold on much longer, and I am not going out there to get mauled by a pig.' I was seriously mad, but then again maybe he was hysterical because he was scared.

'You should have seen your face.'

'What do you mean?'

'When I said it was a wild pig.'

'It was a possum?'

'Yip a baby one, long gone now.'

'There's no pig?'

'Nope.' He sniggered.

'Well stuff you, Sam Anderson.' I threw my bag aside and snatched the torch off him before wrenching the zipper of the tent up.

'Oi go easy you'll break it. It was a joke. What is your fucking problem?'

He was my problem and, ignoring him, I dragged my sleeping bag out behind me before sticking my head back in through the flap. 'I'm going to sleep in the car, and you can take me home first thing in the morning.'

'It was a joke,' he bleated again.

'Not funny.' I didn't bother closing the tent as I headed for the Land Cruiser, and stuffing my sleeping bag onto the driver's seat, I slammed the door but not before hobbling knock-kneed a short distance away to relieve myself. Let me tell you it was a huge relief and there was no sign of pigs or possums as I made my way back to the car to begin the tricky manoeuvre of shuffling inside my bag.

The Sam that had sworn at me tonight was not the Sam I thought I knew. I remembered cowering in my room at the flat Mum and I lived in for a while hearing the 'f' word over and over as Steve flung it at her. It was used in anger and it was ugly. I'd made my mind up I'd never let anyone speak to me the way he had Mum.

I reckon a good fifteen minutes passed before I heard movement. Sam appeared a second later and climbed in beside me.

'Sorry, babe, it was childish of me.'

'It wasn't the pig thing,' I mumbled. The beating of my heart and adrenalin shots of anger had abated.

I could see his face in the moonlight. He didn't understand but then how could he, when I'd never told him. 'It was the way you spoke to me.'

I could see he was still having trouble understanding.

'Sam you *swore* at me.'

'I didn't mean it. I was just annoyed at being woken up and having to go out in the cold.' He shrugged not getting the big deal. 'But hey if it upset you then I'm sorry.'

I didn't like talking about back then but if we were going to move past this I needed to confide in him. 'I promised myself once I'd never stay with anyone who swore at me.'

'Ellie, it's just a word.'

I shook my head. 'No, it's more than that.'

We sat there in the Land Cruiser while I told him how hearing the 'f' word used in anger frightened me. It made me feel small, and powerless. I told him about Mum and Steve and what it was like to hide from the shouting and the other stuff. When I'd finished he pulled me into him.

'I promise, I will never use that word in front of you again.'

He kissed the top of my head. 'I won't hurt you, Ellie, and I won't let anyone else hurt you.'

'You can't promise me that.' My voice was muffled in his chest. 'We'll fight again. We're not perfect. No one is.'

'No, we're not, but we're close to it.'

Now was the moment when I could choose whether or not to trust him. I didn't pull away.

'Can I show you something? It's outside. I promise it's nothing scary.'

That would mean getting out of my warm, cosy bag but I was curious.

I traipsed after him to the edge of the river, a black pool, and wondered what he was up to. He pointed up, and I followed the line of his finger. The sky without the city lights was awash with stars, but the moon was hidden. It was like a vast twinkling carpet.

'Can you see the Southern Cross?'

I shook my head, and he took my hand, guiding it along as he said, 'Look there's the tip and see the two big stars with the little one in the middle next to it, and then go up there to the fifth one.'

'Oh yeah, I see it now.'

'Those five stars are between ten and twenty million years old.'

'Wow.'

We stood in silence, both absorbing the enormity of that.

'I love you, Ellie. I think I have from the moment I saw you shaking your booty when you slipped on that pie the day we met.'

I laughed at the memory. 'I love you too, Sam Anderson.' And we kissed.

The next morning once we'd finished making up, Sam had a nasty case of knee burn, thanks to the punctured airbed.

Chapter 43

That fight with Sam taught me something. It taught me just because you'd shouted at each other didn't mean someone always had to leave. That's something Mum's never understood. I heard her closing the front door. I hadn't moved other than to sit down and cuddle Pete to me since I'd flung all that pent-up rage at her. I'd sat at the table trying to steady my breathing, hearing the water running as she washed whatever it was in her hair out. I heard her tossing things into her case; I even heard it click shut. An Uber showed up not long after that and she'd walked out of the house without saying goodbye.

I was guessing she'd gone to Aunty Paula's and Uncle Colin's. I should have stopped her, but I was still too mad. I had no idea where that anger had boiled up from. It was like sitting on a roller coaster because from the moment I let the lid off it there was no stopping my vitriol. I was sick to death of the past being glossed over when it came to Mum.

My phone rang, and I put Pete down, unsure whether I'd answer but curious to see who it was. Connor. I picked up.

'Hey.' I reached down and stroked Pete who was brushing up against my legs now. He could sense I was still upset.

'Ellie, hi. You okay? You sound weird.'

My voice trembled. 'Yeah, I'm okay.'

'Sure?'

'Yep.'

'Do you want to catch up? I know I said I'd be around to make a start painting your room but I might leave it until tomorrow. The conditions are perfect for a surf out at Sumner. If you want we could go for a walk down the Esplanade later and have a cold beer at the Beach Bar?'

The beach was exactly where I wanted to be. Away from here. The sand, salt air, and the sea always helped clear my head. 'That sounds good. I'll see you there in an hour.'

'Cool.'

We hung up without him telling me where I'd find him. He didn't need to. I knew where he'd be because he and Sam always surfed at the same spot. It was where we'd sent Sam's ashes floating off on the breeze and out to sea.

It was only the Andersons and me and Connor who gathered at the beach to farewell the very last particles of my beautiful man, their son, brother and friend. There wasn't any posturing or speeches, what needed to be said had been said at the funeral. A week after the funeral we'd stood with our arms around each other, lost in our thoughts and saying goodbye in our own ways.

I'd closed my eyes and turned my face to the sun, conjuring his face. I traced the contours of it in my mind's eye, imprinting every detail. My throat grew tight as I pictured his eyes crinkling as he gave me that lopsided smile of his. 'I love you, Sam,' I said out loud. I liked to think he was there with us and that he heard me. Then I silently asked God to look after him. The breeze was brusque and it lifted and carried Sam out to sea. Far, far away.

~

My car slid neatly into a park that a Kombi van with surfboards on its roof had just exited. I could hear the waves crashing on the other side of the beach wall as I locked up and cautiously climbed the steps that took me over it and down to the sand. The water looked inviting with its foaming tips rolling up the beach, and I put my hand up to shade my eyes. There were maybe ten or so black bobbing figures further out and I knew Connor would be one of them, so I spread my towel out and kicked my shoes off before arranging myself on it. The sand was warm between my toes.

My sunscreen and hat were all in my tote bag and I dug them out. I plonked my hat on and slathered on the cream before stretching out. I'd lie there for a few minutes, I decided, until I was good and hot then I'd have a dip. I couldn't stop thinking about all the words I'd hurled at Mum, though, and so I got up, putting my hat and sunglasses back in my bag before sliding my shorts off. I limped past a dad building sandcastles with his toddler. They had ten in a row, and I hoped there wouldn't be tears when the waves rolled in and washed them away. There was a lifeguard in her bright red and yellow uniform checking out what was happening in the water through a pair of binoculars and I was careful to keep within the flagged area.

The water as it rushed over my feet made me gasp; it was so cold! Normally I'm an inch-by-inch girl when it comes to braving our Southern waters, but I threw caution to the wind and waded out until it was deep enough for me to dive under an incoming wave. It took a minute for my body to regulate to the temperature. I gritted my teeth until the stinging in my knee stopped, and then I let the water wash over me, enjoying the freshness. When I'd had enough, I headed back up the beach and lay down to dry off.

The plaster Joel had taped over my graze had held, and my mind was calmer now. I tried to summon up an image of Sam, droplets of water clinging to his hair, goofy grin, the way he used to look when he walked up the beach toward me, surfboard tucked under his arm. What would he tell me to do about Mum? I didn't ponder my question for long. I knew what he would say. He'd tell me that life was too short to hold on to grudges.

I closed my eyes, letting my body relax with his image into the warm sand. I didn't think I'd drifted off but as beads of cold water landed on me, my eyes flew open, and for a moment I didn't know where I was.

'Connor!' I yelped, 'I was just about dry.'

'Sorry.' He grinned, and I could see he wasn't as I pulled myself upright. My hair was probably drying in matted salty dreads, but I didn't care; well maybe I did a little because I used my fingers to untangle the worst of it. His surfboard was tucked under his arm, and he loomed over me in his wetsuit.

'What've you done to your knee?'

I didn't want to tell him the truth because after my argument with Mum the whole mountain biking thing with Joel felt tainted so I lied and told him I tripped over in the driveway.

'Looks sore but the salt water will help. I'm going to stick my board in the van and grab a quick shower. Will you be okay to walk down to the Beach Bar?'

'It's not far. I'll be fine.' I packed my stuff up, smiling as I saw two girls posed on their beach towels nudge one another, their gazes following Connor's lean, muscular form back up the beach to the changing rooms.

Ten minutes later I'd dragged a comb through my hair and gotten changed, and we began walking down the esplanade. People were crawling all over Cave Rock and kids were exploring the cavern below. I remembered paddling along the shoreline around the cave with Sam and how deceptive it can be because one minute I was all ethereal enjoying the wind blowing my hair back and the next I was up to my armpits in the water. I'd gone down a hole, and Sam said the look on my face was priceless, when he'd managed to stop laughing that was. I smiled at the memory as a group of teenage girls giggled their way past us. Their shorts were so high cut that I couldn't help but wonder why they'd bothered with them.

'So apart from a banged-up knee, how's life?'

'The truth?'

'Of course.'

'I thought I was doing okay but then, today I had a big blow-out with Mum.' I sighed. 'It felt like this other super angry being took over my body. I lost it, Connor.' I told him the horrible truth of it all and how I was still none the wiser. 'She was all cool, and calm, and that was worse than her yelling at me. What do you think I should do? Go around and apologise before she decides to get on a plane to go home or play hardball and see if she finally talks?'

He shrugged, his shoulders broad in his T-shirt. *He's got a nice body,* I thought idly and then chastised myself because he was my late boyfriend's best mate, and he'd been a good mate to me too. What was wrong with me? I seemed to have transformed into a walking hormone today. Or rather a hobbling one.

'I think you have a right to know what motivated her to leave and I can understand you wanting to know about your dad, but maybe she has good reason for not talking about him. I think if you push it with her, you'll have to face the fact that you might not like what she has to say. People change, Ellie; you know who she was ten years ago probably isn't the same person she is today. And, she has a point about the timing. You've been through a lot.'

'That doesn't help,' I said moodily eyeballing a wad of gum stuck to the pavement. 'And I don't think there'll ever be a right time.'

The Beach Bar was heaving, which wasn't surprising given the sun had taken on a mellow orange hue as the day began to merge with the evening. The cold beers we ordered went down a treat. We found a space where we could stand on the wooden decking and look out at the water. There was just enough elbow room to raise our drinks to our mouths.

'See that house up there, the two-storey white one with the big balcony jutting out.' Connor pointed toward a cluster of houses nestled into the side of the Port Hills behind us.

'Yeah, it's pretty flash,' I said, imagining what it would be like to sit on that balcony each evening watching the sunset. It would be a view I'd never get sick of—King of the Castle.

'That's where I'm working at the mo, but I should be able to finish your lounge tomorrow and get on with the rest of it later in the week.'

'That would be great. I really appreciate it, Connor.' It was good to move on from the topic of my mother too, and so I launched into a tale.

'Do you want to know what William-Peter got up to this week?'

'But of course, WP stories are always good for a laugh.'

'It's not funny really, but it's the seriousness on his face when he explains himself that gets me. I take him and Saffy-Rose to a playgroup once a week. There are organised activities, and they have a little vegetable garden the kids can help with as well as pet guinea pigs and a rabbit. The supervisor, Jenny, saw him heading outside with a big pair of scissors. When she asked him what he was going to do with them, he said, "I thought Percy the Rabbit looked like he could do with a bit of a trim."'

Connor snorted, and it caused the woman wedged in alongside him to jump; impressively she didn't spill a drop of her wine. 'So he has a future in hairdressing.'

'Quite possibly. It's not the first time he's done it. He had a go at their poor cat Sardine once too. I'll never let him near Pete.' A thought occurred to me. 'Imagine if he decided to lop Saffy-Rose's hair?' I decided that first thing Monday I would round up all the scissors in the Andersons' house and put them somewhere out of reach.

He grinned, then seeing my bottle was empty asked, 'Do you want another or are you hungry?'

'Starving. Shall we have a walk around and see what we fancy?'

'Good plan.'

We opted for Indian, and the conversation flowed, over our respective korma and butter chicken dishes. That's what I liked about Connor. It was never hard work being around him. It was like being with Sam, and if I closed my eyes, I could almost pretend I *was* sitting with Sam.

'How are the plans for the fun run going?' I knew Connor had put them on hold when Sam passed.

'I'm back on track. There's a bit involved. I'm looking at ten kilometres from New Brighton to Sumner in late October. It'll be a year since Sam passed and I thought it would be a good way to remember him.'

'It would be, but ten kilometres!'

'A walk in the park.'

'I'll be on my knees.'

'So you will do it?'

'I can't not; so will Gemma, though she says she's going to walk it.'

'Well if the council vetoes the idea, it won't happen anyway but I've got a good feeling. Once I get the okay from the powers that be, I've got to sort out the logistics of it—all the health and safety stuff will be mind-boggling. Then there's finding sponsors and promoting it.' He looked despondent as he took a swig of his beer.

'You'll sort it. It's a great idea, Connor, and I'll do what I can to help.' I rested my hand on top of his briefly.

We finished our meals, too full for afters, and split the bill. Dusk had settled in, and the esplanade had emptied as people made their way home or to the different bars and restaurants in the area. We were talking about the new *Oceans* film, and Connor was saying that we should check it out, and I don't know how it happened, but one minute we were walking back to where I'd left my car, and the next his arm had slid around my shoulder. It was like slow motion as he turned me so I was facing him before dipping his head so his lips could settle over mine. They were soft and warm, and as his tongue found mine, my arms reached up and wrapped themselves around his neck.

His body was hard against me, and it felt good to be held, and to feel that he wanted me. I was responding enthusiastically, I'll admit it. I wanted him; I wanted Sam, and then it hit me like one of the rogue waves that had pummelled me through the water that afternoon. This wasn't right. I pulled away from him. Connor's skin had a deep flush to it, and his eyes were still glazed. He looked at me, and as his eyes cleared, I saw that he couldn't believe what had just happened, either.

'Shit.' He rubbed the stubble on his chin that a split second ago had grazed my skin. 'Ellie, I'm sorry.'

'Forget it. Let's forget about it. Okay?' My voice sounded weird to my own ears, high-pitched and wired.

'Forget it, yeah.' Connor nodded eager to grasp the straw I was waving.

'Pretend it never happened. Are we good?'

He just stared at me.

'Look I've got to go.' I just wanted to get out of there, and even though I could hear him call after me as I strode the short distance to my car, ignoring the pain in my knee, I didn't turn back. As I turned the key in the ignition, I caught sight of him in the rear-view mirror. His shoulders were hunched, and his hands shoved in his pockets as he walked away. He looked cowed, and all I could think was that in the space of one short day I had fallen out with my mother and just snogged the love of my life's best mate. It was more than a peed-in-my-bowl-of-soup kind of day. I'm sorry, but it had been a total somebody-crapped-in-my-soup day.

Chapter 44

♥

I tossed and turned that night and into the small hours. It didn't help that Pete was snoring down the bottom of the bed, and I finally gave up on getting any more sleep when the birds began to chatter. It was pointless just lying there mulling over yesterday because no matter how many times I went over it all, it didn't get any better.

I threw back the bedcovers, wincing as I swung my legs over the side of the mattress and got up because my knee was sorer today than it was yesterday. I wrapped myself in my dressing gown and ventured out of my bedroom only to be walloped by the silence of an empty house. Silence until, Pete realising I'd gotten up, jumped down from the bed, meowed loudly and ran the gauntlet to the kitchen. He was surprisingly fast for a cat with three legs.

I fed him and while he scoffed his food down I found myself mooching about the empty spaces of my home, a cup of coffee in my hand until, eventually, I wound up standing in the middle of the living room. The floor was level now, the hole in the middle of it long gone. The ceiling and walls are smooth too thanks to the re-gibbing and plastering, and the faint whiff of enamel from the fresh paint Connor applied on Friday was still hanging in the air. Oh God, I don't even want to think about Connor.

At some point today, I was going to have to move the bits and pieces that had been temporarily stored in the kitchen while the work was being done in here back. The food in the pantry would have to be put in boxes, as would all my cutlery and dishes. The table would have to go too because I wanted to give the crew a clear workspace tomorrow. Mum would have helped me with it if she'd been here. Doing it on my own was going to be a gargantuan task. The very thought of what I had to do today made me want to go back to bed and pull the covers over my head. I didn't have the energy.

I wished I could fix my life as easily as Joel and his team were fixing my house. Or, wave a paintbrush like Connor did and for everything to be fresh and new once more. I could feel the quicksand trying to suck me back down again, but I wouldn't let it. So, I steered myself toward the bathroom knowing a hot shower would help. As I stood under the jets letting the water pummel my shoulders I sighed all the way from my toes. There was no anger left inside me now, just a great weariness.

For the first time since I was that little girl who used to dance with wild abandon alongside Mum to those old eighties hits of Madonna's, we'd connected again. It had been a good feeling, but it was tempered by my weariness, my waiting for the inevitable. I could see now that I'd orchestrated it so she left because it was easier than waiting around for her to do it anyway.

As for Connor and that kiss, my face burned at the thought of it but I knew why we'd stepped over that line. We were two lonely, sad people, which didn't make either of us very appealing candidates for Elite Singles, or any other dating websites, but it also didn't mean we were meant to be together. It had only happened because we miss Sam. I couldn't face calling him, not yet. One thing at a time. I would get in touch, though, because I wasn't going to lose him as a friend. He was too precious for that.

I wrote a mental list of everything I needed to fix in my life as I stood under the water, watching it pool at my feet before it gurgled down the drain. Finally I turned the shower off and stepping out of it, decided I'd take action by starting at the top of my list: fixing it with Mum.

I made myself presentable and saw from the time I wouldn't be waking anyone up if I bowled around to Uncle Colin's and Aunty Paula's. 'Bye, bye, Pete.' His fur was soft beneath my fingers and he didn't look up as I gave him a quick pet, too busy washing himself. Outside was balmy and still, but glancing at the arch of heavy cloud sitting in an otherwise blue sky I could see the nor'wester was going to start gusting soon. It would send the handful of yellow-lidded recycling wheelie bins yet to be brought back up their respective driveways skidding about. I got in my car and reversed out on to the street, not seeing any signs of life apart from a scraggy dog snuffling around the gutters as I drove off.

Uncle Colin's car wasn't up the drive when I pulled up; it was Sunday, which meant he'd probably gone to play a round of golf. I knocked at the door a couple of times, but nobody answered, so I let myself in with my key, calling out hello as I stepped inside. I'd leave a note to say I'd popped in if no one was home.

'Out here, Ellie.'

Aunty Paula was sitting in the sunshine with the paper spread out on the table in front of her, a cup of coffee in her hand. She was still in her dressing gown I noticed as I wandered out onto the deck. There was no sign of Mum.

'Morning.' I sat down across from her and tilted my face upwards. 'Gosh, that sun's good.'

'It's lovely. I thought I'd make the most of it before the wind gets up. You're out and about early. There's a pot of coffee on the stove if you want a cup.'

I liked Aunty Paula's home-brewed coffee, and I could smell the familiar Irish coffee aroma mingling with the salty scent of crispy bacon, but I was too uptight for caffeine. 'No, I'm okay thanks. So, how does it feel to be famous?'

'That daughter of mine is being inundated with high-end makeup, hair products and clothes since the video aired. She's even been offered a complimentary full back tattoo.'

My eyes must have widened.

'She declined. I swear though, Ellie, she has her own personal courier van on permanent standby and what does she give me?'

'What?'

'A pair of Spanx that's what.'

Despite the gravity of the reason behind my visit my mouth curved—that was so Gemma.

'You may well smirk, but I told her I wouldn't be starring in any more of her little videos unless she makes it worth my while. There's no show without Punch, I said.'

I had no idea what that meant, but I nodded agreement. 'Fair enough too. Is Mum still in bed?' I looked around as though expecting her to appear in her dressing gown like Aunty Paula.

'Colin took Nicky to the airport before heading to golf.' Aunty Paula glanced at her phone next to the paper. 'She'll be halfway home by now.'

'She's gone?'

'She didn't tell you?'

'No. We had words.'

'She said as much, but I assumed she'd told you she was leaving.' She frowned. 'I think she felt you needed to give each other a bit of space, that it was too much her landing on you. Reading between the lines, I think George was missing her too. I don't think he copes well on his own.'

'So, she's done what she always does and has taken off again when the going gets a little tough.'

'Ellie, that smacked-arse expression doesn't suit you.'

I was a little taken aback and, in my opinion, perfectly entitled to a smacked-arse expression given I'd just been told my mother had jumped ship once more.

'It's not all about you; you know, sweetheart.'

I'm beginning to regret having called around now. 'What do you mean?' I don't get that, who else is it about? Mum was supposed to be here to support me, and at the first little upset, she takes off again. Okay, yes I was horrible, really horrible.

'Nicky was trying and you lashed out.'

I opened my mouth, but Aunty Paula's hand went up to silence me, before I could say a word.

'You're hurting, and you're angry. It's part of the grief process. We all understand that, but you can't treat people the way you treated your mum, Ellie. You'll push those who care about you away if you're not careful.'

I didn't like being told off, and I felt a pang of sympathy for poor old William-Peter who's forever getting in trouble and having to take his punishment. I sat there picking at a wood splinter in the timber top of the table and my eyes began to sting. Self-pity washed over me because everything was going wrong; I was losing everybody.

Aunty Paula's tone softened. 'Ellie, it's important your mum doesn't let herself get stressed—you of all people know that. Things slide out of control when she gets wound up and she's been doing so well, taking her medication, not drinking. She's really been looking after herself and she's in a good place with George. You should be proud of her.'

I did know Mum couldn't afford to get stressed. It's another thing I struggled with because sometimes I'd wanted a mum I could share things with. A mum who could shoulder the load, but I'd always had to watch what I said and did knowing if I upset her I could send her spiralling out of control.

Mum's bipolar. I haven't mentioned this before because it's something I don't like acknowledging. It makes me think back on the times I really hated for her being different. I hated myself more for feeling like that though.

The memories rained down. Mum refusing to get out of bed, and me making my own breakfast before seeing myself off to the new entrants at school. The knot in my tummy during the day over what I'd find when I got home. Would Mum be the happy, exuberant one, the Mum who took good care of me, or the sad, tired one who wouldn't come out from under her blankets? Of wanting so badly to be like the other kids and to bring a friend home to play after school but not daring too because my mum was different from the other mums.

As if someone had pushed skip on a Netflix show the scenes long buried danced past one another, stopping on another random image. Mum arriving at school when I was nine. I was eating my lunch, a Marmite sandwich I'd slapped together myself, and sitting with my friend Alysa on the wooden bench. We had our backs pressed against the brick wall that divided the classroom bays. I'd been eyeing her ham and salad roll; she always had the nicest lunches, but I had nothing to offer for a swap. That was when Mum appeared.

I think she thought she was a wood nymph as she was waving a long scarf behind her, skipping and dancing her way across the asphalt to where we were sitting.

'Isn't that your mum?' Alysa whispered her eyes wide at the sight of her, so young and pretty as she beamed over at me.

'Ellie,' she called flicking the scarf in my direction. 'I've come to break you out. We're going to have a girls' afternoon shopping.'

'Wow! It's times-tables again after lunch. You're so lucky,' Alysa mumbled spraying crumbs. 'I wish my mum would do something cool like that.'

I didn't feel lucky. I felt embarrassed, especially when the teacher on playground duty came and escorted Mum to the office. Alysa knew something wasn't right then, and she ate the rest of her roll in silence, but I remember her offering me her chocolate chip muffin because she felt sorry for me. I'd coveted her mother's home baking for so long that I greedily stuffed it down, but it tasted like cardboard and just made me feel sicker. The lunch bell had gone, and we were trailing back to class when I saw Nan's car pull in the main gates. She'd come to take Mum home.

Aunty Paula's heavy sigh intruded on the past as she rested her hand over the top mine.

'You didn't have it easy, Ellie, I know that, but you can't live in the past, not if you're going to have any sort of future.'

I sniffed and my voice was small. 'I wanted her and me to be okay this time, Aunty Paula. But I've stuffed it all up.' My lip was trembling. 'What should I do?

'Have you ever tried telling her you love her? Because that could be a good place to start.'

I looked across the table at her and felt ashamed. Where Mum's concerned I've always been on the attack. I have never cut her any slack.

Sam tried to get me to but I dug my heels in. I refused to open myself up to a relationship with her. My feelings for Mum were messy and tangled, but if I were to unknot them, I knew that I'd find love at their core. I'd just never been able to say the words out loud.

'Ellie, I think you should go the grief group session I gave you the card for. Sweetheart, you seem to be hurtling along a bad path.'

She was right and that was how I felt—like I was one of those base jumpers about to hit the ground. I remembered what Joel told me, and I nodded.

'Are you nodding yes, you'll go?'

I nodded again.

'Good girl, that's a step forward. Come here.'

We hugged each other hard.

'I love you, Aunty Paula,' I said, in case I hadn't told her that lately, either.

'I love you too, Ellie.'

Chapter 45

♥

I headed straight down to the mall and walked as fast as my sore knee would let me into the Flight Centre. The two staff on duty were otherwise engaged with customers, and I sat down near the wall of brochures, picking at a jagged bit of skin by my thumbnail. I didn't want time to sit here dwelling on what I was planning to do. I wanted to throw caution to the wind and just do it. So, I sent hurry-up vibes over to the left where a couple was bent over a cruise brochure while Jet (I swear I didn't make that up, it was on his name badge) told them that particular cruise line was extremely good value. To the right, sat a man collecting tickets to the Philippines, odds were on him being finished first, so I tossed the vibes in his direction instead.

It worked, and he vacated the seat in front of—I squinted at her name badge—Amy, and my word she was heavy-handed with the contouring stick. Still, at least I could take her seriously so long as I looked at her eyes and not her carefully highlighted nose and cheeks. I took my place opposite her and said, 'Hi I'd like to book a flight to the Gold Coast please.'

Clutching my red ticket wallet ten minutes later, I battled my way through the crowded mall and drove straight around to Gemma's. I was too fizzy to be by myself, and even though it meant I'd probably be up until midnight, the packing and shifting would have to wait until later because I wanted to run my plan by her.

Her door was unlocked, so I poked my head inside and called out a hello.

'I'm in the living room, Ellie, come in.'

I found her standing in her knickers and bra with a puddle of dresses at her feet, clothes of all description strewn across every surface in the room. I felt as though I'd stepped into an illustration for that Hans Christian Andersen tale, *The Emperor's New Clothes*.

'Perfect timing. I've got to pick one of these—' she gestured around the room '—to wear for my post tonight and I can't decide.'

Her lips, I was pleased to see, while definitely plumper were now in proportion with her face, and her eyebrows while still too dark in my opinion at least didn't look cartoonish anymore. 'Where did all this stuff come from?' I stared open-mouthed around me at the colourful array of designer gear.

'Since I posted that video of Mum getting her tattoo done I've been inundated. All these newbie designers, from all around the country wanting me to put their label out there—they want Mum to model, too. I haven't said anything to her about that yet, though, because she's been a total pain in the bum demanding freebies—fame's gone to her head. Here, try this on.' She picked up a black cocktail dress and tossed it at me. It was the kind of thing I'd look longingly at on occasion but never be able to justify the cost. Nor, would I know where to wear it. I was tempted to see if it fit but I was getting side-tracked. Gemma picked up a midnight blue sheath and began sliding into it.

'Did you know Mum's gone back to the Gold Coast?'

I could see by the look on her face that the jungle drums had yet to begin to beat and so zipping her in, I filled her in on our fight and the conversation I'd just had with Aunty Paula.

Gemma slid her feet into a pair of nude heels. 'Is bipolar hereditary?'

'Gemma!'

'Well, you've had more mood swings than Mum when she started with the menopause. And mental illnesses can be, you know. It's nothing to be ashamed of.'

'I'm not bipolar, Gemma; I've been grieving.'

She didn't look convinced. 'I guess.'

'Anyway, I didn't come here for a psychiatric evaluation. I came to tell you I'm going to the Gold Coast on Tuesday. I want to fix things with Mum.'

'Really? Cool. Do you want me to come, because look—' She held up a red one-piece swimsuit.

'Thanks but I need to do this on my own. Besides, I wondered whether you'd keep an eye on Pete for me. He gets fed twice a day and he'd need a bit of fuss, too. And, that is definitely the dress you should wear.'

'You think?'

'I think.'

'And, yeah, I'll feed the cat.'

'Pete.'

She rolled her eyes. 'What kind of a name for a cat is that?'

'The one he was given and it suits him.'

I helped her do her hair, and while I fiddled around with the straighteners, I gave her the rest of the low-down from the last two days.

'You missed a bit there.'

I picked up the rogue wave and jammed it between the hot plates.

'Okay so in brief, you went on a sort of date mountain biking with a gorgeous builder; you fell off your bike and cried like a baby. Right?'

I nodded.

'After that, you came home and had a massive row with your mum, which you followed up by having a snog fest with Sam's best mate. You've outdone yourself, girl.'

I nodded again; I wasn't proud of myself.

'Your knee's a mess, by the way. I bet that hurt, and if it makes you feel any better, I'd have cried, too.'

'It did, but it's not as much of a mess as I feel in here though.' I tap the side of my head.

'What was I saying before?'

'Gemma!'

'Sorry. Listen, when you get back from Aussie do you want me to go with you to this grief group thingy?'

'No, but thanks.' I managed a smile, and our eyes met in the mirror. It was moments like this that I was very glad I had Gemma in my life, even if she did seem to think I was mentally unstable. I was also aware that I'd talked solidly about myself for the last fifteen minutes and as I unplugged the straighteners I asked her how things were going with Regan. 'Any hot dates with the Stud Muffin on the horizon?'

She flicked her hair back off her shoulders and leaned into the mirror to inspect her makeup, flicking an eyelash from her cheek. 'No and I don't get it, Ellie. I've been pulling out all the stops and nada. I even offered to give him a free ticket to Pink. Don't suppose you want to go, do you? I got sent two. I think the promoters were hoping I'd take Mum but it'd be wasted on her.'

I try not to bite her hand off, and I'm grateful. I know my music taste with my penchant for Madonna and John Denver could be deemed eclectic, but Aunty Paula has truly appalling taste in music. 'I'd love to.'

'Ellie?'

'Uh-huh?' I was inspecting her lipstick. It was a brand I didn't recognise, but I loved the colour, and I wondered a little enviously if it was yet another freebie.

'Do you think maybe he just doesn't fancy me?'

That made me look up, and beneath the shimmer and gloss on her face she was vulnerable. This was the side of Gemma Sam had never seen. He'd never really got that beneath her bossy blustering, she was hiding a mass of insecurities. In her expression I caught a glimpse of my idol, my pretty older cousin when her ten-year-old self asked me if I knew why some of the girls at school didn't like her. Horrible little cows they were, jealous the way young girls get when they group together sometimes, and I told her so. 'I think he's playing hard to get that's all,' I told her now.

She stood up and smoothed the ripples of blue clinging to her before striking a pose. 'I'm thinking the Kylie Jenner for this outfit. What do you think?' She pulled the wide-eyed, pouty face and I nodded, pleased to see the Gemma I knew and loved was back with me.

I needed to make tracks. I had to clear out the kitchen for the team to get started in the morning and I told Gemma this.

She picked up her phone, in readiness for her photoshoot. 'You spoken to Klepto Caro yet?'

With everything else that had been going on, Caro had fallen to the bottom of my 'to-do' list. 'No, not yet.'

'It won't end well, if you don't, Ellie, I'm telling you.'

I drove home with my head full of 'what if' scenarios where my boss was concerned, and hoped I didn't look as guilty as I felt when I pulled up at the lights and saw a police car in the lane next to me.

Chapter 46

♥

Monday morning rolled around like it always does and my aching knee meant I bypassed the gym on my way to the Richards'. Caro, dressed in a fetching moss-green trouser-suit greeted me at the door with a box of Lego in one hand, car keys in the other.

'Nice weekend?'

I opened my mouth, but she'd already moved on.

'I ordered it online for Saffy-Rose.' She shoved the box into my hands. 'It's the Heartlake City Playground she's been after, you know the Lego Friends. Have fun. I'm off to Helen Nottage's Ladies who Paint Art Auction. She's fundraising for Hospice.' She sighed. 'It's a fantastic charity, but I seem to spend my life raising money for other people's causes and accumulating pieces of amateur art I don't want. Gotta go, I'm going to be late as it is. Bye.'

I had planned to tell her about my short-notice trip to the Gold Coast tomorrow, but she was rushing and was already halfway to her wagon jabbing at the remote to unlock it. I'd have to sit on it now until she got back.

So while Caro contributed to a worthy cause I spent an industrious morning with her children constructing a tree-house with a climbing wall no less, and a slide. The Dappledawn rabbit-children would love it, I thought to myself wondering if I should bring them over for Saffy-Rose to meet. She would adore them. I side-eyed William-Peter and decided they were probably best left right where they were. Saffy-Rose had put him in charge of the merry-go-round, swings, and seesaw and there was only one moment of high drama when he bounced Mia, the mini-doll figure too high on the seesaw. I defused the situation by breaking for morning tea. That I'd managed to sneak in a packet of double chocolate chip cookies in last week's shop helped, too.

By the time Caro arrived home, the twins were on a nice sugar high, and we'd nearly finished our task. I had also just knelt on Pippa, the Lego dog, and was rolling around holding my knee to my chest. Honestly, Lego should come with a warning on the box that says, 'Always wear protective clothing and footwear when assembling.'

'What's the matter with you?' she asked popping her head around the playroom door.

'I just kneeled on Pippa,' I muttered. 'And this was my good leg.'

'But at least you found her for me,' Saffy-Rose piped up. 'That was good, Ellie.'

'Who's Pippa?'

'The dog.' I pointed to where William was pretending to scoop up a poop.

'That's why I refuse to have Lego in any other room in the house, bar the playroom. Would a green tea help, Ellie? I'm having one.'

No, it wouldn't actually and yes, I know I should've been honest that first time she offered me the noxious brew but Caro and I seemed to have settled into this sort of chatty Japanese tea drinking ritual most mornings. The twins would be alright playing for a bit, so I hobbled through to the kitchen and perched up at the breakfast bar while Caro set about making the tea.

As she put a dainty teacup in front of me, I noticed her nails were a pretty shade of polished apricot and I heard Gemma's voice whispering, 'Say something,' in my ear. I played out a scenario whereby Helen Nottage and her cronies had to run a charity art auction to raise funds to bail Caro out of jail. There was nothing for it. I liked Caro, and this last while we'd been getting to know one another. Our relationship, despite her pretensions, was subtly moving toward being one of friendship. If she were to get caught in the act shoplifting she'd be humiliated, and I couldn't let that happen to a friend, I decided.

'Caro, a little while ago Saffy-Rose told me something that worried me a little.'

'Oh yes.'

'Yes. It's a little awkward.'

She looked bemused over the gold rim of her cup. 'Just say it, Ellie, whatever it is.'

My nails were digging into my palms. 'Okay well, she told me when I was off work after Sam passed she saw you putting things in your pocket at the chemist. Things you didn't pay for. Nail polish, makeup sort of things.'

Caro's face paled, and for the first time it dawned on me she had freckles beneath that perfect veneer and that she might not be a natural blonde. The twins' colouring, after all, came from somewhere.

'What are you getting at, Ellie?' The teacup banged down in the saucer, and the noise made me wince. I kept my eyes on the puddle of yellowy green water pooling in it.

'I'm not sure but I'd hate for you to get in trouble, Caro, and I just thought that if something was wrong, maybe you could talk to me.'

She made a noise, a snort I think; whatever it was it wasn't a nice sound. 'Okay let me get this straight, are you implying that I shoplift?'

I explained about the box of cosmetics Saffy-Rose showed me under her mother's bed and Caro reared up like an avenging angel.

'I think, Ellie, it would be a good idea if you went home for the day.' Her voice seemed to echo and bounce off the white-tiled walls around us, and I hoped it hadn't carried through to the playroom.

My face felt like someone was holding a flame near it and I sat glued to the stool.

'I know you've had a hard time this year, but accusing me of stealing? Really? I think you need a break and for God's sake, use the time off to get help. I think it'd be best if you had the rest of the week off. Give us both a bit of breathing space to assess how we want to move forward with your working here. The twins aren't far off school now.'

Oh my God, I put my hands to my cheeks, which felt like they were on fire now. Was she sacking me? To be honest, I wasn't sure what she was saying, but the fact she wanted me to leave was written loud and clear on her face.

~

I drove a little way down the street, but I was shaking, and I couldn't concentrate, so I pulled over not caring that I was stopped on yellow lines. My heart was racing with what I supposed was adrenalin brought on by what Caro had just snarled at me. I realised that I'd never told her I needed time off to go and see my mum and I also realised that I didn't need to ask now because she'd just given me an indefinite leave of absence. I decided to ring Gemma; I needed to tell someone what had happened and given it was technically her big idea that I open my mouth she was it.

'I think Caro just sacked me.'

'Bloody hell.'

Her voice sounded thick as though she was speaking through a hanky or something. I hoped she hadn't had another date with the lip-filler lady.

'Gemma?'

'Look, Ellie, I'm sorry, but it's not a good time, can I call you back?'

'Sure but did you hear what I just said?' The phone had gone dead, and I stared at it in disbelief. Today was taking on a surreal quality, what with Caro and now Gemma, giving me the bum's rush after I'd just told her I thought I'd been sacked.

I didn't want to stay where I was because the way the day was panning out, I'd probably get a ticket for unlawful parking, so I turned the key and crawled home.

Jonno and Mikey were carting what looked like my new pantry door into the house when I pulled up the driveway. I gave them a half-hearted wave. I'd forgotten all about my new kitchen thanks to this morning's debacle. Oh God, another thought occurred to me, if I had no job how would I make my repayments to Uncle Colin and Aunty Paula?

I had that horrid sick feeling in my stomach; adrenalin had made way for nervous tension. I got out of the car and locked up, before heading inside to be greeted by the sounds of banging, hammering and someone singing loudly and off-key along to the Eagles' 'Hotel California'. I was going to have hole up in my bedroom, the furthermost room from the kitchen, if I wanted any peace.

'Hey, Mikey said you were home. I can't hear a bloody thing in there.' Joel appeared in the hall, mobile in hand. He had a pencil tucked behind his ear, a tool belt slung around his waist and baggy shorts. His skin was tanned against the black T-shirt he was wearing, and I could see the tattoo he'd told me about peeking out from under the sleeve. It was etched across his right bicep, and I tried not to stare. 'Jonno thinks he can sing. You better hope you're not around if "Bohemian Rhapsody" ever comes on.'

I dug deep and raised a smile. 'How's it going?'

'So far so good. The bench top is in, and the boys are hanging the new joinery.'

'Oh great.' My voice sounded flat to my own ears, and I tried to look enthusiastic. 'I'll take a peek.'

'How's that knee doing?'

I was instantly reminded of my explosion of tears. 'It's on the mend thanks and, Joel, about Saturday I'm—'

'It's cool.'

If it was cool why did we both look embarrassed? I wondered as I nodded.

'I've got a few calls to make.' He held up his phone, and I stepped aside to let him pass me by. He smelt of sweat and antiperspirant, gritty real smells, and I wanted to grab hold of him and bury my head in his chest, but of course I didn't.

The kitchen was a hive of activity. Jeff, Uncle Colin's mate who helped me move in, was wiring in my oven, and he waved over. Jonno mercifully didn't seem to know the words to the old Genesis song that was now blaring. He and Mikey looked up from where they were affixing the pantry door and grinned. Pete, unruffled by all the noise and commotion, was curled up in the sunshine on his bed, sound asleep.

'She's coming together nicely,' Mikey yelled over the top of the music.

'It looks amazing, guys. Thank you. You're doing an awesome job.'

I stood there for a moment trying to absorb it all. Nan would find her old domain unrecognisable, but I think she'd approve. The thought of her looking down on what was going on and saying, 'Goodo,' her catchphrase when she liked something, cheered me a tiny bit. The bench top looked so polished and sleek I decided I might never cook in my kitchen again. And all the extra cupboard space the new joinery had afforded would leave no room for excuses when it came to unpacking the box of cookbooks I'd shoved out in the shed. It was all so shiny and fabulous, and I wished Mum was still here to see it. I WISHED I still had a job to pay for it all.

I had a chat with Jeff and then left them to it, disappearing into the sanctuary of my pink palace. I needed to be proactive, and the drapes for the living room still need hemming. It was as good a task as any to tackle. I focussed my mind on that, not wanting to make any mistakes because the fabric was far too pricey for that. I listened to the familiar thrumming of the machine and my mood found flat ground. I even managed to ignore the odd expletive and burst of song I could hear coming from the kitchen.

The sewing calmed me and by the time my beautiful, shimmery curtains were finished, the afternoon was all but gone. I got up stretching and hauled the first of the four drapes through to the lounge. I picked my way around the boxes of stuff I'd carted through yesterday and laid them down on the couch. Straightening I looked out the window. It was a pretty average view so far as backyard outlooks go and certainly not on a par with the Richards' sumptuous—*don't go there, Ellie*—but Sam's crab apple tree caught my eye. Its clusters of tiny red fruit dangled, the flashes of colour amongst the foliage teasing the birds. Its roots were now firmly entrenched in the soil, and it no longer looked spindly and vulnerable. Unlike me, I felt the pin get pulled, and the grenade get lobbed, and I began to cry.

Chapter 47

I'd hidden away in my room until I heard the last of the tradesmen leave for the day and then I'd begun the practical task of packing. 'I'm carry-on baggage only so I can't take you with me,' I said to the Dappledawns who were all lined up outside their cottage eyeing me accusingly. 'Or you.' I felt a stab of guilt looking at Pete, his yellow eyes huge as he sat in the doorway watching me. 'I'm not abandoning you. Aunty Gemma will look after you, and I'll be back in no time. I promise.' How many pairs of knickers should I take? I pondered a second or two settling for five to be on the safe side. The weather was going to be scorching, so I was opting for loose and light in the way of clothes. I'd just begun tossing things in when my phone rang. It was Gemma.

'Hey sorry about today. Where are you?'

'I'm at home packing. I'm flying to the Gold Coast tomorrow remember?'

'I might join you,' she muttered. 'Can I come around?'

'Well, you can't come with me because you promised to look after Pete.' I was too curious as to what was going on with her to be miffed over the brush-off I'd received earlier. 'And yes come over. Have you eaten?' It was just after six, so chances were she hadn't.

'No, you?'

I realised I hadn't since breakfast. 'No and the kitchen went in today. I can't use the oven until I've heated it on low for a few hours. That's what the manual says anyway. Did you want to pick up something?'

'Thai?' Pad Thai and green chicken curry were our go-to dish from our local Thai whenever neither of us had felt like cooking.

'Great.' I didn't know how much of an appetite I'd have but if anything was going to inspire me to eat it was Pad Thai from the Exotic Orchid. 'See you soon.'

I was about to zip up my bag when I remembered my hair straighteners were in the bathroom. All that sunshine and humidity didn't bode well for good hair, with or without them, but the odds were better with. I put them on the top and squished the lid on my wheelie case down before doing it up. Should I text Mum and let her know I was coming? I sat down on my bed and chewed my thumbnail. She might tell me not to come. No, I decided, I'd just turn up and hope for the best. Whatever reception I got tomorrow I'd have to deal with it.

I was giving the kitchen floor a vacuum, picking up the wood-shavings and other telltale signs that the builders had been in when Gemma pulled up the drive. I opened the front door for her, unsure of what to expect, but she looked like she always does. Maybe a little paler than usual, but then again, I could have been imagining that. As promised in one hand she had a bottle of wine and in the other a plastic bag from which spicy, yummy smells were emanating and despite my lack of appetite, my mouth watered.

'Wow, they've done a great job. Is it all finished?' Gemma put the wine and food down on the table that Jonno and Mikey had carried back in before they left. It was thoughtful of them. It had been a mission dragging it out on Sunday by myself with my poor, sore knee and I was grateful.

I could tell by the flatness in her tone and the set of her shoulders as she looked around that just like me when I arrived home earlier, her heart wasn't exactly in it. 'Not quite, they're putting the shelves in tomorrow, and the dishwasher's got to go in too.' I'd sorely missed having a dishwasher. I dug two wineglasses out of one of the boxes stacked in the laundry, located some plates and hunted down some forks.

'Eat first, talk later?'

'Drink first.' She opened the wine and poured two glasses, taking a gulp from hers. 'Can you put that cat somewhere else? He's making me nervous sitting there staring at me like that.'

'It's Pete and he can smell the food. I'll give him a few biscuits so he doesn't feel left out.'

I saw to Pete and while she swigged her wine I served up our meal. So much for having no appetite, I thought helping myself to another heaping of the noodle dish. I was going to use my finger to scrape up the remaining sauce I could see in Gemma's green curry container, waste not want not, but then I remembered the black bean sauce couple all those years ago at Nummy's and refrained.

Gemma was done, and her fork rested on her plate. She knocked back what was left in her glass and then sat back in her chair. 'It's Regan.'

All this performance over the Stud Muffin? 'Did you ask him out and he turned you down?' I supposed that would be pretty embarrassing, but still, there were worse things in life, I mean come on.

'Not exactly no.'

'What then?'

'You know the "Me Too" movement?'

'Yeah of course who doesn't?' An image of gropey, fat men in power suits sprang to mind, and I shuddered. Then, I thought about what she'd said. 'Oh God, Gem, did Regan behave inappropriately at work?' My poor cousin had been sexually harassed by that gym-buffed sleaze bag. Hang on a second thought I thought frowning, I thought she was interested in him, and any attention he sent her way would be suctioned up like the woodchips I'd just vacuumed.

'No not Regan. Apparently I did.'

I shook my head; I must have misheard. 'What do you mean?'

'I mean Regan has gone to head office and accused me of harassment.'

'I don't understand.' It didn't make sense.

'He's laid an official complaint, which head office is duty-bound to look in to. I've been in a Skype meeting with the CEO and Christine Simich, their legal counsel, all afternoon. That's why I cut you off when you called. It's a nightmare, Ellie.' Her voice was laced with hysteria.

I zoomed back over a conversation we'd had where she told me she'd peeked at Regan's file. It hadn't sat well with me at the time but harassment? It seemed like a big jump to get to that and how would he have found out what she'd done anyway? 'What were his grounds?'

'He told them that I showed up at the gym and the pub knowing he'd be there on numerous occasions.'

'But you only went to the gym once.' And look how that went.

'Ellie, the wind will change, and you'll be stuck looking like a bewildered Spice Girl forever.'

I had no idea where she got that from; I thought with a glance down at my Union Jack T-shirt. 'Sorry but I'm struggling with this, Gemma.'

'I did go to The Terrace Club a few times because I knew he'd be there.'

I remembered seeing him there now the night I christened that poor man's shoes.

'I mean that's what you do isn't when you think someone's hot. You show up where you know they'll be? How else does anyone ever get together? When did the lines get so blurred?'

'Did you say that to the head office people?'

'No. I said it was a coincidence. He didn't stop there though, Ellie. He told them that I made inappropriate comments about the fit of his jeans in front of colleagues.'

'And did you?'

'I might have, once—remember the day you moved in here?'

I do recall her calling me from the pub to ask what the definition of a cougar was and I nodded. 'But you know, Gemma, if the shoe was on the other—'

'Ellie! You're supposed to be on my side.'

'Sorry.'

Her voice dropped to a mumble, and I had to strain to follow what she was saying. 'And I might have brushed my breasts across his chest when he came out of the kitchen.'

'Gemma!'

'What! Most men would bloody well love it.'

I don't know what to say. She has a point, but then again I couldn't help thinking we couldn't have one rule for us another for them even if Men were from Mars and Women from Venus.

'Did he know about you sneaking a peek at his file?'

'No thank God.'

'Well, that's something.'

She nodded, and her face was a picture of misery.

'What was the outcome?'

'I'm to attend a restorative justice session with Regan, and they're sending me to a psychologist to talk about—' she made quotation marks with her fingers '—*my issues* and, I'm on probation. I am totally and utterly humiliated.'

'And contrite? I mean can you see that you were in the wrong?' I needed to be clear on this because my cousin had been rubbing her breasts on work colleagues for goodness' sake.

'I guess. I still think he overreacted though.'

'He obviously felt strongly about it.'

'Dickhead,' she muttered.

I thought she might be missing the point.

My imminent grief counselling, which I'd go to when I got back from Australia, didn't seem so bad when stacked up against a restorative justice session and chatting with a psychologist about predatory tendencies.

'Anyway, that's the dirt on my day from hell and don't worry about me I'll be okay. I'm tough.'

I'm not so sure.

'So, what's going on with you and Klepto Caro?'

I remembered with a jolt then that I was unemployed and suddenly the Pad Thai was not sitting well. I filled Gemma in on my own day from hell.

'Well, she can't just fire you, not like that, she's not allowed. I should know.'

'Maybe not but I don't want to be in a toxic environment, and it wouldn't be fair on the twins either.'

'Listen, Ellie, you were already going to go to Australia, so go. I've said I'll keep an eye on the—'

'It's Pete.'

She pulled a face. 'Pete. Sort things out with your mum and deal with Caro when you get back. What time's your flight?'

'It's early. I fly at seven, but I need to be at the airport before five.'

'I'll take you to the airport. I won't sleep tonight anyway. I've got my first face-to-face with Regan at the office, some independent mediator called Raelyn something or other is meeting us there at eight tomorrow morning.'

'Thanks, Gemma, and it will be okay—you know that right? In six months from now, you will have moved on from this moment in time and forgotten about it.'

'It doesn't work like that, Ellie. You of all people should know that.'

Chapter 48

I tried to read a magazine on the no-frills flight over but not even the breaking news that Jen Anniston was yet again pregnant could hold my interest. Imagine getting your picture taken and having headlines shrieking your baby news when in fact you were just a tad bloated. I shook my head. Who'd want to be famous? I tried to sleep for a bit too, but there was a family behind me whose tow-headed son reminded me of William-Peter. He kept kicking the back of my chair, which was another reminder of my former charge, the thought of whom made my throat close over. I couldn't leave things up in the air with him and Saffy-Rose. It wouldn't be fair on either of them.

Wedged in my seat by the window and having angled myself so there was no chance of making conversation with the older woman sitting next to me, her husband squeezed into the aisle seat, I brooded. What would Caro have told the twins about my absence? I went around in circles pondering that before my mind raced over to Gemma's predicament. Her session would have started now. How was it going? Time would tell whether she'd stay on at the Property Pro. Even if things got smoothed over with Regan, word was bound to leak as to what had happened. It would be titillating office gossip, sniggered at during after-work drinks. It wouldn't be an easy environment to stick with. Then again, my cousin was determined, and if she felt it was in her best interests to stay where she was, then she'd rise above all of that and dig her heels in.

I splurged on a coffee somewhere over the Tasman Sea in desperate need of a fix after a restless night. I'd finally gone into a deep, dreamless snooze for what felt like minutes before my alarm shrilled that it was time to get up. The caffeine helped, and by the time we bounced down the runway of Coolangatta Airport, I felt ready to take on the three-bus journey to Mum and the Papadum's apartment overlooking the lagoon in Labrador.

The queues through customs stretched long with grumbling travellers, keen to get on with their holiday, the scent of sunscreen in the air. We kept inching forward until finally I flashed my passport at the surly officer who clearly was not getting job satisfaction and passed through the doors into Arrivals. I wheeled my carry-on case through the crowds and out the doors to the pavement outside.

It was a hive of activity with people milling about as they sorted out how they were getting from A to B and I was immediately drowned in wet heat. I literally felt my hair go ping as it rebelled against it and it took a moment or two for my breath to adjust to the heavy air. I looked around wondering where I'd find the bus. The taxis jostled at the rank, and I was sorely tempted to splurge. The distance I had to travel wasn't great, but it was going to be a roundabout way of getting there via the buses I'd worked out I needed to take. Oh, to sink into the back seat of an air-conditioned cab. Cabs were not for the unemployed though and spying where I needed to head to, I averted my eyes from the cabs and marched forward.

The bus was standing room only. There was a pervasive and oppressing odour of BO, and I held on for dear life, as the driver showed off his accelerating and breaking prowess all the way to Broadbeach.

By the time I'd boarded the bus outside Sea World that would take me to the Gold Coast Highway, I'd decided this unique foot-heavy style of driving must be taught at the Gold Coast's Bus Operating Training School, and I hoped I wouldn't be suffering whiplash by the time I disembarked.

At last I spied my stop approaching and I pushed the button. The bus slowed and jerked to a halt outside a brick community building opposite the park I recalled from my last visit. My shirt was clinging to me as I crossed over the highway to the carpark in front of the park. Squealing children were clambering over the climbing frame or digging in the sand under the shade sails while their mums sat at picnic tables shaded by the trees. The green verge of the parkland dropped away to powder-white sand ringed by the brilliant blue of the Broadwater. I was standing near a young couple stretched out on a picnic mat. If things had been different with Mum and me, Sam and I might have come here together for a holiday. We'd have been like that couple, laughing and stealing kisses on their rug. I blinked against the sheer brilliance of the vista before carrying on my way.

The last time I'd been here I hadn't appreciated the beauty of this place. I'd come on my own under duress, thanks to Sam who'd insisted I take Mum up on her invitation to visit, and I'd behaved accordingly for the week I'd stayed. Now, I felt ashamed of that behaviour. I owed George an apology, too, starting by calling him George and not the Papadum. I knew the bare minimum about him. He was rich, retired and had two grown-up daughters from his first marriage. That was it. If things went well with Mum, I decided I'd make a concerted effort to get to know him better.

I found the path that ran along the lagoon edge and I followed it around, smiling at the sight of the pelicans snapping open their long pink beaks in exchange for a piece of fish. Mum and the Papa—

George's apartment building came into view as I rounded the bend on Marine Parade. It was white and glistened in the sunshine, all twelve storeys of it. I spotted a café and an ice-cream parlour nestled at the base of a near-identical block of holiday apartments where I could plant myself to wait if they weren't home.

The marble-tiled foyer of the Aqua Vistas apartment building was deserted, and it was also blessedly cool. It took a minute for my eyes to adjust to the change in light as I stood by an oversized potted fern, fanning myself. No way was I going to take nine flights of stairs, not when I was already dying of thirst, so I pushed the button and waited for the lift while looking around me. The residents' mailboxes lined one wall along, and a huge photographic print of Surfers Paradise adorned another, the austerity softened by the leafy green plants strategically positioned about the foyer. The lift doors slid open, and a man in a porkpie hat, vest, shorts and boat shoes got out, nodding in my direction. Hoping I wasn't whiffy from my journey, I brushed past him to step inside. As I ascended to the ninth floor, my stomach began to do flip-flops. I hoped I was doing the right thing by just showing up.

By the time I began trailing my case down the hall to Apartment 94, the flip-flops were doing somersaults. My hand hovered over the bell for a split second before I told myself to stop being silly and just press it. Worst-case scenario, Mum would tell me I'd had a wasted trip and to go home. I stood back and waited, half hoping now that no one would be home. The door swung open.

'Ellie, what on earth?' Mum was standing there in a white tank top and her cut-off Daisy Dukes. Her hair was in a ponytail and her face bare apart from the permanent eyeliner. Her mouth hung slightly open at the shock of seeing me there. Behind her I could see George sitting outside on their balcony, the ranch slider closed to keep the hot air out.

'Hi, Mum.'

She swung her head, her ponytail swishing as she called over her shoulder, 'George, Ellie's here.' There was a hint of a plea for help in her voice. I didn't think he'd hear her through the closed door but he did and I watched him get up and lumber inside to see what was going on. I smiled past her at him. 'Hi, George, I'm sorry to just land on you like this.'

He was wearing a pale blue polo shirt, open at the neck, and I could see his signature chunky gold chains nestled amongst the thick matted hair of his chest. He had white shorts on and if he was given a pipe and cap, he could have set off to sail the seven seas.

'Ellie, welcome! How wonderful. Don't leave her standing in the hall, Nicky, invite her in.' He took charge.

Mum blinked and opened the door wider. 'Of course, sorry, I just, well the last person I expected to see was, you. Come in.'

I followed her inside enjoying the cool temperature after the heat outside. The body corporate fees obviously didn't stretch to air-con in the hallways, and George shut the door behind me. 'Are you thirsty?' Mum was already in the kitchen busying herself getting glasses out and using the ice dispenser on their fridge. Her actions were jerky, and her speech was fast as she called, 'Lemonade, or maybe a beer?'

'Lemonade would be lovely, thanks. I came straight from the airport, and I'm parched.' There was an enormous bunch of flowers—reds, oranges, yellows—arranged in a vase on the breakfast bar and the scent from them was heady. I wondered if George had met her with those when she arrived home. What a lovely way to be greeted, I thought looking around. Given their mutual love of bling the apartment is surprisingly tasteful. It's all light and airy with big black and white arty prints.

'Did you taxi?' George asked picking up my case.

'No I got the bus, three of them actually.'

'You should have called. I would have picked you up,' he admonished as Mum gestured for me to have a seat in the open-plan living space. She fluffed around arranging coasters on the glass-topped coffee table before setting the lemonade down.

I didn't want to say I was worried as to what kind of reception I might get, so I said, 'I didn't want to bother you, and the bus was fine.'

'It would have been no bother.' George headed into the guest room where I had stayed the last time I was here.

I sat down in the leather two-seater Mum had gestured to and took grateful gulps of the sweet, cold liquid looking up from under my lashes as she perched down on the edge of the matching recliner. She looked as though she was going to take flight at any moment. There was a wary look in her eyes. 'Who's looking after Pete?'

'Gemma's going to be popping in and out to feed him and to give him a bit of attention. It would have been nice if I could have asked the kids next door if they wanted to earn a bit of spending money but I'd probably come home and find the flat-screen gone.'

Mum raised a smile at that. 'They're alright that lot over the fence. Rough diamonds that's all.'

She was being generous I thought.

'So everything's going alright, you know with the house and well—' she pulled at frayed bit of denim on her shorts '—with you?'

I nodded and put my drink down, there was no point soft-soaping her. 'Actually, Mum, it's not. Things went from bad to worse after you left. I kissed Sam's best mate; Gemma was accused of sexual harassment; I asked my boss if she'd been shoplifting, and she pretty much gave me the sack.'

Mum's black-ringed eyes widened. 'So that's why you're here. You've run away?'

What a tempting thought that was. To never go back and face the music. To while away my days in the sunshine state. I wouldn't be the first person to come and lose themselves in Queensland.

'I haven't run away, Mum. I've come to tell you I'm sorry and that I never should have spoken to you the way I did.'

George reappeared then with a towel slung over his shoulder; he'd changed into Hawaiian print board shorts, which looked faintly ridiculous on a man of his age and with his girth. But I was grateful that he was not the budgie smuggler sort because that would have been the end of me.

'I'm going to go for a dip down in the lagoon and leave you two lovely ladies to it.'

'Alright, love,' Mum said shooting an anxious glance at him and I wasn't sure how I felt about her being nervous about being left alone with me. I couldn't blame her I suppose. He smiled over at her, and I could see the strength and reassurance she gleaned from it. I recognised her response because it's exactly how I used to feel when Sam smiled at me like that.

I gave him a wave and smile and waited until I heard the front door close before turning my attention back to Mum. She'd moved on from fraying her shorts further and was fiddling with her rings. The only one I recognised was Nan's sapphire engagement ring. It was going to be mine one day, Mum had said after Nan died.

'It sounds like you've been busy. I've only been back here a few days.'

I managed a wry smile. 'Mm the Connor thing was a big mistake on both our parts.'

'You'll want to sort things out with him unless you know any other good painters.'

'I know, and I will. He's too good a friend not to.' I hesitated before adding, 'I've agreed to go to that grief group Aunty Paula was on about.' I sounded like I wanted a big pat on the back but the more people I told the more people I'd have to answer to if I backed out.

I got a nod of approval. 'That's good, Ellie.' I watched Mum reach over and pick up her vape-pen from the table. Her hand was trembling as she inhaled on it deeply and the air smelt like strawberries when she exhaled.

I shrugged. 'It's a start.'

We were both tense, the atmosphere was thick with things unsaid and we skirted around them while I filled her in on what had happened with Gemma.

'The world's gone mad,' Mum said, shaking her head and having another puff on her pretend cigarette. 'And what were you saying about your boss, shoplifting?'

That was a whole other story and when I'd finished she leaned over and began rummaging in her handbag on the floor beside her chair. She pulled out her purse and opened it. 'If you're strapped for cash, I can help. I'd like to.'

'No, Mum, put your purse away. I can manage, I'll sort it out.'

Mum looked at me directly then and I felt myself grow a little smaller as she chewed her bottom lip. She used to do that with her lip when I was little and she was about to tell me off. 'See, that's what you always do, Ellie.'

'What?' I didn't know what I was supposed to have done.

'You push me away. You open the door a crack as if you're going to let me in and then you slam it shut.'

'I don't.' Or maybe I did. I sat there as she sprang up, opening the ranch slider and stepping out onto the balcony. She closed it behind her and turned her back to me as she looked out toward the Broadwater. Her hands gripped the rail and the stoop in her shoulders made her seem older than she was.

I didn't want to fight, not this time, and I left her for a minute before getting up to follow her out. The heat as I opened the door and stepped outside was like a slap in the face and I moved to stand alongside Mum. I didn't know what to say but she spoke next.

'You said you wanted to know how I could have left you.'

I wondered if I'd made a mistake coming here because now I wasn't so sure I wanted to know. What if I was right? What if she'd left because she didn't love me enough to stay?

Chapter 49

♥

'I always made bad choices. You were the only good thing I ever had a hand in.' Mum looked over at me squinting against the harsh sunlight before turning her gaze back to the blue water. A pelican was perched on top of the lamppost across the street and I watched it for a minute wondering what she'd say next.

'Did you know I went to Polytechnic for a while after I left school?'

I shook my head.

She smiled and brushed a strand of hair that had come loose from her ponytail and was sticking to her face away. 'I used to love sewing and making my own clothes; we both got that from your nan.'

It was common ground between us I'd never known we had and I looked straight ahead, sad at the thought of all the things that might have been. The pelican must have seen something on the beach of interest because he flapped his wide wings and swooped down to the sand.

'I was doing alright there for a time. I'd go to my course in the day and waitress at an Italian restaurant that used to be near the square in town a few nights a week. I was living at home and Mum and Dad thought that was me, finally on the right path.' She gave me a rueful smile. 'You'd think they'd have known better.'

I smiled back at her even though it wasn't funny.

'My boss at the restaurant, Antony, was about fifteen or so years older than me. God I thought he was it. I was so bloody grateful when he told me I was special.' Her knuckles were white from clenching the rail. 'Because I never felt special, Ellie. I couldn't see why anyone would ever want to take me on with my roller-coaster moods.'

'Oh, Mum.' I didn't know what to say and I reached over and rested my hand on top of hers.

'He had a wife and four young kids, and I should have known better but I was young and stupid, and I thought he loved me. When I told him I was pregnant, he didn't want to know.' She let that sink in and I moved my hand away.

I was the product of an affair with an Italian Stallion. It explained my colouring. I racked my brains trying to visualise all the Italian eateries in town. One or two sprung to mind and I knew I'd be dragging Gemma out for dinner in the near future. I wouldn't be able to help myself. The news could have been worse than him being a married man. I'd imagined a lot worse over the years. There'd been times I was terrified that Steve was my father. 'What was his last name?' I'd need to know if I was going to be staking restaurants out.

She shook her head. 'That's exactly why I didn't want to tell you because where would it have got us? You can't contact him. He made it clear he didn't want to see or hear from me again or have anything to do with you.'

I thought that was unfair but I didn't push it, not for now anyway, and we stood in silence, that hot sun beating down on us. Mum was lost in the past and I was trying to process what she'd just told me. I heard the door on the adjacent balcony open. Boy, whoever that was would be in for some juicy eavesdropping if we didn't head back inside.

'Come on it's too hot out here anyway. I don't know how George can sit out here baking like he does. It's not good for him. I'm forever seeing people with bits chopped off at the mall from skin cancer,' Mum said and I followed her back inside wanting to stand under the air-conditioning unit, arms up in the air like I was worshipping. We took up our previous seats and she picked up her vape-pen again.

'When you were born, Ellie, I made you a promise, that I'd always do my best by you. You were so beautiful.' She smiled at the memory and fiddled around with loading another cartridge into the pen. 'Your nan and pops were besotted with you too but it wasn't easy living under their roof. Mum was quick to criticise and tell me how I should be doing things. I think she was always worried about me having one of my episodes as she called them and I could feel her watching me all the time.' The cartridge slotted in and she took a puff. 'I wanted to prove to them both that I could manage. They were devastated when I moved out and took you with me.'

I knew none of this and I was unable to take my eyes off Mum as her hand fluttered back to her mouth and she inhaled again before carrying on. Chocolate flavour this time, I thought as the vaporised liquid filled the air. 'We were okay, me and you, but then I met Steve, and things went out of kilter in a big way. I don't know why I stuck it out all those years, fear I suppose but I finally hit rock bottom after that last fight.' She rubbed at her temple with her free hand. 'It was only supposed to be temporary—you going to Colin and Paula's. I thought I'd head over here to Australia, get my head straight and then bring you over. We could start a new life here but by the time I felt strong enough you'd settled in with them. You and Gemma were thick as thieves. You were doing well at school; you had friends, a good life. You were happy, Ellie.' She looked at me willing me to understand. 'I couldn't just waltz back in and make you leave all that to come back here with me. Not when I couldn't guarantee things would stay on an even keel. I could never promise you that.' I saw her eyes had filled with tears but I couldn't keep the accusatory tone from my voice.

'Why didn't you come back to Christchurch then? You just said you'd gotten yourself sorted; you could have been closer than the flipping Gold Coast.' I was angry at the thought of all those lost years. I *had* settled at Uncle Colin's and Aunty Paula's, their house—just like 16 Radford Street—had always been a home away from home for me, and Gemma and I had always been close. But I'd needed my mum. I could have handled her ups and downs. I'd weathered them before.

'Steve would have found me if I came back.'

I sat back in my chair then, my stomach tightening as those long sat-upon memories of vicious words being flung sang in my ears. Only this time I remembered the sound of a fist connecting with flesh. I remembered being frightened.

Chapter 50

♥

I look down at my homework spread across my bed and try to focus on the essay I am supposed to have on my English teacher's desk first thing in the morning. My handwritten notes blur on the page, the text growing distorted as my eyes fill with frightened tears. Mum and Steve have been shouting in the bedroom next door for well over half an hour now. I don't know what set things off this time but the pitch of their voices is escalating. The slurs are getting fiercer, uglier.

'You're a fucking cunt, Nicky!'

I flinch and put my hands over my ears, not caring as a tear plops onto the page in front of me, smudging the ink.

'Get off me! Don't touch me!'

'You fucking nutty bitch!'

Mum screams. I can hear the fear in it, and I freeze. I'm too scared to leave my room and see what's happening. I hate myself for not going to help her. I'm breathing in short, frightened huffs. What if he's killed her this time? What then? I hear footsteps and the front door bangs and a few moments later there's the sound of tyres squealing. The sound rouses me, and I reach for my phone. I'll phone Uncle Colin; he'll come. Steve wouldn't touch him. He wouldn't dare. Oh please, please don't let Mum have left me here alone with him. Thoughts tumble on top of one another and before I can make my call my bedroom door bursts open. I drop my phone as Mum, her hand holding one side of her face, pulls my case down from the top of the wardrobe.

'Get your things, quickly. Come on, Ellie, move!'

I do what Mum says, opening drawers and pulling things out at random, my brain unable to process what I need to take with me. I see the Dappledawn family on top of my dressing table, and I put them in the case. Mum's gone, and when she next appears, she has a bag, and I can see her right eye is beginning to close up.

'Are you ready?'

I nod and follow her out to the car. Steve's car's not in the driveway, and there is no sign of him, but the neighbour across the street is peering over at us through their living room window.

'Where are we going?'

'Your nan and pops'.'

I allow myself to breathe then because I know we'll be safe in the house at Radford Street.

Chapter 51

♥

Mum wasn't in the room, but I heard her blowing her nose in the bathroom. She returned with a box of tissues and offered them to me. I took a handful and did the same before wiping my eyes. There was nothing more to be said. I knew the full story now; I'd shut my mind to it for such a long time. It couldn't be changed, but that didn't mean we couldn't change what happened next. It was time to stop rehashing the past and say what I'd come to say. I wanted to this complicated woman in my life. I needed her in my life and I knew she needed me too.

'I love you, Mum.'

Mum's lip was trembling but she looked at me then and reached over. We held each other's hands. 'I love you too, Ellie. I always have but you know I'm far from perfect.'

'None of us are.' And I knew it was true. To put someone on a pedestal and expect them to be so was unfair and besides I'd learned love meant accepting someone for who they were, imperfections and all. You loved them because of their flaws not in spite of them. I didn't know if I was thinking about Sam or Mum, or both of them at that moment.

~

I stayed for a week, and it whizzed by as Mum and I got to know one another again. We did the theme parks and Sea World. We even went to Wet 'n' Wild water park, and honestly, when she came down the hydra-slide and lost her bikini top in the white froth at the bottom, I thought I'd have the kind of accident in the pool I hadn't had since I was too small to know better. She gave me a manicure, and the pale lilac gel polish she used made my short nails look fabulous. I tried not to think about Caro while she painted them. This version of Mum was different from the Hurricane Nicky who'd blown in and out of my childhood.

George fired up the barbeque on the balcony every night and kept us fed. I really liked him. He was warm and generous and he genuinely loved Mum. I didn't want to go home. I was in a warm, Gold Coast bubble, and I didn't want it to burst. I told Mum this the night before I was due to fly out.

We were sitting on the balcony, the heat of the day had gone, and it was growing dark. There were shouts and hoots of laughter ever so often from the restaurants below on Marine Parade and now and then I could make out the dark, eerie outline of bats swooping across the inky sky. Someone, somewhere in the building was frying onions and sausages and it was making my mouth water even though we'd eaten. George was rattling about in the kitchen assembling what he'd proudly announced was his signature dessert, Kataifi. Seeing my baffled expression, he explained it was an almond syrup pastry that his mama had taught him how to make. Mum leaned over and told me it was to die for.

Now she said, 'You've got commitments, Ellie. Colin, and Paula had enough faith in you to loan you all that money to buy and do up Radford Street. You can't let them down. As much as I'd love to keep you here.'

She'd only put into words what I already knew. The old house was mine now. I'd overseen it being put back together and made whole again. I did have responsibilities. William-Peter and Saffy-Rose's faces floated to mind; only they looked a lot more cherubic than they did in real life. Guilt can warp things. I had to see them again, too.

'I don't have a job anymore, though, Mum. What am I going to do?'

'So? You're my daughter, aren't you? We're nothing if not resilient us Perkins women. You'll find one.'

George appeared then, reverently placing the plate with the decadent dessert down on the table in front of us. He looked from me to Mum waiting for us to comment.

'It looks wonderful, George, not too big a serving for me though or I'll have to do an extra Zumba class this week.'

'Wow, George, can I have ice-cream too?' I hoped the extra pounds I'd piled on this week wouldn't count as excess baggage when I got to the airport tomorrow.

~

Mum and I said goodbye at their apartment. Neither of us wanted a teary send-off at the airport. We concentrated on the fact she was going to be coming over in a few weeks to toast the old house when it finally got signed off and insured. I'd decided despite my reduced circumstances, I was going to have a housewarming. Nothing big, just a thank you to Joel, Mikey, Jonno and the other tradesmen who'd worked on it and of course Connor, and my family. This time George was coming with her, and I'd already made him promise he would make Kataifi for my party. He drove me to the airport, and when he pulled up behind the row of taxis, he reached over and drew me to him. It was the first time we'd embraced and I liked the way he smelled of mints and sandalwood.

'I'm glad you're in Mum's life.'

'I'm glad you are too.'

'Thanks for everything, George.'

'You're Nicky's daughter—that means you are like a daughter to me too, Ellie. There's no need to thank me.'

I looked at him, this portly Greek man with all his gold medallions who made my mum so happy and felt immensely warmed by his words.

Chapter 52

♥

I texted Gemma when I landed and made my way outside the airport to wait for her. It wasn't long before I saw her shiny jeep nose around the corner and I waved. She pulled over, and I threw my case on the back seat before climbing in alongside her.

'Thanks for picking me up. How's Pete?'

'That cat has an eating disorder.'

'He does like his food. He's okay though?' I hoped he hadn't been pining for me.

'He is fine. Fill his bowl, give him a pat and he's anybody's. He's a floozy.'

So much for pining for me. I belted in. 'Well thanks for looking after him. I've had the most incredible week, Gemma.'

'You sorted it with Aunty Nicky then?'

'Yeah, things are going to be okay with us.'

She looked at me, her face serious. 'That's the first time I've seen your smile reach your eyes since Sam's accident.' A car behind us tooted, and Gemma wound down her window and leaned out. 'We were having a moment, arsehole!' she shouted before pulling out of the space.

'What about you? How are things at work?' I asked as we headed away from the airport.

'Not great. God, the Sunday drivers are out in force today.' She tapped the steering wheel, and I could see she was itching to hit the horn. I refrained from mentioning that she'd just shouted at someone for being impatient. She was, after all, doing me a favour picking me up.

'I'm not sure what I'm going to do. That Girl has taken off so maybe I should concentrate on that for a bit, give the real estate a break. I've still got a few houses I want to get past the finish line but I don't know.' She shrugged. 'I'm thinking I should ride the Instagram wave so to speak because it's the only kind of riding I'm going to be doing for a while.'

I'll believe that when it happens. 'Wow, it must be going great if you're thinking of making it full time.'

'Yeah the problem is my followers want to see more of Mum, but I'm not sure that *I* want to. I see plenty of her as it is.'

That made me laugh. 'Who'd have thought Aunty Paula would become an Instagram star.'

'Tell me about it. One measly tattoo and she thinks she's the suburban housewife's answer to Helen flipping Mirren.'

'You're okay though? I mean with all that Regan stuff. It's been resolved?' I crossed my fingers he wasn't going to take things any further.

'Oh yeah, you know me. I'm okay even if the restorative justice session was hard going. I did my thing though, ate humble pie and apologised, said I'd seen the error of my ways.'

'And have you?'

She side-eyed me. 'I concede that the boob brushing was inappropriate and I've learned my lesson when it comes to making lewd remarks about the opposite sex to colleagues, but I didn't stalk him. Not really anyway.'

She was halfway there at least, I thought as we cruised into Radford Street; that was something.

'It's irrelevant anyway because I'm totally off men. They are *way* more trouble than they're worth.'

'Fair enough,' I said as she pulled into my drive.

'I'll come in and have a coffee with you before I go. I've got an open home at two. I got you some milk and bread—it's in the back seat.'

'Thanks, Gemma.'

I opened the front door. 'Pete, Mummy's home.'

'He's a cat, Ellie, not your love child.'

I ignored her as I heard him thudding out the kitchen and his familiar hoppy gait coming down the hall. He veered around the corner and scampered toward me. I scooped him up and held him close listening to him purr his contentment. I was home and it felt good.

'Come on, shift it. I'm not standing out here while you and fat cat bond.'

'I was just thinking how this place really feel likes home now, Gemma.'

'Yeah, well that's because it is; you'll be paying it off for years.'

I could smell turps and the metallic tang of paint, the kind that you can almost taste in the back of your throat. Still holding Pete I stepped inside. Gemma shut the door behind us. I hadn't expected Connor to come back, not until we'd met up and smoothed the waters so to speak. I should've known he'd be bigger than that. 'Connor must have been while I was away.'

'Uh-huh.'

I followed my nose, and it took me into my bedroom. I stood in the doorway staring around in disbelief because the ugly walls I'd stripped, that I'd scraped and put holes in and that had surrounded me while I sobbed until I fell asleep exhausted were now an on-trend off-white. No more Pink Palace!

It wasn't just the fresh paint job though. There were stylish blush pink Roman blinds hung where there'd been floral monstrosities. A white lantern-style light shade dangled where a brass and frosted glass globe had dominated. The old duchess Sam and I had fought for drawer space over had been painted white and given new handles. My framed photographs of us together artfully arranged.

'Aunty Paula did that,' Gemma said following my stunned gaze to the duchess. 'It looks good doesn't it?'

I nodded literally struck dumb as I took in my bed. It was dressed in photo-ready plump, soft new linen, with cushions and artful blush throw blankets galore. It was the sort of bed you want to read in, eat toast and drink tea in. It looked divine. The thing I wasn't getting though was I hadn't had a hand in any of this but everything was exactly what I would have chosen if I'd been handed an open chequebook.

'Who's done all this other stuff?' I swung around to Gemma, who was standing there beaming proudly.

'You like it?'

'Oh, Gemma, I love it!'

'Me and Mum did it, but I chose the bed linen. Bedland gifted it in exchange for me taking a couple shots reclining on it for That Girl. I'm diversifying. We wanted to surprise you—don't you dare start crying! And don't let that cat on the bed!'

I paused, Pete hovering mid-air in my arms above the beautiful throw blanket at the foot of the bed. I put him down on the floor.

'They're happy tears. How did you get everything so—'

'Right?'

I nodded.

'I looked at your Pinterest pages.'

It really was amazing and I hoped she could see how touched I was that she and Aunty Paula had done all this for me.

I remembered something as I looked at the bed and Gemma read my mind once more.

'It's still there under the pillow.'

I wandered over to the bed, stroking the sumptuous fabric and wishing it was bedtime now before lifting the pillows. There it was, Sam's shirt. The photos of us might decorate the dressing table but the room with its feminine colours and numerous scatter cushions smacked of me. The time suddenly felt right. I didn't stop to analyse what I was doing. I simply folded his shirt up and walked over to the wardrobe, placing it on the top shelf. I wasn't ready to take it to the second-hand shop yet, maybe I never would be, but moving it to the top shelf was a start.

Gemma gave me a smile before tapping the side of her head. 'Oh, I almost forgot. Connor asked me to tell you when you got back, that he's good with it.' She winked. 'I didn't let on I knew about your lonely hearts session.'

I smiled. 'Thanks, Gem.' Things between me and Connor would be just fine. 'Come on I'll put the kettle on.'

~

Over coffee, Gemma brought up the subject I was hoping to avoid thinking about at least until tomorrow anyway. 'Are you going to phone Klepto Caro and see how the land lies now she's had a week of being on active duty?'

'No.' I tapped the side of my mug with my pale lilac nails. 'Oh, I don't know. I have to do something. At the very least I need to go around and say a proper goodbye to the twins.'

'I think you've been worrying over nothing. I bet you she'll be desperate for you to come back. Just make sure she grovels good and proper before you do.'

But Gemma hadn't seen the look on Caro's face the day she sent me packing. If anybody was going to be doing any grovelling, I had a feeling it would be me.

'Ellie.' Gemma did that mind-reading trick of hers. 'Don't let her bully you. I know her type. She's used to getting whatever it is she wants with a click of her fingers.'

The irony of what she'd just said went completely over the top of her head, and mentally shaking my head, I noticed Pete was sitting in front of his empty food bowl.

'I gave him a generous helping this morning,' Gemma said following my gaze.

'It's nearly teatime.' I got up and opened the cupboard where his biscuits were kept.

'No wonder he's overweight,' Gemma muttered.

'He's not overweight, he's a big cat and he's only got three legs. The poor fella's got to have some pleasures in life.' I shook out a generous helping of biscuits into his bowl. 'There you go, Pete, you enjoy them and don't listen to your Aunty Gemma. That's a boy.'

Gemma drained her coffee. 'Well, I can't sit here talking about your cat's food issues all afternoon. I've got things to do, places to be. Give me a call and let me know how you get on with Klepto Caro.'

'I will and thanks, for everything.' I followed her outside. 'I absolutely, totally love what you and Aunty Paula have done with my room. I'll ring her in a bit and tell her what an amazing surprise it was to come home and walk into my new boudoir. I feel like I'm on one of those home makeover shows.'

I spied a newspaper and a wedge of fliers sticking out of my letterbox. Waving Gemma off, I walked down to the front gate and was about to clear it when I spotted my pint-sized nemesis from over the fence. He was sitting, cradling his elbow a few houses down the street under a tree, the skateboard upturned on the pavement next to him. I could see even from where I was standing that he was crying. *Be the adult, Ellie,* I told myself, knowing he'd probably tell me to mind my own business and not in such salubrious terms either. I walked toward him nevertheless.

Chapter 53

♥

I didn't even know his name, I thought as I drew near. 'Hey there, are you alright?'

He looked up at me, his eyes red and his nose running.

I waited for the inevitable bad language, but there was none. Instead he said, 'I fell off my skateboard.' He showed me the hole in his sweatshirt and the angry graze on his elbow.

'Oh dear, that looks sore. Do you want me to help you home? Get Mum to sort that elbow out for you?'

He sniffed loudly. 'Nah, I'll be in big trouble.'

'No you won't; it was an accident.'

'I will. Mum only bought me this yesterday.' He pulled at his sweatshirt. It was navy blue with a kid in a yellow cap skateboarding on the front of it. 'She'll be pissed I've ripped it.'

'Show it to me again.'

He did so.

'Come on; I think I can fix that for you.' I picked up his skateboard. He looked at me uncertainly and then obviously decided he had nothing to lose.

'I'm Ellie. What's your name?' I asked as we walked the short distance back to my house.

'Cody.' He wiped his nose with the back of his hand before following me up the steps and in through the front door. Mercifully it was still open because if it had blown shut while I was gone, we'd have been locked out.

'You got this place looking nice,' Cody said glancing around as I headed up the hall toward the kitchen. 'What's the cat's name?' he asked sitting down at the table a beat later.

'Pete and he loves being made a fuss of.'

'He's only got three legs,' he said as Pete got up from his cushion, stretching languorously before doing his hoppity-skippity walk over to Cody.

'That's right. He was hit by a car and a lady called Iris who rehomes cats took him in. I've only had him a little while but he already acts like he owns the place.

'I want a dog, but Mum says no because Jackson—he's her boyfriend—doesn't like dogs, and neither do landlords.'

'Dogs can be a lot of work.'

'I'd look after it.'

'What about a fish?'

He looked at me like I was stupid and I moved on. 'Well, you're welcome to come and say hi to Pete whenever you like. How long have you lived next door?'

'Mum only rents it; we've been there two years now.'

I nodded. 'Do you like it?'

'It's alright. Not as nice as this. Mum says we might move in with Jackson soon anyway.'

I hope Jackson, this man who doesn't like dogs, is a kind man for Cody and his siblings' sake. 'I think I've got some antiseptic cream and a plaster somewhere.' I opened cupboards until I managed to locate my first aid kit behind the baked beans on the pantry shelf.

'Here we go. We'll have you fixed up in no time.' I put it down on the table and opened the lid. 'Some Savlon to stop it getting infected and Elastoplast. That will do the trick.'

Cody took off his sweatshirt and sitting in his T-shirt gritted his teeth while I cleaned it before dabbing the antiseptic cream on and putting the plaster over the top. I remembered Joel doing the same for me the day I came off the mountain bike. The memory of those kind, concerned silver eyes made me feel strange. 'All done. You're very brave.'

'Yeah, I am. Not like Dylan, he's a wuss. He cries at anything.'

I guessed Dylan was his younger brother.

'You reckon you can make it look new?' He passed me his top.

'I reckon I can, Cody. Follow me.' I led him through to my sewing room, and he sat down cross-legged on the floor watching while I threaded the machine with matching navy cotton.

'Do you know I used to come and stay here in this house when I was a little girl about the same age you are now.'

'I'm nine.'

I smiled. 'My grandparents owned the house then. My mum and Uncle Colin were brought up here.' I chatted away about what the neighbourhood was like then as I patched the sleeve of his sweatshirt until it looked good as new.

'There we are. All done.' I handed the top back to Cody who held it up inspecting it.

'Awesome, that's dope. Respect, man.'

I'm not up with gangsta speak, but I could tell he was pleased. 'I'm glad I could help.'

Cody put his top back on, gave Pete one last pat and picking up his skateboard at the front door, he headed home. I smiled as he turned back and gave me a wave. See, I told you to watch this space.

I realised the letterbox was still full and after clearing it I carted the pile of papers inside. It was only when I sifted through the junk mail at the table that I saw the envelope tucked up inside it all. I looked for the postmark but there wasn't one, and I turned it over in my hand. There was no return address either. Strange, I thought opening it.

I pulled out a card and looked at it a moment, bewildered, before opening it. It was a deep pink colour with the words, 'I'm Sorry' inscribed in white loopy font across it. A blue flower swirled beneath the inscription. It was simple but pretty, and definitely not off the one-dollar rack. I opened it, my eyes darting to the bottom to see who it was from. Caro's name jumped out at me, and I began to scan the small, neat, handwritten text filling the entire blank space from the top this time.

Dear Ellie,

I want to apologise to you from the bottom of my heart. The way I behaved when you tried to talk to me about, well there is no polite way of putting this although you did try, my stealing, was inexcusable. I steal. I am a thief. There, I said it.

I steal to fill an emotional void. No prizes for guessing what that void is. After you left, I decided enough was enough. I told Doug what I've been doing, and he was horrified enough to agree to attend marriage counselling. He also made me promise to speak to someone about my problem.

Thank you for being brave enough to confront me. It was the shock I needed to acknowledge what I've been doing. I'm so grateful it was you and not Mr Burns who owns my local pharmacy. I don't know if you want to come back but Doug and I want you to come back more than anything and the twins, well you know how they feel. I hope you can see your way to forgiving me and if we can't start again then at the very least we can part on good terms.

Yours

Caro

I closed the card and picked up my keys. 'Pete, be a good boy, I'll be back soon.' He fixed me with those yellow eyes and then his baleful gaze swung to his food bowl.

'Oh for goodness' sake, I just fed you.'

~

Who was this woman standing in the doorway of the Richards' house? Had Caro hired somebody else already, having not heard back from me straight away? She didn't know I'd gone to Australia after all. The woman flung her arms around me. She smelt of shampoo and, what was it? I sniffed again, play dough, that's what it was.

'Ellie, you came!' She released me, and I took a moment to gather myself. Caro had no makeup on, her skin was pale and lightly freckled, and without her lashes' normal coatings of mascara, her eyes looked small and insignificant. Her hair was pulled back into a ponytail, and there was something stuck in it. It was a Cheerio, I realised. She was dressed in joggers and a sweat top, and looked completely exhausted.

'I got your card, thanks.'

She took me by the hand, and I got the feeling that she was terrified I might try to escape.

'William-Peter, Saffy-Rose, look who's here!' she called out, pulling me inside and shutting the door. I half expected her to bolt it behind me.

Two little faces appeared from the playroom; I just had time to register William-Peter was wearing Saffy-Rose's Elsa from *Frozen* dress before they shrieked, 'Ellie!' and careened toward me. They each launched themselves onto a leg, and I reached down and hugged them back. 'It's so good to see you guys. I've been in Australia visiting my mum.'

'You could have told us.' William-Peter broke free long enough to look up at me accusingly. 'I was worried. How's Pete?'

'Mummy did say Ellie was on her holidays, William-Peter.'

'Yes, she did. You don't listen.' Saffy-Rose primly added her bit.

'Pete is really good, thanks. I missed him just like I missed you guys.'

'We've made him a present.'

'Have you? That's sweet of you both.'

They shot back into the playroom returning a second later carrying the cardboard tube from a roll of paper towels. It had been painted black and had a sock stuck to the end that had been stuffed with something. William-Peter thrust it at me.

Caro, explained, 'It's a prosthetic leg.'

I was lost for words as Saffy-Rose pointed to the sock. 'That's his paw.'

Two little faces looked at me expectantly and I took the leg from William-Peter. 'Thank you both from me and Pete. This will make a big difference to how he gets about.'

'You can probably glue it on,' William-Peter said.

I nodded, not trusting myself to speak.

'Mummy's been trying to make play dough, but it isn't like yours,' he confided moving on.

'And she makes horrible things like fish fingers for our dinner,' said Saffy-Rose.

'It's nice to be appreciated,' Caro muttered. 'Come through to the kitchen, Ellie. I'll make us a cup of tea, and we can talk. You'll have to excuse the mess though. You two can have your technology time now if you like.'

The twins squealed, 'Yay technology time!'

'Technology time?'

'It's a new thing I've brought in since you've been away,' she said as the children raced off to the retrieve their devices. 'And it's absolutely not using technology as a form of babysitting.'

I grinned, and she smiled wearily back. 'The only peace I've had since you left is when they're on those bloody things. I did ring an agency, but William-Peter's reputation preceded him. They haven't forgotten what happened last time, and I couldn't get anyone in to help. I've had to do everything myself.'

Caro was not exaggerating when she said the kitchen was a bit of a mess. There were pieces of yellow dough stuck to the floor, and an array of play dough shape implements were scattered far and wide. The lunch things were also still sitting on the bench waiting to be loaded into the dishwasher. I could've told her I didn't want a green tea—it would have been a good moment to come clean about my dislike of it—but she looked so crushed already I decided to keep quiet.

There was a slight sense of déjà vu as she placed my teacup down in front of me. But this time it was Caro who started the conversation.

'So you've been in Australia?'

'Yes, I'd already booked when, well you know.'

She nodded.

'It wasn't my finest few days, Caro. Mum and I'd had a massive fight, most of which was my fault, and I needed to go over and sort things out with her. Then—'

'Then you confronted me about my stealing.'

It sounded so blunt and if you were to look across the breakfast bar at her, she'd be the last person you'd think would have light fingers. Still, it was true, and I nodded.

'And did you make it up with your mum?'

'I did. We have a much better understanding of one another now.'

'I'm glad to hear it.' She took a sip of her tea. 'Oh that's good, I needed that.'

Wish I could say the same.

'Ellie, I said my piece in the card.' She put the cup down in the saucer. 'We need you. I mean look around you.' She gestured around the kitchen, which on my watch was always spotless. It felt nice to be needed.

'I don't want to launch into a big spiel about how miserable I've been.' She gave a little laugh. 'I suspect you find me a little self-indulgent at the best of times.'

'I don't.' I did.

'We've made a large donation to the Eastside Golf Club. Doug got chatting to Mr Burns from the pharmacy once while he was waiting for a script. It's where he plays golf every Sunday.'

I'd have liked to interject here that it probably didn't make up for the hundreds of dollars' worth of cosmetics tucked under her bed but that wouldn't be helpful.

She shrugged. 'It's something and we put all of that stuff, none of it was opened, in a box and had it couriered anonymously back to the pharmacy.'

That's better, I thought.

'It's not all bad though, Ellie. Doug's promised we'll spend more time together and the counselling has got to be a good thing. We'd lost sight of ourselves as a family. My husband's a workaholic, and when he wasn't at the office, he was out on that bike of his. We weren't connecting as a couple anymore, and I felt like I was merely existing in our relationship.'

What was she just saying about self-indulgent? Because there were worse places to 'just exist' than the hairdresser's and the yoga centre. It made me feel a little sad too that not once had she mentioned the fact that her children were being ignored by both their parents in that equation of hers either.

'Please, please, Ellie, come back. We'll pay you more, anything you want. Name it. Oh, and Doug's talking a family holiday to Italy; of course, we'd want you to come with us.'

'It isn't about that Caro.' I hoped I wasn't going to regret saying that because I did have rather a large mortgage hovering over my head and Italy? Yes please! 'And of course I'll come back.' I wanted to be there with the twins until they started school. They wouldn't need me around the same way they do now once they began at Fendalton Primary later in the year. What I'd do then, I didn't know. I wondered if now might be a good time to broach a redundancy package. Then again, that might be pushing things. I mean Italy! I'll tackle finding new employment when the time comes. Like Mum said, the Perkins women are resilient.

Chapter 54

♥

I swung by the Woodland Memorial Garden after work the next day, yawning as I parked and got out of my car. It had been a busy day. The twins were on high alert despite their sugar-free snacks from the moment I arrived until the moment I left. It was excitement at having me back I guess, which was nice albeit wearying. They vied for my attention all day, and by the time I'd cleared up their dinner things, I was seriously considering changing my name. I was thoroughly sick of hearing '*Ellie*' wailed in that way kids do from wherever they might be. Honestly, William-Peter called my name a couple of times for no reason at all other than he liked the sound of it.

As for Caro, she looked much more like her old self when she opened the door that morning. Her war-paint was on, and she was like a prisoner on early release from a life sentence. Her keys were a jangling; there was a skip in her step as she rushed past me calling out, 'Cheerio.' I shook my head watching her go. I wondered what, if anything, would change in the Richards household.

The memorial garden was quiet. People would be home making dinner, I guessed. I could see a woman sitting on a bench a ways off, but apart from her, it was just me and the birds homing into the trees for the evening. I sat down by the rock with Sam's plaque on it. It was so shiny still, unweathered by passing time like some of the other plaques. There was a small posy of ferns interspersed by a dark rust-coloured flower I didn't recognise next to it. It wasn't a feminine arrangement.

'Hi, Sam, I'm sorry I haven't been for a while, but I've been away.'

I know it might seem crazy to sit and talk to a lump of stone, but I could feel him there with me. I had so much I needed to say to him. Things I should have spoken to him about while he was still here. I began by filling him in on Caro and Gemma's misdemeanours, I told him about little Cody from over the fence and then finally I opened up about Mum about Steve and all that ugly stuff I'd bottled up for so long. I talked for such a long time that when I'd finished the shadows from the shrubbery around me were stretching long. I kissed my fingers and rested them on the plaque. I thought that if Sam was looking down at me he'd be feeling pretty proud of how far I've come. It was time to go.

'Bye, my love, sleep tight.'

~

It felt like forever since I was last here, I thought pulling up the driveway of the Andersons' house. I'd been invited for dinner, and then Gina and I were going to go the church where the grief group meets each Monday. I couldn't help but think how weird it was, how totally out there it was that this was how I was going to be spending my Monday nights. Other people would be tuning in to *My Kitchen Rules* or *Love Island*. Not me though, I was going to a grief group with my late partner's mother.

'Ellie, hello! Gosh, you're looking well, love. Come in.'

That would be down to George's cooking. I hugged Gina back.

'You do, too. I mean your hair, it looks great.' She had finally transitioned.

'Thank you. It needs a trim, actually. Now come on in. Phil's in the kitchen; I left him in charge of browning the mince. It's not hard, but he'll still manage to burn it if I don't get back in there. He's probably snuck out for a sneaky cigarette while my back's been turned. He thinks I don't know.' She led the way through to the kitchen chatting all the way. 'We're not having anything fancy I'm afraid—savoury mince. Quick and easy.'

'Sounds perfect.'

I could smell the onions and herbs as I walked into the kitchen and seeing Phil standing at the stove made me pause as I felt a grief grenade being tossed my way. There were certain angles and lights when I could see what Sam would have looked like in years to come. I wouldn't allow the pin to be pulled though, not tonight, and I concentrated instead on how good it was to see Phil. Remember I said he gives the best hugs and I *could* smell cigarettes on him.

'How're you doing, Ellie?' He held me at arm's length. 'You're looking good on it.'

'I'm okay thanks, Phil; you know how it is, good days and bad days.'

He nodded.

'I've just got back from seeing my mum in Australia, actually.' I helped him set the table while Gina served up the meal and I told them about my time on the Gold Coast. I left out the bits about Steve and about Mum's illness—it would have felt disloyal to talk about that stuff with them. Phil told me Lucas was planning on going to London for a while on a working holiday and that Justin had a girlfriend. She was into bodybuilding too, he said. A match made in heaven.

Once we all had a glass of red in front of us, Gina cleared her throat. 'We've got a bit of news, Ellie. It's still hush-hush, but you're family too.'

My eyes prickled at that.

'Mandy's pregnant—it's early days but apart from the most horrendous morning sickness, she's doing well.'

It went without saying that Mandy had morning sickness. Mandy will also have whatever else is on offer throughout her pregnancy, and if Mum thought I'd make a job of giving birth one day, well she's not met Mandy. Still, I felt my heart lift hearing this. 'That's wonderful news.'

There was a light in Gina's eyes. 'It is. Phil and I are very excited aren't we.'

Phil was smiling too. I could see a softening in those hard lines Sam's death had etched on his face. 'We are. It'll be good to bounce a little one on my knee again.'

'You'll have to knock the smoking on the head if you want to be allowed to do any bouncing.'

I smiled at them both over the top of my glass.

~

The church hall when Gina and I opened the doors and stepped inside was an expansive and echoing stretch of timber floorboards and wall panels. A monument to a long since felled rimu tree. If it were winter, it would be freezing in there. Rows of pews were stacked against the wall on one side, and a door with a sign for the toilets was to the right of them. On the opposite side, faded green velvet curtains hid the windows looking out to the carpark. At the far end of the space was another door, and a serving hatch leading through to a kitchen area. It reminded me of twenty-first birthday bashes I'd gone to in the past. Only this time I couldn't smell sausage rolls being heated and there was a low murmur of voices, no loud music, or balloons hanging from the ceiling. The small, hunched group sitting in the circle of chairs in the middle of the hall was a far cry from the crowd of drunken revellers from parties past.

A woman with brown hair, clipped back on either side, stood up. She looked to be in her forties, and her clothes were tidy and spoke of someone who worked in an office. 'Hello, Gina, who's this you've brought with you?'

'Hi, everyone. This is Ellie; she was my son Sam's partner.'

A swivel of heads swung toward us, and I instantly felt self-conscious.

'Well you're very welcome, Ellie—sit down and join us.'

There was no format. Those who felt like talking talked. I'd done enough talking that afternoon at the memorial garden, so I listened. There was Alice, her partner Louise had just died of breast cancer. I could relate to her feeling she'd been abandoned. Travis's son Louis had committed suicide last year, he was only nineteen, and when Travis choked up talking about how he hadn't seen any signs and how he felt he'd failed his son, I cried. Lori was missing her mum who'd died suddenly of a heart attack and listening to her I was so very grateful I had my mum back in my life.

As this mismatched group of people—old, young, and in between—opened up I realised something. What had happened to our loved ones and the roll-on effect losing them had had was tragic but it was also life. As I continued to sit there, my hands clasped in my lap, head bent to one side, I heard not just about the sadness of death but also of the laughter and joy of life. None of these people would change what they'd had with the person they'd lost, not even if they had lifted that piece of paper and learned what lay ahead.

Gina and I linked arms as we left the church hall an hour later and I thought as we followed the others out to the carpark that life can be cruel and unfair, but there are moments where it can be wonderful too. It's those moments we need to seize hold of and cherish and nothing, not even death, can take them away from us. We carry them always in our hearts.

Chapter 55

♥

I'd come to a standstill on the path leading from my back door, a bowl of potato salad in my hands as I watched the tableau playing out in my back garden with a silly smile on my face. Uncle Colin who'd brought his enormous 'boys and their toys' barbeque around, had it set up in the lick of shade afforded by the house. I could smell the sausages he was turning on the hotplate with one hand from here. His other hand was thrust in the bowl of peanuts he'd gotten me to sneak over when Aunty Paula wasn't watching. A bottle of beer was open alongside the bowl.

Pete was sitting at his feet, his gaze trained on the barbeque in case a sausage should suddenly roll off the hotplate and land in front of him. Phil was standing alongside Uncle Colin and from the way he was stroking the side of the barbeque I was guessing he was asking him where he'd bought it.

We were having an Indian summer and the day was hot and still. We'd set up a trestle table in the middle of the lawn with an open mini marquee shading it. The table was Connor's painting table prettied up with a linen tablecloth, it was laden with the plate of buttered bread, bowls of green salad, and coleslaw Aunty Paula, Mum, Gina and I had whipped up in the kitchen, which by the way is a dream to work in.

Although why Aunty Paula felt the need to put green pepper in the coleslaw salad was beyond me. Beside the table were two chilly bins overflowing with wine, beer and bottles of Gemma's awful fruity lolly water drinks that will never, ever pass my lips again.

A heavy bass beat thrummed from the open window in the living room where the speakers were perched on the ledge. I'd had a word with Cody who calls around quite often to say hi to Pete and I'd put him in charge of the sounds. I told him to steer clear of Queen and under no circumstances was he to play 'Bohemian Rhapsody' not even if it was requested. So far we've had nothing but 50 Cent, Jay-Z, and Eminem. Honestly the language! I saw Caro's toes curl in her Tommy Hilfiger sandals when Eminem launched into 'Insane'. I don't blame her. William-Peter's taken a shine to Cody and I had a feeling there would be threats of mouth, soap and water on their way home.

Saffy-Rose was pushing Cody's little sister Taylor around on her trike, just like Gemma used to with me. I could almost hear myself calling out, 'Faster, faster,' my little legs flying around with the pedals until Nan inevitably waded in with, 'Gemma Perkins, be careful! Don't tip her off or there'll be tears.' I smiled at that recollection because Nan was right. I always fell off and there were always tears. She'd make it all better though with a piece of her chocolate crunch slice; it was Pops' and my favourite.

Nan and Pops would just love to see their old garden full of smiling people, laughter and the shouts of children floating on the air like it was today. I pictured them sitting on a couple of chairs in front of the purple rhododendron Nan had so loved. Pops with a social glass of beer in hand, Nan a small shandy. I liked to think they'd be raising their glasses to me, proud of how far I've come.

Cody, Dylan and Taylor's mum Brittney, she of the hipster trackies next door, is okay when you get to know her. She'd dropped the older two of her four kids round here while she and Jackson—who, by the way, has an impressive snake tattoo down his left leg—went to look at a place he liked the sound of in the 'to lets'. I'd be sad to see them go but I've learned so much about myself over the months since Sam died—one of them being that I'm actually quite resilient. Change doesn't frighten me anymore, not like it used to, and besides Cody and I are both on Snapchat. We won't lose touch.

Eminem ramped up and I decided after I'd deposited the potato salad I'd have to request something mellower. I moved across the lawn, which was beginning to brown, the grass crunchy under my feet, to the table smiling over at Justin and his girlfriend, Rose. They're positioned so they've a great view of themselves in the living room windows, which I've polished in honour of today's party. Rose seems nice, if not a little body obsessed. They're heading off to some bodybuilding competition in the States in a week's time together and are on a strict protein diet in the lead-up. The tuna and egg salad in a Tupperware container they'd brought for their lunch was chilling in the fridge.

Zac and Mandy couldn't make it along today. Zac phoned me earlier in the morning to say Mandy had the worst case of morning sickness her doctor had ever encountered. I clucked sympathetically but I managed to get off the phone quickly by pretending someone was at the door. Lucas had already left for London where he'll no doubt try to bed any female under thirty in the legal profession for as long as his work permit allows him to be there.

Gemma was sitting in the shade of the shed on one of the plastic chairs I'd borrowed from Uncle Colin. Connor was sitting next to her, and they were deep in animated conversation. She looked really lovely in her floaty summer dress with its spaghetti straps. The last time I'd been over to ask if their drinks were okay they'd been talking about the fun run Connor was organising. Gemma had been suggesting he draw up a schedule for her and act as her personal trainer. Watch this space! I'm never wrong when it comes to that sort of thing.

Jonno was tapping his foot to the music's beat as I passed by him and Caro. He was pulling the tab on a can of beer and mercifully he didn't seem to know the words to the song. I caught a few snippets of their conversation. Caro was interested in having a gazebo built down the bottom of her garden. A Zen place to drink green tea and admire her roses, no doubt. She'd brought around a beautiful bunch of flowers and an apology that 'call me Doug' had a prior biking engagement.

'That looks good, Ellie,' Mum called out winking. She'd made it saying her potato salad was the stuff of legends over on the Gold Coast. The key was adding crispy bacon and plenty of chopped spring onions, she'd informed me, Gina and Aunty Paula before tipping in a carton of sour cream and muttering about it definitely meaning a Zumba class in the near future. She was standing in the smoker's corner, vape-pen in hand, along with Mikey down the bottom of the garden. I could see he was making a concerted effort to look at her face and not her chest as he chuffed away. Mind you, the amount of cleavage she had on display would have given Pamela Anderson in her red swimsuit a run for her money. 'How's George getting on?'

'He's got the Kataifi in the oven,' I called back. He, Gina and Aunty Paula had really hit it off and had been chewing each other's ears off in the kitchen when I left. Mum gave me a thumbs up.

I put the salad on the table, arranging it amongst the other bowls, and looked toward the house. It was solid now. One day when I've paid more of my loan off, I'll get the outside painted. That can wait though because the stuff that mattered was done. The foundations were strong and the floors straight, the walls sturdy. Inside the fixtures and fittings have been modernised, and in the decor, I've put my stamp on the old place. It's home—my home and I love it.

As I walked back toward the house I spied Joel with a beer in his hand. He was standing near the crab apple tree Connor and I planted. Its once blousy blossoms long since replaced by thick, hardy leaves. He smiled over, and a spark of something warm ignited deep inside me. I smiled back. His white shirt got a big red tick. It was setting off the tan of his skin and he was wearing his favourite jeans, you know, the ones I patched. They were holding up well, I noticed as I moved toward him.

'Thank you so much for the doormat.' It was the second time I'd thanked him. Joel had arrived with a welcome mat as a housewarming gift proclaiming he knew for sure I didn't have one because there was never anywhere for him to wipe his work boots when he'd arrived of a morning. He smelt of apple shampoo and an aftershave I couldn't pinpoint but the fresh, woody scent suited him.

'You're welcome. I like your outfit by the way it's very—'

'Different,' I finished for him, with a glance down at my lime green, lace top. It was a steal, and I fell in love with it the moment I spied it nestling on the rack at the hospice shop. I'd called in with a bag of Sam's old clothes I'd managed to part with. His shirt's still in the top of the wardrobe though. I was wearing a black singlet underneath the lace and three-quarter-length jeans that sat low around my hips, held up by a chunky black belt.

'That's it, but it's also very you. How're you doing?'

'I'm doing well, thanks.' It was true. Sam's birthday passed a few weeks back and a grief grenade had imploded. I'd played our songs over and over but I got through it just like I will all the other firsts as they rolled around. The therapy group is helping, talking about your feelings to people who get you, is a good thing. My eyes flicked to the leaves on my crab apple tree once more but I wasn't going to be sad because today was a celebration and I know Sam would want me to enjoy every moment of it. 'Thanks so much for all your hard work on the house. I'm going to miss having you guys around.'

'It was a team effort and she's a sturdy old girl. She'll be around for a good while yet.'

I looked up at him. His silver eyes held my gaze. I could lose myself in those eyes and I'd really like to kiss him, but I'm not ready yet. I don't want to let him slip away, either.

'Joel, I uh, wondered if maybe in a few months I could give you a call and we could um, I don't know maybe go for another bike ride?'

He smiled down at me. 'How about we make it dinner this time?'

I grinned back at him and then as Eminem let rip with another expletive I decided enough was enough, besides I had a special request.

I marched up to the window and beckoned to Cody, whispering in his ear what song I wanted him play. He wrinkled his nose and I told him I'd give him two dollars if he did what I asked. There was a moment of blissful silence and then Cody's voice bellowed out across the lawn. 'I've got a special request from Ellie. This song is for her mum, Nicky.'

There were a few whoop whoops, I think it was Jonno, and then Madonna's 'Holiday' boomed out. I danced into the middle of my lawn, and my mum came to join me.

The End

Dear Reader,

I'd like to say a huge thank you for choosing to read When We Say Goodbye. If you enjoyed it, and I very much hope you did, then leaving a review to say so on Amazon would be so appreciated. Reviews go a long way to helping other readers choose what book to read next. If you'd like to keep up to date with my latest releases and receive a free e-book of my first novel,

The Cooking School on the Bay, visit my website at www.mich ellevernalbooks.com x Michelle

If you loved When We Say Goodbye then you'll love, The Promise. Available at your favourite Amazon store Read on for an excerpt:

A chance encounter thrusts a lonely and lost young British woman into a web of forgotten promises and lost love.

In the midst of World War II, on the beautiful Isle of Wight, Constance's life was turned upside down by the death of her beloved brother. But when she meets a charming Canadian Airforceman, she dares to hope for a better future. Little does she know, their love will lead to unexpected consequences.

Fast forward to present-day New Zealand, where British backpacker, Isabel's chance encounter with a dying woman sets her on a journey to fulfill a final wish. She must find Constance and apologize for a past mistake. As she returns to England to search the Isle of Wight, the past and present collide, forcing Constance to confront the secrets she's kept hidden for so long. Will Isabel's promise bring closure and healing to Constance?

A heart-wrenching story of love, loss, and the lasting impact of war.

Part One

Verbena officinalis–Blue vervain/Common vervain

From Celtic/Druid culture and Ancient Roman herbalism–a sacred herb associated with magic and sorcery. Means 'to drive away a stone' and was said to remove urinary stones during those times. Used to purify homes and temples and to ward off the plague. Contribute to love potions and can be used as an aphrodisiac.

Used to ease nerves, stress, and depression.
To clear airways and expel mucous.
To aid in sleeplessness, nervousness, obstructed menstruation, and weak digestion.

Using the dark green leaf of the plant, wash thoroughly and dry. Place leaves on baking paper and allow to dry naturally in an open space out of direct sunlight for several days. Turn the leaves occasionally ensuring there isn't any moisture present. Once dried out the leaves can be used for tea or placed in bathwater for a soothing effect while bathing. The vervain seeds can also be roasted and eaten.

The Beginning

♥

Isabel's heart felt as though it would jump right out of her T-shirt as she crouched down beside the mangled car—later she would realise it was down to adrenalin. Now though she leaned in through the window and managed to cradle the elderly woman's head with her left hand leaving her right hand free to stroke the sparse floss of hair. She was careful to avoid the gaping wound from where the blood ran free. The woman's breath was faint and jagged, while Isabel's came in short puffs. She felt as though she'd fallen into a nightmare.

Less than a minute ago she'd been staring out the passenger window of the two-berth Jucy van she was sharing with her friend and travelling companion, Helena. Her mind absorbing and trying to imprint the beauty of the backdrop the Southern Alps provided against the rushing waters of the turquoise river they were crossing.

New Zealand had lived up to its hype, she'd been thinking, spotting the now familiar sight of a hawk soaring low in search of something to eat. It was amazing how much diverse scenery could be packaged up inside such a small country. In just four weeks, they'd seen volcanos, boiling mud geysers, rainforests, a glacier, fjords, mountains, rivers, and beaches to die for but the highlight for Isabel had been the sperm whale in Kaikoura. It had risen out of the water as though to say hello as she leaned over the railing of the whale watch boat, she'd been blown away by its size and grace. That moment was one she would never forget.

Yes, she was so pleased that she hadn't flown straight home from Australia when her work visa was up like so many of her fellow Brits. They were missing out by not coming here she'd mused as the hawk swooped.

She'd met Helena who hailed from Freyburg in Germany through the pub where she was working in Melbourne's hot spot of St Kilda. It had been while clearing tables and tallying up tips that the two girls had hatched the plan to spend a month traversing New Zealand before heading back to their respective countries. What a trip it had been, she'd thought rubbing her temples which were tender after last night's efforts at Pog Mahone's in Queenstown. Helena might have looked like butter wouldn't melt with her big brown eyes and sensible short haircut but she was naughty, and they'd had a right laugh together. They'd not had a moment's snippiness either, which was quite amazing given their close living quarters.

Imagine Dragons was playing on the stereo and Isabel's fingers had been tapping out the tune to "Radioactive" on her thighs. It was hard to imagine that in just over a fortnight she'd be back home in Southampton. Mind you it would be nice to have Mum fussing over her. She couldn't wait to have a hug and catch up on all the news properly. There was something about Skype that made her mum behave like a giggly teenager. It was the way she twiddled with her hair and her eyes kept flitting to her image in the corner. Her dad said she'd never been any different—a show-off in front of a camera who was born before her time. In the age of the selfie, she'd have been up there with the Kardashian clan.

Ahead, the road was a black twisty snake beneath the bright blue South Island sky. There was such a sense of freedom doing a roadie she'd thought, as Helena handled the camper around the corner with the expertise of someone who'd been driving it for the best part of the last month. She was thinking that one day she'd like to do a trip like this down Route 66 in the States, and that was when Isabel spied the car. It was still too far away to register what had happened, but she understood instantly that it was not good.

As Helena slowed and they drew closer, she saw the little hatchback had folded itself around a telegraph pole. The crumpled bonnet was still steaming like an alien ship that had crash landed.

'Shit!' It had obviously just happened, and Isabel wasn't sure if she'd sworn out loud or if it had been Helena.

Her friend braked and veered the camper over to the grass verge.

Isabel's hand hovered over the handle in readiness for the van to stop. 'You ring 111 and get help. I'll see what I can do.' She jumped down from the camper van, racing over to the car hoping for the best but petrified of what she might find.

Now, here she was, willing this poor old woman to be all right. She should not die like this; it would not be fair! To have lived this long and to die in the arms of a stranger on the side of an open road in the middle of nowhere was not how it should end. Isabel was no doctor, but it was obvious the woman was too old to survive the shock let alone her injuries. She watched as the woman's eyes, weighted down by crepe paper lids, fluttered before drifting and locking on hers. That her irises were the same piercing blue as the sky Isabel had been admiring only moments ago, she vaguely acknowledged as she continued to whisper her soothing platitudes.

The woman was trying to summon the strength to speak, a herculean task given the twisted groaning metal wedged against her chest from the impact.

'Shush now, you'll be fine. Help's on its way.'

'Wanted to go back to the Isle of Wight—Tell Constance I'm sorry. Was wrong—should never have left—too late, too late. Tell her for me—'

Her voice held the traces of an accent, almost forgotten it had lived elsewhere so long, but it was one which Isabel recognised as being from her part of the world. The woman's eyes fought to hold on to hers. She knew that she would not let go until she answered her and so she found herself nodding. 'I will; I'll tell Constance.'

'Promise.' The lips formed the words, but the breath behind them was faint.

'I promise.'

A smile flickered then the light behind those bright blue eyes clouded over, and then she was gone.

Chapter 1

Isabel looked around the crowded church hall as she waited behind a gentleman with a thick thatch of white hair many a younger man would be envious of. She was in the line for the tea and coffee although having held back from the initial rush it had thinned out considerably. In the middle of the room were three trestle tables bowed with the weight of the plates of food set out upon them. Seats had been lined up against the wall opposite the entrance from the main building, she noted, and all were taken. It was a good turn-out. People were milling about, some with cup and saucer in hand talking in low murmurs, and they were all strangers to her, every single one of them.

'What would you like, dear?' asked a woman who made Isabel think of apple pie for no reason other than she had a round face with rosy cheeks and a kind smile.

'Oh, um, coffee, please.'

'Coffee it is. My goodness that's an unusual hair colour,' she said looking properly at Isabel before lifting the coffee pot.

'Mmm.' The green colour she'd chosen on her last visit to the hairdressers always garnered second glances, which she didn't mind. She wouldn't have opted for such an unusual shade if she did. It was her way of standing out from the crowd. A crowd in which she was never very confident of where she fitted. She was never sure how she should reply though when someone actually commented. To launch into her reasons for wanting to set herself apart a little seemed far too long-winded for such a straightforward comment.

'And how did you know our Ginny then?' the woman asked, pouring the hot liquid into one of the cups set out on the table.

Isabel didn't want to blurt out the truth, so she said the first thing that sprang to mind. 'I only met her the once, but she made an impression on me, and well, I just wanted to come today.'

The woman was only half listening as she weighed up whether to signal to her catering side-kick, who was beavering away in the kitchen, that she needed another pot of coffee. 'That's nice, dear.' She decided she'd get away with what was left in the pot as she handed Isabel her drink. 'I have to say Father Joyce did her proud; it was a lovely service. Help yourself to milk and sugar.' She gestured to her right. 'And don't be shy with the food; it's there to be eaten.' She eyed Isabel's petite frame thinking she was a girl who could do with a sausage roll or two before turning her gaze to the next person in line.

'Thank you.' Isabel moved over to the tray she'd been directed to, and as she finished stirring the milk and a heaped teaspoon of sugar into her coffee, she wondered where she should stand. She spied a quiet corner near the entrance and opting for that weaved her way through the gathering being careful not to get knocked. If anyone was likely to send her cup of coffee flying, it was her!

Isabel hadn't been sure if she should have come today, but she'd been certain it was something she had to do. It might sound clichéd, but she was seeking closure. She hoped that by attending the funeral of Virginia May Havelock, the woman who'd died in her arms not quite a week and a half ago, closure was what she'd get. They didn't mess around in New Zealand, she thought, taking a sip of her drink and trying not to make eye contact with anyone because she did not want to have to get into a conversation on how she'd met Ginny.

The coffee was weak and flavourless the way coffee always is at weddings and funerals, and she wished she'd asked for tea. It was very different to her limited experience of a funeral in the United Kingdom where more often than not the congregation was mostly made up of family and close friends. Today, it looked as though the whole town had turned out.

She would have felt less out of place if she'd had Helena with her, but she'd left for Thailand four days ago. There was no way her friend was going to miss the Full Moon Party on the beaches of Koh-Pha-Ngan before heading home to Freyburg. One last rave-up before she got back to the serious business of real life. Isabel had planned ongoing with her, but everything had changed the afternoon they'd stumbled across the accident. It was awful, but in some respects, she wished she could rewind to the moment she and Helena had spotted the mangled hatchback. She wished it had been her no-nonsense German friend who'd gotten from the camper van to see if she could help. She would have been able to put the elderly woman's death into perspective and move on.

Isabel, however, couldn't which was why she'd changed her flight and was now heading home via a direct flight to the UK tomorrow instead. There was only one full moon a month, and it had been and gone. Helena had partied hard and staggered on board her Lufthansa flight the following day, texting Isabel to tell her she'd missed a fantastic night. She'd been unable to understand why her British friend wouldn't leave New Zealand before the funeral. 'You don't owe the woman anything. She was a stranger.'

'But I was there when she *died*, Helena. I saw the life go from her eyes. And I made her a promise before it did.'

'Yes, yes, it is very sad, but she was not young, and there was no one else involved, Isabel. People live, and people die, and at least she did not die alone. As for this promise, she is dead—like I said you owe her nothing,' she'd said in her clipped tones.

The thing Helena didn't get was that from the moment the police officer who'd arrived at the scene with an entourage of an ambulance and a fire truck told Isabel the woman's name was Ginny she'd become a real person. She was ninety-one according to her driver's license which had expired five years earlier, he'd gone on to tell her with a sage shake of his head. Ginny was a person who'd had a life and a family and who, thanks to a moment's misjudgment, was now gone. She was also a person to whom Isabel had made a promise. It was that promise that was haunting her no matter what Helena said.

She'd continued to tell her to put it behind her, as she set about making the most of her last couple of days in Christchurch. But Isabel couldn't. Instead of heading out to admire the street art the city was becoming renowned for post-earthquake, her hungry eyes had scanned the paper the hostel supplied in the foyer each morning for the next few days, until the obituary appeared. She'd torn it carefully from the page and had read it so many times over the last week that she knew it by heart.

HAVELOCK Virginia May (nee Moore)
In loving memory of Ginny who passed away suddenly on Wednesday afternoon aged 91 years. Dearly beloved wife of the late Neville, much-loved mother and mother-in-law of Edward Henry and Olga Havelock. Cherished grandmother of Tatiana. The family would like

to acknowledge the support of Father Christopher Joyce of St Aidan's, Timaru who looked after their beloved Ginny in life and in death.

A celebration of Ginny's life will be held at St Aidan's, 160 Mountain View Road, Timaru on Saturday 15 April at 11 am. In lieu of flowers donations to St Vincent de Paul Society, Timaru may be placed in the church foyer.

Isabel's hand shook as she raised her cup to her mouth and a little coffee slopped over the side and down her front. She glanced down at her plain black shift dress bought specially for the occasion. The wearing of black was as foreign to her as was attending the funeral of someone she didn't know. She was a girl who loved colour, and the brighter the better. That was another anomaly about a Kiwi funeral, she thought, wiping off the liquid. Not everyone was dressed in formal black. Satisfied no one would see her mishap she looked up and spied Father Joyce making his way toward her. He wore the white robes of an Anglican priest, and despite his attire swamping him like a tent, it did little to hide his rotund frame. His wispy grey hair floated up with each purposeful step, and he had a serviette in one hand, cakes, a savoury and club sandwiches on a plate in the other.

'The parish ladies have outdone themselves,' he declared upon reaching her. The smear of cream on the top of his lip gave away the fact he was on second helpings. 'It's a spread our Ginny would have approved of. Have you partaken, my dear?'

'Erm no, I haven't had much of an appetite of late.' It was true, Isabel had not been sleeping well and not just because of the comings and goings at all hours in the hostel dormitory. She'd been running on empty for the past week.

Father Joyce nibbled on his club sandwich, declaring ham and egg to be his favourite combination and that she really should try them.

Isabel smiled politely as he dabbed at his mouth with the serviette. She was pleased to see the cream was gone because she'd been afraid her gaze would have kept slipping toward it the same way it would a large pimple or such like. The more you tried to pretend it wasn't there the more you stared.

'I don't believe we've met. In fact, I know we haven't met. I'd remember meeting a young lady with green hair.' He chortled. 'Are you a relative of Ginny's?'

'No.' Isabel's hand had automatically moved to her hair which she tucked behind her ears, a nervous habit. She hesitated and then decided to come clean. She couldn't tell a lie to a man of the cloth not even the teensiest of white ones. 'I'm Isabel Stark. I'm here on holiday from the UK, and my friend and I came across Ginny's accident just after it happened. I tried to help—but it was too late for that, so I held her head in my hands while my friend rang for help. I tried to soothe her before she uh—' Her voice caught in her throat as it closed over at the reliving of such a raw memory.

'Oh my, my.' Father Joyce reached out and rested his hand on Isabel's upper arm. From anyone else she'd only just met she would have flinched away from the gesture finding it intrusive, but from this man with his kindly buttonlike eyes, it was comforting. 'To witness the passing of a person in the circumstances such as you did must be terribly traumatic. But how very wonderful you were there, Isabel, for Ginny, to ease her passing.'

Isabel bit her bottom lip; she hadn't thought about it like that. She hoped her being there had helped in some small way.

'She'll be greatly missed you know. She was a force of nature our Ginny. You'd never have believed she was over ninety. I don't think she believed she was over ninety!' He gave a little snort. 'She was always happy to bake for the new mum's in the church or to pop a meal around if she heard someone was poorly. She kept herself busy too by volunteering in our local St Vincent de Paul second-hand shop here in Timaru.'

'She sounds like she was a wonderful person, and your eulogy was lovely by the way.'

His eyes twinkled. 'Ah. Now you see what I didn't say was Ginny was a woman who in later years, did not suffer fools gladly, and whose tongue could be more acerbic than a sharp lemon vinaigrette at times. But you don't say those sorts of things now do you. None of us is perfect, and she was no exception, but she was also incredibly generous of spirit with a heart as wide as the Clutha River, where I hail from.'

Isabel smiled. 'She was human then.'

'She was human, and we all have our foibles.'

'You said you met twenty years ago when you spoke about your friendship with her during the service.'

'Oh yes, it was when she brought a cake, carrot cake it was with proper cream cheese icing, to the manse not long after I took over the parish after Father Samuel retired. She'd clashed once or twice with him, something to do with the flower arrangements, I think. I never did get the full story, but she was hoping to get off on a better foot with myself. Father Samuel didn't have a sweet tooth like me.' He patted his girth, resplendent over the purple belt. 'Carrot cake with cream cheese icing is the fastest way to my heart.' His laugh was low and rumbly like an engine starting, and Isabel couldn't help but smile.

'We two sat together and put the world to rights over a cup of tea and many a generous slice of her cake over the years. I know she missed her son, Teddy, dreadfully I'm afraid; he was her only child which made it worse. I know she would have liked more, but it wasn't meant to be. I used to tell her, "Your children are only on loan, Ginny, they're not yours to keep." He spoke very well today, Teddy I mean, don't you think?' He cast his gaze around the room as though seeking him out.

'Yes, he did. I liked the story he told about the height of his mum's pavlovas and how she lost the title of being a ten-pound pom.'

'Having earned the respect of the local farmers' wives by winning the Biggest Pavlova competition at the annual country fete,' Father Joyce finished for her, chuckling at the tale before snaffling his slice of banana cake.

Teddy's hair, Isabel had noticed as he spoke, still whispered of the ginger, sandy colour of his youth, despite his years. The only clue to his age was in the wrinkles fanning out around his hazel eyes when he smiled and the way his hair had receded ever so slightly. There was a greying too around his temples. He was a tall man but lean and obviously kept himself in shape. There was a gentleness to his features, and he looked she decided, her inventory not quite done, like a nice man.

His suit even to Isabel's untrained eye was obviously tailor-made. It was clear by his confident manner that he was used to public speaking and he'd peppered his eulogy about his mother in a way that had managed to be humorous and eloquent at the same time. Isabel had been rather taken aback at the sight of his wife as he sat back down though. She'd leaned in and kissed him on the cheek, a glamorous vision who was at least half his age. A young girl sat by her side.

Isabel had passed by them as the congregation trailed from the church into the hall and the family of three stood at the entrance of the hall shaking hands, accepting condolences, and thanking people for coming. She hadn't the heart to say who she was and how she'd encountered Ginny and so she'd simply said, 'I'm sorry for your loss,' to which she'd received a sad smile and nod.

'I'll miss Ginny's pavlova almost as much as her carrot cake, and I think it's always a good thing to laugh at a funeral. A person's life should be celebrated.' Father Joyce said, finishing his sarnie. 'Yes really, rather good,' he mumbled, despite his mouthful.

Isabel was unsure if he meant laughing at a funeral, or if he was referring to the sandwich once more. She saw his eyes flit in the direction of the trestle tables where the plates of food were slowly being depleted.

'I rather fancy one of those ginger gems before they all go,' he said.

'Is a ginger gem like gingerbread?'

'They're a little crustier on the outside than gingerbread, but they melt in your mouth on the inside.'

'Sounds rather delicious.'

'Are you tempted, my dear, because if you do, then I can. Raewyn Morris, she's my secretary, has been keeping an eye on the afternoon tea proceedings, and she'll slap my hand if she sees me going back for thirds. I'm supposed to be trying to lose a few pounds.'

'I am partial to all things ginger.'

'Oh go on, Isabel,' he urged conspiratorially.

There was nothing else for it. Who was she to deprive Father Joyce of a ginger gem? Isabel returned after nearly sending the contents of her plate flying, thanks to the stray foot she tripped over on her journey back from the trestle table. Thankfully she was righted by the owner of the stray foot's helpful hand and returned with the two ginger treats intact.

'You almost lost those,' Father Joyce said in a tone that implied that would have been sacrilege indeed as he helped himself to one of the gems.

'I'm a proper klutz—always have been,' Isabel said as he looked furtively over at an angular woman standing near the cheese roll-ups. Her hawkish gaze was elsewhere.

In two bites his little cake was gone. Father Joyce wiped the crumbs from his robe and Isabel listened to him describe the woman whose gaze she had held until she passed while she ate hers at a much slower pace than the priest.

Chapter 2

'I rather think Ginny looked upon me as a stand-in for Teddy given we're of a similar age. He's a mover and shaker in the world of finance; does something or other in banking and lives in Hong Kong. I must say he strikes me as one of those men for whom retirement is a foreign word.'

It was a bit pot calling the kettle black Isabel thought, given the priest must be somewhere in his early seventies himself.

'His wife, Olga, is Russian, and they have a daughter, Tatiana, who's about to turn fourteen. I had the most heart-warming chat with her before the service; she's a charming young lady you know. A credit to her parents.' Father Joyce looked around making sure none of his parishioners were within earshot, but crowd in the hall as the afternoon wore on was slowly thinning. Nevertheless, he leaned in closer to Isabel and said, 'Between you and me it was a cause of consternation for Ginny when her son married Olga. That he should marry a woman he not only met on the Internet but who was half his age and so late in life too. Well,' he tapped the side of his nose, 'let's just say Ginny had rather a lot to say on the subject. I told her she should be happy he'd found love. Not everybody gets a second shot at it.'

'Had he been married before then?'

'Yes, his first wife passed away from a prolonged illness ten years after they were married and there were no children. He, as I understand it, threw himself wholeheartedly into his finance career and did not come to terms with his grief for a long time. On the occasions I've met with him over the years when he's been home visiting his mother, it was clear to me he's devoted to Olga and Tatiana. They both gave him a new lease of life.'

'She's very beautiful,' Isabel said spotting Olga, a willowy brunette, across the room in conversation with a woman who looked very staid by comparison in her tunic top and leggings.

'Yes, she's a beauty all right. That didn't impress Ginny though. She felt that at his age he should be retiring and spending his time on a golf course, a golf course preferably somewhere in the South Island of New Zealand near his mother. She didn't approve of him embarking on fatherhood along with the trials and tribulations of keeping a younger woman happy when he was of pensionable age. She was heard to mutter more than once, "Who did he think he was—Donald Trump?"'

Isabel suppressed a smile. Melania and Donald *had* sprung to mind when she initially saw them together.

Father Joyce finished his remaining savoury before continuing. 'Do you know Ginny remarked to me the last time Teddy, Olga, and Tatiana had been to visit that she didn't fancy Tatiana's chances of becoming the prima ballerina her mother seemed to have her heart set on. In her words, the poor sod who had to perform the pas de deux with her granddaughter would surely be left bowlegged were he to attempt a lift! A little unkind but humourous nonetheless, and I knew that at the crux of the comment was a wish for what was best for Tatiana.'

Isabel looked around until she spied Teddy. By his side was a solidly built young girl standing with the awkwardness of an adolescent who doesn't yet know where she fits in the world. Isabel knew that feeling well, except she no longer had the umbrella of her teenage years to hide under. The young teen standing next to her father looked like she'd be much more at home in a pair of jeans than the frilly ensemble she was currently decked out in. Isabel watched her as she tugged at her skirt with obvious irritation. It was hard to imagine the poor girl in a tutu.

'Ginny felt her daughter-in-law was trying to relive her childhood dreams through her daughter and that it was ludicrous to push a style of dance on poor Tatiana that required one to be sylphlike. She wondered whether perhaps with her granddaughter's sturdy frame, she might be better suited to women's rugby. "The New Zealand Black Ferns were doing ever so well on the world stage," she was fond of saying. Ginny loved her rugby; she felt it made her a proper Kiwi when she wrapped her All Blacks scarf around her neck and cheered the boys on.' Father Joyce looked off into the distance lost in his memories for a moment before lamenting, 'Funny that she should feel the need to be a 'proper' Kiwi given she spent more of her life here than in your part of the world.'

'Do you know where she hailed from in the UK?' Isabel recalled the traces of an accent, the slight rolling of an 'r' dropping of an 'h' she'd picked up as Ginny spoke her last words.

'Southampton originally.'

Goosebumps prickled her arms; she wasn't surprised she was from the South East she had managed to say that she wanted to go back to the Isle of Wight, but the same city as her? The coincidence sent a shiver coursing through her. 'I'm from Southampton.'

Father Joyce sensing he had a captive audience was only too happy to continue with his musings. 'Well now isn't that a coincidence, and it was definitely Southampton because I remember she mentioned it in conjunction with her being from the city from which the Titanic sailed forth. She didn't talk much about her life before coming to New Zealand. Although we got onto the subject of the war one day and she did remark that she'd gone to live in the town of Ryde on the Isle of Wight at the outbreak of World War Two. Ginny said it was deemed safer than the port city, and she married a local lad while she was there on the island.'

If Isabel had had antennae, they would have been quivering. Here was the connection Ginny had to the Isle of Wight.

'She never told me his name, but she did tell me she was pregnant when the news arrived that her husband had been killed in battle. The poor fellow, like so many other young men of the time, didn't get to celebrate his twentieth birthday or the birth of his son.' He shook his head, and the wisps of hair floated up briefly before settling back down on his scalp with a silent sigh. 'After his death, she felt she couldn't stay on the island with all its ghosts of what might have been, so she returned to the mainland with her son. It was there she met Neville who adopted Teddy. He was still a wee babe, and the three of them immigrated to New Zealand in the mid-forties along with the rest of the ten-pound poms wanting to put the war years behind them.

'They bought land upon arriving here and farmed it until Neville died. It wasn't an easy life she was always quick to mention, but it was a good life. She tried to run the farm on her own for a while after Neville passed but it was too much, and she sold up. I think it always saddened her that Teddy didn't come home and step in where his father left off, but he had a different path to follow. She'd downsized and moved into Timaru shortly before I arrived in town.'

Isabel seized the break in his story. 'Father Joyce, just before she passed she asked me to promise her something.'

He peered closely at her. 'I can see whatever it was she asked of you is weighing heavily on your mind, Isabel.' Then he did a little jiggle ridding himself of the crumbs that had settled on the front of his robe before turning his attention back to Isabel. 'You're welcome to share that promise with me if you think it might help.'

'She asked me to find someone called Constance and to tell her she was sorry—she should never have left. Those were pretty much her words, and the only clue she gave me was that she'd wanted to go back to the Isle of Wight herself to say sorry.'

'Now that is interesting,' he rubbed his chin, 'because there *was* something on Ginny's mind of late. She wouldn't allude to what it was other than to say she needed to go back to Ryde—there was someone she had to see. She must have been referring to this Constance she mentioned to you. She wouldn't tell me why she wanted to go back, but there was a desperation about her this last while which I can only put down to her age and the realisation that nobody lives forever. In fact, the day she died a suitcase was in the car as well as a return ticket to the United Kingdom. Did you know that?'

Isabel shook her head; she'd been in too much shock at the time to pay attention to anything other than Ginny.

'No, why would you? Teddy, told me he was most perturbed by this as he knew nothing of her plans.' Father Joyce laid a hand on her arm once more. 'Isabel, Ginny, for all her endearing attributes was also a woman with a stubborn streak. I believe it was this unwillingness of hers to listen to those who knew better that saw her continue to get behind the wheel. This was despite being told she was endangering others each time she did so. It's a blessing that nobody else was hurt in the accident as she wouldn't have been able to rest in peace had there been.' He nodded and raised his hand in a wave to signal goodbye to one of his parishioners who'd paused as though wanting to interrupt but had thought better of it. 'Mrs Mercer, a gossip of the highest order if you give her an in,' he mumbled out the corner of his mouth.

Isabel watched in amusement as the older woman, in a pair of black trousers that fitted a tad too snuggly—and would cause concern were she to attempt to bend over—scuttled over to join a small party also making their way toward the exit.

'You do realise you're in no way obligated to fulfill your promise to Ginny, don't you, my dear?'

Her attention turned to Father Joyce once more.

'You did more than enough by being there and offering comfort in her final moments, and it was very good of you to come today.'

'It wasn't, really; I think my reasons might be rather selfish. I was hoping by coming that I'd be able to move forward from what happened that afternoon. I haven't been sleeping well, you see.'

'Oh, dear, dear. Nightmares?'

'No, I thought I might have bad dreams, but I feel like I haven't been dreaming at all. It just takes me forever to drift off because my mind keeps replaying Ginny's last moments over and over.'

He patted her arm. 'It will get better. It might just take a bit of time. Do you think coming to the funeral today has helped?'

'I don't know, Father Joyce. I really just don't know.'

Read on by visiting Michelle Vernal, The Promise at your favourite Amazon store.

Printed in Great Britain
by Amazon